Why do I get all ...

It's not like I'm anyone's idea of ultimate evil. I'm a convenience store cashier, for Chrissake! I don't need more than a pint of the red stuff a week, and I try to get it in daily doses. Preferably with someone who knows what I am and doesn't mind a little nibble, although if I don't have a girlfriend, it's kind of expensive paying for a fifteen minute simulated quickie each night, just so I can get my few ounces in.

"Will that be all, ma'am?" I might not be much of a vampire, but God help me, I'll be a polite one.

"You are *so* staked, sucker." She even tried to fake the Buffy accent. With her Texan drawl, it didn't work.

I smiled at Miss Grrrl Power Wannabe Slayer, a nice smile that didn't show my fangs. "Pardon, ma'am?"

She shoved the dowel a little closer to my liver while I rang up her Doritos. "Enough with the talking, it's, like, time to die."

I really did not have time for this. I don't get sick pay, and there's no way I was going to go to a hospital. The kid was worse than the potheads who did their best to buy out our stock of blunts each night. At least the potheads were harmless.

—*from "Night Shifted" by Kate Paulk*

Also Available from DAW Books:

Blood Bank by Tanya Huff
Tanya Huff's *Blood* books centered around three main characters: Vicki Nelson, a homicide cop turned private detective, her former partner Mike Celluci, and vampire Henry Fitzroy, who is the illegitimate son of Henry VIII. Not only are the three of them caught in a love triangle, but they are, time and again, involved in mysteries with a supernatural slant from demons, werewolves, and mummies. Here are all the short stories featuring Henry, Vicki, and Mike, and as an added bonus for fans of the TV series *Blood Bank* includes the screenplay for "Stone Cold," the episode Tanya herself wrote for the *Blood Ties* series along with a special introduction by Tanya, detailing her own experiences with the show.

Enchantment Place edited by Denise Little
A new mall is always worth a visit, especially if it's filled with one-of-a-kind specialty stores. And the shops in Enchantment Place couldn't be more special. For Enchantment Place lives up to its name, catering to a rather unique clientele, ranging from vampires and were-creatures, to wizards and witches, elves and unicorns. In short, anyone with shopping needs not likely to be met in the chain stores. With stories by Mary Jo Putney, Peter Morwood, Diane Duane, Laura Resnick, Esther Friener, Sarah A. Hoyt and others.

Witch High edited by Denise Little
There are high schools attended by students with special talents, like music and art, or science and mathematics. But what if there was a school that catered to those rarest of students—people with the talent to perform actual magic? The fourteen original tales included in *Witch High* explore the challenges that students of the magical arts may face in a high school of their very own. If you think chemistry is difficult, try studying alchemy. If you ever fell victim to a school bully, how would you deal with a bully gifted with powerful magic? If you ever wished for extra time to study for those exams, could the right spell give you all the time you could possibly need? These are just a few of the magical adventures that will await you when you enter Salem Township Public High School #4, a place where Harry Potter and his friends would feel right at home.

BETTER OFF UNDEAD

Edited by

Martin H. Greenberg
and Daniel M. Hoyt

DAW BOOKS, INC.
DONALD A. WOLLHEIM, FOUNDER
375 Hudson Street, New York, NY 10014

ELIZABETH R. WOLLHEIM
SHEILA E. GILBERT
PUBLISHERS
http://www.dawbooks.com

First Printing, November 2008
1 2 3 4 5 6 7 8 9

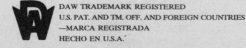

DAW TRADEMARK REGISTERED
U.S. PAT. AND TM. OFF. AND FOREIGN COUNTRIES
—MARCA REGISTRADA
HECHO EN U.S.A.

PRINTED IN THE U.S.A.

ACKNOWLEDGMENTS

Introduction and *Section Introductions* copyright © 2008 by Daniel M. Hoyt

A Grain of Salt copyright © 2008 by Sarah A. Hoyt

The Poet Gnawreate and the Taxman copyright © 2008 by Dave Freer

The Infernal Revenant Service copyright © 2008 by Laura Resnick

Mummy Knows Best copyright © 2008 by Esther M. Friesner

Genius Loci copyright © 2008 by Chelsea Quinn Yarbro

Ah, Yehz copyright © 2008 by Thranx, Inc.

Gamma Ray versus Death copyright © 2008 by Carrie Vaughn

Museum Hauntings copyright © 2008 by Phyllis Irene Radford

My Tears Have Been My Meat copyright © 2008 by Nina Kiriki Hoffman

The Perfect Man copyright © 2008 by Fran LaPlaca

Two All Beef Patties copyright © 2008 by Joseph E. Lake, Jr.

That Saturday copyright © 2008 by Devon Monk

Walking Fossil copyright © 2008 by Robert A. Hoyt

Night Shifted copyright © 2008 by Kate Paulk

Twelve Stepping in the Dark copyright © 2008 by Rebecca Lickiss

Gooble, Gobble, One of Us copyright © 2008 by Charles Edgar Quinn

Bump in the Night copyright © 2008 by Amanda S. Green

Separation Anxiety copyright © 2008 by S.M. Stirling

CONTENTS

Flesh

Undead

INTRODUCTION

Daniel M. Hoyt

Undead. The word immediately evokes the image of a vampire, a supernatural being existing beyond human mortality, mercilessly feeding on the blood of the living. The vampire's ironic reliance on human life in order to cheat death underscores the dichotomy between vampires and humans. Is it any wonder that vampires are often depicted as tortured and tormented?

But what if they weren't such emotional wrecks? What if they actually *liked* being undead? What if being undead were *better*?

This idea has been acknowledged in modern entertainment: the vampire photographer, Otto Chriek, in Terry Pratchett's Discworld novel *The Truth* (2000), as well as the semi-regular Discworld zombie, Reg Shoe; Mel Brooks' vampire spoof movie, *Dracula: Dead and Loving It* (1995); Joss Whedon's unapologetic vampire Spike in the TV series *Buffy the Vampire Slayer* (1997-2003).

Although it's not clear when the term "undead" first came about, this modern romantic vision is generally credited to Bram Stoker's *Dracula* (1897) over a century ago. Over time, the ranks of the undead have expanded from the titular vampire in Stoker's novel

1

to include entities that were once alive, but are now neither alive nor dead in the classical sense. Stoker's Count Dracula was also a shape-shifter—taking the forms of a wolf and even inanimate mist during the course of the novel—so this explosion of undead tropes isn't surprising, but a natural progression from the Count's mythos. (Although, ironically, shape-shifters are *not* traditionally considered undead!)

Given the broad scope of the modern undead and a burning desire to prove that being undead isn't necessarily all that bad, I asked eighteen writers—some well-known and even iconic in horror and supernatural fantasy, some fresh faces, and some you'll be surprised to find in this anthology—to surprise me with stories where it's *better* to be undead than alive.

Naturally, some of those stories are lighthearted, even humorous. But not all of them—just because it's better doesn't mean it isn't *creepy*. What follows are adventures in four realms of the undead: the highly-anticipated AFTERLIFE, the ghostly world of SPIRITS, the walking dead FLESH of zombies and revenants, and the traditional UNDEAD of vampires and others like them.

I hope you'll enjoy the journey.

AFTERLIFE

Many people believe in an afterlife, but few think of it as being peopled by the undead—yet that's exactly what it has to be. If there *is* an afterlife, be it heaven or hell or something else, it's peopled by the former living, acting much the same as if they were still alive. In other words—undead. Four writers embraced this concept to provide glimpses of afterlives worth believing in.

Sarah A. Hoyt takes us on a wild ride through part of the eighteen Chinese hells, complete with supernatural contracts. When Dave Freer mixes up a poet, a witch, a dentist and a taxman, it can only end up in a bar. Our communal frustration with the IRS resonates with Laura Resnick's tale of sin, judgment, and penance. And only Esther M. Friesner can make mummies seem this attractive.

A GRAIN OF SALT

Sarah A. Hoyt

My name is Hui and my surname is Fang. I was born in the year of the Fire Pig, at the time of the Quin Shi Huangdi Emperor, on the banks of the Yellow River, in a village of no significance.

I was my father's only surviving son. But since my father was only a secretary of the rank 6-A to the local court and since by great misfortune on the year of my birth the Emperor fined all his functionaries throughout China twenty silver in cash for *pestering his Majesty with unneeded petitions*, there was no money for my schooling.

Still my father taught me at home the principles of Lao Tze and the *Classic of the Mountains and the Sea* and many other excellent works, which he bought by forsaking a portion of our weekly rice.

Thus I grew up hungry but learned. I could write a perfect hand and improvise on the spot an erudite poem to a lotus leaf and there was every hope that when I stood the examination I might get a post with the provincial ministry.

To great misfortune, just before my twentieth birthday I was waylaid on a deserted road on a night when the moon suddenly vanished and all became pitch black.

At my death I was given the name Heng.

* * *

We have found this auspicious site, which is suitable for the grave of Fang Hui Heng. We use 99,999 strings of cash as well as five-colored-silk as offerings of good faith to buy this plot of land.

To the east and the west, it measures five steps; to the south and the north, it measures ten steps. To the east is the green dragon's land with the element of wood and the season of spring; to the west the white tiger's land, whose element is metal, whose season is autumn; to the south is the red phoenix, whose element is fire and the season of summer; to the north is the Great Tortoise, whose element is water, whose season is winter, and in whose power lies immortality.

The imperial guard shall patrol the four borders. The deputy of the grave mound and the earl of the tomb shall seal it off by pacing its borders; the generals shall make twisting paths through the fields so that for one thousand autumns and ten thousand summers no spirit will find its way back from the dead. If any dare contravene, they shall be imprisoned by the Two-Thousand-Bushel-Captain-of-the-Underworld.

We have prepared meat and wine and fruits and the sacrificial food. These things are a contract of our sincerity.

Once the land is paid for, the order will be given for the workmen to build the tomb. After the deceased is buried, that will guarantee good fortune and peace for ten thousand thousand years.

Someone finished reading the document, and I came awake with a start. At first I saw nothing. Blinking brought me a vision of a smoky, dark cavern, where many people clustered and something made a sound like metal rubbing on metal. The sound was barely audible, drowned out as it was in the screaming, shrieking, and begging of a thousand tongues.

Closer at hand, I had other problems. For one, I

was shackled, my hands and feet held by boards pierced with holes, then tied to each other by strong ropes, so that I could only walk in the smallest of steps and could not move my hands at all.

Worse than that, on either side of me were two men. At least I assumed they were men. They looked like clouds formed entirely of ice and curling snow.

In front of me stood a functionary in silk robes, holding a document and glaring down. "How do you plead?" he said.

I realized suddenly, in dismay, that he had the head of a tiger and multiple necklaces of jade. His eyes looked like deep-set fires, burning at me.

"How do you plead, you miserable debt-skipper?"

I remembered the contract read at me. A tomb contract. I supposed my father had ruined himself in providing well for me in the underworld. But none of this explained why I was shackled and guarded. Or why I was being called a debt skipper by a creature with the head of a tiger.

The tiger's tongue lolled out in an expression or distaste or perhaps of madness. "Answer me."

"I . . . milord," my voice emerged creaking and trembling like a metal spring too long held immobile.

"Kowtow to the Lord Ping Deng Wang, ruler of the Ninth Court of Feng Du," the dark cloud creature next to me bellowed. It reached out and grabbed me by the neck, pushing me forward, into what could be a kowtow—or just as well a full-bodied sprawl, held only by the boards that served as shackles.

Being that close to the ground, I could tell it was neither stone nor dirt nor paving, but a sort of black ice. And being that close to it, I might as well pretend I intended it as a kowtow. I looked up. Feng Du. I was in Feng Du—the hell of eighteen levels where souls suffered punishment for their sins in life. How had it happened? Surely my parents had done everything to ensure I would suffer no such fate. And I had not sinned in my life. Indeed, I had had too little time to live, much less to sin.

And the tiger-headed gentleman facing me was none other than Ping Deng Wang, the Lord of the Iron Web, who held you fast while the lords of the underworld reviewed your sins and decided on the appropriate eternal punishment.

I abased myself, hitting my head on the floor three times. "Oh, Lord Ping Deng Wang, sublime Lord of the Iron Web," I said. "This miserable one does not know what his crime is. He died before he was twenty summers and is not aware of having committed any of the nine unforgivable sins."

"Silence!" The guard to the right of me—was he a Two Thousand Bushel Captain? Such were usually the officers of the courts of the underworld—put his foot on my neck. "Do not lie to the Lord."

"You and your wife, Yen, have not ever paid the bill for your land and therefore you are liable to punishment as debtors."

I should have been terrified. I was terrified. Nonpayment of debt was a serious offense. More serious, though, was the mention of a wife, Yen. I'd died at twenty, unmarried. How had I acquired a wife?

I did not dare ask the tiger, who turned to one of the officers near me and said something. He did not address his words to me, and I could not hear him through the shrieking of the damned and the rubbing of metal on metal.

The two guards grabbed me and lifted me, then threw me. I flew through the air, through darkness and cold. The cavern could not be that large, but it felt as though I flew through thousands of years of darkness, till I hit something. The something was a web made of iron strings. I clung to it, unable to move, like an insect in a spider's silk.

At the same time, with a twang of metallic strings, she landed beside me.

She was small and lithe, with a body like a graceful spring stream, skin the color of the whitest lotus, and eyes and hair as black as a summer night. Around her waist was a girdle of bright green jade beads.

"Who are you?" I said.

"I am Yen," she said. "I am your wife."

"I have no wife," I said, pitching my voice so she could hear it over the mayhem around us.

She was the most beautiful creature I'd ever seen, and at any other time, I'd think myself the most fortunate of men to have acquired her as a wife. But right then my heart was speeding at the thought of the torments ahead. Would they send me to the forest of iron, where every leaf of every tree is a blade? Would I be commanded to climb the trees and cut myself to ribbons over and over again? Or would I fall under the purveyance of the Fifth Hell, which was ruled over by Yen Lo Wang, where they gouged out your heart and boiled you in oil?

It was hard to concentrate on Yen's lovely features and disconcerting to realize she did not look in the least troubled by our location or our fate. "You had no wife when you died," she said. "But your parents were approached by people who said their daughter had died without marrying. For a very small price, they allowed your parents to celebrate a wedding between your body and my bones, that you might have company in the underworld."

I thought about it. It was not unusual. Not unusual at all. In fact, some villages had a matchmaker for the dead as well as one for the living. It gave the parents someone to call their kin, and it provided the dead with that companionship they would otherwise have lacked in their afterlife journeys.

That I'd ended up with such a pretty bride was pure luck. It was clear she remembered our spirit-wedding, too, and I wished I did.

"My people thought your parents were honest. Why would they not pay their debt?" she asked.

I shook my head. "My parents would always pay their debt. For years they labored to pay a debt to the emperor."

She squinted and wrinkled her nose. Indeed, she had the loveliest nose I'd ever seen. "Very well," she said, at last, as though she were conceding a profound argument. "Very well. We shall go to the Fifth Hell, then, and—"

"Not the Fifth Hell," I protested. "I do not wish to have my heart gouged."

She gave me a pitying look, as though I were a poor thing without understanding. "Neither do I. I meant we should go and consult the records of our souls and see who's been tampering with them." She squinted at me again. "I do not belive any of this is natural, from your sudden death to this," she gestured with her head towards the surrounding immense cave with its iron web and its prisoners screaming in anticipation of the agony to come.

"But," I said. "we cannot. We are attached to this web."

But she only smiled at me, and as she smiled, a buzz came out of nowhere. A cloud of insects surrounded me—flies and grasshoppers and june bugs. They surrounded me till I could not see. I opened my mouth to scream and it was filled with insects.

The insects lifted me, held me, carried me.

Like being thrown across the cavern, it went on much too long. It was like I was flying for a thousand thousands of years, with insects all over me. I was afraid to scream, for fear they would penetrate my body and I would burst from the insects.

I tried to remember if this was a torment of the eighteen hells, but I could not. And then, suddenly, I was set down. A buzz sounded all around me, and the insects left.

I blinked the eyes I had closed to keep the creatures off my pupils, and looked around.

We were in a deep tunnel. There were no insects anywhere. I was out of the shackles, and Yen was standing right beside me, smiling as if she'd done something very clever.

"Who?" I asked. "How?"

She pulled back a lock of her long, glossy black hair. "It's something I do," she said.

So I was married to a woman who could command insects? This did not seem to be the right time to dispute it, though.

The tunnel ended in a large iron door, locked with a giant seal.

From behind us came the sound of pursuers. No doubt they did not like someone escaping their iron web any more than a spider would like its meal walking off. Hell apparently was an ordered place, with documents for everything. They could not just have souls wandering at will through the places of torment. If they could not capture us, the demons would have to pay heavy fines, or perhaps be thrown to the torments themselves.

"We have exchanged the iron web for a worse place," I said, tearing at my hair. "Now we shall be sent to the Sixth Hell, where the screaming torture of Lord Bian Cheng Wan will punish our escape."

She frowned at me, and I was not sure I would not prefer the screaming torture to her displeasure. "Do not be daft," she said. "The seal is a letter. It is the letter of absolute closing, which bars it against any intrusion. All you have to do is change the letter to be one that opens."

"All I have to do?"

"Certainly!" she said, and tossed back her head with the grace of a queen. "I heard you were the best calligrapher in the prefecture, able to draw letters as well as the high court calligraphers. Show me."

"But I have no brush," I said. "And no ink."

She reached down to the floor, and with her nails tore flakes of the black ice. It melted in her hand, becoming liquid and black like the best ink. Then she gave me a lock of her hair held in a tuft for a brush.

I worked fast, remembering my letters. It was hard because my hand was shaking, and I could hear our pursuers coming ever closer. But Yen stood there as though she trusted me to do it, and what else could I do? It was either write the door open or start enjoying the screaming torture.

"Hurry," she said. "They're almost upon us."

Without turning, I could sense them there, their large bodies, their heavy muscles. Without turning, I could imagine the confusion of fangs and teeth and everything that the most accomplished painters of a thousand generations had drawn in scrolls and murals of the underworld. My shaking hand finished turning the upturned tail of the letter that meant "closed against all" into a downward tail that meant "open to all."

"There," I said, but my quick-witted wife had already reached past me to push the door open and shove me through, yelling, "Run, run, run."

And then her voice stopped, because the place we entered had no air at all. It was like walking inside a red hot furnace with no air in it.

Around it, all over, people stood and lay, gasping, flopping like fish out of water, until they fell, blue and still, only to be poked by demons that revived them so that they could be suffocated again.

It was the Eighth Court of Feng Du, ruled by Du Shi Wang. I never saw the gentleman, but I heard his voice vibrating forth through my brain, in this place with no air.

Intruders. Catch them.

I did not fancy suffocating any more than I fancied having my heart gouged out. I ran so fast I overtook Yen.

My chest felt like it would burst from not breathing. In another moment I would fall, flopping, to the ground. We hit a huge door, made of wood, locked with the symbol of the green dragon. Almost fainting—feeling as though my eyes would pop out of their sockets—hearing the clamor of many demons closing in on us down the narrow tunnel, I bowed to the east, "Lord of Spring," I said soundlessly, miming the words with my lips. "Whose color is green and who lives in the East, you are our only hope, and you are a lord of air and life. Grant us air and life; let these miserable supplicants through."

I could not believe it when the door opened.

Yen could, because she was through it before me, taking big gulps of air. I threw myself through the door, shoving it closed behind me and hoping it would at least delay all those demons. I must have pleased the Lord of the East, because though I could hear the demons pound on the door on the other side, trying to get through, he held it fast against them.

I was so relieved by this—trembling in tiredness at our flight and in gratitude for our escape—so happy to be breathing air again, I did not notice the smell for the longest time.

When I did, it was like the smell of ten thousand butcher shops rolled together. There was screaming, too—more screaming than I'd heard when the river overflowed its banks and flooded our village.

I realized this was the Seventh Court of Feng Du, where evildoers were put through mincing machines, then made whole again only to be ground up once more. Looking up, I could see the place was full of people being shoved feet first into mincers and of blood-splattered demons intent on their work.

This was the domain of Lord Tain Shan Wang, and as I thought this, Yen pulled at my arm, and I heard the voice of the Lord of Grinding scream, "Intruders! Get them."

Blood-splattered demons abandoned their grinding machines and headed for us, leaving their victims screaming, half ground.

We were already running, fast, through the dark corridor. Turning a corner, we were faced with a door of polished diamond on whose surface were inscribed the words *a perfect poem.*

"What does that mean?" I asked Yen.

"It will open for a perfect poem. I heard you were the best poet in three prefectures."

"How can I make a poem like this?" I asked, gasping and trembling, while the blood-splattered mincing demons closed in on us.

"Would you prefer to be minced?"

From the depths of my mind I pulled all the talent that my father had ever imagined I had, and I shouted with my whole strength:

"Amidst the flowers a jug of wine
I pour alone lacking companionship
So raising the cup I invite the Moon
Then turn to my shadow which makes three of us
Because the Moon does not know how to drink
My shadow merely follows the movement of my body
The moon has brought the shadow to keep me com-
pany a while
The practice of mirth should keep pace with Spring
I start a song and the moon begins to reel
I rise and dance and the shadow moves grotesquely
While I'm still conscious let's rejoice with one another
After I'm drunk let each one go his way
Let us bind ourselves for ever for passionless journeyings
Let us swear to meet again far in the Milky Way."[1]

[1]Substantiating the theory that every perfect piece of art exists independent of the artist, this same poem—hastily shouted by Fang Hui and not recorded in hell—would later be recreated, word per word, by the incomparable Li Bai.

The door sprang open and we ran in. We could hear the screams, and I remembered this was the Sixth Hell, ruled by Lord Bian Cheng Wang, and the domain of the screaming torture. With it ringing in our ears, it was difficult to hear him ordering the demons to seize us, but I was sure he was doing just that. I ran as fast as I could, and I came upon a door that was made of ice. Try as I might, my nails scraped on it, and there was no indication on how to open it.

I turned to Yen, but she only smiled and reached past my shoulder, to touch the door. The door went from ice to water to vapor in a moment, and she pushed past me, her heavenly soft skin rubbing against my body.

"How could you do that?"

"Does it matter?" she asked. "Come, this is the Fifth Hell. It has sixteen departments of heart gouging and boiling oil, but it also has, deep within, the files of life, where every soul's destiny is recorded."

I thought it mattered. Pieces of our adventure were gathering in my mind and adding up to a very odd picture, but I had no time to think because Yen pulled me through and, with a word, caused the door to reform into ice behind us.

The blood-splattered demons hit against the ice, and we were now in another corridor and at least no one was saying we should be seized.

Yen put her tiny, well-shaped finger to her red lips to signify that I should be very quiet, then led me, on tiptoe, down a hallway and past another and yet another, till we got to the lowest level, where a correct functionary looked up from behind the desk.

For a moment I was afraid he was going to scream that we should be seized. But instead, he asked, "What is your business?"

Yen was working with her fingers at her waist unfastening her girdle. I was about to ask her what she was doing, when I understood her plan.

Any functionary, anywhere, could be bribed, and the jade girdle was worth a king's ransom, in heaven, hell or earth.

She held it in front of the keeper of the records, and spoke, softly, "We want to consult the records of souls and the archives of deaths."

The functionary looked perfectly normal, but his eyes were beady and small like a pig's. He now squinted them at us, then bowed once. "You may consult."

His hand moved so fast to snatch the girdle that it was almost impossible to see. We left him exclaiming over his prize and moved forth to an immense cavern, filled with pigeonholes carved in the stone. Each pigeonhole contained a hundred or more well-rolled scrolls; the cavern extended to seeming infinity.

"We'll never find it," I said.

"Do not be ridiculous," Yen said, and she moved, assured and calm, among the pigeonholes. "They are of course organized by district, county, and prefecture, and by year and month and hour, too."

"But what are you looking for?" I asked, bewildered, walking after her in the immense cavern.

"Your records, of course," she said. "Ah, let's see, here they are. Year of the pig. . . ."

She knelt, pulling at several scrolls. Meanwhile I'd had time to think. There was a legend of a creature that could turn into a multitude of insects, a creature who would command water, a creature who owned a green girdle.

In a time so long ago that only fragments of the story had been taught in my time, a goddess had fought the god of the granary. He'd invaded her land and she'd tried to convince him to share it. When that failed, she had seduced him, every night. And every morning she had disappeared by turning into a cloud of insects that blocked out the sun and blinded him.

He'd defeated her by giving her a girdle of vivid green jade, which allowed him to see her even in the darkness. Then he'd shot arrows and killed her. I felt my hair stand on end.

She was squatting on the floor, her perfect buttocks resting on the back of her perfect heels, reading a scroll as though it were the most fascinating story.

"Yen," I asked, my voice cracking. "Are you the Goddess of the Salt River?"

She looked up and smiled at me, then back at her scroll, "Listen here, Heng. You were not supposed to die at twenty. In fact, you were supposed to live till you were ninety."

"You did not answer," I said.

She smiled again. "You'd have married a woman named Na and—"

"How could it be, though," I said, trying to convince myself I was dreaming. "You said that my parents bought your bones from your parents. That means . . ."

"Not my parents. Just my people. Na would have given you five daughters and three sons. And you'd have been a secretary first grade. Oh, I bet your father would have been proud. And you'd—"

"I would not have attained a provincial post?" I asked, offended.

"No. Just a local one. And you'd have lived in the village all—"

"Unauthorized entry into the most secret records," a voice boomed, reverberating off the walls of the cavern. With that much power and potency, it could only be the voice of Yen Lo Wang, Lord of the Fifth Hell. He had once been the Lord of the First Court of Hell, but he'd been so lenient too many souls were getting into Heaven, and so he'd been sent to the Fifth Hell, where he found joy in gauging hearts and pouring boiling oil onto the guilty souls.

"Seize them."

The sound of running feet was everywhere, from every recess of the cavern. "Where do we run?" I asked Yen.

"We do not run," she said, and smiled. "Nowhere to run. They're coming at us from the east, the west, and the north. Our backs are against the wall to the south."

"We'll be caught," I said. "And after all this we'll be sent to the Hell of Ice, which is in the Second Court of Feng Du and whose lord is Qu Jiang Wang."

She shook her head. "Not if I can help it. Only remember, when the secretaries reach us, there are perfect jade disks hanging on leather thongs from their necks. I need one of those."

"Why?" I asked, confused at my wife, who was a goddess and who spoke in riddles. She'd just given away her jade girdle and now she wanted a jade disk?

"They are Pi disks," she said. "And through them we can speak to the August Jade Emperor."

"What?" I asked. "Why?"

"Because there's been an administrative error only he can correct."

I'd have asked more, but I could now see the secretaries. An army of them, running towards us. There were thousands. Millions. We'd never have time to speak into the Pi disk.

"When you get the disk," Yen said. "Scream into it that you are Heng, married to the Goddess of the Salt River and that your life was cut before your time."

"You are insane," I said. "We will not have time."

"Just do it," she said, and smiled at me, revealing her perfect, pearly teeth.

And then the secretaries were upon us, screaming, shouting, reaching.

Blindly, before they could immobilize me, I grabbed the jade disk of the nearest one—a perfect disk the

size of my palm and the color of the purest amber—
and pulled on it, desperately.

I felt the leather thong break at the same time that
a cloud of insects covered me.

I managed to shout into the jade disk, "My name
is Heng. I'm married to the Goddess of the Salt River.
My life was cut short. My tomb money stolen. It's an
administrative error."

And then darkness engulfed all.

Pang, echoed a golden gong from amid the rosy
mist that surrounded us. The scent of roses was everywhere and warm breezes caressed my naked body.
Yen stood beside me as unruffled as ever, her hair
flowing like black silk down her back. In front of us
was a perfect lotus flower the size of a village.

Slowly, slowly, while I stared in confusion, thinking
it must be a dream, the petals of the lotus opened to
reveal a giant white palace. It was laid out with pleasure gardens. Peacocks strutted in the gardens and
called out their sudden screams.

Without any words, I felt we were being ordered to
enter the palace. I think Yen must have felt the same,
because we stepped forward, side by side, onto the
petal of the flower and through it, into the gardens.

There was a sound of giggling from my left. I
glimpsed, amid flowering rose bushes, several young
women playing and throwing petals at each other in
a pool of water.

"Those are the concubines of the Jade Emperor,"
Yen said, with the faintest tone of disapproval in her
voice. "They are not for you to gawk at."

I tore my gaze away with some regret, and instead
followed my wife down the garden path to a broad
white stone staircase and up it to a salon filled with
the most august beings I could imagine.

There were people and dragons, phoenixes and

other fabulous creatures all of them mingling with men and women of such perfect countenance and dress as had never graced any land in the world.

And in the middle of it all, in splendor, sat the August Emperor of Jade, in a white throne shaped like a lotus flower.

I immediately fell to my face and started kowtowing. I was somewhat surprised that my wife was doing the same by my side.

Laughter, like a low rumble shivered through the marble floors. And then a voice said, "Get up, Heng and you too, Yen. You may approach the throne."

I stood up and approached, shivering, because majesty and eternity rolled from the August Emperor of Jade.

"Speak your case," he said. "You and your wife have laid hell half to waste. In fact, there has not been such an uproar here since the Monkey Trickster got into hell. This disorder cannot be allowed to continue. And therefore I agreed to listen to you."

Yen spoke. "Heng has been robbed of most of his life," she said. "He was killed at nineteen, when the scroll of his life said he should have lived to ninety and sired many sons."

"You have this scroll?" the Jade Emperor asked, leaning forward.

She bowed and proffered it. He read it, then looked up. "And you, Mistress of the Salt River, how came you to be here with him? How came you to be married to him?"

She looked embarrassed. "My people sold my bones to his parents, that they might perform a wedding with his corpse and thus—"

"How came you to have people, when you'd been dead that long?"

"I was buried with my jade girdle," she said. "And all my effects. On the bank of the river. After centuries some robbers found my bones. It was not hard to talk in their minds and strike a deal with them. In exchange for my keeping my girdle, they could have all my cups and vessels and my earthenware boat. And they could sell my bones to someone who needed a bride for their son in the afterworld."

The Jade Emperor frowned. He turned to a functionary standing at his elbow and whispered something. The whisper was repeated, from one end of the salon to the other, till it came to the end of the room.

For a moment everything was quiet. Then the golden gong sounded again and someone announced, "Qi Lin answers the Emperor's summons."

Into the room came a unicorn—a creature that I'd only seen in paintings. He had the body of a deer, the hooves of a horse, and a single, perfect, spiraling horn on his forehead. His body was a scintillating ivory.

"Lord Qi Lin knows the truths that are hidden, and he accuses the guilty and punishes the innocent," the Jade Emperor said. He proceeded to give a summary of my situation, and to ask the unicorn, "Who waylaid Heng in the dark night?"

The unicorn looked up and managed to look amused, though his features were not at all like a human face. "Two malefactors whose names are well and truly forgotten and so should be. They died years ago, and they are being punished in the Pool of Filth, in the Second Feng Du court, under Lord Qu Jiang Wang. They also stole the money to pay for Heng's tomb, thereby leading to Heng's being here, on an underworld court procedure brought by the seller of the land, who is seeking an eviction."

The Jade Emperor was quiet a moment. His hand caressed his ineffably brilliant face. "But who ordered those crimes?" he asked. "Who suggested it?"

"The Goddess of the Salt River spoke in their feeble minds," the unicorn said.

"Ah!" the Jade Emperor said, turning to my wife. "Defend yourself if you can!"

"Indeed, I cannot, save to say that I was once more

powerful than you," she said. "I once ruled the earth and could stop the sun rising in the sky. When humans were nomadic and there was no idea of planting and no knowledge of the seasons, I ruled them and their heaven and hell. But then came the Lord of the Granary, with his fields and domesticated animals, and he tricked me into accepting his girdle, and thus he killed me.

"I was a goddess, and as you see, the span of my life should have been forever. And I offered to share my domain with him, but he killed me by stealth." She produced another scroll from somewhere. "As you see, my scroll did not list a death date." She showed him the scroll and he took it and read it.

His sublime fingers drummed on the arm of his venerable chair. "I see only one way to resolve this," he said. "He lost the life he should have had and he must be compensated. She lost her life and she must also be compensated—but she must be punished also. We will give him immortality to compensate for his mortal life. We will give her immortality also, but to punish her she must continue to be married to this boy who was once a mortal."

Thus spake the Most Venerable Jade Emperor of the Heavenly Golden Palace, the Supremely High Emperor of the Heavens, the Holder of Talismans, Container of Perfection and Embodiment of Dao, The Most Venerable and Highest Jade Emperor of All Embracing, Sublime Spontaneous Existence of the Heavenly Golden Palace.

A thousand years later, I'm not sure Yen considers me such a punishment.

With her knowledge and my academic talent we live very well indeed, on a palace at the edge of her river, surrounded by peacocks, attended by servants and amid gardens of surpassing delightfulness.

Truly, though she might have stolen my other life from me, I cannot grudge it. The happiness my wife has given me far surpasses what I could have attained in a long life in my village.

The only restriction she puts on my happiness is not permitting me to keep concubines. But when we enact the fifty known positions of pleasure and the thirty-two refinements of joy, I am sure no other women, no matter how many, could surpass the exalted acrobatics or the tender affection of my wife Yen, Goddess of the Salt River.

THE POET GNAWREATE AND THE TAXMAN

Dave Freer

He was short, balding, and cadaverous. The latter was a lot more typical of my usual clientele than the short and balding part. Mind you, as I always say, it takes all sorts to make an underworld. Vampires with bad breath, werewolves with mange, overweight sylphs crying into their Bloody Marys—I get them all. For some reason they come and tell me their troubles. Being the late-day barman at the Open Crypt Bar and Grill has its downsides, but the tips are good.

I'd never had quite such a cheery customer, nor one with a seersucker jacket in a loud check, neatly pressed trousers and argyle socks before. Nor one with two such large demons as bodyguards.

"You look to be very good spirits today, sir," I said, polishing glasses as he helped himself to peanuts from the bar.

"Oh, I am," he said, smiling jauntily, revealing a gap where he should have had a front tooth. "It's another lovely day. Mind you, I haven't always been happy about being undead."

I nodded. "I always thought there might be some

advantages to being dead. Takes a bit of getting used to, though, sir."

He tasted his martini. Smiled again. The missing tooth was very distracting. "When I was alive people always told me I'd be better off dead."

"In one sense they're completely wrong," I said grumpily. "Being dead has been a financial disaster zone for me, except from a taxation point of view."

He sniggered, as if enjoying some private joke. "They said nothing was sure except death and taxes."

"Well, looking at us, they were wrong about that, too. Another drink, sir?"

He looked at his pocket watch. "So hard to keep track of time these days. Yes, I'll have another. After all, I've got time to kill now," he said, showing that despite having lost a tooth, he still had good solid long canines. We both laughed, and I wondered if he was a vampire. Mostly they're more aware of appearances, though.

I poured. It was a slow morning. No one else was in the place except for an old hobo zombie quietly falling apart into his beer at the far booth. They came in to keep cold, and they could nurse a beer for a full hour. I mean, I understand. There but for the job go I. I just wish they wouldn't shed so much. My martini-swigging customer's two demons were drinking vodka to keep their spirits up, but they hardly counted. It was just the two of us, chatting. "One of the problems," I said, "about being undead is that your sense of time goes to hell in a handbasket."

He chuckled. "You've got to keep up with progress, barman. These days I believe it goes FedEx. Faster, cheaper and more reliable. They deliver or arrange delivery anywhere."

"Ah. Well, I daresay. Hell has always been avant-garde, if you take my meaning, sir. When I joined the ranks of the undead we only had the Pony Express."

"Mine began further back still. But I try to keep up. Fascinating developments in my old field."

"And what was that, sir?" I asked out of politeness. He was going to tell me anyway. They always did. You'd be surprised how many were in real estate.

"I was a tax collector," he said, suddenly looking like a predatory bird.

"Oh." Once I might have shied away. But the undead don't feel quite the same way about things that trouble the living. "Don't see a lot of your kind in here."

He shook his head. "Mostly they go straight to hell. It's being damned that often. But I got unlucky."

"Unlucky?"

"Yes." He nodded thoughtfully. "You know, certain professions should be exempt from taxation. They contribute so much to the whole of society that it is unnecessary to tax them. Or at least damned stupid to do so. Writers, dentists (when you need one, no one is more valuable), and . . . er, witches."

"And bartenders. No one appreciates how much fine psychological counseling we do. Still, I'll agree. You don't want to interfere with witches. Or writers. I write a bit myself under a pen name, sir," I said tentatively. One never knew when someone might become a new reader.

"True. Bartenders are undervalued. When your glass is full, that is," he said, meaningfully.

I refilled his glass. "On the house, sir. I had a brush with a witch myself once."

"Thank you. Yes, you'd think people would be more careful, but we never were. So what do you write?"

"Fantasy, sir. Bit of horror every now and then. They say that you should write what you know," I said, and licked my canines.

"For art, catharsis, or money?" he asked, steepling his fingers.

"Money," I admitted. "Not that there is much in the short fiction market nowadays. But it's an unliving, when I add it to my pay here. It's not like I have to keep body and soul together like those poor mortals trying to do it. And there's a certain satisfaction in seeing your pseudonym in print."

He nodded. "Money is at least an honest reason for trying to sell it. Your problem really lies in the marketing. You can get rich from writing, if you have some really innovative marketing."

I didn't want to talk about innovative marketing, since the boss nearly fired me for selling copies of my self-published collection to late morning drunks. It was going so well, too, until one of them was sick on my magnum opus and I got a little . . . upset with him. Do you know how hard it is to dispose of undead body parts? They keep trying to wriggle back together, fingers digging their way out of wet concrete, legs hopping out of the seething acid. "So you tried to tax a witch, did you, sir?"

He shook his head. "Worse. Taxing witches is just . . . well, look at me. It was something I would never have considered doing. However, I was misled. You see, Miss Maggie Inplank was not just a witch. She was a witch, a dentist, *and* a writer of sorts. A poet."

"Very touchy, those," I said sympathetically. "Like to feel their work is being taken seriously. And it just doesn't sell."

"Hers sold very well. She had her marketing perfected," he said sourly.

I had to admit I was interested. I still had 982 copies of my book cluttering up my coffin. Anything that could sell poetry . . . "And how did that work, sir?"

"Very well. She always sold at least one copy, and at times up to a dozen of them, to everyone she quoted her book to."

Enlightenment dawned. "They paid her to stop? I'm

surprised you were the only one cursed undead. Poets don't appreciate that attitude."

He shook his head. "No, she did far worse to me than being merely cursed to spend all eternity on earth. Being undead was a sort of side effect of what happened to me. They were all very polite, really. Even me . . . at the time. In a manner of speaking. I did say she had three professions, didn't I? She used that fact. She had one of those modern dentist's chairs. With restraints. Modern back then, I mean. Nowadays they don't use them much, but back then it was the most essential mod-con any dental practitioner could own." He took a long pull of his drink. Touched the gap in his teeth. "No one went until the pain was close to unlivable. Anesthetic was half a bottle of gin."

I reflected that he was well on the way to being anesthetized now. But it was a neat trick if you could get customers with money as a captive audience, and half drunk to boot. "Well, *some* poetry—and I wouldn't want to say this in public—is not too bad, you know. I've got some Yeats. . . ."

He shuddered. "Aches. I had those, too. Believe me, her epic iambic octometric dithyrambs were enough to cause them, even if the tooth hadn't kept me awake for a week. Her sales pitch went something like this. First she tightened the straps on my wrists and ankles. Then she said 'Open wide.' She said it with this mighty big pair of long handled pincers in her right hand, so I was fairly nervous about complying . . . and as soon as I did it, I realized the pincers were a feint. I was so busy watching them that I hadn't been aware that in her other hand she had a handful of rags. She shoved them between my jaws so I couldn't bite. 'And now to soothe you,' she said, 'a quick recital of my latest ode. You'll enjoy it. It has great literary merit, not like that tosh written merely to entertain.' I tried to protest. 'Uunghh!! Mo oofff,' I said. 'How kind of you!' she said. 'It's not everyone who is in a position to get a personal recital from me, you know.' I certainly did know. What I didn't know, she soon told me. 'It's been very well received. And not just because my brother Henry is the local magistrate. Hanging Henry they call him. Mind you,' she cackled, waving the pincers in my face, 'He's never had to hang anyone twice for not honoring their signed contracts,' she said, exchanging the pincers for a book order form. Then she took up a slim puce calfskin-covered volume and began to read to me." The former taxman shuddered, and took a long pull at his drink.

"Ah." I said. "Puce calfskin, eh. Covers make a lot of difference."

"A padlock would have been a good addition to that one. Anyway, after some twenty generations . . . well, minutes, she paused, closed the book reluctantly, and said: 'Inspiring, isn't it? I'm glad you agree. Now, I can have this rotten tooth out fairly painlessly in a moment . . . I hope. I'm sure you'd like to order a copy of my book first, though. It always steadies my hand, knowing that I've made another fan. Of course, a copy for your mother . . . and they make great presents for your extended circle of friends and relations. There is a slight discount for orders of over twenty copies. Let me hold the order form for you. I'll put the quill in your hand. How many would you like?' she asked me."

The taxman shook his head sadly. "Does 'Uonnnne!' sound like 'a dozen' to you? Well, it did to her. And true enough, she had the tooth out in two shakes of an ant's whisker. I hardly felt it happen. Just the sudden relief."

"An aching wallet is a great distraction," I sympathized.

"Yes. But she really was good at it. A compensation for the poetry, I thought. I should have suspected magic. But once the pain stopped . . . I started wondering."

"About poetry?"

"Something that is poetry to me, anyway. It seemed this was a major stream of taxable income. I was foolish enough to say so when she let me out of the chair.

He sighed. "She screamed at me. 'What? You want me to PAY YOU!' It was a sweet moment. And then she waved the discolored and rotten tooth in my face. 'What do you think this is?' People often seem to take taxation so hard."

"Unreasonable of them," I said. "They seem to want something back for it, too."

"A ridiculous idea. But I must admit that as I thought her merely a writer and a dentist, and I had no need of a dentist right then . . . I was a little flippant. 'A considerable relief,' I said to her. 'I paid you for that. You insisted on money upfront . . . but it appears to me that you are, according to my records, not paying any taxes on your second stream of income. There will have to be fines and penalties levied. . . .' " He sighed again. "I should have noticed the danger signs. The thunder before the lightning. But I didn't. I was thinking of those twelve copies of *Selected Poems* by Maggie Inplank that I had just bought."

"Well, most of us have twelve relations we don't like. . . ."

He wasn't listening to me. He just continued his tale. "She was incandescent, and I must admit I was enjoying it. 'Relief!' she said. 'Don't you think works of literary merit are worthy of tax relief? It's my duty to educate and uplift readers with my art. You are looking for trouble.' With my tooth in one hand and her little puce book in the other . . . the Poet Gnawreate hung over me like a dark cloud. But in my line of work you get rather used to threats. They come just before pleading. I probably shouldn't have made my little jest then. But people always found me so droll. They always used to laugh at my little jokes. 'Well, perhaps for something of merit. But not your potty poetry. And there is a special clause about up-lifting for profit . . . a haha . . .'

"Well! In an instant, her hair stood out straight. Her bun swirled up into a great fan, all by itself. I nearly died right there, and saved myself a great deal of trouble, because one hairpin plunged a full two inches into the oak of the chair and pinned me there by the ear. Her face went very white. She raised her arms and a dark nimbus formed around her. I stopped thinking it was a joke right then . . . and realized just how right she was about trouble . . . but it was too late to tell her. She held my tooth and her book aloft."

> *"For bitter and for verse,*
> *I damn you with my curse,*
> *In sooth, in truth I bind you with this tooth,*
> *The hole, your soul my toll, until I see it whole."*

"I see what you mean about the poetry," I said, pouring him another drink.

"It got worse. She put the tooth back. And I found I was shrinking. Stiff-backed, limp-leafed. Bound into a collection of three epic poems: *Malocclusion, Caries, and Decay*. Doomed and trapped there until I could give her the whole tooth. . . ." He shook his head. "I was undead with a toothache . . . and not even able to get some relief from it by actually dying. Being undead goes on longer than being alive does." He downed his drink.

I poured him another. The boss could take it out of my salary if he liked. "But you plainly got out," I said, feeling my own jaw in sympathy.

"Eventually. It took me two hundred years. Still," he said, smiling, showing the gap in his teeth, "things are looking up. I'm enjoying being undead without the ache. And I got the time knocked off eternity, because I've already had two hundred years of damnation without relief. No relief from pain and none from the poems. I don't know which was more agonizing."

"So how did you break free?" I asked, curious. That was plainly a powerful spell. It could be a trick worth knowing.

"More luck than skill," he admitted. "You know, life as a haunted limited edition folio of three epic odes by a literary poetess of the early nineteenth century was not an easy one. I had to be read to communicate—by moving the letters around. Otherwise I was limited to eerie, tortured moans and a bit of poltergeist work. I was part of the Poet Gnawreate's estate. She died a wealthy woman, thanks to her clever marketing and tax-free status. Childless and unmarried, though, so the estate had to be divided among her relations."

"So what happened?" I asked, curious.

"Well, the cousin who inherited me, together with her house, didn't last the night. Old Maggie found my moans a pleasure to listen to. He didn't. He was planning to burn all her books. But I ran him off by midnight. He froze to death," said the tax man with some satisfaction.

I nodded. "No finer feelings. Should have been more sensitive about literature. If he'd read you . . ."

"Yes . . . but it took a while to find anyone ready to do so. More people write poetry than read it, alas. I saw more of New England than I wanted to. In display bookcases. On shelves in kitchens. Above smoky fireplaces. In some damp chests. I must have been responsible for half the reports of haunted houses in America. No one ever looks at old books as source of ghosts. I was thrown away once . . . but retrieved by an upwardly mobile scavenger. Mostly people keep old leather-bound books, they just don't read them. I did trips out west, and even a voyage to Bermuda. Pleasant climate. Hell on books. My pages got quite foxed, and it lowered my moan an octave.

That was quite nice in its way. I could shake walls when the tooth was really driving me mad."

"No problem with exorcists, then?" I asked. I'd had a brush with them myself once. That's one of the problems of being undead. Everything eventually happens to you, and it's very hard to live a regular life. Or open a bank account.

The tax man pulled a face. "One of them—a do-it-yourself fellow—thought I'd do for the book in bell, book, and candle. Give me a proper religious practitioner any day . . . that was close. It would have done dreadful things to me. I got him just in time with a poltergeisted tea-pot. I thought the cycle of haunting would never end. But eventually I ended up in a secondhand bookstore. I'd just about ruined the bookseller when a deaf dentist came in and perused his stock."

"It's like shaking a piggy bank. Eventually you get a coin out."

"Yes. Mind you I'd gotten very tired of shaking, even shaking walls. But finally I'd struck the jackpot. Except he wouldn't open the book. Just thought the title looked amusing, drat him. And I didn't dare drive him mad or shake the walls. I had to modulate my moaning. I poltergeisted any other books out of the place. And he just kept buying more. It took me a full year to get every other book out of the house, before I could get him to open me. And then I could only alter my print in rhyme. You try doing that all the time. It's like running in slime. It's a crime. . . ." He sighed. "Sorry, one of the aftereffects of the spell. I'm a poem in remission."

"You got liberated, though."

"Eventually. It happened like this: picture the scene."

"My girlfriend has left me. My friends won't visit. The cable company has refunded my subscription. I've lost four hearing aids this month. I have bought thirty-

one paperbacks this week. Every one has gone missing. My life is mess," said Dr Jim Edwards to the slim
leather-bound book that was his sole companion in
the house's smallest room. "*Malocclusion, Caries and
Decay.* Three epic poems by Maggie Inplank. If that
doesn't move me, nothing will." He opened the book.
He was one of those souls so conditioned to reading
on the john that he found it nearly impossible to go
without one.

> *"Your various problems are
> many,
> Your pleasures are few,
> If help to me you render any,
> I'll help you too. Awoooo."*

"Good grief. And she got this published? What has
it got to do with malocclusion?" said Dr Edwards,
looking faintly nauseous.

*"A hole in my tooth was my woe,
And to the witch dentist I didst go,
With a toothache in this book she trapped me,
Set me free, I'm in pain pain pain pain, aieeeeeeee!"*

"I swear the letters moved. And what rot. It's
enough to induce constipation. . . . Holy mackerel!
The toilet roll is levitating! Who the hell locked the
door? Help!" And he tried to break the door down.
It took him a while to look back at the floor. To the
toilet roll, which had unraveled to form letters.

"HELP
BOOK"

As he watched, "BOOK" turned to "LOOK" . . .

and he pounded on the door frantically. There was no one else in the house, and it was a good solid door.

Eventually, desperation made him pull up his trousers and open the book.

> *"From this book of poetry,*
> *You must set me free,*
> *And liberated you too will be,*
> *Ahhhhh, Aroooooooweee.*
> *I'm in pain, pain, pain,*
> *Please fix this tooth again."*

He sat down on the only available throne. "A haunted book of poetry. With a toothache. I have finally gone crazy." He reached into the pocket of his white coat, pulled out a vial, broke the top off, and poured it onto the pages. "Novocain. Just what every slim folio of self-published poetry needs."

> *"Thank you! Oh the wonderful relief,*
> *The tooth has given me much grief."*

"It's talking to me. The damned book is talking to me."

> *"You and I never will be free,*
> *Until whole is made the tooth that bound me."*

"Oh, now I'm supposed to do a root canal on a poetry book? What about a simple extraction? I'll tear your pages out until you let me go."

> *"Your death would be chilling*
> *But a filling would be thrilling*
> *And to let you free I'd be willing."*

"And just how do you do a filling on a poem? Anyway, do you have a dental plan?"

"Dental man, be a gentleman,
Help a poem without a dental plan
Or finish your life in the can.
Of letters I the tooth can make.
Fix it and remove the ache
And free I'll let you break."

He felt in his pockets. "Open wide. Ah. I see the problem. You really should have taken better care of your teeth. First filling I've done with magic marker."

"Now in a pentacle the book you place,
Certain magic symbols you must trace,
Needs must I should go down to hell,
Make a deal with the devil, before all is well."

"I'm a dentist. Not a Satanist. There is a difference, you know."

"If rid of me you want to be,
You'd make haste
Not in idle debate, while waits my fate
My time do waste.
Being meek, Maggie Inplank, I must seek
The last hurdle must be faced."

The dentist drew the pentacle and the circles nine, and the symbols of summonsing. He had to escape the bitter verse.

I'd heard a lot of tales here as the late-day barman at the Open Crypt, few with worse poetry, but not many stories in that league. "Worth a pint of gin, that yarn," I had to admit.

"Ah, but it wasn't over yet," said the tax man. "I had my tooth, and the devil was not going to let me speak in verse, so he gave me a temporary body, but he didn't have my soul. Maggie the witch had that, and I had to give her my now-whole tooth before she would set me free."

"His Infernal Majesty couldn't have liked that too much. He's never been too happy about the soulless undead."

"Too true. But I pointed out a few things to him. How taxation was second only to direct demonic intervention for presenting the temptation to sin, as well as generating huge amount of blasphemy, which is music to his ears. Then I made him an offer . . . so he let me speak to her. Released her from the awful torment by honest criticism, and literary award assessment on merit."

"I'm surprised she agreed to free you. You must have been one of her last remaining works in print."

"Well, you know what they say. Literary prostitution is more a case of haggling about the price—whether you take it in satisfaction, fame, money or all three, or just a get-out-of-hell ticket. I must say she looked a sight, her soul lashed with red pen. But she recognized me right away, in spite of my being in a borrowed body. The soul sees clearly. 'You! You philistine! You called my work potty poetry!' she screamed at me.

" 'I have the whole tooth for you,' I said, doing my best to keep it friendly.

" 'Too late,' she said nastily. 'I'm dead and in the pit.'

" 'You could free me,' I suggested.

"She hadn't changed a bit. 'No. Not unless *you* free me,' she said. 'I want my life back, and literary fame.' She always drove a hard bargain, even on extractions.

"The Devil shrugged. 'It is a pity. It was a tempting offer you made me, tax man. But no one gets out of Hell.' he said.

"I'd really got onto his Infernal Majesty's level by

now. We were kindred spirits of sorts, I suppose. 'Your Majesty, the literary arts? How many does that send to perdition?' I asked.

"The Devil must have consulted his accountants via his bluefang, because a few seconds later he said, 'Many. But poetry less so these days. The smart damnation is into pseudo-intellectual angst-prose and shock-value sexual deviancy.' His Infernal Majesty looked at me thoughtfully . . . and nodded. 'I suppose so. But she'll have to change fields to the high-yield area, and operate under a pseudonym. I won't have all writers thinking they can get away with this,' said the devil.

"Miss Maggie looked sour. 'Well, I still won't give his soul back. I'm a poet at heart. It's the highest art, although I will admit literary prose can be very moving. And that's a mended tooth, not the whole one.'

" 'You may have custody of my soul,' I offered. 'As long as you liberate me from the verse fate. Just think of all the wonderful sneering you'll be able to do at lesser literary forms. All I want is to be free of the dusty, yellowed, foxed, lonely pages of *Malocclusion, Caries and Decay.*'

"She thought about it awhile. Then she turned to the devil. 'I'll need glowing reviews . . .'

"The Devil smiled, showing long yellow fangs. He'd be needing her or my friend Dr. Edwards soon. And hell gets few dentists. 'I can even get you on daytime TV. It's full of my employees,' the Devil said."

The tax man finished his drink. "And that was that. She's a major literary figure now, sneering happily at fantasy and science fiction, last I heard. And here I am, too, free of her poetic justice. I believe she's found literary fiction just as rewarding, with her fine grasp of marketing. And the Devil's well pleased by the numbers she's driven to perdition."

"And you?" I asked, looking at the demon bodyguards snoozing in the booth. "What price did he demand of you?"

The tax man gave me his gap-toothed smile again. A very predatory happy smile. "We made a bargain—both parties got what they wanted. You see, I was able to point out that the soulless undead were technically his property. Heaven doesn't want them. And thus, even if he was not able to claim their souls . . . they were subjects of his. Liable for taxation. Many of them work among the living with souls to part with, and hell doesn't mind indirect taxation. I've got my old job back." He looked at his watch. "Ah. The bank is open. I have to drop in on the ogre of a manager. Then I've got a shape-shifting toad at the local school board. We have a bloodsucking attorney on the list next, with a final visit to a banshee diva at the opera house. They're in arrears."

He laughed. "I'm better off undead. But *they* aren't, now that I'm here. Death may not be sure, but taxes are."

THE INFERNAL REVENANT SERVICE

Laura Resnick

Death was not turning out to be the picnic that I had expected.

"What do you *mean*, I'm not being admitted to heaven?" I demanded of the celestial bureaucrat who greeted me at the security checkpoint outside the waiting room to get into the registry hall to sign up for the angelic inspection that was required before being admitted to the Divine Presence for final approval and an I.D. card valid for eternity.

"That tone is quite unnecessary, sir," the winged official said frostily.

"Listen. . . ." I looked at her nametag. "Listen, Lucy—"

"Saint Lucy the Chaste, if you please. I find that it's best to keep things formal when dealing with petitioners for entry into the afterlife."

"But I'm already *in* the afterlife!" I said. "I'm dead. I swear to God."

She flinched. "We don't do that *here*, sir."

"Sorry," I said.

"Try not to let it happen again."

"Look, I'm here because I died, Saint Lucy, so how can I be a *petitioner*—"

"Saint Lucy the *Chaste*," she said firmly.

"That's quite a mouthful."

She arched her brows. "Nonetheless . . ."

I silently begged God for patience. "My point is, my life is over, I'm dead, so this *is* after my life. You know: afterlife. I'm here already."

"No, you are currently making the transition between your life and eternity," she said, as if speaking to a particularly slow-witted child. "And in order to enter *the* afterlife, you're going to have to fill out the correct application for an entity of your classification and be routed to the right department."

"But isn't heaven the right department, Saint Lucy?" Seeing her frown, I added, "Er, the Chaste. Tell me, what do your friends call you?"

"I'm afraid it's going to be several millennia before you find out. According to my records . . ." She flipped through some pages attached to the clipboard she carried. "You're scheduled to go to holding for the next ten thousand of your earth years."

" 'Of your earth years'?" I repeated. "You sound like someone from a *Star Trek* episode."

"Do you want me to give it to you in metric time?"

"What's metric time?" I asked.

"Perhaps you see my point."

"Oh. Yes. Okay." I frowned. "But . . . ten thousand years? I think that must be a mistake."

"On the contrary. In eternity, that's a mere drop in the bucket. And He Who Rules On High has determined that it's a fair penalty for your sins."

"What are you talking about?" I said.

"The Maker of All Things has judged that you should spend ten thousand years meditating upon your misdeeds before your application to heaven can be considered."

"My *misdeeds*? Oh, wait a minute! Is this because I didn't pay that parking ticket?"

"Hmmm . . ." Saint Lucy the Chaste flipped through her paperwork again. "Unpaid parking ticket, unpaid parking . . . Yes, here it is. Listed under Moral Infractions, Minor.''

"No way!" I said. "That was a totally bogus ticket! I was in a store, only twenty feet away, *getting change for the parking meter,* when some cop came along and started writing that ticket! And when I got back to the car and explained, he wouldn't *stop* writing the ticket! Wouldn't even acknowledge my presence! It was completely unfair!''

"Nonetheless, the Lord God Almighty is a supporter of law and order (he's also a fan of that clever TV show, though he doesn't like the spin-offs as much), and you were unquestionably in the wrong when you chose not to pay that ticket.''

"*Unquestionably*? How can you say that?''

"The Master of the Universe judges that you were wrong. Therefore, you were *wrong*,'' the chaste saint said. "And you're going into holding.''

" 'Holding?' What does that mean? Limbo?''

The saint rolled her beatific eyes. "We don't have limbo anymore. Don't you keep up on current events?''

"Oh, right. I guess I heard about that in the news while I was still alive.''

Lucy the Chaste shook her head in exasperation. "The Vatican gets a whim, and *we* have to shut down an entire dimensional plane. You have no idea how much red tape is involved.'' She sighed. "I really hate popes.''

"Then I guess you mean I'm going to purgatory?''

"Bingo.''

"So you've still got that place?'' I said.

"Yes. At least, we've got it until yet another new Bishop of Rome wants to flex his muscles by messing with our system.''

Trying to get things back on track, I said, "Look, in all fairness, and not suggesting that I deserve special treatment, I have to say that ten thousand years in purgatory seems a little harsh for an unpaid parking ticket."

"Oh, that's merely *one* of your sins."

"What are these 'sins' you're talking about?" I asked. "I know I'm not perfect, but I certainly wasn't a *bad* man. I was a good husband and never unfaithful. I was a decent father, even when the kids were teenagers and didn't exactly inspire feelings of paternal affection. I ran my business honestly, I gave to charity, I recycled . . . Oh, wait a minute. Is God punishing me because I fudged some of the deductible expenses on my business taxes?"

"Oh, no, of course not!" the saint assured me. "Since the Internal Revenue Service is a tool of Lucifer and its employees are his minions—"

"Really? I always suspected as much!"

"—the One True God does not frown on mortals who challenge that evil organization's dominion."

"Ah! So . . . you know how I died, right?"

"If you did not die rescuing virgins or puppies, I don't need to know," said Saint Lucy the Chaste. "It's irrelevant."

"Not so fast," I said. "I died of a heart attack induced by the stress of trying to clear up yet another IRS screw-up. They were harassing me for not filing taxes that I had indeed filed, and that I repeatedly showed them *proof* I had filed. One day, after speaking to six bureaucrats in a row who all insisted there was no one in the entire IRS who could help me with this problem, and that they had no supervisors, and that there was no such thing as a complaints department there . . . I got so frustrated and agitated, I had a massive coronary on the spot."

"Oh, so that was *you*? I heard about that." Saint Lucy the Chaste seemed to warm up to me a bit. "Evil can be *so* trying to deal with, can't it?"

"You said it, sister. And the bastards are probably harassing my wife, now that I'm dead. Er . . . can I say 'bastards' here?"

"In general, we frown on profanity, but the Lord of Hosts is lenient in instances where it was obviously provoked." The saint patted my hand.

"So if I may ask, Saint Lucy the Chaste, why do I have to spend so long in purgatory?"

"Hmmm, let's see . . ." She referred to her records. "Oh, dear. It appears that you haven't voted in a national, state, or local election for the past eighteen years."

"I'm being kept out of heaven for *that*?"

"Not voting in a democratic society?" she said. "You abandoned a moral duty! For eighteen years!"

"Have you *seen* the candidates we've had for the past eighteen years? As a citizen, I refuse to be forced to choose between the lesser of two evils."

"Speaking of evil . . ." Lucy frowned as she glanced over my records. "Ah, *now* I see why you're going to purgatory for ten large."

"What did I do?" I tried to see the entry she was looking at.

She glared accusingly at me. "You worked for an oil company!"

"Huh? No, I ran my own real estate business for thirty years."

"Before that."

"Before that, I was an accountant in a mortgage company."

"*Before* that."

"Before . . . Oh, *wait*. You mean . . ." I realized what she must be talking about. "Oh, my God."

"Watch your tongue."

"You're kidding, right?" I said.

"We never kid about taking His name in vain here."

"No, I mean about why I'm going to purgatory."

"We never kid about going to purgatory, either," said Saint Lucy the Chaste.

"It was a summer internship!" I said.

"At an oil company."

"I was twenty-one years old!"

"And working at an oil company," the saint reiterated.

"For ten weeks! *One* summer. In their accounting department. I had to get *some* sort of professional experience on my résumé before graduation if I wanted to find a decent job!"

"The follies of youth," said Her Chasteness. "In the end, everyone pays."

"I'm going to purgatory for ten thousand years because of *that?*"

"The Lord God feels ten millennia will give you sufficient time to meditate upon your misguided professional commitment to big oil—"

"It was ten weeks!" I cried.

"—in a universe where He provided you with an abundance of alternative energy sources to choose from."

"At ten thousand years," I said, "that's one thousand years in purgatory for every week I spent on that internship! And I didn't even learn anything there!"

"Sin catches up with everyone in death," Lucy said.

"Oh, for God's sake." I saw her expression and added, "Sorry. I'm a little agitated."

She pulled a few papers from her clipboard and handed them to me. "Fill these out. I need to process you."

I looked at the forms. "Ten thousand years. Jesus." She flinched.

"Sorry, sorry," I said. "So who'll be keeping me company in purgatory? A gazillion oil company executives?"

"Oh, no," she said reassuringly. "We don't let *their*

sort into purgatory. They're routed straight to . . . you know." She pointed down and leaned forward to whisper, "The other place."

"They go straight to hell?"

There was a bolt of lightning and a deafening crack of thunder.

"Wow!" I blinked. "I guess that's another word I'm not supposed to use here?"

"It's considered to be in bad taste."

"So purgatory is full of . . ." I shrugged. "Interns?"

"It's full of people who need to meditate on their sins."

"Sounds like a charming place to spend the next ten thousand years," I said morosely.

The saint gave me a sympathetic look. "Take heart. You're in eternity now. Ten thousand years isn't long."

"It sure *sounds* long."

"No, no, not at all. Most people are in purgatory for much longer than that."

"Really?" I said.

"Oh, yes." She perused my records again. "You see, you really *were* a good man. If not for that one youthful sin—"

"It was an *internship*."

"—you'd be out of purgatory by his time next week. Even in metric time."

"Jesu—er, gosh! You're saying that *one* incident accounts for virtually my entire sentence in purgatory? In that case, I repent! I repent right *now*. Fully and unconditionally!"

"I'm afraid there's more to penance than that."

"Look at my record," I insisted. "I never worked again in oil after that. I worked in mortgages, then in real estate. I sold affordable homes to hardworking middle class people. I installed solar panels in my own house and drove a hybrid car. I was one of the good guys!"

"Yes, but—"

"I loathe the oil industry!"

"So does Yahweh, but—"

"I spit on big oil! Ptooey!"

"We don't spit in heaven."

"We're not *in* heaven," I pointed out.

"Oh, right."

"But in a fair universe, we could continue this conversation there, instead of in purgatory," I said. "Come on, Saint Lucy the Chaste. How about giving a guy a fair break?"

"Well . . ." She bit her lip, then said, "To be honest, the Master of the Universe can be a little harsh when it comes to the sins of nonrenewable energy sources."

"Is that a fact?"

Saint Lucy the Chaste leaned close to whisper, "It just bothers Him so much that mankind failed what He thought was an easy test of free will. You know. On the one hand, lots of sunshine, it's right there, and it doesn't pollute anything. On the other hand, a finite amount of oil, it's way underground, and it's pretty hard to wash off egrets. The Lord God thought it was a no-brainer and you people would all make the right choices without a struggle."

"The Lord God didn't count on profit margins, did He?" I said.

"There's a flaw in every grand plan," Saint Lucy the Chaste said with a sigh.

"Look," I said, "I acknowledge that my life was not entirely without sin, but do you think you could cut me some slack?"

"Hmmm." The saint tapped her quill pen on her clipboard. "Well . . . all right. I'm really not supposed to do this for anyone who worked in oil, tobacco, or Hollywood, but you seem sincerely repentant, and the rest of your catalogue of misdeeds is fairly minor. So I will file a petition with purgatory management to enroll you in a work-release program."

"Work-release?"

"Yes," she said. "Technically, you'll still be assigned to purgatory, but you'll only need to check in with them once every metric annum. And if you get a good report from your work detail, you can reduce your sentence by up to sixty per cent."

"So I'd have a chance of getting into heaven in a mere . . ." I took deep breath. "Four thousand years?"

"Yes. I can see by your expression that you think that still sounds like a long time. But you'll be doing important work. And time flies when you're busy. Whereas I've heard that time passes rather slowly in purgatory."

"Yeah, I suppose that sitting around and contemplating your misdeeds would tend to make minutes feel like hours." I frowned and asked, "But what does 'work-release' mean in the afterlife?"

"You will return to the earthly plain."

"I'm going to be reincarnated?"

"No, that's a different classification. You will maintain your present, eternal, unearthly form. In performance of God's work, you will probably come into contact with earthly beings—"

"You mean people?"

"Yes, people. But you will not go back to being a person."

"What will I be? An angel?"

She snorted. "Goodness, no! Only saints become angels, and only with special training." She chuckled at my naiveté.

"So what will I be?"

"People have a variety of names for entities who are on earthly visitations as part of various departmental work-release programs in the afterlife: ghost, spirit, poltergeist—"

"Oh, my God! Er, sorry. I mean, those things are real? I thought they were just stories."

Saint Lucy the Chaste sighed. "I've been telling

Yahweh for metric decades that we need to make the nature of these entities clearer to mankind, in hopes that people would pay more attention to their work. But He's been in such a snit about global warming, He claims there's no point in trying to *reason* with mankind, we're better off just scaring them."

"So that's what I'll be doing? Scaring mankind?" I looked down at the puffy white cloud I was standing on. "Boy, I don't know, Saint Lucy the Chaste. That doesn't sound like very noble work. I want to reduce my purgatory sentence, but I really don't want to harass people. Couldn't I do something a little more like community service? Maybe clean up—"

"Hang on," the saint interrupted me. "Message from the Lord God."

"Huh?" I looked up and saw a plump, winged cherub fly up to Lucy's ear to whisper something to her.

The saint listened for a few moments, while the fluttering of the cherub's wings made a faint humming sound.

"Ah-hah! Splendid idea!" Saint Lucy smiled at the cherub. "The Maker of All Things always knows best, doesn't He?"

The cherub chirped and giggled, then flew away.

Saint Lucy the Chaste said to me, "The Lord of Hosts has suggested the perfect work detail for you."

"He knows?" I looked around. "I mean, He knows we're talking about this?"

"Of course! He knows everything. He's omniscient and omnipotent. Also ubiquitous." Lucy added, "He also speaks more than two thousand languages. But I digress."

"He knows I'm trying to reduce the purgatory sentence he slapped on me? And He's not angry?"

"Yahweh gets bad press," the saint said. "He's much more merciful and forgiving than organized religion would lead one to believe. Since you seem truly repentant about the oil thing, He has suggested a work-release program that I believe you can join with true enthusiasm.''

"Which is?''

"The Infernal Revenant Service.''

"I'm going to be a revenant back on earth?''

Saint Lucy nodded. "Your job will be to torment the minions of Lucifer and to protect mankind from them.''

"Oh? Hey! That sounds fine. I could feel good about doing work like that.''

"Given your own experiences with the spawn of, er, the other place—''

"My experiences with *who*?''

"The Internal Revenue Service,'' she said.

"Oh. Right.''

"Considering that, the Lord God thought this would be the right work-release placement for you. The Infernal Revenants are assigned exclusively to the IRS, and it's a big job.''

"I see,'' I said.

"I'll help you fill out the necessary paperwork in purgatory, and after you've served one week there for that unpaid parking ticket—''

"That *bogus* ticket.''

"—you can join the Infernal Revenants and start haunting the servants of Satan—''

"Otherwise known as the IRS.''

"—and wreak havoc on their evil works.''

"So what do I do? Rattle chains, fiddle with the lights and electricity, leave messages in blood on the walls, that sort of thing?''

"That sounds like a good start,'' the saint said. "But there'll be much more work than that before your service culminates in your application for entry into heaven. Yahweh would like to see the Infernal Revenants send the children of Lucifer back to the fires whence they came by the end of this metric millennium. So there are big plans in the making. Your team captain will fill you in on the details when you report for duty."

"Excellent!" I said. "The Lord God sure knows His stuff. There's no work-release detail I'd rather be on. The IRS caused my fatal heart attack, after all! They're the reason I'm here now instead of vacationing in Hilton Head with my family."

"Ah, but remember," the saint cautioned me. "Haunting the IRS isn't vengeance. It's a sacred duty."

"Understood, Saint Lucy the Chaste. Now let's get started on that paperwork, so I can report for duty!"

And whether it's duty or vengeance, I expect the next four millennia to pass rather quickly now.

MUMMY KNOWS BEST

Esther M. Friesner

"Well, what do you think, Ms. Cyprien?" The dapper young man turned off the DVD, sat back against the sofa cushions, and smiled at Ashley. His skin, dark as finely polished mahogany, contrasted dramatically with the soft white leather. "I like to believe that I provide certain additional customer services that our promotional materials simply can't equal, but every time I show that video to a client, it does my job for me."

Ashley Cyprien crossed, uncrossed, and re-crossed her legs, a nervous habit she'd picked up early in her career when said legs had been the most bankable thing in the young starlet's life. "I—I'm afraid I'm still not sure about all this, Mr. Smith," she said.

"Smith is so formal. Please, call me Tchet-Ptah-auf-ankh." He leaned forward and kicked his smile-power up a notch.

"Um . . . I can't."

He laughed without condescension. "Then call me Chet. Now, how soon would you like to tour our facilities?"

Ashley's legs flailed back and forth once more. "I don't need to do that."

"Then you've decided to go ahead with the transformation as soon as possible? Wonderful! I admire a woman who knows what she wants. I so seldom see beauty, intelligence and determination in one—"

"I mean that I don't need to do that *yet*." Ashley blushed, loath to interrupt her visitor's spate of flattery. "I'm still not convinced that your company's service is something I really want to commit to—"

"It's the brains thing, isn't it?" Chet was suddenly solemn. Ashley didn't reply. Her involuntary shudder told the story. He nodded sagely. "I thought so. It's always the brains thing that's the stumbling block. I said it was a bad idea to put the brains thing onscreen, but you know how it is: in this day and age, most folks already know about it, and there's always a fuss about truth in advertising." He sighed and rubbed the back of his stylishly shaved head. "At least it was okay to use animation to get the message across. When it's a cartoon mouse undergoing the procedure, no one runs away screaming."

Ashley lowered her eyes. "I almost did."

Chet's smile was warm and reassuring. "Almost doesn't count. Ms. Cyprien, I wish I had a dollar for every one of your fellow actresses who shot out of their chairs even *before* we got to the brains thing. Some of them ran out of the room, jumped into their cars, and burned rubber getting away, even though I was making my presentation in their own homes! But you! You stayed. You're a heroine, Ms. Cyprien; a real heroine."

"No, I'm not." Ashley tried to sound embarrassed, but a note of pride crept into her words. "I'm still all grossed out by the brains thing. I know it's part of your culture, and I respect that—honestly, I do! It's just so . . . icky. No offense," she added quickly.

"None taken." Chet stood up and spread his arms wide. "Ms. Cyprien, look at me. Please." He turned around once, slowly, giving her ample time to take in every aspect of his person. He was strikingly handsome, with high cheekbones, a sensuous mouth, a trim, muscular body, mesmerizing dark brown eyes, and the lithe grace of a Bengal tiger. He filled out his Armani suit in ways just this side of legal in some of the less liberal states. "What's wrong with this picture?"

"Nothing." Ashley wasn't just saying that to be polite. The little dab of drool at the corner of her mouth testified to her sincerity.

"And yet, would you believe that it has now been over four thousand years since the skilled professionals of the Beautiful House removed *my* brains through my nose and fed them to the sacred cats?"

Ashley let out a yelp and ran out of the living room.

Chet smacked his palm with a fist. "Curse it, I moved too fast again! I was sure I had her, and then I had to go and say the bit about feeding brains to cats. May the dark god Set be my witness, compared to some of the stuff these people plop into their cats' feeding bowls, brains are a step up. A whole *flight* of steps! When will I learn?" His scowl deepened and he muttered, "It had better be soon. I'm running out of time."

"Chet?" Ashley's timid voice sounded from just beyond the doorway. She edged back into the living room. "I think I've changed my mind. I'm not interested in becoming a mummy any more. Ever. Please don't take it personally. It's just . . . just . . ." She scanned the air for a cue card that wasn't there. "It's just that I'm not worthy of that sort of eternal life." She sounded relieved.

Chet shrugged. "The customer is always right," he said, apparently untroubled at the abrupt loss of a potential client. "It's quite true: eternal beauty and fame isn't for everyone." He popped his promotional disc out of the DVD player and headed for the front door.

Her hand closed on his shoulder before he'd gone three steps. "I said eternal *life*. What did *you* say?"

"I said *beauty,* Ms. Cyprien." It was all he could do to suppress the urge to smirk in triumph when he turned to reply. In his boyhood days he'd been one of the best anglers on the Nile, as many an unwitting perch had found out just one tug of the hook too late. It was always simply a matter of using the proper bait. "Eternal beauty and—for those whose chosen careers are enhanced by such things—the fame that logically accompanies imperishable loveliness." He caught sight of her perplexed expression and simplified his pitch. "Mummification has always been about preserving the body. When that body is supremely beautiful—as yours is, if you don't mind my saying so—our process freezes that beauty in time. It will not fade. It *can*not. Ms. Cyprien, once you agree to undergo the transformation, you will always be as young and exquisite as you are now." He took a step closer, lowered his voice to a seductive purr and breathed in her ear: "*Always.*"

She made a small, helpless sound. "Oh, I'm *so* confused! I mean, what you're saying, what the DVD said, it all sounds so wonderful, but—" She looked ready to run away a second time. "—but don't I have to be dead first?"

He was pleased to notice that, for all the signs of impending panic and flight, she was making no immediate move to step away from him. "We prefer the term Eternity Enhanced. And really, how dead is *this*?"

With the skill born of thousands of years of practice, he slid his arms around her and kissed her, warmly, deeply, and thoroughly. When a man has walked the earth for millennia, he gains a certain level of adroitness at reading the subtlest signals of amatory encouragement and waiting willingness that women sometimes send out. From the moment he'd walked into her home, he'd noted the way Ms. Cyprien looked at him. She'd been broadcasting on the Wow-You're-Hot-Take-Me-*Now* Channel from the get-go. Once in his embrace, she didn't put up even the pretense of a struggle. When he eventually tried to break the clinch, she clung to him and would not let him go.

Finally, she collapsed against him, panting. He stroked her hair with adept fingers. "I'm sorry, Ms. Cyprien," he said. "That was inappropriate. I hope you won't report me to my superiors?"

She shook her head weakly and pressed her face into his chest. Her hands became talons, clutching his shoulders. "I want—I want more proof," she murmured.

"Proof?" he asked innocently.

"That you're not dead." She raised her head and looked him in the eye, her face flushed and slack with lust. She began dragging him toward the open spiral stairway. She hadn't given him a tour of her Beverly Hills home when he'd arrived, but it was fairly obvious that where there was an upper level, there were bedrooms.

His lips twitched into a fleeting smile. "The customer is always right," he repeated softly.

Afterwards, he traced hieroglyphs on her stomach with trickles of the excellent California merlot she'd brought out halfway through their passionate encounter. "Well, now I *really* hope you won't report me," he said, licking wine off his fingertip.

"What's it worth to you?" she asked lightly, attempting to interest him in a romantic rematch.

To her chagrin, he sat up and turned away from her. "What do you think it's worth to me, Ashley?" he asked. His voice shook just a bit, striking exactly the right note of male vulnerability without doing a nosedive into wimphood. "Because if you guess it's worth anything less than my life—my continued existence—you'll be wrong."

Her felt her cool fingers close on his arms but he refused to face her. "What do you mean, Chet?" she asked. There was genuine fear in her voice. He bit his lower lip. Really, it got harder and harder not to smile when they danced so prettily at the end of his line!

"If I do anything—*anything* of which my superiors disapprove, they will . . . kill me."

She nestled her chin on his shoulder and put her arms around him. "But they can't do that! It's not fair! This is America! You're already dead!"

Steadfastly he refused to meet her gaze directly. He knew exactly how noble and long-suffering he looked in profile and he was going to use it. "I may be . . . dead, as you choose to put it, but I assure you, this is as dead as I wish to be. There are greater deaths. I have already experienced one of them, and as dreadful as it was, compared to my present condition, it's nothing next to the even worse death I would have to endure if my superiors find any fault with me."

He felt Ashley's arms slip from around his neck as she sat back on the bed. "Chetsy, I'm a little, you know, confused?" she said in a daddy's little girl voice entirely inappropriate to her age. "I mean, I know you're not *dead* dead, and that you could be, sorta-kinda, *deader* than now, but the way you're talking, it sounds like you could actually get to be even *deader* than *dead* dead. I don't get it."

Chet pinched the bridge of his nose and muttered a prayer to Thoth, the god of wisdom, to lend him patience. "Ashley, do you want to know how I came to work for the Beautiful House?" he asked, giving her the slightest of glances. When he saw her nod, he went on: "You know what I am. You know when I died."

"Um, a long, long time ago? Like, when Cleopatra was doing Marc Antony?"

"When Cleopatra reigned over Egypt, I had been in my tomb for at least two thousand years."

"In your tomb?" Ashley's voice shrilled with alarm. "I thought—I thought that after you got made into a mummy, you didn't have to stay in a tomb. You're not in a tomb now. I don't want to go into a tomb! I hate cemeteries! I can't wear my favorite shoes there because the high heels keep sinking into the grass."

He had her in his arms again so quickly that she didn't see him move. "Hush, my darling, hush. I promise you, this lovely body will never see the inside of a tomb. You must let me explain. You must . . . trust me. Will you do that? Can you?" She nodded again, and he rewarded her with a kiss, and then something more than a kiss.

At the next intermission, he resumed his story. "Progress is a marvelous thing, beloved. It is a kind of magic, and it works its spells upon the dead as surely as upon the living. The art of the priests who prepared me for the grand voyage into eternity did everything within their power to ensure that my soul would reach its destination, the Field of Reeds, which is what we call the blessed realm where the god Osiris rules. They gave me the scriptures of the sacred Book of the Dead to take with me on that journey, as a part of the linen strips they wound around my body and as inscriptions on the walls of my tomb and written on papyrus scrolls sealed inside clay jars near my golden sarcophagus."

"Ooooh, gold?" Ashley's eyes shone with a fresh love-light. Chet barely suppressed his annoyance when he noticed that it was several hundred watts brighter than any of the burning looks she'd given him. "Were you, like, a prince or something?"

"What I was is all in the past," he replied. "I would rather not speak of that now. It is the future that concerns me, as it should also concern you, my adored one."

"Then why are you telling me all this *other* stuff about the past if you say you don't care about it?" Ashley pouted like a cranky four-year-old.

"Ah, now it seems you wish to argue with me,"

Chet said smoothly. "How sad. I must be boring you, or why would your divine face now be touched by— is that a wrinkle?" He kissed her right between the eyes with the swiftness and venom of a cobra's strike.

"What wrinkle?" she cried, distraught. "Oh God, please, not that! Do I really have a wrinkle?" She was pleading so pathetically that he almost felt real affection for her.

"My mistake. It must have been a trick of the light." Her touched her forehead with one fingertip. "There's nothing there."

"Honestly? You're not just saying that?"

"I could never lie to you."

"Well, okay. Go on."

"As I was saying, when a person embarks upon the trip to Lord Osiris' realm, he must pass through many challenges, encounter many perils, but the wisdom in the Book of the Dead provides him with all the knowledge he needs to come through every encounter successfully."

"Oh! Like cheat codes for winning Super Mario Brothers!" Ashley beamed over her own intelligence.

Chet sighed. "Sure, why not. Although I doubt Mario and Luigi ever had to confront the Devourer of Souls. She is a most fearsome beast, part lion, part crocodile, and part hippopotamus, and she—are you *laughing*?"

Ashley looked guilty even while stifling more giggles. "Hippos are funny."

"You might change your mind about that if you ever saw the size of their teeth at close range," Chet remarked. "However, the Devourer's teeth belong to her crocodilian aspect. They are more than sufficient for rending unlucky souls into utter oblivion."

"Oh! That's *awful*." Ashley shivered. "Why doesn't someone stop her? Can't that Irish guy do it?"

Chet's thin brows drew together. He didn't need to ask *What Irish guy?* He was already all too familiar with the way Ashley's mind worked. "O-S-I-R-I-S, darling, not O-apostrophe-Cyrus. He is the ever-living god of the dead and the first to be mummified. His wife and queen, Lady Isis, did it to restore him to life after his evil brother Set slaughtered him, tore him to pieces, scattered his bloody remains across the lands and the waters, fed his manly parts to a fish, and—"

"Are you making this up as you go along or are you just trying to convince me there are worse things than the whole brains-through-the-nose bit?" Ashley demanded.

"Love, what I tell you is as true as the final judgment that awaits each soul who comes into Lord Osiris' presence in the Hall of Two Truths. For it is there that a man's heart is placed in the Scales of Thoth, to be weighed against the Feather of Ma'at, goddess of Truth. The heart that is blameless is light as that Feather, but the heart heavy with sin can't survive the test and is thrown into the waiting jaws of the Devourer. Now do you see why I prefer to stay on *this* side of the final journey and judgment?"

"Wouldn't you pass the test?" Ashley asked fearfully.

Chet shrugged. "Who can say? Can any of us know what will displease the gods, what they will consider a sin? The matter is no longer in my hands. You see, my love, the soul's journey may be brief or lengthy. Time in this world and time in Osiris' realm are not the same. My final fate had not been declared when I found myself brought out of the slumber of ages, my self and my body reunited by heartless beings. They used the spells of a powerful magician who had discovered the secret for making one's existence as a mummy—" He spread his hands wide. "—what you see before you now."

Ashley's eyed opened wide. "I do!" she exclaimed. "I *do* see! I understand *everything* now. They must be the ones you work for, your superiors, the Beautiful

House guys! Oh, you poor baby, if they make you do bad things, those mean old gods might not forgive you even if it wasn't your fault at all! I mean, you didn't ask to be born. Reborn. Whatever." She flung herself upon him, a veritable tidal wave of compassion.

"Such a good heart," Chet murmured, smiling. "So loving, so tender. If only it could be mine for all eternity."

Abruptly she pushed herself to arm's length away from him. "Oh. Em. Gee."

"Oh? Er? What?"

"I'll do it," Ashley said. She struck the same resolute pose she'd been laboriously coached into for her role as Mimsy Gillifoil, the blind amnesiac nurse in *The Heart Forgets What It Wants.* "I'll have the procedure. I'll go to the Beautiful House, I'll become a mummy, and then I can become the most famous actress ever, *for*ever, and I'll earn so much money that maybe I can buy off your bosses and you can be free again and we can get married and be happy and—"

He silenced her with a kiss. "My heroine," he said fondly. There was a flickering in the air, the rapid movement of his hands as a pen and a stack of legal-looking papers whisked onto the bed between them. "Sign here."

While she inked the contract, Ashley said, "Wow. You are so fast with your hands. I mean, not in the bad way. Which isn't really so bad either." She giggled. "Oh, you know what I mean. It was like you made this contract appear out of thin air. How did you do that?"

"Simple." He took back the signed papers. "I'm a magician." She was in the middle of making an extraordinarily lame joke about his magic wand when he stilled her lips yet again, in self-defense.

The waiting room of the Beautiful House was decorated in a style Chet thought of a *haut* Eurotrash, a palette of gray, black, and scarlet with chrome accents and furniture that oozed irony and ennui. This was no mean trick for a sofa to pull off, but the Beautiful House specialized in the impossible. Where else could a dead man sit thumbing through a copy of *Vogue* while studiously avoiding eye-contact with a very irked goddess?

Chet was faking fascination in a glossy ad about overpriced wristwatches when the goddess finally lost her patience. "Oh, drop it, you worm!" she snapped. "You're not fooling anyone. We both know what you want to do."

Chet slowly shut the magazine and settled it in his lap. "Why, Ma'at, my dear, I can't begin to imagine what you mean."

"Don't lie to me!" the goddess of Truth roared. She leaped to her gold-sandaled feet, divine wrath rendering her dark beauty almost incandescent.

"I never do," Chet said calmly. "The truth is that I can't *begin* to imagine what you mean because I've already done so. Indeed, we both *do* know what I want to do, so I'll do it." With that, he tilted his head back and let loose a loud, gloating laugh. Then he raised his right forefinger and thrust it at the goddess' face. "*One* more, O divine Ma'at! That's all I need to fulfill our bargain, and then there is nothing you nor any of the gods can do to force me to face judgment in the Hall of Two Truths!"

The goddess gritted her teeth. "If I hadn't witnessed it, I would never have believed it. Ninety-nine thousand nine hundred ninety-nine hearts! Ninety-nine thousand nine hundred ninety-nine souls! Ninety-nine thousand nine hundred ninety-nine women without the brains that Bast gave a kitten!" Her furious gaze drifted toward the door leading to the treatment rooms of the Beautiful House. "When are you going to tell *this* one?" she asked.

"No hurry." One corner of Chet's mouth lifted in

a wry smile. "It's funny, but I rather like her. Too bad we didn't meet after I'd met my goal. We might have had a *real* future together. I could have spared her, but I needed her too much. You women do have such a strange *hunger* to be needed. I suppose that's what makes you such tender-hearted things."

The goddess slapped the smirk from his face in two thunderous claps, forehand and backhand. "I curse the day your deceitful soul entered the Hall of Two Truths, Magician!" she shouted. "I condemn it to the oblivion that awaits you when the Devourer of Souls finally feasts on your wicked heart!"

"You're just angry because I put one over on you," Chet said, touching his smarting cheeks gingerly. "It's not every day that a mortal manages to be quick enough to snatch Ma'at's sacred Feather right out of the Scales of Thoth and replace it with a sorcerously crafted one guaranteed to balance against the most sin-laden heart in all Egypt." He placed one hand on his bosom, bowed his head in a show of false modesty, and added: "Mine."

"Gloating bastard," Ma'at snarled. "Foul mage. When you felt your death approaching, you used your powers to enslave the minds of the funerary priests so that they wrapped that blasphemously created plume in your burial linens! And because you were able to switch the two feathers, Lord Osiris ruled that for my inattention to duty, I must bargain with such scum as you to retrieve my own! The stench of that humiliation still clings to me. Deceiver! Betrayer!" Then she added the worst insult she knew: "*Liar!*"

"Tsk, tsk, tsk. If you keep misusing that word, you're going to embarrass yourself. Have you forgotten, my lady? I touched your Feather: I *can*not lie any more, lest the bargain be annulled. You were there when Lady Isis herself made that pronouncement." His eyes narrowed in a sly look. "Or is that the worst humiliation of all, O Goddess? That I have been able to convince so many women to give me their hearts using only the truth?"

"A fine *truth*," Ma'at said scornfully. "I've been watching you, Magician. All that talk of a gold sarcophagus, of the heartless priests who raised you from death's slumber, of what your superiors would do to you if you failed them—!"

The powerful mage Tchet-Ptah-auf-ankh snorted in a thoroughly impertinent manner. "You've watched, but you haven't listened. Then again, if you were an *attentive* deity, you wouldn't be in your present fix, would you? I said I had a *golden* sarcophagus, and so it was: painted. The girl said 'gold' because that was what she wanted to hear! I never said *priests* brought me back to life, merely heartless *beings.* And so they are: I made them myself, my life-sized *ushabti,* the hollow clay images of servants meant to do my work in the afterlife. But why waste them there, when I had the power to animate them before I died and instruct them to restore me with my own spells when the time was right?"

"You pour a drop of beer into the Nile and claim that the river is a drunkard's paradise!" the enraged goddess cried. "And how did you *dare* claim your life would be forfeit if you displeased your superiors in the Beautiful House? You run this place alone, with the help of your *ushabtis!*"

"Great lady, I never said I had superiors *in the Beautiful House*; merely *superiors.*" He gave Ma'at a bland, pious look so deliberately provoking it would have made a stone dog foam at the mouth and added: "The gods."

"Miserable slime, Truth is not one of your clay creatures, to be shaped to suit your selfish purposes. It is the flower *and* the flower's scent, the light *and* the shadow it creates, what is said *and* what is left unsaid! You pick it apart like a roasted goose and feast upon only the pieces you like best, but it is the Devourer of Souls who will feast upon *you*!"

At that moment, the door opened and a glassy-eyed man walked stiffly over to Chet. "It is done, O Master."

Chet stood, rolled up his copy of *Vogue* and thumped the man smartly on the head. It made a sound like an empty flowerpot. "Excellent. Tell the client I will be with her shortly."

As the *ushabti* trudged off, Chet turned to Ma'at and asked, "Would you like to meet her? You could be the one to tell her your precious *Truth*: that as soon as I persuade one last woman to give herself into my power as she has done, then all one hundred thousand of them shall accompany me back to the Hall of Two Truths, and there I shall offer up their hearts to the Devourer of Souls as the agreed-upon price for my safe passage to a blissful eternity! It will be quite spectacular. Thousands of those women—no, more likely *tens* of thousands—have been living happy lives, convinced that they've found the secret to immortality. I'm afraid there will be tears."

"I *will* tell her!" Ma'at cried heedlessly. "I'll tell her, and the two of us will find enough of your other victims to tell the world about you, to make sure that you fail to find the last heart you need to fulfill the bargain! I'll—"

"You'll do nothing," the magician said. "Because Lord Osiris decreed that one word of revelation out of *you* would nullify our agreement and send me straight to the Field of Reeds, happily ever after. Of course that would also release the spirits of all those devoted ladies, save them from the Devourer . . ." He pretended to give the matter serious thought. "You could save them all, but not without saving me. Any hope of that happening, O Ma'at? Tell the *truth*, now." He laughed and fled just seconds before the goddess threw one of the *haut* Eurotrash table lamps at him. It smashed against the closing door.

Alone in the waiting room, Ma'at flung herself down on the sofa and howled.

"Hush, dear, you'll shatter the *ushabtis.*"

The goddess of Truth looked up to see the unutterably beautiful face of her sister-goddess, Isis. Osiris' queen perched on the arm of the sofa, wrapped in the splendor of a thousand stars and shod in a pair of Manolo Blahnik pumps.

"O Isis, what am I going to do?" Ma'at wailed. "We never thought that little monkey-tweaker would ever find *that* many women who'd follow him so blindly, even beyond the bounds of death, yet now he's just one heart away from his goal! He'll rub my nose in it for eternity! You're the one who used wisdom and magic to bring your husband back to life as the first mummy, so why couldn't you have stopped Tchet-Ptah-auf-ankh from becoming a mummy on his own terms? Why did you let that piece of camel-spit usurp *your* wondrous lore for *his* lowdown ends?"

Isis shrugged her delectable shoulders. "If we tried to stop mortals from turning every divine gift into a pile of dung beetle balls, we'd never get anything else done. Don't worry, Ma'at. Tchet-Ptah-auf-ankh won't get within *sniffing* distance of the Field of Reeds. You know how much I hate people who turn my beautiful art of mummification into something nasty. Remember what I did to those Hollywood cretins? As if you could make a proper mummy just by wrapping someone in linen and dropping him in a coffin! Tanna leaves, my butt!"

The goddess of Truth dared to feel a slight stirring of hope in her immortal breast. Not only was Isis the queen of the gods, resourceful, powerful, wise, and skilled in magic, she also had one immeasurable advantage over Ma'at when the situation called for getting down, dirty, and done: she could lie like an eat-all-you-want-don't-exercise-and-lose-twenty-pounds-in-five-days diet guru. "What will you do to him?" she asked Isis.

"Nothing. I can't. My Ossie made a universal oath of nonintervention part of the whole give-you-back-your-real-Feather bargain, remember?"

"Then how—?"

Isis smiled. "Sometimes the best goddess for the job is a woman."

Even a man who has spent untold ages in the tomb needs his beauty rest. Thus it was that the sorcerer Tchet-Ptah-auf-ankh was roused from sleep by the bedside telephone one fine morning a short while after Ashley's transformation. The voice on the line was sweetly feminine, though unfamiliar, and the words were music to his ears.

"Mr. Smith? My name is Bambi LaRue. I work with Ashley Cyprien. I've got to say, I'm really impressed by what a fabulous effect mummification's had on her career. They just can't seem to get enough of her, offers everywhere she turns, and the money's obscene, even for Hollywood. Sure, it's the novelty of it all, but who cares? Anyway, I think it'd be a smart career move for me to get the work done, too, so how about it?"

Chet frowned, feeling a bit like a cat that's woken up to find a live mouse trying to force his jaws apart. "Ms. LaRue, are you sure about this? I mean, did Ashley happen to describe the part of the procedure where we put the sacred cats on standby, take a hook, and—?"

"The brains thing?" Bambi giggled. "I've done worse. And Ashley's still the same, brains or no brains, so I'll be okay. Look, Mr. Smith, it's real simple: movie-making is a tough, hungry, ugly business.

No one gets out alive. You need an edge if you're going to make it to the top. I want Ashley's edge and you're going to give it to me."

"You're a very . . . decisive woman, Ms. LaRue. And Ashley doesn't mind the thought of you becoming her competition? Stealing that novelty value you mentioned?"

Bambi sighed deeply. "Oh God, the silly bitch was right: you must be in love with her or you wouldn't be trying to put me off. That or you're the world's worst salesman. Cute, but I don't have the time to do your job for you. Good-bye, Mr. Smith, it's been—"

"Wait!" Chet found himself clutching the heavy, retro-styled receiver with both hands. "Let's talk."

As a magician, Chet could smell the presence of the gods. When he met Ms. LaRue, he made sure to determine that she had nothing otherworldly about her before taking things any further. She was an unnaturally beautiful young woman, a type as common to Los Angeles as minnows to a pond, but she was otherwise clean. She was also a lot more intellectually gifted than Ashley. Chet almost regretted what an easy sale she'd given him. It would have been fun to seduce her and have an intelligent bed partner, for a change.

But business was business. Like Bambi, he didn't have time to waste. Not yet, anyway. There were six months to go before his millennia-old bargain came due. If she hadn't shown up on his doorstep, figuratively speaking, he could have met that deadline in a walk, but getting everything done ahead of time would be a coup. He reveled in the thought of showing up early in the Hall of Two Truths and saying something smug to Ma'at as he presented his swarm of stand-in hearts.

But the journey to Osiris' kingdom hadn't lost any of its perils in the intervening ages. He'd need time to prepare the proper spells to gather his enthralled women, to open the way to the afterlife, and to shield everyone from the dangers of the trip. The magic itself wasn't going to be the main problem. What was going to take time was the *shopping*.

Once Bambi signed on the dotted line, Chet whisked her off to the Beautiful House, handed her over to his top *ushabti*, and beat tracks for the farmer's market. Having purchased all the ingredients for casting spells of utmost darkness and hideous power, plus a chopped salad for lunch, he set to work.

Bambi emerged from the Beautiful House as a card-carrying member of the undead to find a super-stretch limo awaiting her. Ashley leaned out the window and actually *said,* "Yoo-hoo!" From the front seat, Chet beckoned, and she could do nothing but obey.

The trip to the Hall of Two Truths was the same as always—ordeals, beasts, government checkpoints—but in good time Tchet-Ptah-auf-ankh once more stood before Osiris, the other gods of the underworld, and the Devourer of Souls. He greeted them all with a show of feigned reverence, but could not resist giving Ma'at a contemptuous smile when he saw the goddess staring at him, clutching her sacred Feather protectively.

"As promised," he said, waving at the long line of women in his wake. "And well ahead of deadline. No pun intended, Lord Osiris."

Like the earthly pharaoh, the king of the afterlife carried a crook and a flail as his emblems of office. With the crook he gestured for the Devourer of Souls to come forward, with the flail he commanded the unlucky women to line up and give themselves to the monster. Anubis, the jackal-headed god who guided the dead, performed the formality of reaching into each lady's chest, murmuring a word of apology before removing the still-present heart, and tossing it to the Devourer. This repeated ritual was no Aztec sacrifice.

Anubis withdrew the hearts without bloodshed—after all what blood did the mummified women have left? As each heart went down the Devourer's gullet, its former owner vanished, though not before sending Chet a pitiful look of complete betrayal.

At first, the victims' poignant plight caused the implacable gods themselves to look on with compassion. Some were even seen to wipe away a tear. But somewhere around Victim #24,978 the emotional impact began to fade. Tedium gave sympathy the boot. Yawns were stifled. Eyes wandered. Someone set up a hounds-and-jackals game board behind Osiris' throne. The king of the dead gave the guilty parties a perfunctory glare of disapproval, then declared that he'd play the winner. Woman after woman went to her doom memorialized by the divine equivalent of *gosh-that's-a-shame-what's-on-the-other-channels?* In some respects, the gods of Egypt were only human. Only Ma'at stood as unblinking witness as the Devourer feasted and, in the mortal world, the remaining months until the magician's deadline slid away.

As for the instigator of the whole sorrowful scene, Tchet-Ptah-auf-ankh hadn't even bothered to watch more than five of his victims lose heart before he strolled off in search of Imhotep, the mortal architect whose creation of the first pyramid had elevated him to godhood. He wanted only the best talent to design his estate in the Field of Reeds.

He was just debating the placement of the wine cellar when a great commotion filled the Hall of Two Truths. The space before Osiris' throne was chaos. The gods were shouting. The Scales of Thoth was spinning like an amusement park ride. The remaining women were rushing around, shrieking. The lord of the dead was waving his crook and flail like a cheerleader's pompoms, vainly trying to restore order. And in the center of it all, jackal-head Anubis had the Devourer of Souls in a fearsome, inexplicable embrace.

The monster struggled in his grasp, leonine forepaws thrashing, hippo hindquarters pedaling madly, toothy snout gaping wide while a sickening gray tint crept across her crocodilian features.

"What—?" Chet cried just as Anubis jammed his bunched fists into the Devourer's midsection once, twice, thrice, and Bambi LaRue came shooting out of the monster's mouth.

Anubis set the Devourer down. "She was choking," he explained.

"What is the meaning of this?" Osiris bellowed. "Why did you feed my Devourer a whole woman? You know she only eats hearts, for the heart is the vessel of the soul!"

"Lord, I tried to feed her this woman's heart," Anubis said. "It's just that, well, I couldn't seem to find it. I rummaged around in there for the longest time, and it was holding up the line. It's all very nice for the rest of you, but I've been doing all the work here, and I'd like to have a little *me* time before the next century, thank you very much. So I decided to chuck everything down the chute and let the Devourer sort it out for herself. I figured once she got the heart, the rest of the package would vanish, like it always does. I don't know what went wrong."

"I do," said Isis. She stepped down from the royal dais and went to help the regurgitated woman to her feet. "*So* nice to see you again, dear." She gave Bambi a double air-kiss. "Wasn't that a *fabulous* little studio party? I'm *thrilled* you took my suggestion to ask Ashley about Mr. . . . Smith's services. I realize we're off to a rocky start, but being undead *will* give you a big leg up on the competition in the long run."

"No worries." Bambi wiped crocodile drool off her clothes. "I've gone through worse. There was one time I had to tell Tarantino that—"

"Darling, before you go on, do me a teensy favor?" Isis engulfed Bambi in her irresistible charm. "Would you mind telling everyone here what you do for a living?"

"Don't hold things up with your silly theatrics," Chet cut in. "You're only trying to put off my moment of triumph. *I* can tell you what she does for a living. She's just another actress."

"*Enh!*" Bambi did a good imitation of a quiz show's *wrong answer, stupid!* buzzer. "I'm no actress, sweetie. I'm a producer."

"So *that's* why I couldn't find her heart!" Anubis exclaimed. "D'oh!"

Somewhere in the universe a time's up gong rang. The Hall of Two Truths filled with a fluttery roar as the broken bargain restored the spirits of all the women the Devourer had already . . . processed. The magician stared in horror as all his victims fled back into the mortal world.

The goddess of Truth grinned full in his face. "One hundred thousand take away one equals *what*, O Tchet-Ptah-auf-ankh?"

He didn't have the chance to pull out a calculator before a very cranky lion-hippo-crocodile chowed down.

SPIRIT

Ghosts. Haunted houses. Spirits running amok among us. Spirits are the incorporeal form of the undead. Sometimes they walk among us, oblivious of their deaths, and sometimes they only touch us briefly, but they always fascinate us, as evidenced by numerous movies and books, ghost tours in New Orleans and small Western towns, and even Halloween.

Chelsea Quinn Yarbro shows us a side of Pacific Island cultures we might not want to face. Alan Dean Foster catches up with a famous personality whose living joke becomes his undead "life." Carrie Vaughn proves that death doesn't have to be the end when you've got an important job to do. Even a haunted museum's secrets can be surprising, with Irene Radford's deft storytelling.

GENIUS LOCI

Chelsea Quinn Yarbro

"And this part of the house is called the gullet," the proud owner declared as they went up the stairs.

"Who lived here before you bought the place; do you know?" Agatha Pomeroy asked her niece, Bronwyn Sallister, as she followed her up to the second floor. This was her first visit to the new house and she was very impressed with what she saw of the refurbished Queen Anne Victorian.

"You mean before it was restored?" Bronwyn stopped on the landing, allowing her aunt to catch up with her. She was dressed in a mauve silk blouse over beige wool slacks, her light-brown hair pulled back from her face into a ponytail. For thirty-eight, she was in fine condition, burnished with health and fitness. As a part-time librarian for the local historical society, she had achieved a place in the community she enjoyed.

"Yes. That's what I mean," said Agatha. "From what you said, it was transformed by the renovators." She had taken off the long, pin-striped jacket of her traveling suit, revealing the lace-fronted blouse with a high, frothy neck. Her slacks were a bit wrinkled from the long drive, but she felt neat enough not to need to change clothes yet. A trim woman of middle height,

Agatha Pomeroy was striving to keep from admitting her fatigue, but the five-hour drive had left her feeling a bit frayed, and it showed.

"It had been very rundown," said Bronwyn, finding it impossible to imagine her glossy, elegant house anything less than what it was. "It was built in 1894, you know. The man who owned it before the restoration company bought it didn't bother with it, or so I'm told. He was retired and spent most of his time in Santa Barbara, I understand, with his son's family. He only came back here two or three times a year, and never stayed more than a month. He said he didn't like the place, or at least, that's what my across-the-street neighbor told me. She's been in her house for thirty-nine years, so she knows everyone."

"Why didn't he like it?" Agatha wanted to know.

"According to Mirabelle, he claimed the house was haunted." Bronwyn laughed to show her opinion of such nonsense.

"This Mirabelle—your neighbor?—does she have an opinion? Does she agree it's haunted?"

"She hasn't said. Not that I've asked."

"You'd think she would have," said Agatha musingly. "If she told you so much in the first place."

"If you want to know, ask her when you meet her," said Bronwyn, clearly not interested in Agatha's line of questioning.

"If she's lived here for so long, she must be about my age, unless she was born here," said Agatha, who was fifty-seven, the youngest of Bronwyn's three maternal aunts.

"Oh, no: she's eighty-eight, a long-time widow. I'll invite her over, if you like," Bronwyn offered as she resumed the climb. "As you see, four bedrooms, each facing a different direction. I've put you in the south bedroom. Martin and I have the north bedroom—it's the master suite, I'll show it to you after you see your room. Then there's the east room, which we've made

Martin's study, and the west, which is our second guestroom, for when Martin's kids are here." She smiled and stepped onto the gallery that surrounded the stairwell. "It's as if this is the heart of the house, isn't it?" The gallery was lovely, the elegant quartet of fanlights in the square cupola above banishing all darkness. "Come." She turned right, with Agatha behind her.

"Was this part of the original house?" Agatha asked, looking upward.

"Yes, but there were only two very small windows in the cupola and a really hideous chandelier hanging down from it. The whole place was very dark." The renovators had shown her a photo of it, and she had been shocked. "The stairwell was almost always in shadow and . . . claustrophobic."

"Then this is really an improvement," Agatha remarked, and went into the bedroom where she would be staying for two weeks; it was large, with a bay window overlooking the adjacent house, a fanlight above the bed, and two skylights that revealed the luminous blue May sky, all making the room bright and airy. But as Agatha entered the room, she had one of her *notions*—an impression that began at the base of her spine and ran electrically up it, combined with a sense of being watched—and she decided in that instant she knew why the former occupant had stayed away from the house. She hadn't felt anything like it since the dig in Turkey, four years before when she had been working on excavations near Kutahya, and had stumbled into an ancient villa.

"The bathroom is next door, just turn left as you go out the door," Bronwyn went blithely on. "The blue towels are for you. There's an extra blanket in the closet, and you can plug in your computer behind the desk. The small armoire has a television, and we have satellite."

Agatha could only nod.

"These switches control the lights. This knob controls the shades on the skylights, if you want to have a more muted morning," Bronwyn said, demonstrating how to work the sliding switch. "You can have partial sun, or no sun at all, if you want to sleep in."

"No," said Agatha, not wanting to be in the dark in this house. "I like rising with the larks."

"As you wish." She went back out to the gallery. "Our room is directly across from yours. The master bath is *en suite,* and there's a walk-in closet with a dressing room."

Agatha did her best to look enthusiastic.

At four-thirty that afternoon there was a knock on the door and Bronwyn, who had been setting out salad-makings and salmon to marinate in lime and tequila for dinner, looked over at Agatha. "If you'll excuse me, I'll be right back."

"Fine," said Agatha, who was polishing the good silver for their dinner.

There was a flurry of conversation at the door, and then Bronwyn returned to the kitchen accompanied by a small, bird-thin woman in khaki slacks and an olive-green cotton sweater; she carried a tray of canapés along with a bottle of Golden Owl chardonnay. Her bright eyes peered out of a nest of wrinkles, and she grinned at Agatha. "Welcome to Auburn, Missus Pomeroy." She handed the tray to Bronwyn, and surged toward Agatha.

Agatha turned away from the sink, and reached for a towel to dry her hands. "I'm guessing you're Bronwyn's neighbor," she said, trying to match the wattage of welcome the newcomer displayed.

"Mirabelle Trask," she supplied, taking both of Agatha's proffered hands in hers. "So nice to meet you. Is this your first visit to Auburn?" Not waiting for an answer, she glanced at Bronwyn. "Why don't I find us some wineglasses and a corkscrew, and you can just leave things in the kitchen while we all have some chardonnay."

Bronwyn shrugged. "All right. Give me five minutes. You two go into the living room while I finish slicing the tomatoes. The wineglasses are in the glass-fronted cabinet in the dining room."

"Very good." Mirabelle plucked Agatha's sleeve and, taking the bottle by the neck, prodded her toward the door to the dining room. "We'll be in the living room. Don't dawdle."

"Certainly not, Mirabelle," said Bronwyn, laughing her best social laugh. "I'll be right in."

Mirabelle hurried to the glass-fronted cabinet and removed three white-wine glasses, then winked at Agatha as she took a corkscrew from a drawer. Artfully holding the glasses, the bottle, and the corkscrew, she rounded on Agatha. "I hope you like chardonnay. I have a real fondness for it, particularly Golden Owl." She bustled into the living room, and plunked herself down on the sofa. "Come. Sit down. Let's toast your visit."

Agatha, feeling a trifle overwhelmed, did as she was told, choosing a handsome Maguire chair for herself. "I haven't had Golden Owl before," she said, to prove she was paying attention.

"I love it—the flavor is so intense." Mirabelle had already set down the glasses and bottle, and opened the bottle. "I hope you will, too."

Agatha took a sip, finding it a little oakier than she liked, but she said, "It's quite good," which was true enough.

"The vintner teaches at Cal Davis, and his vineyard is in Yolo County, back in the hills," said Mirabelle, and leaned back against the sofa cushions. "Here's a welcome to you, and the hope for a pleasant stay."

"Thank you," said Agatha. "To new friends."

"So, have you been to Auburn before?" Mirabelle asked.

"I have, but not for many years," said Agatha.

"Bronwyn tells me you're a professor?" Mirabelle pursued.

"At Cal Poly, in San Luis Obispo: archaeological anthropology." She smiled. "The semester's just ended."

Bronwyn appeared in the kitchen door, the tray of canapés in her hands. "Here I am," she announced and brought the tray to the coffee table and set it down. "Has Agatha asked you anything about this house yet, Mirabelle?"

"Not yet," said Mirabelle, eyes bright with anticipation.

"Well, she probably will," said Bronwyn, taking the glass Mirabelle had just poured for her. "I can't remember half of what you told me about the place, so I rely on you to fill her in. Chin-chin."

They sat and talked, making the usual gambits of first acquaintance, and comparing experiences. Mirabelle had a raft of questions to ask Agatha, who answered them with just enough reserve not to feel she was divulging too much to her talkative neighbor. Finally, about an hour and a half later, Mirabelle considered the empty tray of canap s, and said, "Well, time to stop grazing." She looked directly at Agatha. "What did you want to ask about this house? You must have questions. Not that the place is anything like it used to be. Still, there is the matter of the genius loci, isn't there? The spirit of the place."

Startled by such direct questions, Agatha answered without shaping her inquiry. "Is the house haunted?"

Mirabelle gave the question some consideration. "Well, Jim Riggins certainly thought so, but he felt it was something more than haunted. And he didn't like it."

"You mean he thought it was possessed?" She was surprised to her herself say this; just the idea made her queasy.

"He didn't use that word," said Mirabelle, enjoying

herself hugely. "He said the house was the embodiment of something, or someone, and that it wasn't well-inclined toward him."

"Do you agree?" Agatha pursued, thinking *in for a penny, in for a pound.*

"Not entirely, no," said Mirabelle. She gazed into the middle-distance, then said, "Jim served in the South Pacific in World War II, and spent some time on one of those islands near Australia—I forget which one—and he brought back a thing called a Spirit House; it's something the natives make to house the souls of their dead. It's not like a grave, it's like a new corporeal form, so that the spirit can continue to live—sounds like something right up your alley: these houses *are* the people they're made for. Most of them are model houses, very complete. Well, Jim thought the spirit in the house he brought back got out of its miniature house and took over his. The whole house was imbued with the spirit, he used to say. He had been told that the Spirit House was for the first chief to come out of the interior and deal with Europeans, but he thought that it probably wasn't true. He said one of the natives had sold it to him, along with some tiki-gods." She pondered a bit. "I don't know if he was convinced that the spirit was a good one or something malicious; he only said it had occupied his house, made this house its body, so to speak."

"You'd think the renovation would put an end to it," said Agatha.

"Yes, you would. But it could be having the house restored served to restore the spirit within it—you know, like a closet full of new clothes." She laughed. "So long as the building is standing, I imagine, if Jim was right about it, the spirit will continue to . . . live." She managed a bright smile. "Not that I put much stock in what he said."

"That's a bit . . . unnerving, thinking that such a ridiculous thing might be believed," said Bronwyn, getting up. "I have to do more on dinner, or we won't eat until after nine. If you want to sit and chat a while longer, it's fine with me." With that, she took her wineglass and the canapé tray and made for the kitchen. "I'll put this in the dishwasher for you, and return it tomorrow."

"Bronwyn isn't comfortable with these kinds of conversations, is she," said Mirabelle.

"I'm not entirely sanguine myself," said Agatha.

"It could be a lot worse," said Mirabelle with an artful shudder. "You could have one of those demonic things—you know, like the Amityville house: the one they did the movies about? They weren't just scary films, you know. There truly was a house and very nasty things happened there."

"Did anything nasty happen here?" Agatha asked, trying to sound simply curious.

"Not that Jim ever mentioned." She put the empty bottle aside. "But he didn't tell me everything. It had him spooked, that's for sure."

"So there could have been some kind of event?" Agatha prompted.

"It's possible, I suppose, but in Auburn, spooky doings wouldn't remain unnoticed for long. In a town like this, they'd probably want to make it into a tourist attraction," said Mirabelle, getting to her feet and smoothing the front of her clothes. "It's been great fun, Agatha. I hope we do this again soon." She raised her voice. "Bronwyn, thanks so much!" Without waiting for a more formal farewell, she made for the door and let herself out.

"Sorry I wasn't able to get yesterday off," Martin Sallister said as he sat down to brunch the next morning. He was a pleasant man in his mid-forties, his dark-blond hair thinning, his glasses now bifocals. His demeanor was content to the point of smugness. Beside his plate were two Sunday papers—the *Sacra-*

mento Bee and *The New York Times,* ready for reading; he had gone out to pick them up an hour ago, to get ahead of the Saturday crowds. "Sometimes they give us half-days on Friday, but not yesterday. We're up for our annual office performance review, and it's been hectic, I can tell you." He smiled at Agatha. "We're glad you're here, Aunt Agatha." Reaching over to pat her hand, he added, "I hope you slept well."

"Well enough for a strange bed," she said obliquely. There had been the ongoing sensation of being watched, but not with any ill intent, so eventually she had been able to sleep, although lightly. This morning, she had had an uneasy few minutes in the shower for the same reason—she felt observed, and it flustered her, as a goat might feel when there were lions about.

"Well, that's good." He grinned at Bronwyn in the kitchen, and changed the subject. "The word around our office is we're twelve percent ahead of last year. That means the Roseville office is ahead of the Sacramento office, for a change. We'll get bonuses for it."

"That's good news," said Bronwyn, bringing in a platter of Hangtown Fry, the fried oysters artfully folded into the scrambled eggs and bacon. "Something fairly local," she said, and set it down in the center of the breakfast table. She beamed at Martin, who continued to grin.

Agatha took her napkin and dropped it in her lap, then reached for a slice of multi-grained toast. "This looks wonderful, Bronwyn," she said, loving the rich aroma of the steaming dish.

"Mimosa? Coffee? Tea?" Bronwyn sat down at the foot of the table and looked at Martin. "I'll have a mimosa. One-third champagne for me, if you please."

Martin reached for the carafe of orange juice and poured out a generous amount into an oversized flute. Then he took the bottle of champagne and topped off the glass. "Aunt Agatha? Which would you like? A little mimosa, or something less alcoholic? Name your poison." He indicated the options that flanked the platter.

"I'll have a mimosa and then coffee," she said, mildly annoyed that he should call her Aunt Agatha when they were only in-laws.

"Half and half?" Martin asked, meaning orange juice and champagne.

"Thank you," she said, and watched the ritual of pouring, finding Martin's style of hospitality a bit officious.

"We're really glad you're here, Aunt Agatha," Martin went on. "We hope you'll make it a habit, coming up to visit us now that we're in this wonderful house. You have a lot of time off in the summer. You could make a longer stay, couldn't you?"

"Thank you," she said as Bronwyn served up the Hangtown Fry. She lifted her glass and dutifully said, "To you both."

Martin touched the rim of his glass to hers. "That's very gracious. To you, Aunt Agatha."

Bronwyn beamed as she finished serving the breakfast. "I'm so pleased that we have this time together."

"So am I," said Martin, and looked encouragingly at Agatha. "We haven't got to know each other very well, and it's time that changed."

"Yes; yes indeed," said Agatha, and set her glass down so she could eat, devoting herself to the merest small-talk until the eggs, bacon, and oysters were all gone. Then she said, making an effort to sound academic, "I was thinking about what Mirabelle said yesterday, about the Spirit House the former owner brought back from the South Pacific."

"Oh, please," said Bronwyn. "Let's not indulge in that kind of fantasy."

"I wasn't thinking about the haunting; I was thinking about the Spirit House. Does anyone know what happened to it? Did the owner take it with him, or the renovator? Or is it here somewhere?"

"What can it matter?" Bronwyn asked impatiently.

Agatha persisted, keeping very calm. "It's just that an artifact like that could be valuable to a university or to a museum. It shouldn't be lost."

"There are some boxes in the basement that the renovator didn't remove," said Martin. "You can have a look, if you like."

"Oh, Martin, I just hate the thought of something like that still being here. I'm not superstitious, but something like that is just so . . . so *unpleasant.*" Bronwyn gave a ladylike shudder.

"That's just the point, my dear," he said to Bronwyn. "I think Aunt Agatha's right. After all, she should know about these things, shouldn't she? If we can find the Spirit House, I'm sure there's a museum that would be grateful for the donation, and we'd get a nice tax deduction for it." He smiled and nodded to Agatha. "I think you've hit on a very good notion. Thanks for the suggestion. I'll help you go through the boxes later today, or first thing tomorrow, whichever you prefer."

A little taken aback, Agatha said, "I suppose this afternoon would be as good a time as any."

Martin nodded crisply. "You're on. Let me pour you some coffee—do you like cream or sugar, or both?"

"Black, please," she said, suddenly dismayed at what she had got herself into.

Far more than the rest of the house, the basement showed the building's age; dark beams hung low, with any number of hooks and improvised shelves on them for tools and storage. Martin had turned on the lights, but he also offered Agatha a flashlight, saying as he did, "There isn't much light in the corners, as you see."

"Yes, I see," said Agatha, switching on the flashlight and taking comfort in its beam, although it revealed little more than ancient cardboard boxes and cobwebs. She was glad now that she had insisted that she and Martin wear latex gloves—who knew what kind of creepy-crawlies lurked in those very old boxes?

"Yes. There they are," Martin said, shoving past Agatha and reaching for the top box. "There's writing on the lid," he told her, using his flashlight to illuminate the faded letters. "J. Riggins. Jackpot!" He reached to pull down the box—the uppermost of four in that stack, pulling at the lid, and revealing two large scrapbooks and a photo album. He made a sound of disgust and set it aside, reaching for the next box in the stack, doing a swift count of the remaining boxes. "I count nineteen of them left."

"Don't be so hasty," said Agatha, removing the photo album and flipping through its pages. She was about half-way through the heavy black pages when she came upon a series of snapshots taken during World War II, the first one captioned, *Honolulu, March 19th, 1942.* Encouraged, she slowed down and perused them carefully. On the fourth page of war pictures she found what she had been looking for: an angular young man in a Navy uniform standing on the steps of a South Pacific house. He was next to an older native man in a printed regional skirt topped off by a G.I. blouse and a number of wooden necklaces; the islander was offering the young naval officer what looked to be a model of a house very similar to the one in front of which they stood. The line of the front of the house made it appear that they were in front of a grinning mouth. Both men were looking pleased. Agatha held up the album. "Martin. This is very useful. This is the Spirit House. It not only shows us what we're looking for, it provides a kind of provenance—you'll need that to make a donation. You can prove the item wasn't stolen, and that could be important."

Martin stared down at the photograph. "Looks kind of flimsy—the real house, I mean, like it couldn't do more than keep off the rain," he said, for the first time allowing a little doubt to slip into his tone.

"Most of the inhabitants of the South Pacific islands don't need to stay warm; they need to stay cool," said Agatha, finding a loose clipping and using that to bookmark the page in the album.

"I suppose you're right," said Martin, pulling up the lid of the second box. "Shi—oot!"

"What is it?" She set the album aside, and went to where he was bending over the open box.

"Uniforms. A pair of shoes. Useless!" He clicked his tongue in disgusted disappointment.

"Not necessarily," said Agatha, as much to keep Martin working as to encourage him in his hope for a windfall. "There's bound to be an historical society that would be glad to have these for display."

Trying not to seem too dissatisfied, Martin put the lid back on the box. "Do you really think so?"

"Of course I do." She reached for the third box in the stack, a bit put off by his obvious greed.

"Or maybe I could sell them on eBay? What do you think?"

"You probably could," Agatha agreed flatly.

"I could probably sell a *lot* of this stuff, couldn't I?" He smiled again, and began a pile of the first two boxes near the foot of the stairs. "Come on—there's seventeen boxes to go."

They were on to the fourteenth box when Martin gave a long whistle of discovery. "Looks like this is the one. It's not in very good shape; stored on its side." He pointed his flashlight straight down and revealed a finely woven mat of some kind of vegetable fiber. Newspapers from 1951 surrounded the item; he tossed them aside and pulled the thing from its resting place.

It was about the size of a microwave oven, beautifully detailed even in its neglected condition. The front was readily identified: there was a wide verandah spread out on either side of four central stairs leading up into the house itself. A railing along the verandah stood up on little posts like teeth, the railing collapsed where the thread holding the rails on had rotted. The main rafter supported a kind of bamboo thatch, and the woven-mat walls, even though they were brittle and cracked in a few places, had not fallen apart. A number of squat gods no bigger than the last joint of Martin's little finger were ranged about the little house, posted at every door and window.

"Now, this is more like it," said Martin. He looked over at Agatha. "What do you think?"

"I think it's remarkable," she answered, staring at the Spirit House; it was in fine condition, considering its haphazard storage. "It's the one in the photo, that's for sure."

Martin laughed out loud. "Six boxes of collectable stuff, and this." He put the Spirit House down carefully on the workbench under the largest of the basement windows. "I should have thought about this when we first moved in. Thanks, Aunt Agatha. I owe you one."

Agatha took the Spirit House from him. "If you don't mind, I'd like to take a look at it. If it's as unusual as I think, there are a couple colleagues I'd like to call—to get an idea where you might donate it. You'd like it to go someplace with a fine reputation and a superior collection, wouldn't you?"

"Why can't you handle it yourself?" He gave her a sudden, hard look.

"Because the South Pacific islands are not my field of specialization. If this were from Turkey and at least two thousand years old, I could find you just the right place with a couple of e-mails. But twentieth century and South Pacific? I only know it's a good piece. I'll call a couple of museums, and I'll e-mail a colleague in Australia. I should be able to get you solid information by Monday."

Martin considered this, finally nodding. "That's okay with me, then. But it has to go to a place where I'd get a tax deduction. Keep that in mind, Aunt Agatha."

She bit back the sharp retort and said only, "I'll bear that in mind."

It was Tuesday morning before Constantine Hildred called from the National Anthropological Museum; his call, coming at that hour, told Agatha that he was about to leave his office for lunch.

"I got your e-mail about the Spirit House and the photos you attached," he said after a quick exchange of pleasantries. "Tell me more about this find."

"Well, as far as I can tell, it was acquired by the former owner of this house some time during World War II. We found it on Saturday, packed away in the basement," she said as she went to the desk where she had set up the Spirit House next to her laptop, grinning contentedly out at the room. She said nothing about the disturbing dreams that had filled her sleep for the last three nights—not that they mattered. She logged into her e-mail, just in case.

"Yeah, I got that from the old photo you attached with the rest. Go on."

"It's rumored to be haunted, but given what it appears to be, that's hardly surprising," said Agatha.

"Tell me about the little gods in the Spirit House; it'll help me identify where it came from."

Agatha picked up a small magnifying glass and peered into the little house. "They're the usual small, squat gods. The carving looks as if it might come from the Philippines or Indonesia."

"Can you tell me anything about them that's more

specific? Don't worry. I'm interested in the piece, but I want to know what kind of thing I'll be getting. I don't want any trouble with it."

"Why should this be trouble? Are you worried about provenance?"

"More about the nature of the thing," said Constantine.

"More national treasure issues, you mean?" she asked.

"Ethnic ones, anyway," he said.

"Okay, Conny." She lifted her magnifying glass again. "There's two that are female—long breasts, and one with a bone in her hand. There're carvings along the main rafter, very intricate. Would you like me to photograph them and attach the photos to an e-mail?"

"How soon can you do it?"

"I've got my camera right here," said Agatha, ready to put it to use.

"Okay. Take a couple and send them along right now. And while you're at it, take another of the front of the house, if you would."

"Glad to," said Agatha, lifting her camera and taking a half-dozen photos. She attached them to her e-mail to him and sent them on their way. "I gather the previous owner didn't like the Spirit House," she repeated while she listened to the keyboard click from Conny's office.

There was a long silence, and then Hildred said. "Small wonder."

"Why?" Agatha asked with an uneasy glance at the Spirit House.

Hildred took a deep breath. "Because the people who made it are cannibals."

AH, YEHZ

Alan Dean Foster

Archie had not known that some of the money was spoken for. Even if he had, he still might have been tempted to take it. A starving man will hesitate before stealing to eat, but an alcoholic in desperate need of a drink will swipe anything unguarded that is left for the taking.

So it was with Archie. He had paused only briefly before scaling the fence that walled off the cemetery from the street. It was two in the morning, a time that downtown was devoid of tourists and safe to attempt a quick snatch and grab. Having worked the same location on several previous occasions, there was no reason to suppose anything would go wrong. This time something had. A concerned citizen objected to him absconding with the loose change.

A citizen who happened to be very dead.

There was nothing dormant about the deceased's outrage, however. As a frantic Archie scooped up the last of the scattered coins, sending pennies and nickels bouncing and rolling across surrounding gravestones, a rapidly expanding humanoid shape writhed and coiled itself right up out of the grave that lay beneath the last forlorn dime. Ashen and angry, heavily bearded and clad in the tattered clothes of a bygone age, it howled curses in English and screams in banshee as it chased a terrified Archie back over the fence. Which is to say that Archie went over the fence. His pallid pursuer went right through it, shades of the dead being able to pass through solid objects with little difficulty.

In contrast to its ghostly owner, the heavy cane the angry specter swung at Archie possessed a disconcerting solidity. Descending in a potentially lethal arc, it connected painfully with his right shoulder and nearly brought him to the ground as he continued shoving the purloined coins deeper into his pockets. For the life of him Archie could not imagine what he had done to provoke the horrific response from the usually indifferent earth. Why now, why on this night, had one of the long-buried chosen to rise up and come after him? What aspect of his early morning theft had transpired differently?

None of that would matter if the phantasm, or boogeyman, or ghost, or whatever kind of horror it was that was hot on his heels, actually caught up with him. His throbbing shoulder was testament to that. If that flailing spectral club came down on his head . . .

A sensible person might have considered giving up the money. But a sensible person did not filch coins from national monuments in the middle of a chill November night. Archie needed to live, yes, but in order to live he needed to drink. He needed to drink more than he needed to eat. He hung onto the pocketful of coins and kept running.

Not many people chose to stroll the streets of downtown Philadelphia at two in the morning. Those who did and happened to encounter the hysterical Archie saw a young man older than his years, unkempt and cheaply clad, running pell-mell down Church Street toward the river while constantly looking back over his shoulders. Presuming him to be afflicted by some possibly dangerous variant of the DTs, the other nocturnal walkers understandably gave him a wide berth.

"Give me back me money, y'no-good thief! I'll break yer bones, I swan I will!" Cane held high, the outline of the ethereal specter feathered slightly as it rounded a corner before collecting itself once more.

Not in the best of health to begin with, Archie raced on. In the absence of wind, muscle tone, or conditioning, he could only rely on fear to give strength to his pounding legs. Now even that was beginning to fade.

A light gleamed just ahead, the warm inviting glow of a bar, open even at this hour. Another time Archie might have wondered why any bar stayed open so late. Now he saw only a potential refuge from the cold, forbidding streets and the inexorable wraith that was steadily closing the distance between them. But even if he ducked inside, what was there to prevent his pursuer from following? He would find himself cornered. Worse, any barkeep working at this inhospitable hour would be in no mood to give shelter to an obvious drunk. He had to make a decision fast: run on past or go inside?

The figure standing just outside the doorway settled the matter for him. Puffing away on a fat cigar, the smoker's attention was understandably drawn to the fleeing Archie. Sizing up the situation, the portly figure straightened. His voice was somewhat grating and his words oddly drawn out, but it was their content rather than their context that persuaded Archie.

"Over here, boy! Get in behind me!"

Archie did not have to be told twice. Completely out of breath as well as options, he stumbled to a halt behind the hefty figure and tried to shrink himself into invisibility. In the event of catastrophe he could still try hiding inside the open bar.

Confronted by this unanticipated interposition, the ghostly figure of Archie's pursuer slowed to a halt, his cane still held threateningly high in one half-skeletal fist.

"What manner of interference is this?" he hissed.

"This be no business of yours, sor, and I'll thank ye t'mind yer own business and stand aside so that justice may be done in this matter!"

"All in good time, my good man, all in good time." The cigar migrated from one corner of the smoker's mouth to the other. He glanced briefly back down at the malnourished youth cowering behind him. "Now then, what's this pitiful young man done to merit such blatant hostility? Not that I've any inherent objection to the deliverance of a good beating, but there ought to be cause."

"Cause?" Grimacing, the hovering shade revealed ragged, broken teeth, the consequence of some hundred plus years of slow disintegration. " 'Tis cause ye want, is it?" Lowering the cane, he angrily shook the tip in the direction of the cowering Archie. "Stole money that were given t'me by the good people of this city, he did! Helped himself to it without so much as a by-your-leave!"

Again, the stout smoker looked back at the younger man trembling behind him. "Is what this memory of a man says true, m'boy?"

Archie hesitated, then found himself nodding miserably. "Yes—yes, I took some coins. I've been doing it for a long time and nothing ever happened, ever!" He peered out from behind his protector. "I don't know what I did different."

Adjusting the high hat he wore, his sapient shielder nodded sagely. "Well then, m'boy, just give this decrepit dozer his money back and be done with it, yehz? If it's just food that you need, or shelter . . ."

Abandoning himself to confession, Archie did something remarkable. He told the truth. "I can't—I can't do that, sir. I—you see, I haven't had a drink in *days.*" He licked his lips to emphasize his discomfort. "I've got the shakes real bad, and I just—I can't."

His protector's eyes widened slightly. "A drink is it you need? Ah, yehz. Why, that changes everything."

He turned back to the floating, and increasingly impatient, eidolon. "Have you no sympathy for the lad, then, my good man? Have you no understanding, no compassion? Why, what we are confronted with here is nothing less than a crisis of the human spirit! Why, not to assist the lad would be to deny the very essence of his humanity, yehz!"

The cane threatened. "I want the money he took off me grave!"

"Is it not better to . . ." The smoker paused. "Wait just a moment now. Off your grave, you say?" He looked back at the wretched figure crouched down behind him. "M'boy, did you plot to steal coins off this man's plot?"

"I always take money off Franklin's grave," Archie protested reluctantly. "It's mostly pennies, which are supposed to bring the thrower luck, but not everybody knows that. Lots of times they throw dimes and nickels, and sometimes quarters." His expression brightened ever so slightly. "Sometimes you can scrape together enough for a bottle!"

His interlocutor nodded understandingly, then raised a hand and pointed at the waiting wraith. "I ask you now, m'boy: does this desiccated rag of suppurating, degraded flesh in any way resemble the noble Franklin?"

"Hey, just a minute now . . ." the apparition began angrily.

Peering out from behind one of the older man's legs, Archie regarded his pursuer hesitantly. "Uh, no. No, he doesn't."

The cane shook violently in their direction. "My name is Thaddeus James Walker, you young fool! Mayhap old Franklin doesn't care about the coins that the credulous fling onto his gravestone, but I care about the ones that come my way. You've no right to take them!"

"Ah yehz," Archie's savior muttered under his

breath, "Saving for a glorious spending spree in the hereafter, are we? Planning to open an account at the Philadelphia Savings and Loan for the Long Demised?"

"Well . . ." The drifting phantom looked suddenly confused. "That be beside the point. Theft is theft!"

"Yehz, yehz, I do not question your overall analysis of the situation, my friend. But can you not make an exception for this poor lad you see shivering behind me, of whom I suspect he is about to pee in his pants? Take it from one who knows, sir, his need is dire as it is true. Can you not leave him free to indulge himself this one night? You have my personal assurance the offense shall not be repeated."

The flickering, cane-wielding shadow hesitated. Then he lowered his weapon. "Well—all right. But just this one time." He shook the heavy stick in Archie's direction and Archie flinched, drawing back behind his protector. "I'll do it on your word, William. But only this one time. If I ever see him stealing from me again I'll cave his skull in. You can be assured of that!"

Having delivered those final words of warning, the shade of the long-dead and much desiccated Thaddeus James Walker whirled about and did not so much stride off into the darkness as evaporate into the night.

Shaking as much from need as fear, Archie slowly straightened. "I—I don't know how to thank you, sir! I—was that a real ghost?"

An arm swung around Archie's shoulder as his new friend guided him toward the beckoning doorway. "What's real and what's imaginary, m'boy, often stumble across one another in a burg as old as this. As for thanking me, why, you can buy me a drink. Have your illegitimate nocturnal perambulations garnered you enough for that?"

Archie licked his lips. All he had were the coins he

had managed to scrabble together. But—he owed this man his life. "I'll make sure there's enough."

"Excellent—yehz!"

They entered the bar. Though well-lit, it was deserted and silent save for the clink of glasses as the bartender cleaned and stacked. He eyed Archie briefly, then smiled at the older man, who was obviously a regular.

"What'll it be tonight, Bill?"

"Something celebratory, yehz, to wish this young man well. Whiskey, as good as you can muster. In other words, dispensed from a bottle with a label." Beaming behind a bulbous nose that Archie could now see was rosy as the blush on a Catholic high school girl's cheeks, the man set his cigar aside. "And you, m'boy—what'll you have to celebrate your survival to drink another day?"

"Whiskey also. Straight up." Digging into a pocket of his worn jeans, Archie pulled out a handful of coins and dumped them on the counter. The alert bartender kept any from fleeing.

There were a lot of quarters this time, and by the tail end of the third shot Archie felt comfortable enough with his savior to put an arm around him. Luckily he was by now too tired and too drunk to freak when instead of being halted by the expected bone and muscle his lowering arm passed completely through his new friend to emerge in the vicinity of his portly but decidedly insubstantial waist. Archie was not so inebriated that his eyes failed to widen slightly.

"Ah, c'mon—c'mon now! Don't go telling me you're a gheest—a ghost, too?"

Raising his half-full shot glass high, his savior offered a salute. "William Dukenfield's the name, m'boy, and I can't deny that I'm little more than a shade of my true self. How else d'you think I succeeded in deterring the homicidal shadow that pursed you? Takes one to persuade one, yehz." He gestured at their surroundings. "This present existence is my blessing and my curse, you see, because it's nothing less than the very one I repeatedly asked for when I dwelt among the living. It was just a recurrent joke then. Well, the joke's been on me ever since, yehz, but to its credit I have to confess it's not been a bad one." He downed the remaining contents of the glass in a single swig.

"Another one, Bill?" the bartender asked quietly.

W. C. Dukenfield studied the counter. "Alas, my noble dispenser of aged and purified grains, I fear that our young visitor here has at last exhausted his night's takings."

"This one's on the house," the bartender responded, smiling. He eyed Archie. "You too, son."

Wavering slightly, Archie started to respond instinctively, pushing his shot glass forward—and hesitated. "Two ghosts in one neat—in one night. Tha's two too many. Maybe—maybe I ought to cut back a little, y'know? I mean, the next time it might not turn out so well for me, y'know?"

"Ah, my boy," Dukenfield declared brassily, "it would be a shame to lose you to that stolid whore sobriety. Conversely, you're a bit too young to be following in such footsteps as mine. Take it from one who knows, you really might consider drying out for a bit. Get a life first, so to speak, and then decide at your leisure how much cleansing lubrication it really requires."

Archie stared at his empty shot glass for a few seconds, then released it and took a step back from the bar. "I—I'll do it! I'll go to the shelter tomorrow and sign up for counseling. I've been meaning to, for months. All I needed was a reason." He shook his head, as if trying to return to reality. "Ghosts—two ghosts. No more for me. No more. I need to . . ." his eyes came up to meet those of his savior, "I need to get a life, yes."

"An occupation much overrated, in my opinion," his spectral and slightly sloshed friend declared with conviction, "but then no one ever paid much attention to my opinion. Only to my jokes, yehz. Good luck to you then, m'boy, and if you should ever find yourself in the neighborhood again, be sure to drop by to share a tipple. You're buying." He turned away as the barkeep set a freshly filled shot glass down in front of him.

Suffused with unexpected resolve, Archie turned away. He needed no stiff-necked counselor to tell him that if he found himself being pursued by a ghost, much less spending a convivial evening with one, it was time to get off the bottle. His life hadn't always been like this. He just needed something to kick-start conviction again. Something as elemental and convincing as being chased down dark streets by an angry ghost, and then finding himself sharing drinks with one.

At the door he paused to look back. "You said— you said that this existence was one that you asked for." Raising a wavering but slowly steadying hand, he gestured at the interior of the establishment. It struck him then that the décor was—period. 30s or maybe 40s, he decided. "How does—how does one die and end up in a place like this? In a bar."

"A bar?" Taking a short slug from his freshly-filled glass, Archie's rescuer focused beady but intense eyes on the younger man standing in the doorway. "Why, it's not just the bar, m'boy! I roam where and when I please. Otherwise I'd not have known your intemperate pursuer. There are quite a lot of us in this town, you know. After a while one gets to know many of one's own kind. Franklin now, he tends to keep to himself. Taking apart a computer, I understand. But on the right nights some of the rest of us often get together and have a little party, yehz.

"What happened to me, not that you need or deserve to know, was that for years people kept asking how I felt about death and dying, so in a little piece I wrote for *Vanity Fair* back in '25 I declared, more or less, that on the whole, I'd rather be in Philadelphia. Yehz." For a second time he raised his glass in salute.

"And do you know what? When I shuffled off this immoral mortal coil on Christmas Day back in '46, I found myself not in heaven, not in hell, not even in Los Angeles, where they interred the sodden remains of yours truly. And it's here I've been ever since. Good luck to you now, m'boy, and remember one thing always: keep well clear of children and dogs."

"I'll do that, sir, and—thanks."

With that, Archie went out of the bar. But not into the Wilderness. And he was forever thereafter a happy man for never forgetting the advice.

GAMMA RAY VERSUS DEATH

Carrie Vaughn

Ray paced along the computer banks and sensor readouts, around the steel table that formed the centerpiece of the Command Room, passing the wide double doors to the hangar and returning to where he started. Something on that last mission had gone wrong, but he didn't know what. He should have known—he'd been in the middle of it—but his memory went fuzzy right at the good part. He still didn't feel right, like he was drifting. Like his mind wasn't all here. His feet were numb against the floor. The fact that the team wasn't back for the debriefing increased his worry. Where were they?

And what had happened?

Hours seemed to pass before the doors to the hangar opened and the team filed in.

"Finally," Ray muttered, but his worry didn't diminish. He'd never seen his teammates like this. The five of them wore civilian clothes, nice suits and dresses. Even Gadgeteer wore a skirt, and Ray had never seen her in anything but jeans and T-shirts when she was off duty. Heads bowed, shoulders slumped, they moved slowly, like they were sleepwalking. One by one, they found their seats around the table. They didn't say a word.

And no one looked at him. No one saw him. Ray swallowed and tried to quell a fluttering in his stomach. Experimenting, he waved a hand in front of Mr. Steel's face. Not even a flinch, and Steel had super reflexes to go with his super strength.

Then Gadgeteer, the spunky young woman who maintained the team's equipment and did amazing things with copper wire and chewing gum, said, "I can't believe he's gone." She was staring at the one empty chair around the table. Ray's chair.

"Oh, no," he said. "No no no, that can't be right. Guys, I'm right here, I've been waiting for you—"

But no one heard him. He looked at his hands—they were solid. But when he grabbed the back of the empty chair to pull it away from the table, nothing happened. He couldn't feel the stainless steel frame and padded back. His hands skittered off the surface and it didn't budge. He could walk, but couldn't feel the floor—because he drifted an inch or two above it and only made the motions of walking.

They'd been a team for five years. They'd been through everything together, every kind of scrape, trouble, disaster, supervillain, and alien invasion. They'd had some close calls. But they'd never lost anyone. Until now, apparently.

Ray looked at the five of them. Their leader, Mr. Steel, was hunched over and silent; Tessa sat rigid and frowning; Cheetah, the super-fast woman with flame-colored hair, bit her lip and crossed her arms stiffly; and Gadgeteer. Even Jetstream, the team's loner, sat with them for this moment. They hadn't just lost someone. They'd lost their invincibility. They were mortal again. They were falling apart before his eyes. Because of him.

"God, Ray," he murmured. "What are you going to do?"

"It was good of the city to put up the plaque," Tessa said. The athletic black woman sat at Mr. Steel's right. Usually, the telekinetic was the one rallying the team, shouting directions and encouragement. The team's second-in-command, she had the enthusiasm to carry them all. Ray had never seen her so subdued.

"He'd have hated it," Gadgeteer said, sniffing. "He wasn't engraved marble and lilies, he was neon and cheap beer. None of that service was about him!" She put her hands over her face, and the room was silent but for her stifled crying.

Somehow, his heart broke, even though he was dead and shouldn't have felt anything. He knew she had feelings for him, and he'd always liked her. He'd never known what to do about it except laugh it off. They were always so busy, fighting one crisis after another. And now—

This had all become one big, stupid cliché.

He slunk to the corner, crossed his arms, hunched in on himself, and watched. He was still in his fighting suit, the specially designed heat-resistant, gray-toned body glove that could withstand his radiation blasts. He was ready for action. Would always be ready for action. If he had to die, why couldn't he just . . . stop? Vanish out of the universe. Why couldn't it be over? That would have been far better than watching his team—his friends, the best friends he'd ever had—go through this.

"He would have wanted us to get back to normal," Tessa said. "He wouldn't have wanted us to sit around moping."

"I don't care," Gadgeteer said. "I don't care anymore what he'd have wanted. It's been over a week and it hurts worse now than it did when it happened. I just keep thinking about everything . . . everything that I *miss*. I keep finding his *things*, I keep—" Her face was red. Her dark hair was loose, but ruffled. Like she'd been standing in a breeze at a funeral. "I'm sorry. I can't do this right now."

"Annie—" Mr. Steel said, but she stood and left,

almost running out of the room to the door that led to the living quarters.

"Let her go," Tessa predictably said, laying a hand on Mr. Steel's arm as he stood to run after her.

Jetstream, the raven-haired hotshot flier, scowled. "It shouldn't have happened. If I had gotten to him sooner—"

Steel shook his head. "We've been over this a hundred times. There was nothing any of us could have done."

"But if I hadn't—"

"It wasn't your fault," Steel said.

Jetstream slouched over the table and quickly wiped his eyes.

One by one, they drifted away to grieve privately. Tessa rose, second to last. Touching Steel's shoulder, she said, "Are you all right?"

He pursed his lips in a wry smile. "I will be, eventually."

"It wasn't your fault, either," she said, and walked away.

When he was alone, Steel stood before the giant monitor over the computer bank. "Retrieve archive footage," he spoke the command. "Gamma Ray. File dated May first."

He'd been over it a hundred times, but went over it again. Ray stood nearby, watching the video screen with Steel.

The footage must have come from a TV news crew, maybe one that had found a vantage on a building opposite the park where the battle had taken place. The angle looked down on the clearing between the City Museum and the wooded bike paths to the south.

Professor Terrible's killer machine emerged from behind the museum building. The thing had been huge, as big as the building itself, and made of nearly indestructible titanaloid steel. Built like a tank, it moved on treads that could mow under any obstacles, climb stairs, rumble through water, and adhere to the sides of buildings. It had a dozen appendages bearing blades, laser guns, cannons, rocket launchers, microwave emitters, and sensor and communication arrays. They had assumed that Terrible himself was inside the armored core of the machine, operating it like a tank.

They'd been wrong. Terrible wasn't anywhere near the place. The thing was a robot, set to its most destructive capabilities and let loose in the middle of the city.

Ray—Gamma Ray as he was known and loved by the public—arrived on the scene first. They'd known Terrible was on the move, and he'd happened to be the one investigating the warehouse from which the robot emerged. When he understood the machine's power and the gravity of the situation, Steel had radioed Ray to fall back and wait for support. Ray had disobeyed the order. He didn't want to see the robot trash the museum, as it had seemed bent on doing. Firing blasts of energy from his hands, he managed to distract it. All its sensor dishes and receptors swiveled to focus on him, and Ray led it to the clearing. That was the image Steel watched now: Ray, a tiny bug next to the monster, bracing for an attack.

Ray remembered thinking that if he could just hit a weak spot—find a key sensor, a video receptor, a control antenna—and destroy it with a well-placed blast, the fight would be over. He never doubted that he could beat the thing singlehanded.

Then—something had happened. He didn't remember what. The world had gone fuzzy, like bad TV reception. Then, a moment later, he was pacing the Command Room, trying to remember what had happened. He watched the video replay, intensely curious.

On screen, he blasted the thing. Standing braced, visible energy beams—white light, searing with intensity and difficult to look at—blasted from his hands. But they didn't strike the robot's metal skin. The machine had a force field, and the beams deflected, putting a hole in a nearby building and setting a tree on fire. Ray had apparently been ready for this, because he danced out of the way and tried again. The shield seemed automatic, and it had no weaknesses.

In the video, Ray could be seen speaking into his headset, relaying information to Steel. Steel had the audio recording cued up.

"—can keep it distracted, it won't do as much damage!"

Steel's recorded voice shot back angrily, "No, Ray, get out of there. We need to set up a trap. You can't take this thing by yourself!"

"I know that, I'm not going to! I'm just going to keep it busy!"

"Jetstream's on his way, wait for him—"

"Too late!"

The robot brought to bear an appendage that looked like a post-hole digger, something designed to drive into the ground, dig, or smash an opponent to dust. Ray was fit, athletic, tough. He dodged the crushing blow when it pounded toward him and kept firing beams at the thing. The monster actually became flustered, flailing its limbs, pivoting to keep Ray in its sights. Jetstream flew into the frame then and became a second insect harassing the metal beast.

Ray moved behind it and blasted the joint of an appendage with one of his beams, hoping to catch him off guard. But the monster was ready for him, and swiveled one of its gadgets into place to block the beam.

It didn't just block the beam. Ray could imagine— could almost remember, even though the memory of this scene had been erased from his mind—the feeling of surprise as the robot collected his own energy beam in a parabolic dish, and fired it back at him.

The beam of radiation caught Gamma Ray directly. He shivered for a moment, his arms flung out, limned in an aura of glowing, white-hot energy. Then, his skin and hair charred and smoking, he flew back, smashed hard against the street, bounced, and rolled, coming to a rest with his back twisted, his limbs wrenched at unnatural angles.

Watching, what was left of Ray observed with detached satisfaction that the suit seemed to hold up to the blast just fine. It wasn't the radiation that killed him, but the force of the fall onto the road. Broken back at least, probably neck as well, and limbs, skull— everything broken.

Mr. Steel leaned on the table, his head bowed, and listened to the rest of the radio chatter. Jetstream reported the whole thing, shouting that Ray was down. Steel kept yelling at him to get Ray out of there, and Jetstream kept saying that it was too late. The panic and desperation in their voices made Ray's heart ache. The others arrived in moments and battled the thing into submission. Gadgeteer struck the final blow by rigging a localized EMP that froze it.

But Ray was already gone.

He considered: maybe his reflected blast had converted his body to some form of conscious energy, that he was somehow still alive and they only had to figure out a way to convert him back to his physical form. But it was right there on screen: he'd left a body. A scorched, shattered, dead body. They'd buried that body.

So now what?

After dark, after everyone had gone to bed and the computers were left humming and processing surveillance data from all over the world, ready to sound the alarm if need be, Ray tried an experiment.

He'd use his powers to write his name on the wall of the Command room. They'd come in the next day, see it there, and know he was still alive. Or still around, at least. Then they could work together to figure out how to get him back to a physical form. It had to work. He knew it would work just like he knew he could take on Professor Terrible's machine all by himself. Hell, the blast of radiation would activate the sensors and get the team in here in seconds. Then he wouldn't be alone anymore.

He decided the wall with the hangar doors would be best. It offered the clearest space, and if something went wrong there wasn't any infrastructure behind it to destroy. He'd just blow a hole into the hangar, which was designed to take a beating anyway.

Across the room from the wall, he stood feet apart, legs braced, and rubbed his hands, his ritual of preparation. It was certainly good to be doing *something* again. He straightened his arms, closed his hands into fists, and thought, *now*.

Nothing happened.

Usually, he felt a surge of power in his gut. It flowed up his spine like a gust of hot air, burned through his arms, collected in his fists and fired out in a blast of directed energy. Now, he felt no surge. Nothing welled up in him, no power blasted through him.

He'd had that power since he was a teenager. Not having it felt . . . wrong. He felt empty. Insubstantial.

His legs folded under him and he sat down hard. Or pretended to. He was still a matterless form that didn't actually make contact with the floor. That was it, then. His power had died with his body. He really was finished.

Time passed and confirmed Ray's fears. He didn't sleep, didn't get hungry, cold, hot, or tired. He was permanently wakeful, permanently insubstantial. Timeless.

He wandered though the team's complex, observing, alone.

He tried. He had to be able to do something, or what was the point of even being here? Rattle a doorknob, make the lights flash, anything. If he was still here, there had to be a reason. Unfinished business or the violence of his death anchored him here. If he could find the reason, maybe this stupid, truncated existence would end.

But he didn't want to fade away, go to wherever he was supposed to go. Fade off into whatever afterlife waited for someone like him. Or fade into nothing at all.

He wanted to be part of the team again.

He needed a plan. He had to find a way to tell them he was still here. Mr. Steel had the great planning chops on the team. It was why the others deferred to him more often than not. Ray was the spunky comic relief. No wonder he'd been the one to die. More tragic that way, he thought with a huff.

The team had resources. Computers, high-tech vehicles, alien artifacts that might have sensors that could detect unusual energy signatures—his, for example. Maybe he could influence the temperature of a room. He only had to find the thing he *could* do, then use it to make his presence known.

And since he had all the time in the world, he simply tried everything.

He tried the computers first. He couldn't make the keyboard do something simple like type "Hey guys, it's me" on the screen. His fingers skidded over the keys. But if he put his hands on the front panel and leaned, he passed through, into the machine's innards. Then, he was at a loss. If he couldn't type, he certainly couldn't do something like pull out wires and circuit boards to crash the whole thing. In fact, he couldn't feel anything at all. Just the strange, muted sensation he felt every time he tried to touch something solid. Maybe if he thought hard enough, concentrated—sort of like he did when he used his power—he could influence the system on some level.

He closed his eyes and imagined pushing energy

through the computer circuits. Pure thought. Ecto-plasm. Whatever.

"Hey!" Something shocked him, like a static charge, and he flinched back. But nothing visible had happened. He lurked in a corner to wait.

Something *had* happened. When Mr. Steel tried to access the system the next morning, he frowned, tapped at the keys a few times, then called Gadgeteer on the intercom. "Annie? Something's wrong with the computer."

"I'll be right there," she answered.

When she arrived, Steel said, frustrated, "I can't access the archive."

She only had to fiddle with the system a moment, her head stuck under the very panel Ray had pushed his ghostly hands through, before she emerged victorious.

"Just had a burnout in one of the processor's circuits," she said cheerfully. Ray was a little sad that she'd returned to her chipper self so quickly after his death. Had it been quickly? How many days— weeks—had it been? He hadn't kept track. He couldn't tell. She continued, "I'll replace it and everything'll be all right."

And it was all right, and no one gave it a second thought.

When Jetstream made pasta for supper, Ray stuck his face in the steam over the pot of boiling water. He had this idea that maybe the shape of his head would form in the mist. One of the women would look over and scream in surprise, but then one of them— Gadgeteer, probably—would recognize him. Then they could all work together to figure out how to get him out of this predicament.

But it didn't happen like that. He held himself over the pot, and the steam wafted in a new pattern for a moment. No more so than it would have if someone had opened the door and let in a draft. No one noticed that the steam moved without a draft.

He couldn't do more to the team's equipment than short out a circuit or two. He could access the closet of alien artifacts, and he even made one of them ping by holding his hand inside it for a minute, but his teammates attributed it to an electrical quirk.

Despairing, he invaded his teammates' privacy. Namely, Gadgeteer's.

Late at night, he sat by her bed. Even in the dark he could see clearly. Technical journals and schematics lay spread over her comforter. Occasionally one slid off when she shifted or turned over. A glass of water, an intercom, and a couple of half-dismantled gadgets of undetermined purpose sat on the night stand. Then her. She was even cute asleep, wearing an oversized T-shirt, curled up under the covers, hugging her pillow, her hair splayed around her. She frowned a little.

What the hell was he doing here? Then it occurred to him: that's exactly what this was. Whatever he'd done, no matter how much he'd tried to fight for what was good and right, no matter how much he'd tried to follow Mr. Steel's example, his faults came out in the end, and he'd landed in hell. He'd watch his team, his friends, forever, and not be able to help them. Not be able to do anything.

"I'm sorry, Annie," he said softly. "I don't even know why. I'm sorry I never said anything. That I never told you how I feel about you. I'm sorry I got myself killed. I've been trying to find a way to tell you. To tell you everything. But I guess it's too late. I miss you. I just wanted to tell you that. Even if you can't hear."

He reached out to smooth a strand of hair from her face. Didn't affect the hair at all, of course. But he sensed something. A change in the sensation on his fingertips, an anomaly in the air. He felt more than a little creepy doing it. Here he was, watching her sleep, and she didn't even know it. Now he wasn't just dead, he was a pervert. Maybe he belonged in hell.

She turned, lifting her head, and her brow wrinkled. "Ray?"

Ray pulled his hands away and stood back. His heart should have been pounding. If he still had a heartbeat.

She was still asleep, he was sure of it. Her eyes were closed, her body still snugged under the covers, her face still crinkled in that pursed, thoughtful look, like she was in the middle of a dream. Maybe it was just a dream.

Then, in her sleep, dreaming, she brushed her hand across her cheek, right where his hand had been. "Ray," she whispered.

"Annie?" She was just having a dream. It was only a dream.

He knelt by her bed and touched her hand like he would have if he was alive. Like he should have when he was alive. A light touch, fingers brushing along her wrist until his hand lay alongside hers, their fingers twining.

And he felt something. Her warmth pressing against him. Her hand moved, her fingers shifting against his, and he felt the pressure of it. Somehow, by some cosmic weirdness, they were holding hands.

"I miss you, Ray," she murmured, then sighed as she sank deeper into sleep.

"Oh, Annie."

The next morning, she looked a mess when she came to breakfast. She stuck her hair in a pony tail without brushing it, still wore the T-shirt she'd slept in, with sweatpants and bare feet. Shadows made her eyes look sunken.

Ray stood back and watched. He couldn't take his eyes off her.

Tessa asked, "Annie, are you okay?"

"I'm fine. I didn't sleep very well," she answered.

"Any reason why?"

"Thinking. You know. Still thinking of Ray."

Sitting around the kitchen table, the others nodded in understanding, heads bowed.

Staring at her empty plate, Gadgeteer continued. "It's like I can still feel him. Like he's looking over my shoulder. Like he's still here. It's felt that way since the funeral."

Ray gaped. He *knew* it; he knew he had to have some influence and wasn't just floating around here.

"Why haven't you said anything?" Ray said. No one heard. But he was hopeful, for the first time since the funeral. He rushed to kneel by her chair and put his hand over hers, where it rested on the table.

"We all feel like that," Steel said.

"No." She shook her head. "I mean last night, I could have sworn he was right there. Like he's not really gone. I just . . . I don't know." She stared at her hand—his hand. Like she could feel him touching her.

"Please, Annie," he whispered, all his attention turned on her. "Please, believe it. You can figure this out, I know you can." His insubstantial flesh looked solid to his own eyes, but the edges where his hand folded over hers seemed vague, until he couldn't tell where the lines of his hand ended and hers began. He could speak to her, contact her. He knew it. "Please."

The others watched her as a look came into her eyes—a focused, thoughtful expression. Her inventing look, Ray always called it. It meant the problem she was working on would soon be solved. She'd pulled them out of so many scrapes in the past.

She glanced to her left, where he knelt beside her. Almost like she could see him. Maybe she could.

"I have an idea," she said, and rushed away from the table to her workshop. Ray watched her go and wanted to laugh.

He grinned at the others. "I knew it. I knew she'd figure it out. You just wait, you'll see."

The other four team members sat in awkward silence, stealing glances at one another. Finally, Mr. Steel said, "I hadn't realized how much it's affected her. I thought she was doing all right."

Tessa said, "She loved him, you know. Never said a word about it, but she did."

Cheetah looked up. "Did he—"

"I think so," Jetstream said. "I'm pretty sure he did."

"I did," Ray said. "Of course I did. I was just too stupid—"

"Is she all right?" Steel said. "Because if she isn't, I'll take her off duty. I don't want her getting hurt."

"No, you idiot!" Ray said, just like the old days, like he always argued with Steel when they were sitting around this very table. "She's doing her thing, fixing problems. She's *fine*."

Tessa shook her head. "I think that would make it worse. This is all she has now."

Tessa was always the smart one, the real brains behind the outfit. Ray leaned on the table next to her. "Listen to her. Let Annie work!"

Steel sighed. "All right. But I want everyone to keep an eye on her. If you see anything that seems wrong, let me know."

Ray rushed after Gadgeteer.

Her workshop was marvelous chaos. The size of a three-car garage, it barely had enough open space to walk across it. She managed to keep pathways clear between various supply cabinets and work areas. Gadgets as large as car engines sat shoved in corners, dismantled. Three tables were covered with smaller devices, all in various states of repair. Boxes with dials sticking out of them and wires trailing away were everywhere. Scorch marks painted the ceiling and walls in a couple of places, results of some less-successful experiments. A blow torch, arc welder, a lathe, a band saw, soldering gear, and other machines Ray couldn't identify made up the heavy equipment. But in the end, give Gadgeteer a pair of nail clippers and a coil of dental floss, she'd create a device that could move the world.

She was already working, searching through bins on a set of shelves, pulling out wires and transistors, dials and other, less identifiable electronic detritus. She piled the supplies on one of the work benches, then strapped on her tool belt and got to work.

"Ray, I don't know if you're really here . . . Geez, what if this is all in my head? I'm going crazy. Maybe this is all wishful thinking and I've gone completely crazy. Ray, I don't know if you can hear me . . . but if I have gone completely crazy, I'm blaming you. I mean really, leave it to you to get creamed by your own radiation blast." She actually smiled.

So did Ray. He stood on the other side of the work bench. "Hey, I apologized for that already."

"I know you didn't mean to. Nobody could have seen that coming. But you know what I mean."

"I think I do," he said. It was easier to blame somebody: Professor Terrible's killer robot, Jetstream for not getting there in time, Steel for not having a good game plan. Hell, he could blame Gadgeteer for not stopping the robot in time. But he wouldn't. In the end, he'd been the one in the wrong place at the wrong time. It was just one of those things. In this line of work, he couldn't expect to live forever.

She didn't hear him, didn't respond. But it didn't matter.

He watched her work. A few hours into the project, Mr. Steel stopped by. "Annie? I just wanted to check in. Make sure you're okay."

"Can't talk, working," she said in a monotone, without turning around. Steel left, looking worried, and Ray wanted to throttle him. Didn't he recognize her when she was at her best?

As she often did when she was working, she forgot to eat and fell asleep at the work bench, slumped over, head resting on folded arms, screwdriver still clutched in her hand. She was sleeping when Tessa brought her a sandwich. She set the plate down and lightly touched Gadgeteer's hair. "Poor kid," she murmured, then started to turn away.

Ray was waiting for her. He grabbed her wrist, or tried to. As always happened, matter became slippery and uncertain under his touch. She passed right through him. But she paused, shivered, and rubbed her arm, the very spot he'd touched.

"She's right, Tessa," Ray said. "Listen to her. I'm still here. I'm *right here*."

Tessa shook her head and walked away.

Annie hadn't invited the rest of the team to watch the test of the pair of model devices she'd built, but they came anyway. They all wanted to see what she'd been up to for the last week of tinkering. They all had a look of pity in their eyes.

She explained the devices. "Theoretically, a ghost should leave some kind of trace on the environment. Radiation, a psychokinetic trail, something. So it's just a matter of building a sensor sensitive enough to detect the smallest trace of such evidence."

"Haven't people already tried this?" Jetstream said. "There've been ghost hunters doing this sort of thing for ages."

"But they're not me, are they?" she said, smiling. "This one, I've programmed using the last EEG reading taken of Ray's brain. If that pattern still exists, is still active, it should find it. The second I've programmed with the spectrographic signature of his energy beams. It's unique to him. If he's here, any part of him, then that signature should be here too."

They looked like any of a dozen gadgets she'd created over the years. Small, square, metallic, definitely not pretty to look at. They tended to look jury-rigged and vaguely unreliable, with multicolored wires looping out of them and mismatched buttons. These each connected to a remote control with an LCD screen. She pointed the first one toward an open space and switched it on. The screen on the remote lit up; that was all. Only Ray heard her murmur, "Please, help me out with this."

He stood right in front of the sensor. He stood far away. He jumped up and down, waved his arms, shouted. Gadgeteer stared at the screen like she might develop laser eyes and bore a hole through it. But nothing happened. She picked up the device, aiming it in one hand, holding the remote in the other, and walked around the room, sweeping it back and forth, a ghost-hunting Geiger counter. Ray kept in front of it the whole time, even gripping the machine—at least as much as he could in this state. Still nothing.

Jaw set, Gadgeteer put the first device aside and switched on the second one. No one said anything; the tension in the room was brittle. No one wanted to be the one to tell her she was crazy to think this would work.

"Come on, come on," Ray muttered. "Work, dammit!"

But this was the device designed to read his radiation blast signature. He no longer had that power. He had no reason to think it would detect him without it.

Again, not a click, not a blip, nothing. When Gadgeteer set the sensor back on the table, her hands were shaking.

Tessa tried to sound comforting. "Annie, I know you miss him, we all do, but—"

"Don't—just don't even start," she said, her voice low.

Ray was desperate. "Annie, don't give up, please. Come on, I'm right here, you know it! You'll find a way to prove it!"

He touched her hands where they covered the device. And something happened. A faint run of static sounded from the sensor, and the screen on the remote flashed green. Gadgeteer froze. Hand in hand, just like they had been the other night, they stood, and the sensor hissed his presence.

She glanced up, and they met each other's gazes. At least, he imagined they did.

"Did you see that?" she said.

"What's it mean?" Steel asked.

"It's detected a trace of Ray's radiation burst!"

"Where?"

"I don't know." She picked up the sensor and started moving. Ray backed away, and the static and activity on the screen stopped. Gadgeteer shook the machine.

"What happened?" Jetstream said.

"I don't know."

Ray had a suspicion. The sensor by itself wasn't enough. *Him* by himself wasn't enough. Slowly, she panned the device over the space by the work bench. He stood next to her and held the device with her, as much as he could. His hands, her hands, both over the machine, making contact. That was the key, he was sure of it.

Again the device gave off a signal.

Gadgeteer laughed. "It's working! He's here! I told you!"

Then, something else happened. They both saw it because they were both staring at the device. Gadgeteer watched the sensors, and Ray was watched their hands—which had started to glow.

"Annie, what's that?" Steel had donned his commanderly voice. It happened whenever he confronted something he didn't understand, that he thought was dangerous.

"I don't know," Gadgeteer said, watching the glow, a white light that surrounded both their hands and the device. "Maybe the sensor is overheating. He must be really close."

Right beside you, Ray thought. Holding you. He recognized that silver, super-hot glow. It was part of him. "No, Annie," he said by her ear. "It's not the sensor doing this."

He felt the familiar surge, the well of power growing in him, ready to be released. But now, he felt it through her. He still had the power—but he needed someone else's life to energize it. Hers.

"Okay, Annie, hold on, here it goes!" He stood behind her, wrapped his arms around her, held her hands in his, and braced. Just like before, just like the old days, he felt the power surge through him, and her. The energy collected in her hands and blasted away from them, a burst of light that struck the steel wall on the other side of the workshop.

They stared at the blackened, smoking space on the wall, where part of the metal had melted, dripping to the floor.

"Holy . . ." Jetstream muttered, trailing off.

"That machine, it's duplicating Ray's powers," Steel said.

"No, that's what I've been trying to tell you. It's Ray. He's here!" She was both crying and smiling. She put down the device and offered her hands. Ray cupped them in his, and they glowed. They'd practice, she'd get the hang of it. And he was back in the game.

"Oh, Ray," Tessa said.

"It's great to be back," Ray answered. Gadgeteer laughed. The glow in her hands reflected back to her face. Maybe she'd even learn to hear him, one of these days.

Then the alarm rang.

Steel rushed to the networked computer terminal in the workshop and called up the report. Full of determination, he reported to the others. "Zombies are attacking the city power plant."

Jetstream said, "Good timing. Ray's powers always worked great against zombies."

"Annie," Steel said. "Can you handle it? Can he handle it?"

"Yes yes yes," Ray said. "Of course we can!"

"Yes sir," Gadgeteer said. "I think we can."

"Then let's move it!"

When Gadgeteer raced for the hangar with the others, Ray was right beside her.

MUSEUM HAUNTINGS

Irene Radford

David Walker Stanley IV woke up. The first fluttering of his eyelids showed him the attic bedroom of his grandfather's house. He'd curled up, dripping wet, into a fetal position. One little stretch of his stiff legs ended abruptly at the foot rail of the small iron bedstead.

"I'm still alive," he said aloud, to test his voice. He pinched his thigh to make sure he wasn't still dreaming the nightmare of jumping off a cliff into the river.

"Failed again. I have got to be the most incompetent suicide ever." He grinned. Just the way he planned it.

"And I'm free of the old biddies. They might have declared me incompetent when I graduated from college, just to keep my money, but they can't control me any more."

He'd mailed his lawyer a will bequeathing any remaining assets to himself, under a different identity he'd spent five years building.

He angled his body differently and stretched again. This time his knees straightened and his feet dangled off the side of the thin mattress. Bright sunlight filtered into the room through the cracked shutters on the dormer window. He watched dust motes drifting

in the sunbeams. They spotlighted the faded and peel-
ing red wallpaper.

He'd awakened this way in this room for most of
his first ten years of life. Then Grumpy had died, leaving him the house and a generous trust fund, and only
the bank as his guardian.

A door banged somewhere below him. He risked
peeking out through the broken slat on the shutter.
The side yard below him, now a paved parking lot,
had a small red sedan parked in the back corner.
Blackberry vines crept over it.

"Damn, they're opening the museum today." He
thought every small museum in the state closed on
Mondays. "Why'd the aunts sell this place, anyway?"

Aunt Betty and Aunt Freda didn't believe the stories about Grumpy's hidden treasure. David did. He'd
seen it once, on his eighth birthday, and sort of remembered its hiding place.

He'd been fifteen when they sold. His aunts had
partied away most of his trust fund by that time and
needed the cash from the only remaining asset in
order to maintain their lifestyle.

They'd justified their expenditures on David's education, sending him to one boarding school after another, always inflating the tuition and expenses by a
factor of ten. Their drinking, wild parties, and syco-
phant husbands—four for Betty and three for Freda—
were why he'd gone to his grandfather and not them
when his missionary parents died of some exotic fever
before he turned three.

The town of Stanley Mills had made the only bid
on the house, well below the inflated asking price.
Five years of neglect on a one-hundred-fifty-year-old
house with six bedrooms, four stories—counting the
attic—and two acres of land had taken its toll. Repairs
to roof and plumbing, updating the furnace and electricity, restoring overgrown landscaping and roses

gone wild cost more than the difference between the asking price and the town's offer.

Two years later Grumpy's house became an official museum. The town had even hired a hotshot workaholic curator with a Ph.D. in U.S. history. More important, she knew how to write grants for operating funds.

Too bad her abusive husband killed her the following year. Multiple stab wounds. David had read everything concerning Grumpy's house.

"I thought I had twenty-four hours to search for the stash," he muttered. "Guess I'll just have to hide out and sleep for another twelve hours until she leaves."

Ten years of renovations and tourist traffic had probably repaired creaking stair treads, opened walls, changed doorways and who knew what else.

Tonight he'd reacquaint himself with his childhood home. If lights showed through the windows, the locals would believe his trespass just another ghost. The place was supposed to be filled with them.

He loosed a long yawn that started in his toes and stretched upward. Another nap. He opened a low cupboard door that let into a triangular storage space beneath the eaves and curled up in the sleeping bag he'd stashed there a month ago.

Keely Kora Ramsey unrolled the morning newspaper and spread it out on her antique rolltop desk as she had every morning for the past ten years. She stopped skimming the headlines, her coffee cup halfway to her mouth, and read the sidebar on the left with community news.

"Heir to the Stanley fortune succeeds at suicide after two failed attempts."

Then, in smaller type she read on:

David Walker Stanley IV, 27, was seen jumping from the top of Cemetery Ridge into the Whistling River last

*night around midnight. Chief George Miller, head of
the water rescue division of the Stanley Mills Fire Department, said he'd never heard of anyone surviving
that jump. Stanley's body has not been found. His com-
panions said he'd been drinking.*

*Stanley is survived by two aunts, Elizabeth Stanley
Bronson and Frederica Stanley Carlisle. Mrs. Bronson
told local authorities that her nephew had tried to commit suicide twice before, once by an overdose of pain
medication the day he graduated from college, and
again by slitting his wrists on his twenty-fourth birthday. "I guess he really didn't want to live," she said.
"He's been on medication for depression for years."*

A private memorial service is planned for Thursday.

"Poor fool." Keely shook her head and continued
reading, coffee forgotten. But her eyes kept coming
back to the sidebar.

"Wonder if he'll come back to haunt this place?"
she muttered. "Along with his damned cat."

Then she went about her day, dusting, fluffing
feather tick mattresses, setting out change in the till,
and cataloguing new acquisitions.

Strange, she didn't remember the beaver felt top
hat or the silk opera cape coming through the normal
donations. "1870s. Good condition, only a little shattered around the hem of the cape. Beaver felt worn
on crown. Grosgrain ribbon at brim modern replace-
ment."

She automatically recorded her notes on a standard-
ized form. For now she had to leave the donor and
the estimated value blank. One of the high school
work-study students could transcribe it later with that
information. Keely didn't trust computer records. Too
many hard drives crashed and floppy disks degraded.
She liked the tactile sensation of writing on paper with
a favored pen.

A fleeting shadow darted from the butler's pantry through the kitchen to behind the dining room drapes, setting the heavy brocade to swooshing. Dust bunnies the size of her fist skittered in the wake of the lilac point Siamese cat that refused to die. Or stay dead.

Keely frowned. She didn't like cats. Sneaky beasts, too smart for their own good and always behaving as if they owned their humans instead of the other way around.

No sense in chasing after an animal that wasn't really there.

The shadows grew longer as the sun dropped behind the line of hills to the west of town. Keely waved her dust cloth a little more frantically. Her heart beat faster in agitation. Night was coming.

She was supposed to lock up the museum at five and go home.

"If I'm quiet and don't turn on any lights, who will know if I don't leave? I'll just heat up a frozen dinner in the employee microwave," she reassured herself as she had every night for many, many nights. "I'm safe during the day when people are around. Will pretends to be very loving and solicitous then. But at night, he'll . . ."

She wouldn't think about the bruises on her body, or the broken ribs, or the threats with a wickedly sharp knife.

Even with her education and sophistication she hadn't chosen love wisely. Never again would she trust love at first sight. And so she hid every night where Will Ramsey couldn't find her, wouldn't think to look for her.

"I'll just move my car down to the theater parking lot and walk back."

David woke up cold, achy, and still damp on the short iron bedstead. Darkness reigned in the small attic room. He stretched until his foot banged into the foot rail. Then he angled his legs sideways to dangle off the thin mattress.

After several minutes, his eyes adjusted to the darkness and he picked out the shapes and shadows of the child-sized furniture, the toys piled around a painted chest and the beloved, threadbare teddy bear that had comforted him through many nights. Grumpy had owned the bear first, then David's father, and finally David himself. The aunts had insisted he leave it behind when he moved in with them. They bought him a new one that didn't shed fur and had hypoallergenic stuffing. But it had no personality, no history, no sense of family, and tradition.

He walked across the room and reached for the bear. The sound of footsteps on the stairs stopped him dead in his tracks. Who was in the house? Everyone should have gone home hours ago. He edged quietly over to stand against the wall, behind the door.

The door creaked open a few inches. It stuck halfway open; the settling house had thrown the frame out of alignment.

A small, round, fur-covered face with long white whiskers peeked in.

"Lilac!" he cried, forgetting to be quiet. "Oh, kitty, I thought you'd died long ago."

"Mew?" The delicate lilac point Siamese cat looked up at him. "Meower," she continued, letting him know that he'd been gone far too long and she resented him, and longed to be held because she was lonely.

"Oh, Lilac, I missed you, too." He stooped and picked her up, cradling her against his chest. "You must be the oldest cat on record, Lilac." She'd been old and slow, no longer interested in hunting, only in warm laps and a puddle of sunshine to sleep in, when he moved in with Grumpy. The aunts had tried to put her to sleep but she ran away, as old cats are wont to do.

The cat began purring as she rubbed her face against his arm.

He held her tighter, letting her animal warmth fill him with the love he'd been missing for a long, long time.

"Who's there?" a woman asked from right outside the door.

David and Lilac stilled, going cold with fear.

"Just my imagination. These old houses creak and settle. The wind in the trees always sounds like whispering," the woman continued. She rattled the door latch and pushed against the door.

David closed his eyes and willed himself to invisibility. When he opened them he found the woman—shapely and slender, in her late twenties with curly brown hair that made her look like a poodle—staring at him with big hazel eyes. Her mouth fell agape, showing a few straight white teeth.

All he could think was that she'd had expensive orthodontia. So had he.

Lilac pushed at his chest and leaped away. Her hind claws scratched his arm painfully. He rubbed the raw wound, surprised that his fingers came away clear of blood.

"Don't come near me, I'm going to call the police," the woman said. She deepened her voice and tried to sound stern, but it came out shaky and frightened.

"Don't do that. Please." David reached an imploring hand, stopping just short of touching her.

She flinched.

"I won't hurt you. I just need a place to hide out for a few days."

"Why?" She backed toward the window. A bit of moonlight filtering through the broken shutter slats outlined her trim body, but masked her face in shadow.

"I'm David Stanley. I used to live here. Please let me stay here."

"David Walker Stanley? The paper said you jumped off Cemetery Ridge last night."

She sounded more curious than frightened now.

"I faked it. I'm trying to escape my family. They poisoned me and made it look like failed suicide six years ago and they've tried twice more since. Now they're trying to put me in an asylum so they can control my money without question."

"You can't take it with you," she quipped, almost laughing.

"In this case I can. And will."

"Smart trick if you can pull it off."

A bit of light glinted off the whites of her eyes as she opened them wide.

"Tell me how? That might be just the trick to get away from Will."

"Will?" David didn't like the idea of this lovely woman belonging to another man. He couldn't explain the sudden flare of jealousy over someone he'd just met, didn't even know her name. It was just there, filling him with rage, as if he had a right to the emotion.

"My . . . my husband." She turned her head away, as if embarrassed.

"You need to get away from him," David said flatly. "Does he hurt you?"

She gulped and nodded, still looking at the cobwebs in the corner.

"I'll kill the bastard!"

"No, please. He's dangerous."

"I can take care of myself." David took two determined steps toward the closed door.

"He's got a very large hunting knife. He knows how to use it."

Something clicked in David's brain. He went cold all over. Colder than he'd been when he woke up damp and cramped. "How'd you get through the door without opening it?"

*   *   *

Keely had to pause a moment to follow David's leap of topics. "Why did you ask that? I don't follow."

He shrugged and looked pointedly at the small gap between the door and frame.

"Just answer my question. You not opening the door means a lot. To me. It should have stuck half way open."

"I planed off the bottom during the restoration. It doesn't stick any more. I also oiled the hinges. It opens and closes easily."

"Oh." He looked so disappointed, as if he'd hoped she'd walked through the closed door.

"I'm not a ghost, if that's what you're wondering."

"If you aren't a ghost, then who are you?" He bent over and petted the cat that stropped his legs.

It purred loudly. A real cat. Not the ghost reported by her interns and docents. She'd have to get someone to take it to the shelter. She couldn't have a real cat scratching fine wood and shedding all over priceless antique furniture.

"I'm Dr. Keely Ramsey, the curator."

"Aren't you kind of young?"

"That, sir, is none of your business. Now will you leave my bedroom or should I call the police and have you removed?"

"Your bedroom!" He sounded outraged at the thought.

"It's the only place I have to hide from Will." She hated the frightened whine in her voice. "This floor is closed to the public. No one comes up here any more, not even to dust." She swiped at a cobweb in the corner. "I leave it dusty in case someone does look. And I keep some clothing in that cupboard." She pointed to the triangular space below the dormer.

"I thought it strange to find some women's clothes hanging in there," David said. He stroked his chin in thought. "Toiletries?"

"In the bathroom up here. Where else? It's fitted out to look antique, but all the plumbing works."

She watched him pluck at his knit shirt. It clung to his body as if wet. And a nice body it was, too. He must work out.

Will had a nice body, too. That didn't make him trustworthy, or kind, or even a gentleman.

But this young man, so close to her own age, had kind eyes. *He's not trustworthy. He faked suicide,* she reminded herself.

"Mind if I get a bath and a shave?" David asked. "The river left its mark on me."

"Do you have fresh clothing?" Keely didn't want to risk running down to the Laundromat, though she supposed she should wash some of her own things as well.

"Stashed a few things along with my sleeping bag some time ago." David waved toward the cupboard. "I visit the museum incognito often."

"Very well. But don't come back to this room. I'm going to bed and don't wish to be disturbed. I've had a long and trying day." She felt exhausted, no longer had the strength to remain standing, though she couldn't remember why she should be so tired.

What had happened today that was so unusual?

David wandered through the big house, shadowed by Lilac. He forgot that he was still cold and damp as he revisited memories he thought he'd lost. Grumpy's room with the big four-poster bed where David had curled up with him when thunder or nightmares frightened him. Grumpy would read to him or tell him stories until he fell asleep. Always, David woke up the next morning in his own bed, carefully tucked in by Grumpy.

He barely poked his nose into the rooms where the aunts had slept when they visited on holidays, or when they needed a loan. One of the guest rooms had been converted to storage, two others housed natural history exhibits and Indian stuff, and yet another had pioneer cabin things. One small room toward the back of the third floor had become a maid's room, complete with mannequin in Victorian black uniform with a wraparound white apron.

Next to Grumpy's room he found a ladies' private parlor. He couldn't remember how Grumpy used it when he lived here. Closed off, he guessed. Grumpy didn't want to visit his wife's rooms after she died. He'd have to ask Keely what they found there when the town took over.

On the main floor the dining room looked as it should, with the long mahogany table and twelve chairs, all set with white linen, polished silver, and the good china. Everyday china and serving dishes filled the sideboard. Cobwebs connected the crystal stemware. They needed a good washing. Someone neglected their curatorial duties and he suspected it wasn't Keely.

The housekeeper's rooms off the kitchen had been converted to an office, complete with file cabinets, desk, three-line telephone, computer, copier, and employee lounge with modern microwave and coffee pot. A long work table stretched across another pantry where new donations and artifacts were sorted, measured, and recorded. Plastic boxes below held needles and thread and some other restoration equipment.

Satisfied that the staff knew how to run a museum, even if they were a bit lazy in the cleaning department, he aimed his steps toward the library and study. New research books on local history, costuming, cooking, and restoration filled one wall. Otherwise, Grumpy's massive collection stood undisturbed but lovingly dusted. Good. He hated to think about the books falling to ruin from neglect.

Finally he approached the study. He held his breath until it hurt, then gathered Lilac into his arms and stepped over the velvet rope installed to discourage tourists from entering. The cat purred a moment, then jettisoned herself out of his arms. She immediately began sniffing around the corners of the room.

Grumpy had kept everything he valued most in this room. It still smelled of his pipe tobacco and musty old books.

David tiptoed toward the west wall, where two sets of French doors opened onto a flagged patio and the lawn beyond with islands of roses dotted about. They smelled rich and wonderful and welcoming on the night wind. Soft moonlight turned the garden into a fairyland.

Between the two doors, an alcove with a window bench jutted out onto the patio.

He'd curled up here often with Lilac, puzzling his way through homework and favored books while Grumpy sat at his desk with his accounts and stock reports. He sat in the window embrasure a long time, drifting in his memories of this room, of being loved and cherished.

Eventually he remembered his purpose and looked about for signs of something out of alignment, some hint as to which wall of books hid the entrance to a secret room.

He couldn't remember. With closed eyes, he tried to recreate the memory of the late night, so many years ago.

On the occasion of David's ninth birthday, Grumpy had drunk quite a bit of wine at dinner, even letting David have a few sips, watered down. Quite an end to a day filled with cake and ice cream, friends, animal balloons, games, and a magician. David thought he smelled again the alcohol on Grumpy's breath, along with his pipe tobacco and spicy hair tonic.

He traced the steps they had taken from the door to the desk to . . . his mind twisted and refused to lead him further. "Once more into the breach," he quoted, closing his eyes and walking the path again. This time he ended up standing to the right of the sofa, facing the fireplace. Ceramic logs lay there now, in imitation of the real fire that had crackled merrily most evenings during David's time in the home.

"Okay, now if I were going to hide a door . . ."

"What are you looking for?" Keely asked from the doorway.

"I thought you were asleep," David hedged.

"I did for a time. Now I'm awake. What are you looking for?"

Did he trust her? "Something my grandfather left behind. Something he wanted me to have but was afraid to let my aunts know existed."

"If it was in the secret room below this one, we found it when we re-did the plumbing. It was empty."

"Oh." David sagged. All his plans for naught. No money to start a new life. Nothing. No place to go. He crumpled onto the sofa, staring at the endless rows of books, the fake fire, the new carpet and drapes.

"Why didn't you get a restraining order on your husband and divorce him?" He had to make conversation, just to keep going. He thought he knew the answer, but he had to ask.

She looked agitated, pacing from desk to windows to far wall and back to the desk. "He threatened to kill me." She gulped. Tears came to her eyes. "He'd have done it, too. He's a lawyer. Smart. He's defended enough murderers to know how to get away with it. He knows how to make people mad enough to make mistakes and get evidence thrown out."

"You must be scared out of your wits. Couldn't you go to one of the shelters?"

"He'd find me."

"But here? Isn't this the obvious place to look for you at night as well as during the day?"

"I . . . I . . ." She moved faster, twisting her hands together, searching every shadow and starting every time the cat moved.

"Let me ask you this, Keely: How long have you been curator here?"

"A long time. Since the town bought the house." She relaxed a bit but continued her anxious prowl of the room.

"Twelve years," David mused. "I met you at the dedication."

"That long. My, how time flies." But she looked confused. "Could your grandfather have moved his 'treasure' before he died?" She changed the subject and looked much calmer.

"He might. If he thought my aunts would find the room. They mentioned more than once that the old mausoleum should be torn down."

"There you have it. As soon as he got sick—cancer, wasn't it—he took measures to secure it for you. Where else could he have hidden it?" She tapped her lips with her finger.

He noted that she had a near-perfect manicure, except for one small chip in the nail polish at the tip of her index finger. Beneath that nail was an old dark stain that looked like dried blood.

"There's a place in the dressing room off Grumpy's room."

"I've been all through the built-in drawers. I had to inventory everything left in the house, including your grandfather's underwear."

"But did you pull out all of the drawers and look in the cupboard behind them?" New hope brightened David's mood. The whole room looked lighter, as if dawn approached while the moon was still up. "Let's go look." He stood, eager and happy again.

"What got you interested in history?" David asked, just to make conversation. He knew she wouldn't talk about her life with Will.

"Oh." Her eyes sparkled with enthusiasm. "I'm not sure when it started exactly. I've always listened to the stories of old-timers, prowled ruins and museums and cemeteries."

"What were you looking for?" They ambled together toward the kitchen and the back stairs, as if the grand staircase was reserved for someone else. Someone, older and more dignified, who used to live there.

"Connections, I think." Keely paused and looked about at the antique fixtures and wallpaper, portraits painted and photographed, the polished wood floors and high ceilings. "I like to look at the way people used to live, what they believed, their attitudes, and follow them forward to see how the past has shaped our lives today."

"Give me an example." He smiled down at her, liking the companionable air between them, the almost instant "fit" of their personalities. The sense of trust that came out of nowhere when neither one of them had a reason to trust anyone.

Correction: neither one of them could trust their families, but strangers could become instant friends because they didn't have the power to hurt you. Not like family could.

"Okay, did you know that the phrase 'bustle along'—meaning to move hurriedly and with ostentation—has many sources, but our modern meaning refers to a woman wearing a bustle, and usually a tight skirt. She couldn't move very fast because when she hurried, the bustle swayed in a most unbecoming and obvious manner?"

David laughed. "I've got one for you, but not as funny. Street names. A lot of them come from the pioneer family that originally lived on that street."

"Yes," she chortled. "And if you study wedding announcements of prominent families in the past the guest list reads like a local road map."

They continued to trade anecdotes as they approached the master bedroom and its attached dressing room. Most of the long narrow room—just wide enough to fit a single bed across the end under the tall window—was made narrower by built-in shelves and drawers.

"We don't open this room to the public. The door to the hallway is always locked; in fact, I don't remember there being a key when I started work. Easier to control traffic and access if the only entrance is through the bedroom."

"What happened to all of Grumpy's clothes?"

"Is that what you called him? Grumpy? From what I've read, he was not the easiest man to get along with."

"We got along just fine. I loved him," David said wistfully.

"Most of his clothes were too worn and threadbare to display. Valuable to the researcher, though. They are in climate-controlled storage off-site. That's why the shelves are filled with ledgers and document folders that we need to keep but aren't current," Keely explained.

David slid down to sit on the floor, his back to the cupboard. Anxious as he was to find the stash of Confederate gold his multi-great-grandfather had hidden against the day the South rose again, he wanted to prolong this moment, this sharing with Keely. He hadn't allowed himself to share his life with anyone since Grumpy had died. What sense in making friends when he'd spent five years planning his escape to a new life, leaving them all behind?

Suddenly he didn't want to leave Keely behind.

But he had to.

She couldn't go with him. She could never leave the museum she loved so much it had become her sanctuary.

So he patted the floor beside him, inviting her to sit. She did. They talked and laughed until long after the moon set. Better to spend one night talking to a ghost than alone for the rest of his life.

Keely awoke on the narrow child's bed in the attic, as she had every morning since she'd made the decision not to go back to Will and the house of luxurious horrors he'd built for them. As she stretched, just fitting with the crown of her head against the top rail and her feet pushing against the bottom, she wondered if any new donations had come in to the museum.

Her hand brushed soft fur. She jerked it back and squeaked in fear, expecting to find a mouse had crawled into the ticking and chewed its way out.

The cat lay tucked into the back of David's knees.

David. Such a lovely young man. The spitting image of his grandfather's youthful portraits. Polite and caring, smart and eager to learn new things. Why hadn't she met him years ago, before she met Will?

Because years ago he'd have been a teenager and she was finishing up her dissertation.

Carefully, she wiggled off the bed so that she didn't disturb David and his cat.

Maybe this should be her last night hiding out here. She should leave the place to David. After all, he could never leave it, since this was the beloved place his spirit had chosen to return to after death. He'd run away from his emotionally abusive family only to find death. He just didn't realize it yet. He might never realize that he'd died in the cold dark waters of the river.

Knowing him made her realize she could run no longer. She had to stand up to Will and expose him for the cruel brute he truly was. Would the world believe her? They would if she showed a judge and the press the latest round of bruises, broken bones, and knife nicks.

A strange sensation of *déjà vu* washed over her. She felt like she had stood here before, made this decision before. . . .

Nonsense. She needed to get to work.

She longed for the taste of steaming waffles with melted butter and sweet maple syrup. And apple sausage on the side. Oh, and the taste of fine coffee with real cream and sugar, and orange juice thick with pulp. But she dared not show her face anywhere in town where Will might find her. She'd done that before and he dragged her home to another round of abuse. Oh well, she'd make do with instant oatmeal in the microwave and generic coffee.

"I'd best get ready and hide the evidence that I've been here all night," she muttered on her way down the stairs.

David woke up cold and damp on the iron bed of his childhood, feeling as if something were missing. Lilac pressed up against his knees, as she had always slept. He stroked one finger along her silky head, wondering . . .

Keely.

He sighed with regret that he must leave her as soon as he found the treasure. Somehow they'd never gotten around to looking last night. She was just so much fun to talk to.

Another time, another place, another life, he'd look forward to spending a lifetime talking to her, laughing with her, holding her. Making love to her.

But no. That could never be. She was dead and didn't know it.

Should he tell her? He didn't know which would be crueler: to make her continue hiding in fear of a man sitting on death row in the state prison or to force her to accept her death.

The smell of coffee made his mouth water. He wandered down the back stairs in search of the water of life.

Voices drifted up from the kitchen. The staff had arrived already. He and Keely must have slept later than he thought. He considered creeping back upstairs and hiding out again. The sight of Keely standing to the side of the doorway, obviously eavesdropping, drove him on.

She half turned to him and beckoned him to stand beside her, hidden from view.

"I see our resident ghost has been busy, Marla," a mature female said cheerily. "Half my work in measuring, assessing, and recording the new donations is done already."

"Resident ghost?" Keely whispered. Her naturally pale face went whiter. "I did that work myself."

David touched her arm, in compassion. She had to find out someday.

"You don't suppose, Veronica, that Keely comes back. . . ." a younger girl said. Presumably Marla.

"She was found dead here after her husband stabbed her seven times," Veronica added. "Interesting that she crawled back here to her place of employment rather than go to friends, or the hospital, or even the police."

"She loved this old place and her work. Loved it more than she did her husband. And that's why he killed her," Marla insisted.

"Anyway you look at it, even as a ghost she's a more capable curator than Marshall Gibbs," Veronica snorted.

"Don't let him hear you say that!"

"Oh, he won't grace us with his presence until he's damn well good and ready. Plenty of time for us to get the real work done before he starts complaining about the dust. Always complaining that we never dust. As if we didn't have anything more important to do, like give tours to the public."

"I dust every day," Keely sighed. "And it never gets better." She looked sadly at the dingy dining room through the swinging door, now propped open, and the cobwebs that stretched from glass to glass, to plates, to chandelier. "Is it true?" She raised sad eyes to David. "Am I dead?"

"I'm afraid so," David said gently. "I read about your death in the papers. I sent flowers to your funeral because you were kind to me when we met at the dedication. I'm sorry you had to hear it like this," David whispered.

She shrugged. "I think I knew that. I've had a while to get used to the notion. I just didn't want to admit that Will had won."

"He didn't win. He was tried for murder and convicted. His last appeal was rejected last month," David consoled her.

He had a funny feeling that he shouldn't be able to hold her hand. Nor should it feel warm in his.

"Did you read in the paper yesterday that David Stanley killed himself?" Marla asked.

"Such a waste," the woman said, accompanied by the sound of a newspaper fluttering to the table. "The Stanley family must be cursed. First his parents, then his grandfather. Now David. All dead before they should have been."

"Too much money and no reason to work for a living," a man snorted. He sounded officious. The back door banged behind him. "At least now I won't have to deal with his weekly emails 'advising' me on how to run my own museum. He thought he knew more about the displayed artifacts than I do."

"At least they found the body yesterday afternoon. I hate to think of the family not having the closure of a proper funeral and a grave to place flowers on," Veronica continued.

David's already-cold body grew colder yet. And stiller. He couldn't hear his own heart beat.

"I suppose we should issue a statement of condolence and send flowers," the man sighed, as if the duty were onerous. "Work out the proper wording for me, Veronica."

"You know, Marshall, a little compassion would be nice," she retorted.

"I did not know the man, nor his family. How can I feel anything for them but contempt for ruining each other's lives and wasting their grandfather's hard-earned fortune." A door slammed.

David stared at Keely bleakly.

"You must be devastated," she said, squeezing his hand.

"I don't know what I feel. If I feel anything. Except that I'm glad to be here in this house. I love this house. I loved the time I lived here. And I think I could love you." He cocked her half a grin.

She giggled. "You know, if we weren't both haunting this place, we'd never have met, never have been able to be together. I'm . . . I was fifteen years older than you."

"But now we're almost the same age. I'm glad you waited around for me."

"You won't need your grandfather's treasure any more."

"It'll still be fun to look. Rearrange things a bit now and them, give the ladies a bit of a scare." He bent and kissed her cheek.

She stared back at him in wonder. "We can touch!" She placed her hand on his chest as if checking for a heartbeat. Then she smiled shyly and kissed his cheek. "I'm looking forward to having a long, long time to learn to love again."

They broke apart and ran back up the stairs hand in hand. The cat scampered after them.

"Did you hear someone on the stairs?" Veronica asked Marla.

"Yeah, and I thought I heard laughter, too."

"That's new. One more story to add to the 'Haunted Halloween Tour.'"

"Now if she'd just dust half as well as she catalogues donations . . ."

FLESH

Zombies. Revenants. The walking dead. Flesh-eaters. They've been a staple of horror movies and novels for generations, staggering and lurching their way through our literature mercilessly for so long, they almost seem real. These five stories show us just how real they can seem in the flesh.

Nina Kiriki Hoffman chillingly shows us that it's a matter of perspective that being undead can be better. On the lighter side, every woman's dream of a perfect man is realized by Fran LaPlaca. Jay Lake twists the zombie tropes into a shockingly plausible tale of what happens when zombies are commonplace. For Devon Monk's protagonist, there are more zombies than meet the eye. And Robert A. Hoyt spins an engaging yarn about a zombie that could have been titled "My Dinosaur Blue."

MY TEARS HAVE BEEN MY MEAT

Nina Kiriki Hoffman

I looked away from my husband's coffin, past the other mourners and the murmuring priest, and saw the white glimmer of a ghost over my daughter's grave.

The day was cloudy and cool, and smelled of stale water and decaying flowers. I held a bouquet of white lilies. Their Easter odor made me feel faint. Mother had pressed them on me to give me something to do with my gloved hands; before she handed me the flowers, I had not been able to stop tugging at the buttons on the cuffs of my black dress. "One more twist and one of those will come off," Mother had muttered, and closed my hands around the lace-printed plastic holding the lilies.

"We sorrow with our sister, Nicolette," said the priest, "but we hold out hope of heaven for our dear brother Joseph."

I clenched my fist around the flowers, felt the strong stems crunch in my grasp. Joe and the hope of heaven? Not very likely.

But my daughter, Miranda: she should be in heaven by now. What was haunting her grave, and why?

It wouldn't be proper for me to leave my husband's graveside in the middle of the service and go to my daughter's. I wanted to save Miranda from whatever might be bothering her, but I had never been able to do that in life; why should anything be different now?

Mother gripped my shoulder, pressed her thumb into the knotted muscles. She misinterpreted my tension, as usual, I supposed. Despite all evidence to the contrary, she thought Joe and I had had an ideal marriage. She had always liked him, relished the little attentions he paid her. Joe could be thoughtful if he decided it would gain him anything; he had remembered Mother's birthday, her favorite cologne, her taste in flowers and colors. Mother was the one who had made all the funeral arrangements. I had been too shaken after Joe's death. Mother told me she and Joe had talked about his wishes at some point, which I thought strange when I had any thoughts at all. She had picked a mortuary I had never heard of.

Mother probably thought I was grieving for Joe now, when all I wanted was to see him buried so deep he couldn't come back.

The gravedigger cast a shovelful of earth on Joe's coffin. I clenched the flowers tighter.

"Earth to earth, ashes to ashes, dust to dust," the priest said.

If Joe had ever been earth or dust or ashes, I would have been able to stand up to him. He had been flesh and blood and bone, muscular, taller and more powerful than I. Often enough he had proved that to me. Worse, Joe had been mind. He had been able to outwit and disarm me with words, even more than he had hurt me physically. He convinced me he loved me while I watched the bruises color my skin. He convinced me that everyone we knew despised me and only tolerated me because I was inside the edge of Joe's golden aura. He convinced me that without him, I was nothing. He did it so well that after I poisoned him, I had thought I might fade away.

I squeezed the lily stems again, taking comfort from their crunch. I was still solid.

I shifted my shoulders, and my mother's hand slid off. Joe had followed Miranda into death. Oh, God. Could he hurt her there? Was that why there was a ghost over my daughter's grave?

"The Lord be with you," the priest said, and most among the mourners murmured the response, "And with thy spirit." "Let us pray," said the priest.

I prayed, while the priest led people in the Lord's Prayer and then talked his way through other prayers about love, God, Jesus, and mercy. I prayed Joe hadn't found some way to cheat death and come back to haunt me—he'd hinted at such a thing, just before he died.

Joe had lost his greatest power over me after he pushed Miranda down the stairs. It took me time to realize it, though. I spent ages in a gray world after my daughter died. I didn't care about anything except visiting my daughter's grave. Nothing could hurt me enough to punch through the walls I had built, not until I realized, with dull shock, that three months had gone by and the blood hadn't come.

I used the home pregnancy test in a restroom at the local college, where I did not attend classes. Joe went through our trash; I couldn't chance evidence at home.

When I knew I had started another child, I woke up.

"Would the widow like to cast a flower on the coffin?" asked the priest.

I took one of the broken-stemmed lilies from the bunch and dropped it on Joe's coffin. He had always hated that scent.

"It's all right to cry, Nikki," Mother murmured.

I couldn't manage a tear. The gravedigger dropped more dirt into the grave. The priest took my hand, patted it, led me away.

"Wait." I broke from him and went back to Miranda's

grave. The specter no longer hovered above it. I
wanted to leave Miranda a token; I always did when
I visited her. I held nothing but the lilies, and I didn't
want to leave her one of those. I left one of my black
lace gloves on her grave.

I glanced around the graveyard to see if Randy, the
night watchman, was nearby. He and I had become
friends since Miranda died. But of course he wasn't
working now, in daylight; curiosity hadn't brought him
to my husband's funeral.

There was a reception afterward, at Joe's and my
house. Mother put the flowers from the service around
the living room. I stood in the double doorway and
looked into that room, the perfect place for Joe to
have his business acquaintances over. The cream carpet was deep and nubbly. I had had it Scotchgarded
while Joe was away from home. He would have been
horrified that anything shielded his treasures from
him, so I hadn't told him. There was a sculpture in
one corner he had paid twenty-five thousand dollars
for, a lumpy bronze pillar that reminded me of a fat
woman wrapped in a metal cocoon. The couches were
slim on padding, long on pale woods and shimmery
off-white upholstery. The bleached coffee tables' legs
tapered to slender points. You couldn't put your feet
up on any of this furniture. It seemed designed to
break under pressure.

Mixed with all this cool-colored distance, the various flower arrangements looked overblown and distasteful, though most of them were pale or pastel, too.

How Joe would have hated it.

Mother had set up a buffet—a coffee urn, an array
of white porcelain teacups and saucers, coffee whit-
ener and artificial sweetener, and three plates of
skinny, unadorned cookies. Not many of the mourners partook.

Joe's mother and father, shadow shapes at the
graveside service, came to me. I had left the lilies in

the limousine; I found my bare hand tugging at the button on my opposite cuff as I strove to retrieve the comforting distance I'd maintained most of the day.

Grace, Joe's thin, wispy mother, patted my arm, her features crumpled like paper, her eyes leaking plentiful tears. Rudy, Joe's father, patted my shoulder. He was a big bluff man, eaten away with age. Every time he lifted a hand, Grace flinched.

"Nicolette, you're welcome to live with us," Grace said. She stopped patting my forearm and gripped it. Her fingers dug into my flesh like talons.

"That's right, honey. You just let everything go and come on home with us. We'll take care of you," said Rudy. He stopped patting my shoulder and rubbed it instead, his big hand moving in small circles. His breath smelled of soured coffee.

"Nicolette will be fine," Mother said. She drew me out of the clutches of Rudy and Grace, settled her arm around my waist. "I'll stay here with her as long as she needs me."

"Is that what you want, honey?" Rudy asked.

I nodded, though it wasn't remotely what I wanted. What I really wanted was to burn down the house and everything in it, collect all the money I was owed— Joe's life insurance, homeowner's, everything. Then I would change my name and move somewhere else. I would hate to leave Miranda's grave, but to save the new child, I would move to where no one knew me. Nicolette, Joe's shadow wife, could die; I would give birth to a new self, one who could be a strong, protective mother. Child and I could live someplace warm, where there were colors.

For now, having Mother around was much easier than dealing with Grace and Rudy.

Rudy closed his hand on my shoulder, shook me. He didn't manage to shake me loose of Mother's embrace. "You sure, doll?"

I nodded.

"Well, all right." Rudy's fingers pinched my shoulder muscles tight against the bone. I would have a bruise tomorrow. "But anytime you need any little thing, doll, you call us. Grace and I feel like you're our responsibility."

Finally he let go. I leaned against Mother. Grace patted my cheek. At last they left.

Mother's arm around my waist felt like a lasso.

"I never liked that man," she said.

"Thanks for saving me, Mother."

Her arm tightened, then dropped away. "Well," she said. "Let's go talk to the people who really loved Joe."

After that, I stood by the door and accepted condolences from Joe's business acquaintances and poker buddies. I heard murmurs from their women, who whispered to each other, but not too softly. "Not a single tear," one said to another, and, "She didn't deserve a man like Joe."

I had played bridge with them, barbecued for them and their husbands during the summer, cooked roasts and turkeys and potatoes for them in the winter. All the people Joe invited over so he could store up favors, people he had ordered me to cater to. I had never talked to them about anything real.

Well, only one. Helena Whittaker. After Miranda died, I had had to talk to someone, and she sat beside me during Miranda's funeral; her black-gloved hand rested over mine on the pew between us. Joe sat on my other side, his face buried in a white handkerchief. I was surprised later when I found it in the laundry, damp; I tasted it, and found salt. Real tears. During Miranda's funeral I had been so bowed under the weight of my own grief I had no time for what Joe was feeling. Only the warmth from Helena's hand had penetrated my shell.

Later, Helena found me in the restroom of the funeral home. I had cried. She laid a handkerchief over her shoulder and put her arms around me, let me sob, listened to my wails of "why?" When I was exhausted and had run out of tears, she carefully folded up the tear-soaked handkerchief and stowed it in her coat pocket. We left the restroom together. She stood beside me as I faced Joe. I reached for the strength she had lent me. Instead, I saw her nod to my husband and turn away.

As she left the house today, she studied me, her head cocked. Her lips firmed. She shook her head, brushed my hand, and slipped out the door, her huge and befuddled husband stumbling down the steps in her wake.

The others left, couple by couple.

"You should get some sleep," Mother said.

I let her push me upstairs. She drew a warm bath for me—the first time she had done that in an age—and pulled my clothes off, gently. I felt boneless, passive. She settled me in the water, then brought me a mug of warm milk. "Drink this," she said. "It'll help you sleep."

The milk tasted strange, a little sour, though she had put honey in it. I took one sip and poured the rest into the toilet when she was out of the room. I didn't flush, because she would have noticed. I just closed the lid.

Mother bustled about between the bathroom and her guest bedroom. She muttered to herself.

She looked at the empty milk mug and smiled. "Are you relaxed yet, dear?" she asked.

I closed my eyes. "Yes," I murmured.

"Well, let's get you to bed." She helped me stand—and I needed help; I felt limp—dried me off, wrapped me in a robe, and dragged me into the master bedroom, where she had turned down the sheets on the wrong side of the king bed I had shared with Joe.

"But that's—" I tried to tell her. She pushed me down onto the bed and I thought, why fight it?

Mother worked the covers over me, then tucked them in so tight I couldn't move. She kissed me on the forehead and turned out the light. "Rest well."

After the door clicked softly shut, I worked my arms free of the cocoon she had wrapped me in and jerked the covers loose. I so wanted to sleep. I had waited years for a night free of Joe's presence or the menace of his potential presence. But I had to go back to the cemetery and check my daughter's grave.

Mother was a light sleeper, and I knew she was listening to make sure I was quiet and controlled.

I slipped from the bed, stepping carefully on the throw rug Joe kept by his side of the bed. He had hated cold feet. That obsession helped me now by muffling my steps so Mother couldn't hear. I crept to the closet and pulled out my longest, warmest coat. It covered my nightgown from neck to mid-calf. I grabbed a pair of fleece-lined winter boots, hugged them to my chest as I slipped out the door.

Down the hall, a line of light striped the floor beside Mother's room. She had left her door open a crack. To listen for me, I thought, and was surprised at the rush of bitterness that flooded through me.

I heard murmuring from her room. Was she talking on the phone? But she was speaking so low. Did she actually have a visitor? If she did have a visitor and wanted to keep it secret, she should close her door. I wavered between creeping closer and listening to see whom she was talking to and leaving, but finally I opted for leaving. I had to check with Miranda.

Three of the stairs would creak if I stepped on them; I knew this from the nights when Joe passed out in front of the television downstairs and I sneaked down to check on him and contemplate covering his head with a pillow. After a few times when he wasn't passed out enough to ignore me, I figured out how to walk the stairs without alerting anyone to my presence. I used this knowledge a lot after Miranda's death, when I went to visit her.

The front door was a problem. It creaked when any-one opened it, even though I had oiled the hinges.

Sometimes I thought it wanted to let everyone know how unhappy it was.

I went to Joe's study and slid the big window open. Silent. He'd paid a carpenter extra to smooth the window's glide. He liked things smooth. I was sure he left the front door creaky just to keep track of me.

I sat on the sill and put my boots on, then dropped to the flower bed below. I wasn't going to be able to get back in through the window; it was too high off the ground. I had my key in my pocket, but I would probably spend the night on one of the chaises on the patio. I'd done it before.

The cemetery was five blocks from the house. We hadn't bought the house with that in mind, but after Miranda's death, I had walked out my bereavement on the sidewalks between our house and the cemetery. I knew the cracks in the cement, the staples on the telephone poles that bore witness to missing animals and party plans people had wanted to broadcast to the neighborhood. I knew which dogs barked when someone passed. Joe had never known where I went on my frequent walks, but still, he had resented them, and tried to stop me. He wanted to take away anything that meant anything to me, but I had often managed to slip out for moments at Miranda's grave. I gave her my tears.

I zigzagged between sidewalks tonight to avoid all houses with barking dogs and made it to the cemetery without problems. There was a place in the hedge I knew to slip through. Vandals had found it before me, and Randy, the night watchman, checked it regularly; tonight he was nearby, leaning on a headstone and smoking a clove cigarette. "Mrs. B," he said. "Thought I might see you tonight. How's it going?"

"Not so well, Randy."

"Mr. B," he said. "That got you broke up?" He sounded doubtful.

Randy knew me. "No. It's Miranda."

"Oh?" He followed me as I headed for my daughter's grave.

"Do you see ghosts, Randy?"

"Hear 'em now and then. At least I think that's what makes that talk in the ground. I'm walking past a lot of graves of a night, and sometimes there's a murmuring. I figure it's ghosts sorting stuff out, but I don't listen too close. None of my business."

"I saw something like a ghost during the funeral today."

"What'd it look like?"

"Something pale over Miranda's grave. I have to see if she's all right."

"Okay." He turned on his four-D-cell flashlight and lit the path for us. No hesitations; we'd come this way before.

Randy had a gentleness to him. For a big man, he was careful. He never touched me except to grasp my elbow if it looked like I was about to trip. He knew how to be silent when a person wanted to disappear inside oneself, and he knew how to be company when one was walking away from a grave and having trouble pulling oneself out of the ground. He never mocked me. Randy was the closest thing I had to a friend and a counselor. I wished I could help him, but I didn't know how.

Maybe Joe had left me something good, something I could give to Randy.

"Want to be alone, Mrs. B?" Randy asked. The flashlight shone on the words MIRANDA BROUSSARD, BELOVED DAUGHTER; SHE IS IN A BETTER PLACE NOW.

"No, Randy. Thanks. I'd rather have you with me, if you can stay."

He glanced around the cemetery, away from the cone of light from his flashlight. It was a half-moon night; mist rested in rags here and there. I didn't see any movement.

"Go ahead," said Randy.

I knelt, my knees on the grass over my daughter's grave. There lay the dark glove I had dropped earlier in the day. "Miranda," I whispered. "What troubles you? How can I help?"

"Mama," whispered someone under the ground. "Run away."

"What do you mean?"

"Run away, Mama. He's coming back."

I glanced behind me, toward Joe's grave, where fresh, mounded earth lay, a little too tall for the ground, and not yet covered with squares of turf.

"How can that be?" I whispered. I put my hands flat on my daughter's grave. This was the first time I had heard her voice since Joe killed her. I felt a terrified delight. "Miranda. Are you all right?"

Randy switched off his flashlight, leaving us in darkness. "Someone's coming."

I hid behind my daughter's headstone. Randy moved to a nearby tree and blended his silhouette with its shadow.

Someone in black was approaching. A faint breath of perfume traveled before her. I recognized Mother by the scent of White Shoulders. She looked large in the darkness; she was wearing some shapeless overgarment with no arms, and at her side she carried a bulky bag.

I gripped the edge of Miranda's rough-hewn granite stone.

Mother stopped at Joe's grave, dropped the bag. She rummaged through it, came up with three candles, and lit them. She dripped wax onto a white plate and stood the candles upright on it. They glowed red. She laid other things out before her, but I couldn't see what, except a white square of cloth, a handkerchief, which she snapped open. "Her tears," she muttered.

I remembered Helena Whittaker's nod to my husband after I cried on her shoulder. Had Joe known even then that this day would come? Sent Helena to collect my grief over the loss of my daughter? Who was the man I had married?

"I'm sorry, Joseph," Mother said after she had arranged things on my husband's grave. "I don't know what's become of her. I drugged her milk the way we planned, but she didn't drink it. She's out roaming around like the faithless girl she's always been. My blood will do just as well."

"Run," whispered Miranda.

I couldn't let go of the chill rock. I couldn't rise and run.

Mother started a small fire on Joe's grave; I could see the dancing light on her face. She chanted, held things up to the night sky, then dropped them into the fire. One of them glowed in the darkness: the handkerchief.

Had my mother always been a witch? How could I not have known?

Cold invaded my clothes, chilled my feet. Joe had said something at breakfast the day before I poisoned him, something that frightened me. Something about our wedding vows lasting beyond the grave. "You'll always be mine. Always, Nicolette."

Part of me had thought: why do you even want me when you think so little of me? Part of me had thought: this has to stop, now, before he knows about Child. I can't bring Child into this kind of bondage.

What if Mother could bring Joe back? If he was somewhere beyond dead, could he die again? Would I ever be rid of him? What would he do to Child?

Mother lifted a knife that gleamed in the flickering light. She cut across her left forearm, held her arm so the blood flowed, black and wet in the firelight, onto the grave.

"Run," Miranda whispered again.

Mother's murmurs rose louder. I heard words, but I didn't understand them, until she said, "All the conditions are now fulfilled. Joseph, rise. Walk again with Death at your shoulder."

A great shifting in the dirt, as though from below something opened a door.

My pale, embalmed husband sat up out of the ground. My mother reached down to help him out of his grave. In the flickering light of the small fire he looked ghastly, his eyes black pits, his hair perfect, his face catching hell's orange from the flames. Soon enough he had gained solid ground, and was dusting grave dirt from the pleats of his pants.

"Thank you, Trudy," said my husband. "That was quite refreshing." He grabbed my mother around the waist and pulled her to her feet, then pressed his lips against her mouth. She tried to scream, but his kiss muffled her. She struggled in his grasp for a little while, then went limp. A few moments later, he dropped her. "Well preserved," he said, and wiped the back of his hand across his mouth. "Fine wine. She aged well. Nicolette?"

I could not move, even for Child. No: I had to move for Child. But I felt frozen solid. I could not rise.

Joseph walked past the red candles on his grave, strode toward our daughter's grave.

"Too late now," whispered Miranda.

"I'll be with you," I whispered.

"No," she said. "You aren't dying in innocence. You won't come where I am. Wherever you go, though, remember I love you."

"No use trying to hide," Joseph said. "I can smell you, Nikki." He took a deep sniff. "Ah, lilies. When did you start wearing the smell of lilies, Nikki? It doesn't suit you."

I felt dried, a husk, an empty cocoon. I had killed my husband and changed my direction. Miranda told me that I was a night creature, a moth, while she was a butterfly, a creature of day. We would be in two different worlds after I died. "Take care of Child?" I whispered.

"I will," whispered my daughter's spirit.

"You should smell of almonds and orange blossoms," said my husband. He reached behind Miranda's headstone, grabbed my shoulder, and hauled me to my feet. "How long did you plan my death, my dear? You should have spent more time. I didn't suffer. Very little art was involved. I always hoped I'd have a more dignified murder."

"Sorry," I whispered to the ground.

I should fight. I should fight for Child: but then I thought, Child, half his, and half mine. I am a murderer, and this man, my husband, is worse. Perhaps it would be a mercy to Child to die now.

"Oh, well. You undoubtedly did the best you could; it's all of a piece. Pitiful. And now you pay. I'll need souls to sustain me in my new state, and a wife to help me survive, pathetic though your help has always been. I need to bind you to me again. Give me a kiss."

He set his lips on my neck, and their touch was the chill behind chill. He sucked the warmth up through my skin.

I closed my eyes, wondering what he was doing to me.

He pressed his lips to mine and breathed into my mouth a taste of rot and darkness, a hint of desire, a sullied joy. I wanted to spit out the taste, but he pinched my nose until I had to breathe it in. My stomach lurched. Below it, I felt a flutter. Joe was changing me again. What was he doing to Child?

The clunk of Randy's flashlight connecting with my husband's head came as a shock to both of us. My husband staggered back, and Randy struck him again and again. "Get back, you freak," he cried. "Mrs. B, go, now!" He shoved me.

I ran, though I feared it was too late.

At the gap in the hedge, I looked back, saw that

Joe was choking Randy. Randy, who had been kinder to me than anyone else after Miranda died. Randy's arms flailed, but he couldn't seem to get a grip on Joe. Joe leaned forward, pressed his mouth to Randy's shoulder. I remembered the chill he had breathed under my skin.

I should protect Child (but perhaps it was too late for both of us). Randy deserved help, too; he hadn't polluted his life with bad choices, as far as I knew. I ran back, stopping only long enough to pick up a stick under a cedar tree.

"Joe," I said, just before I hauled off and hit his head with the stick. I beat his back, jabbed at his face until his mouth loosed from Randy's shoulder. He turned to me, annoyed, but he didn't let go of Randy's neck. Randy was limp now, his head sagging.

"Leave the boy alone. I'm the one you want."

Joe laughed. He released Randy, who collapsed in a coughing heap on the ground. "I want you, and I want a hundred more. I'll need new people every night. I'll have you in a different way. I'll finish what I've started, and then you'll never be able to leave me."

He reached for me, and I hit him with the stick. He laughed again, wrenched the stick from my grasp and crushed it in his hand. "You don't understand what I've become," he said. He embraced me. His arms were cold and heavy, but he did not hug too hard, the way he had before he died. I felt as though clay had risen from a pit and wrapped itself around me, and I thought, oh well, maybe this is all I deserve.

Was it all Child deserved? I tried to lift my arms, push Joe away, but the weight of his embrace trapped me tight.

He would let go of me. Once he had changed me, he would let go of me, and I would find a way to hurt him. He would turn his back on me sometime. I kindled anger inside me, fed it the stored fuel of all my rage at how Joe had treated me. My anger held back the invading chill of Joe's kiss. To protect Child, to protect all the other people Joe might hurt, I would find a way to stop him.

I smelled something burning, the fuel not wood, but cloth. I opened my eyes: light flickered behind Joe, and then flames raced up the back of his best jacket, spread across his shoulders, ate into his hair. He released me and staggered back, with a cry like the screech of metal scraping across metal. He dropped to the ground and rolled on his back, but it was too late. His hair was alight; the smell changed to scorched hair and cooking flesh, at once repulsive and almost inviting, and the flames ran over him like water.

I swayed, took a step to steady myself. Randy was on his feet. He came around Joe's rolling, rocking, screaming body with its consuming flames, put his arms around me, supported me and pulled me away. We staggered toward the gatehouse. The flicker of Joe's fire stained the headstones as we passed them.

Randy led me around back of the gatehouse. For the first time I saw his apartment, a small room with attached kitchenette. He settled me in the one chair, an ancient red cracked leather La-Z-Boy, filled a kettle from the tap, and put it on the hotplate. He settled on the bed nearby, facing me, his elbows on his thighs and his big hands dangling between his knees. His neck was a mass of bruises in the shapes of fingers and palms. Joe had ripped open his uniform. There was a blood-dark mark on Randy's shoulder where Joe had kissed him.

I pressed my hands to my belly, where Child rested, infinitesimal yet. Had Joe's touch killed Child, or changed Child into something other than human? My mouth still tasted foul, and my stomach roiled. I put my hand over my mouth.

Randy opened a closed door, revealed a tiny bathroom with commode, sink, and shower. I went in and threw up. He offered a glass of water to me when I had finished retching. I rinsed and spat, rinsed and spat. I couldn't get the moldy taste out of my mouth, but my stomach settled. Shadows still clouded my thoughts.

Randy helped me into his chair. I leaned back and closed my eyes. Presently he touched my shoulder and handed me a mug of herbal tea. "Peppermint," he rasped. "Settle your stomach."

"Thank you. Thank you, Randy, for everything."

"Yeah, well." He drank from his own mug, coughed, lit up another clove cigarette with a lighter that had a Harley Davidson logo on it. My salvation. "You get some rest, Mrs. B. I gotta go tidy up. Hate these revenant nights. The bad ones are always messy. You want I should bury your ma with your husband?"

I swallowed my surprise, thought, then said, "Yes, all right."

"More tea in the pot on the table if you want some, and sugar, too. Don't you worry, Mrs. B. Sleep if you can." He put a blanket over me and went out.

I huddled under the blanket and thought again of the dark charge Joe had sent through me with his kiss. Had it reached Child?

I hoped not.

THE PERFECT MAN

Fran LaPlaca

Rob Zombie was playing on the radio, and Oliver's head was pounding. *What in hell did I drink last night?* His eyes were glued shut, but he didn't feel up to opening them anyway. But, God, would someone *please* turn that horrible music *off*?

"Hey! Hey, Fancy Boy, he's waking up!"

Oh, my God, Oliver thought. The western twang in that voice is worse than this so-called music.

"Stop calling me Fancy Boy," an irritated voice said. "I know he's waking up. Give him a minute, you dumb redneck."

"Hey, new guy?" This was a third voice.

What the hell?

"Hey, new guy!" the third voice said again. "Cat got your tongue? What's your name?"

"Oliver," Oliver tried to say, and he heard the word, but he knew he hadn't opened his mouth.

"Oliver, huh? Maybe Ethan should call you Fancy Boy, too, that's a fancy-schmancy name. What's your line of work, Oliver?"

"I'm a lawyer."

What in hell was he doing, so hung over he couldn't even open his eyes, talking to a bunch of . . . of what? Voices in his head?

"Ha! Voices in your head! That's a good one, Ollie." That was the third voice again. "M'name's Ike, by the way, and the voices aren't in your head. They're in Mario's head. That's Fancy Boy, as Ethan so elegantly calls him."

What in hell did that mean? Oliver decided he didn't care. The pain was beginning to fade a bit, and he tried again to open his eyes.

"You can't do it," said a new, depressed voice. "They're not your eyes. I'm Zach. I'm a poet, and I was the answer to the sensitive part of the ad."

He hadn't been stupid enough to do shots of tequila again, had he? Oliver strained his memory, but all he could dredge up was a pair of gorgeous brown eyes, and a significant amount of cleavage.

Great. A hooker. She drugged me, and now I'm probably on a boat to Singapore. A white slave. I'll have to service some old, ugly hag for the rest of my life.

"Oh, she's no hooker. She's a doctor, actually."

How many guys were in this room/cabin/black hole?

"Six now, counting you. And I'm Brett. Brett Jamieson."

"Brett Jamieson," Oliver squawked. "The movie actor? You've been kidnapped, too?"

"Not kidnapped, no," the rich, velvety voice of the movie star answered. "Murdered, pal, murdered. Just like you."

Good lord. The last time he'd been this drunk was . . . Oliver couldn't remember *when* he'd been this bad. Murdered. He would have shaken his head, but couldn't seem to do that, either.

"It's true," the second voice said. "And I'm Mario. Call me Fancy Boy and I just may murder you a second time. I'm the good-looking part of the ad."

"Mario's the only one who's not really here," the cowboy explained. "He's just the body. Sense memory, Zach thinks. I'm Ethan, Ethan Corbett. And we've all been murdered, ol' son. By those ever-lovin' brown eyes and great big knockers you're still dreamin' about.''

"And what part of the ad are you?" Oliver said sarcastically.

"I'm the rugged, outdoorsy part," Ethan said with a chuckle. "And since Brett is the romantic part, and Ike is the sense of humor, you bein' a lawyer and all, I figure you must be the intelligent part. Which means," Ethan said gleefully, his twang becoming even thicker, "that we're complete."

"What does that mean?" Oliver asked. "And why can't I open my eyes?"

"I told you," Zachary's disheartened voice said. "They're not your eyes. They're Mario's."

"But if Cowboy's right," Ike said, "and we're complete, then Mario should be able to open his eyes. C'mon, Fancy Boy. Try."

Oliver felt like he should hold his breath in anticipation, and it was only then that he realized he wasn't breathing. As soon as that thought hit him, he began desperately to try.

"Stop it," Mario yelped. "I can't do two things at once!"

"But I'm not breathing," Oliver said in a panic.

"You're dead, bonehead, of course you're not breathing," Ike snapped. "I thought you guys said he was the intelligent part. Are all lawyers such idiots?"

"Shut up, Ike." Brett Jamieson sounded just as commanding as he did when he played John Banning, Bounty Hunter. "Oliver has no idea what's going on; of course he's upset. We all were at first, remember? We need to get him up to speed." In his "good cop" voice, he said, "Oliver, how much do you actually remember? Do you remember Cordelia?"

Cordelia! That was her name. And she'd been spectacular. Oliver had had trouble believing she was really interested in him.

"I was at a fundraiser," he said. "I was seated next to the mayor's wife."

"Melba?" Mario asked. "Melba Davison?"

"Yes," Oliver said. "You know her?'

"Every little black root, Ollie, every little black root on her head."

"Mrs. Davison isn't a natural blonde?" Oliver said.

"Oh, hell no," Mario said. "I was her stylist for five years. She may be blonde on top, but that's the only place. Was this the museum fundraiser?"

"Yes."

"How did she look? I can't imagine who she's going to now; she always said she'd rather go bald than change salons. Was it up, or did she wear it down?"

"Mario, no one here besides you gives one fat flying anything about how the mayor's baggy wife wore her hair last night," Ike broke in. "Except maybe Brett, and we are just *not* going there. Would you please shut up and let him tell Oliver what's going on?"

"Fine. Whatever." Mario fell silent, but Oliver could *feel* his resentment.

"Thank you, Ike. So, Oliver, you were at the dinner. You met Cordelia. Dr. Cordelia Rogers. And she came on to you like a ton of bricks, yes?"

"Well . . . yes," Oliver admitted.

"And she suggested, perhaps, that you leave the fundraiser early, maybe have a nightcap at her place?"

"Yes," Oliver said. "How did you know?"

"She picked me up at the opening of the Shake-speare in the Round series. My agent made me go, said it would be good for my image."

Ike laughed. "If only he could see you now, huh? John Banning, badass Bounty hunter!"

"Shut up," Brett said. "She picked you up in a bar, Cranefield."

"I was performing," Ike shot back. "I work for my money, Jamieson."

"What do you do?" Oliver asked. "Are you a

bouncer?" He wanted to kick himself for getting sucked into this hallucinatory conversation, but he was sure if he tried, they'd only tell him his feet belonged to the faggy hairdresser.

"I'm not a fag, Ollie. Suggest that again, and I'll kick your ass from here to next week. And you're right, they are my feet, so I can do it."

"Yeah, but it's your ass you'd be kicking as well, Fancy Boy," Ethan said, laughing. "But I'd purely love to see you try."

"I'm sorry," Oliver said. *Now I'm apologizing.* "Okay. So this knockout, Dr. Cordelia. She picked up all of you? You all know her?"

A chorus of assents came.

"So what happens next? I remember offering to get a cab, but she said—"

"She said, 'No, don't bother, I have a car.' And then she took you to her place and poured you a glass of champagne, yes?"

"Hey, I didn't get no champagne," Ethan complained.

"Dom Perignon," said Oliver, feeling a bit smug. "And that's the last thing I remember. She *did* drug me, didn't she?"

"She did, indeed," Zachary said with a sigh. "And then she cut your head open and removed part of your brain."

"She did *what*?" Oliver screeched.

"Well, it's the perfect man thing, ain't it?" Ethan said. "She wants the perfect man, so she thought she'd make herself one."

"By taking my *brain*?"

"Stop shouting, it's giving me a headache," Mario said. "And she only took a part of it."

"Oh, shut up, Mario. You're the only one who's not even supposed to be here. Dr. Miss-Perfect-Legs Rogers didn't want the brain of a guy who works in a hair salon," Ike said, his voice rising. "All she wanted from you was your body. You might remember she didn't take a slice of your brain. In fact, she just ripped your brain out and threw it in the trash!"

"Well, I notice she didn't choose *your* body," Mario snapped.

"I knew this would happen," Zachary said gloomily. "They never stop."

"Wait, wait," Oliver said. "Why'd she only take part?"

"Well, it's the ad, we done tol' ya already," Ethan said. "Didn't she show you the ad?"

"No. Wait. Maybe. I don't remember. Just tell me," Oliver said, raising his voice again.

"The ad," Zachary said with another deep sigh. "I answered it first. 'Single, professional woman, attractive and smart, looking for a man ready to commit. Must be sensitive, yet rugged and love the outdoors. Intelligence and sense of humor required. Romance and good looks a plus. And above all, must be faithful.' I'm sensitive," he said. "So I called the number."

"He never read the part about sense of humor required," Ike said. "Mr. Doom and Gloom."

"Wait. You answered an ad in a singles column, and it was some whacked-out female doctor who killed you and took your brain?" Oliver wished he could shake his head in disbelief.

"Well, yes. I read her sonnets," Zach went on. "And when she told me about her dog, I cried."

"Oh, the dying dog bit, yeah, she tried that on me. Didn't work," Ethan said. "But I took her hiking. She really does have great legs."

"You answered the ad, too?"

"Yep."

"Oliver, do you mind?" Brett asked. "We really want to see if Mario can open his eyes now."

"Go ahead," Oliver said faintly. If this wasn't a dream, if any of this was real, he was so screwed.

"No, not screwed, Ollie. Dead. Dead as a doornail."

"Mario?"

"Hang on," Mario said. "I'm—"

And then suddenly, a light so bright, all six voices cried out in pain.

"Close them, close them!" Ike shouted, and the light was gone.

Oliver was afraid the panic that raced through all their minds might cause cardiac arrest. He knew his heart must be racing.

But it wasn't.

"No heart, Ollie. God, for a lawyer, you're awfully thick. We're dead, numbskull."

"Heh, numbskull, good one, Ike," Ethan chortled.

"Wait a minute. If we're dead, but we're in Mario's body, and Mario can open his eyes now, then isn't Mario still alive?"

"No," Mario said, sadly. "She killed me first."

"Then how did you just open your eyes? Or, wait, maybe you didn't. Maybe we just all wanted you to so much, we imagined it. That has to be it." Oliver wished he could nod.

"Yep, he's a lawyer, all right."

"Shut up, Ethan. Mario, try it again. But slower."

And a faint sliver of light appeared.

"I'm squinting. Is it too much for anyone?"

A chorus of no's.

"Okay. Here goes."

And the sliver of light became larger, bit by bit, until Oliver realized he was staring up at a ceiling.

"Excellent," Brett said. "Now see what else you can do."

Mario grunted a few times.

"I think I must be strapped down. I can feel my arms and legs and all, but I can't move them. Can't move my head, either."

"What about talkin'?" Ethan asked. "Can you talk?"

Uh . . .

"Oh, great. The one in charge of the body is a freaking Neanderthal."

"Shut up, Ike," Oliver snapped. "He's trying, for heaven's sake."

"Thanks, Ollie," Mario said. "I think I need a drink of water or something."

Oliver could hear him trying to clear his throat.

Hello?

The word rang out clearly, and Oliver didn't recognize the voice.

Mario could talk.

"Okay. I have some questions."

"Of course you do; you're a lawyer."

"You may not have much respect for my profession, Ike, but apparently Cordelia Rogers does. She chose me for my intelligence. And if she chose you for your sense of humor, all I can say is, she didn't know you very well." Oliver was tired of Ike's constant complaints.

"What are your questions, Oliver?" Brett asked.

"First, if Mario is dead, how can he open his eyes and talk? And why are all of us in his head? And more importantly, how did we get here?"

"Number one, we don't know. Zach says it's Mario's body's sense memory. Could be, I'm no expert."

"Well, I'm not, either," Zachary broke in. "But it's all I could think of. I believe your body remembers what it's been through in life. The pleasures, the pains. And maybe, just maybe, your soul is more than just feelings and emotions. Maybe it's touch and taste, and what you see and hear. And your body stores all that."

"But if that's so, why don't all dead people keep talking and moving and all?" Oliver asked.

"Because their brains are dead," Brett answered. "Now, Mario's brain is dead, too, but he's got a new one. Ours. Which brings us to your other two questions. Why are we here, and how did we get here.

Well, why, we don't know. We figure all those preach-
ers were dead wrong, if you'll pardon the pun. The
soul is not immaterial. The soul is in the brain. Now,
the how part, that would be the lovely Cordelia."

"She's a brain surgeon," Ethan said. "And she fig-
gered out what parts of the brain controlled the quali-
ties she wanted in a man. So she found men with what
she wanted, us, and took out the parts of our brains
she liked."

"Brains don't work like that," Oliver said.

"Well, I plumb hate to disagree with you, Ollie,
but I'm thinkin' they do. I mean, how else do you
explain us?"

Oliver had no answer. "How do you know all this?"

"Every time she adds another piece of brain, she
sits and talks to us, telling us all about it. She talks a
lot." Zachary sighed. " I'm surprised she's not here
yet."

"It's still daytime," Brett pointed out. "She's probably still at the hospital. She'll be home soon." He
sounded eager and Oliver wished he could frown.

"Excuse me, but why would you care? She killed
you," Oliver said.

"Why? Because I *do* recall my night with Dr. Cordelia, before she killed me, and quite fondly. She is
one hot mama."

"Oh, yeah," Ethan said happily. "And now we can
see again."

It wasn't long before Dr. Cordelia Rogers showed
up. First they heard the tap-tap-tap of her high heels
in the hall outside the room. Then the sound of a
shower running, and Oliver remembered with sharp,
shocking clarity the sight of her slowly unbuttoning
the silky little dress she'd worn to the fundraiser dinner. He could feel the other men's growing impa-
tience, and was faintly surprised to feel it himself.

Finally he heard more footsteps, softer, lighter, and coming this way.

"Close your eyes, Mario; we don't want to scare her off," Brett said hurriedly, and the darkness returned.

Cordelia entered the room, and Oliver felt a surge of excitement. He was unsure how much of it was his, and how much belonged to the disembodied voices that he still wasn't quite sure he believed in.

"That's ridiculous, Oliver," Brett whispered. "If you don't believe in us, then the excitement is all yours."

"Why are you whispering?" Ike asked. "It's not like she can hear you or anything."

The radio switched off, silencing the only sound they'd heard for an hour before Cordelia arrived. Oliver heard her moving closer.

"How are we feeling today?"

Dr. Cordelia's voice was a low contralto, though the words were typical, irritating doctor-speak.

More sounds, a chair being moved closer, and then suddenly, shockingly, Oliver felt a warm hand on his arm.

"*My* arm, Oliver," Mario hissed. Apparently it didn't matter what part of the brain controlled the sense of touch; every single one of them felt the hairs on Mario's arm rise at the delicate touch.

"Oh!" She sounded pleased. "You felt that. Excellent. Can you hear me?"

"Open your eyes, Mario," Ethan begged. "I want to see her again."

Oliver felt a surge of jealousy. The other guys all seemed to have clearer memories of Cordelia than he did; whatever else they shared, apparently a group memory was not part of it.

Mario opened his eyes, and there she was.

She was gorgeous, all right, just as good-looking as Oliver remembered. A beautiful smile broke across her face.

"Can you see me? Can you hear me?" she asked.

"Yes," they all said, though only Mario's voice sounded.

"Speech, too! That's wonderful," she said happily. "I wasn't sure, with this last addition, but it was the best I could do. There's not a lot to choose from in this town."

"Wait a minute," Oliver said. "What's that supposed to mean?" Nothing came out aloud. He could hear Ethan and Ike laughing.

"What about movement?" she asked. She reached over Mario's—their?—body. "Let me unstrap you. It was only for your own safety."

Then the most glorious thing happened. Her hand stroked their—Mario's? Oliver's—arm as she unbuckled the restraining strap. It was as if a jolt of electricity shot through their entire body. Their—Oliver decided it was less confusing to think of it that way—arm jerked, and Mario groaned at the pleasure. She smiled again at his reaction.

"Well, the parietal lobe is certainly working." She unstrapped their other wrist and then unbuckled the strap holding their head in position.

"Would you like to try to sit up?"

"Yes," they all said in unison, and the woman slipped one arm behind their shoulders. Mario put their arms on hers, and they sat up. Since they were at bed level, and she was leaning over, that put their face right between . . . well it was a very pleasant view, very pleasant indeed, even if she did move away a second or two later.

"Wait here," she said, and she raised the bed and adjusted the pillows. "I'll be right back." And she left the room.

"Did you smell that?" Brett said happily.

"Smelled like soap," Ike said. "So what?"

"Soap? You stupid idjit. That was soap and Woman. Geez, when Zach tol' me I was dead, I never thought

I'd miss smelling things so much. I wonder if she's got a horse."

"What?" Oliver asked. "You can't be serious?"

"Yeah," Ethan went on, oblivious. "Or leather. Maybe she has some leather. I plumb love the smell of leather."

"She has quite a bit of leather, actually," Brett told them, and Ike choked.

"Oh, Lord, don't you dare, you prancing little freak," Ike said.

"Shut up, all of you. Mario, look around the room," Zach ordered.

Mario complied, and they saw that, aside from the hospital bed they were reclining on, and several pieces of medical equipment that surrounded the bed, it looked like a fairly decent place. A large room, with long, vertical windows on one side, the door Cordelia had gone through on the other, and directly across the room, a sight that made even Cordelia's amazing cleavage slip from their communal thoughts.

A large plasma high definition television hung on the wall.

"That's gotta be fifty inches," Mario said reverently, "with virtual surround sound, too."

"Sixty," Brett corrected him. "I had the LG fifty. This one's bigger."

"What in hell does brain surgery pay, Hoss?"

"A hell of a lot more than riding bulls, and do you have to say things like *Hoss*?"

"Yeah, I do," Ethan answered. "I wonder where the remote is. Must be a game on somewhere."

"Definitely," Mario agreed. "Hey, you guys all died after me. What are the standings? The Sox were down two last I knew."

Ike blew a raspberry.

"You don't think they can pull it out again, do you? Be effing real."

"Twenty says they make it to the playoffs, jerk."

"You're on. Boston's so lame it's a wonder they can play at all."

"Ollie, you're the newest. Who's in the lead?"

"Er, I don't follow sports, guys."

"What?"

Both Mario and Ike sounded shocked.

"I knew it," Ike said derisively. "Lawyers are all stick-up-their-butt jerks."

"Shut up," Zach whispered. "She's coming back."

"Okay," Cordelia said breezily as she came back in. She had changed her clothes again, and was wearing her doctor's coat. A stethoscope hung around her neck. "Feeling more alert, are we?"

"Yes," Mario said for them all, though Oliver felt a pang of disappointment that she'd buttoned the white coat all the way to the top.

"I just want to check a few things, and ask you a few questions," she said briskly as she unbuckled the remaining straps that held their legs immobile. She pushed up their hospital gown and placed the stethoscope on their chest and listened closely. A frown marred her lovely face, and she sighed.

"Well, it couldn't be helped, I suppose. I had hoped the circulatory system might jumpstart, as it were, once the brain was back to normal capacity, but I guess we can't have everything, now can we? " She sat back and observed him. "Still, we have visual, auditory, speech, and touch."

"And smell," Mario said.

"Really?" She seemed quite pleased. "That's more than I'd hoped for. What about movement? Are you ready to try and get up?"

"I think so, yes."

"All right, but first, you must have some questions. Like who I am, and who you are. Yes?"

"She doesn't know we're all here," Zach said.

"Should we tell her?" Oliver asked

"No," Zach and Brett said immediately, while Ike said, "Hell, yes," and Ethan drawled, "Why not?"

But Mario and Oliver made it four to two, and Mario opened their mouth to answer her.

"Yes."

"Hmm. A man of few words," Cordelia smiled. "I like that. Well, my name is Cordelia, but you can call me Dee. And do you know what your name is?"

Six names rang out in the shared brain, and Mario finally just said, *"No."*

"Well, don't worry, hon, that will come. If not, we'll just think up the perfect name ourselves. Now lean on me."

Mario took her arm, carefully swung their legs off the bed and stood, a little shakily. After a moment, Cordelia—Dee—led them across the room and back. By the time they reached the bed again, even Oliver, who was the least used to this new way of living, could feel the strength returning to their body.

"Are you hungry?" Dee asked.

All six considered this.

"No."

"For nothing?" she said as they sat back against the head of bed.

"Ask her for the remote," Ike urged. "I saw it on the table over there."

"How 'bout a beer?" Ethan suggested, but then Dee began unbuttoning her long, white doctor's coat.

"Since your sense of touch seems so . . . sensitive . . ." She leaned in, and Oliver realized that under the long, while coat was . . . well . . . Dee, and nothing else. "I thought we'd try another little test," she murmured, and her long, red fingernails trailed down past the edge of their hospital gown.

"Don't you dare close your eyes, not once, Fancy Boy," Ethan said.

Oliver agreed wholeheartedly.

*   *   *

"That was nice," Dee said later, satisfied.

The guys agreed.

"Did you enjoy it?"

"Yes," Mario said immediately, without waiting for a majority.

"Damn, I wish Mario smoked," Ike complained sleepily.

"Now, we need to get a few things straight," Dee said a little more briskly. "First of all, your name. I've been thinking. You're the perfect man, aren't you? I mean, I made you. You're sensitive—"

"That's me," Zach sighed.

"—intelligent—"

"Me," Oliver said, smugly.

"—romantic—"

"Number one in the box office," Brett bragged.

Ike said, "Yeah, but does she know you like to wear women's panties?"

"Women's panties?" Oliver yelped.

"They're very comfortable, especially the silk ones," Brett said stiffly.

"—you have a great sense of humor—"

"Should I tell her the one about the two blondes in the bathtub?" Ike sniggered.

"—you're rugged and manly—"

"She ain't never seen *Brokeback Mountain,* has she?" Ethan said

"—and," she continued, stroking their chest possessively, "you're drop-dead gorgeous."

"And I can do her hair, too," Mario said. "She'd look so much younger with a different cut."

"So since you're the perfect man, you need the perfect man's name." She paused, then said, "Dwayne."

Silence.

"Don't you like it?"

"Dwayne?" Mario answered, timidly.

"Dwayne . . . that's a jerk's name," Ike said.

"A redneck name," Ethan said. "And don't even think it. I ain't no redneck. I'm a cowboy, and it just ain't the same thing."

"Oh, say you like it," Dee begged. "It would mean so much to me."

"Oh, God, she's gonna cry," Zach said. "She won't stop. She cried about the damn dog for three solid hours. Don't let her get started."

And sure enough, her eyes were filling with tears.

Oliver panicked. "Mario, tell her it's fine. Tell her it's fine."

Mario said, "*Dwayne. It's . . . it's like I've always known it. Like I've been Dwayne forever.*"

"Wow," Brett whispered. "That was good, Mario."

"It was me," Zach said proudly. "I did that."

"You? How?" the guys asked in confusion.

Zach said, "I just did it. It was a sensitive moment. I mean, come on, I'm the sensitive part, remember?"

I wonder if I can do that, Oliver suddenly thought. Take over. I'm smarter than they are, after all. It should be easy, if Zach can do it.

"You might try to remember, Oliver, that we can all hear your thoughts," Ike said. "And I'm starting to think old Ollie here is a bigger jerk than Dwayne."

"*We* are Dwayne," Brett said, and it was quite a while before any of them realized that Dee had fallen asleep.

"Hey," Ethan said. "*We're* supposed to fall asleep, not her."

"We can't," Brett reminded him. "We're not alive anymore, so really, sleeping is sort of out of the question."

"Do you think she'd mind if we watched some TV?" Mario asked. But just then Dee gave a very unladylike snore, rolled over, and pinned them to the bed quite neatly.

"Now, remember, Dwayne, you mustn't leave the apartment," Dee told them in the morning as she dressed for work. Their hands kept trying to slide up under her blouse and she pushed them away in exasperation. "Stop it. I have a cerebral aneurysm at nine A.M. sharp, and I don't have time for this." The look on her face softened and she said softly, "But be waiting for me when I get home. Maybe some soft music, candlelight? There's a bottle of Dom Perignon we can open."

"*Can I wear your panties while you're gone?*" Dwayne said, and Dee's mouth dropped open. "*I'm just kidding, my dearest,*" he added quickly. "*Hurry home, beloved. I'll be counting every minute until you return.*" They licked the inside of her ear slowly and sensuously, and she shivered in response.

"I'll be home as soon as I can," she promised, and they watched her leave, a tender smile pasted on their face until they heard the lock click into place behind her.

"Can I wear your panties?" Oliver shrieked. "Are you insane?"

"I just wanted to see if I could take over, like Zach did last night," Brett said. "And are you seriously telling me you never once wondered what it would feel like to wear silk underwear?"

"Hell with all that," Ethan interrupted. "Let's go try out that big screen TV."

"Wait," Ike said. "I know we don't need to eat or nothing, but I was thinking. It couldn't hurt to try, could it?"

"To eat and drink? But how would we . . . you know . . . get rid of it afterwards?"

"We'll worry about that when we have to," Ike said. "I saw some beer in the fridge."

"Okay, but hurry up." They picked up a TV guide they found on the coffee table. "There's a Knicks game from last night being rebroadcast in five minutes."

*   *   *

Dwayne heard the door open, nearly ten hours later, and an exhausted Dr. Cordelia Rogers made her way into the luxurious apartment. Her eyes opened in horror. An empty pizza box lay on the floor next to a container of kung pao chicken, a dozen empty beer bottles were lined up like bowling pins on one side of the room, and Dwayne sprawled in the recliner, a football game on the plasma TV with professional golf in the picture-in-picture.

"We're screwed," Zach whispered.

Brett said, *"Let me handle this, guys."*

Dwayne stood. The look in his eyes was borrowed from John Banning, Bounty Hunter that time he'd seduced Holly Hunter in *Dead Men Tell No Tales*.

"Dee. Cordelia, my dearest. I must apologize for the mess, darling. But I waited and waited for you, all day long. I missed you terribly." By now he was at her side, and his hand stroked her cheek gently, then moved behind to remove the clips that held her hair back. "Why, Dee, do you hide this wonderful hair?" Her hair fell to her shoulders, and Dwayne saw her horror beginning to fade. When Dwayne slid his hands lower, stroking her back and pulling her in close, her pupils widened.

"That's good, keep it up," Ike said.

"I'll take care of this mess, dearest. You need to relax. Let me run you a hot bath, then you soak while I clean this up. Then—"

For a moment, his hands slid down, cupping her derriere and pulling her even closer. "Then I'll join you in the tub," he whispered in her ear, and she sighed in pleasure.

As soon as she was safely ensconced in the bubbles, Dwayne hurried out to the living room and rushed through the room. The beer bottles he tumbled into a plastic bag with the pizza box, the Chinese take-out went in the fridge, and the TV went on mute.

"Dwayne? I'm waiting, love. Will you be much

longer?'' Her voice was sultry, and Dwayne took one last, longing look at the TV screen.

"Coming, darling."

"Man, it's going into OT," Mario whined.

Brett was firm. *"I'm the romantic part, and if we want to keep all this, well, then we have to make some sacrifices."*

"Sacrifices?" Oliver said. *"Were any of you paying attention last night? That woman is incredible. And now she's naked, and wet, and covered with bubbles. This is just a football game."*

"Just a football game?" Mario shouted as Dwayne stepped into the large, steam filled bathroom.

Dwayne, with Dee's eyes on his every move, slowly began to remove his clothing, almost in a striptease, and her face flushed as she watched.

"Just a . . . football game?" Mario repeated half-heartedly.

Dwayne watched intently as the bubbles began to disappear, and certain portions of Dee's very wet, very soapy body could be seen.

Dwayne unbuttoned his cotton lounging pants and slid them to the floor, stepping towards the tub with a lazy, sexy smile.

Dee shrieked. "Are you wearing my underwear?"

TWO ALL BEEF PATTIES

Jay Lake

I used to be a skinny guy with asthma, a pot belly, and a skin condition that kept my dermatologist in boat payments. Girls made me stutter, and my palms sweat badly whenever I had to shake hands. My name might as well have been Wilson. I was a network installer—ran low-voltage wiring through drop ceilings and down cube walls. Lot of dust in that line of work, played hell with my asthma, but it paid well and people mostly left me alone after they signed the work order.

That was fine as far as it went, though the only dates I had were with suicidegirls.com, and most of my friends were avatars online. You can have a lot of fun that way, but it never felt quite right. I pretty much gave up watching television, because even the losers on prime time had better lives than me.

Then the Unrapture came. That's not what anybody who goes to church calls it, of course, but it struck the rest of us as funny. The dead came stumbling out of emergency rooms, morgues and mortuaries one summer afternoon. Accident scenes changed in a hurry.

People freaked out, then got over it pretty fast. The dead people can't be their own next of kin, so the quick got to inherit Aunt Millie's nest egg, while still having Aunt Millie around.

It got me back to watching TV, once *Survivor: Dying to Get Off the Island* aired. Turns out the dead are real good at a lot of things that play well on reality TV. Except for *American Idol,* of course.

The dead don't sing so good.

Knowing that dying wasn't necessarily the end of the ride made some people careless. Not everybody got Unraptured, far from it, but enough people did that the same kind of folks who planned on winning the lottery figured that falling off the roof while skeet shooting drunk wasn't going to slow them down much.

It's hard to shamble down Burnside Street moaning "brains, brains" if your own brains had been spattered across the back patio. Coming back from the dead required being pretty much whole. That much the Holy Rollers with their horror of organ donation had gotten right.

Me, I didn't have a death wish so much as a lack of a life wish. Even the dead were cooler than me. I couldn't get into their bars, either.

I can't tell you that I did it on purpose, but one day I accidentally jumped some Cat7 network cable to the commercial 240v feed. Maybe I didn't care any more. Maybe I was tired of who I'd been for twenty-seven years. Maybe I wanted to be on TV.

What I got was a view into the afterlife that made my eyeballs spin while my ears crackled louder than feedback at a Fourth of July punk rock festival.

Two all-beef patties, special sauce, lettuce, cheese, pickles, onions on a sesame seed bun.™

"Jeremy."

I looked up. Everything felt wrong. There was no other way to describe it. My tendons had been unstrung and taped in backwards. My muscles were knotted like a sailor's nightmare. Thinking *hurt*.

"Jeremy."

It was a paramedic. Well, at least a gal in a white suit with a penlight.

"Wha . . . ?" My voice was wrong, too.

"Ok, buddy." She smiled, first time a woman had looked me in the eye and done that since Mrs. Bagby's math class in tenth grade. "I'm required to recite you your Pratt Rights. You are now dead. Your estate has passed to your designated heirs or next of kin. A court may take control of your estate according to the rules of your home state and county. You have no rights to your former residence or funds, though you may have limited claims on personal effects. You are no longer a citizen of the United States, but as a decedent on United States territory you will automatically be issued a work permit. Even though you are no longer a citizen, you still bear tax liability."

She dropped a sheaf of papers on my chest and patted it, and thus through the papers, me. "The Pratt people will have someone around with a kit and a starter funds grant. Good luck."

"Wha . . . ?" I wasn't coming up with much new material.

Mr. Chua, who'd hired me for the job, leaned over. "You're going to miss your delivery date, kid, if you don't get back to work."

"Right," I said.

And that was it. I was dead.

With three days the junk mail started filling up my PO box. I was living—well, residing—in the back seat of my Scion xB, but no one had taken away the box. The post office apparently didn't care about my recent transition.

It was weird stuff, too. Come-ons for all-new wardrobes, pre-packaged according to my afterlife goals.

Did I finally want to make it big in the horror movie industry? How about the poker tour, where the dead had a distinct advantage due to excellent facial control and a total lack of sweating?

Likewise banking services. My credit cards were gone with everything else, but there were people out there happy to take on a 100-year commitment from me. Apparently we dead people had no limit on our life expectancy.

So to speak.

The more interesting material was employment-related. Looking at the ads, come-ons and letters, I found the dead were a lot more risk-tolerant. Work on oil platforms, as salvage divers, as helicopter linemen; some jobs I'd never even heard of, that paid staggeringly well. They required no experience for Pratt-qualified applicants—the politically correct name for the dead.

I didn't have to string wire through ceilings any more.

On the plus side, I didn't have asthma any more either.

Once I realized that, I decided to try going to a dead bar.

Thaw frozen patties, dust with ground black pepper, broil in oven for seven minutes, serve over hamburger rolls with Velveeta cheese, mustard and onion, garnished with salt and vinegar potato chips.

"New, huh?" Angel, the bartender at the Revenant Agent was a Portland hipster. Dead, but still a hipster. She had tattoos that glowed and writhed with some chemical that almost certainly wasn't approved for human subjects.

"Does it show?" I asked. No stutter, no sweaty palms. This dead thing wasn't half bad, was it?

I'd come down in the mid-afternoon, right before happy hour. I'd worked overnight on Mr. Chua's wiring job, for lack of a need of sleep and lack of a place to not sleep in, so I had the time. It seemed better this way.

"You look surprised." Angel smiled. It was cute on her oh-so-pale face. "The new fish always have a stunned expression."

"Yeah. I'll have . . ." I stopped. I didn't know what it was I drank. When I was quick, I never could cope with the bar scene and I'd never been invited to a lot of parties. Dead, well, what did the dead drink?

"You'll have an Edmonton Oiler," she told me.

"I will?"

"Yeah." That smile again. "I'll bet you haven't eaten since you passed over, right? You need some intake, but there's not much you can digest anymore. Mostly soft tissues like calf's brains, and some lubricant to keep it moving. An Edmonton Oiler is just canola oil mixed with brown sugar and rock salt. It works for most of the new fish. You'll find your taste."

My lips puckered at the thought. "What's that taste like?"

Her smile quirked. "It doesn't matter. You can't taste anything anyway."

I found work doing high-voltage wiring under hazardous conditions—the upper floors of high rise buildings in progress, out on dam facings, helicopter-accessible wilderness sites. I didn't have a sense of vertigo or a fear of heights any more, while my hand-and-arm strength was easily three times what it had been.

In other words, I could hang on to myself, hang on to my tools, and had little worry about falling off, in or under whatever I was working on.

I worked maybe ten days a month, and netted more

than twice what I'd made when I was alive, even after paying my taxes. Though the dead had to file quarterly, for some reason.

The rest of the time, I barhopped.

Sex wasn't a big thing among dead. For one thing, nobody seemed to have orgasms. There were a few tantric types searching for a way, and maybe they'd find one. There were plenty of quicks willing to give it a shot, for the sake of the thrill. The kinds of people that used to sneak into morgues for a peek at the cold, blue flesh, I guess. But we didn't go to bars to hook up, not in that sense.

We went to bars to get away from the rest of you.

Me, I went to bars looking for something to taste.

An Edmonton Oiler goes down smooth. Turns out that whatever it is that does work in our digestive systems seems to benefit, a lot, from the vegetable oil. The rock salt is mostly for texture, and the brown sugar for those of us who can still taste it.

Most drinks in a dead bar are about texture and strong tastes. We're trying to beat the ashy slickness that lies on our tongues and in the ruins of our stomachs. We're trying to find something that zings. Those few people without senses of smell or taste weren't bothered so much, but the rest of us craved something.

Maybe it was because we had no thrills. No sex, no sense of danger, what was there to chase? A lot of the buzz of socializing was missing, though that wasn't much different for me, of course.

So we looked for texture and taste.

Spices. Flavors. Liqueurs. Strong scents. Subtle influences. Fluids, liquids, gels, semisolids, stews, stocks, crisp, crunchy, cold. Dead bars tried it all, and dead spent their time finding new and different ways to do it. And we were having fun doing it, having a social death together.

Me, I tried them all. Nothing tasted like anything. And so, in time, I began to dream of food.

*   *   *

*Ground buffalo meat, crispy pepper bacon, Schwarz
und Weiss Amish blue cheese, fresh-sliced tomatoes,
bread and butter pickles, romaine lettuce, topped with
a fried egg over medium on a toasted onion roll.*

I got an SMS on my cell phone—VOODOO DO-
NUTS 6AM. It was from a number I didn't recognize,
but still . . . this was how a lot of dead raves went.
Six in the morning seemed an odd time, but it wasn't
like we slept.

September in Portland and the rain was already rat-
tling with the promise of winter. We go for damp more
than cold in this part of the Northwest, but I remembered hating it when I was alive. Now I found myself
downtown in the predawn gloom amid a crowd of
dead in front of a door set into a brick wall. A pair
of frightened bakers looked back from the other side
of the glass.

"God damn them, sticking this in our faces," someone next to me muttered. Srini, his name was. I hadn't
known him when we were quick.

"Bastards!" someone else shouted.

A woman wailed: "I want to taste chocolate again."

Fists were pounding on the glass door when the
sirens began to wail a few blocks way. We smashed
the glass, then fled into the morning, trailing rainwater
and flour and wishing we could have tasted something
besides ashes and defeat.

It went on like that a while into the autumn—dead
raids on bakeries and farmers' markets. The memory
of the smell of food was making people crazy, I guess.
I tried to stay away, mostly succeeded, spent my time
hopping through dead bars and increasingly obscure
ethnic restaurants looking for the one spice, the one
ingredient, the one thing that would make a difference
from the canola oil and calf's brains I'd been living
(or dying) on.

* * *

I think it was the chocolate that drove the flash mobs. Our little excursion to VooDoo Donuts had been just the beginning. As the weeks grew colder, the attacks grew more widespread. Polls showed a reversal in acceptance of the dead by the quick, who were growing increasingly uneasy, and with good reason. We were, too. Calf's brains and canola oil only went so far as a diet. Most of the dead women and many of the dead men would have killed for chocolate.

Me, I'd exhausted my survey of Laotian and Kazakh and quiche restaurants. I'd tried everything exotic between Grant's Pass, Oregon, and Bellingham, Washington, and as far east as Lewiston, Idaho. You'd be amazed what can be found out there.

As the attacks increased, I saw more "NO DEAD" signs in the windows of shops, restaurants, even gas stations and hardware stores. At first they were small, hand-lettered placards, but soon someone was printing slick, glossy flyers with a help line on them: 1-888-DEAD-STOP.

These people had a point.

But it wasn't chocolate for me. It was the fatty foods—pizza, Mexican, cheeseburgers. When I ran out of ground squirrel in fennel and créme Suisse, I was back to those old American favorites.

They all tasted like nothing in my mouth. I might as well have been eating ashes and stale chewing gum.

So I retraced my steps, driving highways and country roads and gravel tracks looking for the perfect burger. When I was forced to stay home due to paying jobs, I scoured the Internet and Powell's Books for recipes, ways to approach ground beef. My search for exotic cuisines had been replaced by my search for exotic ingredients, or new ways to combine old ones.

Anything to get the taste of canola oil out of my mouth.

If I succeeded, it wouldn't be chocolate—not hardly—but it might bring us dead back to some of the simple joys of life.

Lean ground sirloin mixed with soy sauce, finely chopped cilantro, white pepper and an egg, pan-fried in a cast iron skillet, served on Texas toast and topped with onion crunchies, jalapeños, shredded lettuce and chipotle mayonnaise, with a side of pico de gallo.

"Hey, Jer."

It was Angel, on the phone. She and I ran into each other once or twice a month, even though she wasn't working at the Revenant Agent anymore. Being dead was a big social asset in the Goth scene, if you had the right chops in the first place.

"What's up, girl?" I was mashing a blend of pork and buffalo in the skillet, working with leeks, garlic and pickled jalapęos. Somewhere along the way my geekiness had sloughed away like old skin. I wasn't sure when or how, but I wasn't going to argue if a twentysomething cutie wanted to call me up.

Of course, she'll be a twentysomething cutie for all of eternity at this point.

"Anything taste good lately?"

I worked the meat blend and sighed into the phone.

She laughed, with an edge to her voice. "I'll take that as a no. I maybe got a line on something in the taste way. Meet me tonight at Rimsky-Korsakoffee House?"

"Sure. See you there."

She hung up, I kept frying meat for a while. What was left of my heart just wasn't in it.

Rimsky-Korsakoffee was in a converted Victorian in southeast Portland—unmarked, unremarked, an invisible business that had long catered to college students, aging liberals and Portland hipsters not terminally caught up in their own irony. That it was a dead joint now surprised no one.

Angel was sitting at a little carved dining table, something Depression-era from the look of it, half-hidden by a red velvet curtain which looked to have survived a moth attack. She'd ordered us both Edmonton Oilers. Mine had been served in a Flintstones jelly jar, garnished with a stalk of rhubarb.

I sat down and poked at my drink. "Breakfast of champions."

"Yeah, well." She seemed subdued. "We're eternally free and eternally young. The least we can do is stay in training."

"Hey, I'm the pessimist here."

Another sigh. She reached down and pulled a Little Oscar onto the table. "Pessimize this, Jer."

"Would if I could." I sipped my Oiler and nodded at the cooler. "What is it?"

"New secret ingredient. I got it from Kevin."

Kevin was a militant dead rights activist who was probably behind the chocolate mobs, as well as a number of other nuisance activities. Probably a few criminal ones as well. "Oh joy, did he rob a slaughterhouse?"

"Look." Her eyes met mine, then dropped away. "Don't think of it that way. You're the only one of us who cooks."

I found that hard to believe. "Everybody's got a kitchen."

"They're full of canola oil and mice, for the most part."

And the various calf brain products which had begun to reach the market, I thought.

"So I cook. Not like I eat it."

"Just try this. Make one of your burgers."

I cracked open the cooler and looked within. Four bundles of white butcher paper, unlabelled, sitting among bricks of dry ice. "Okay. . . ."

"Good." She grabbed my hand a moment, a gesture

echoing the days when we were both quick and someone like Angel would never even have noticed me in
the room with her. "Go make something of it."

*Equal portions ground sirloin, ground lamb and
ground beef. Mix with finely chopped ginger, white
wine, paprika and mustard powder. Broil and serve
with hoisin sauce and wilted spinach on toasted arti-
sanal bread with a side of wok-fried snow peas.*

The meat was rough-ground and fairly loose. Not
dense muscle tissue, then. It was also as much gray as
red, like pork could be. I didn't think very hard, just
worked it in the bowl. I knew I'd need a binder for
it, so I crushed some stale sourdough baguette, and
threw in an egg as well. Since I didn't know what the
meat was supposed to do, I went very light on the
herbs and spices—just a little ground parsley and some
onion salt.

As always, I pretended I was going to be able to
taste it when I was finished.

While the meat was setting up, I thinly sliced a
Yukon Gold potato and pan-fried the resulting discs
in canola oil with a heavy sprinkling of rock salt and
paprika. I set those up to drain, slapped a ciabatta roll
brushed with olive oil into the broiler and fried the
patty in my trusty cast-iron skillet.

As it cooked, something started happening.

My mouth began to water.

I watched the meat darken and sear. It continued
to have a grayish color, like pork, but the smell was
heavenly. The patty developed a brown crust where
the meat met the juices in the pan. I almost pressed
my face into it, drinking the smell, swallowing it down.
My mouth watered, twitching in a way that I hadn't
felt since before I died.

When it was all cooked, set on the plate and ready
to eat, I almost cried. Instead I took a big bite of the

burger. Taste exploded into my mouth, meat and spices and the crunchy ciabatta all combining.

Even the potatoes tasted right.

I cried as I ate, the burger running down my chin and across my hands, warm and full in my fingers, everything I'd missed since leaving the living behind.

Screw chocolate, this was heaven. Food *is* better than sex, and now I really did want to live forever.

Eventually, I reached for the phone to call Angel. The dead were going into the meat business.

Pureed human brains mixed with ground human muscle meat. Mix with bread crumbs and a fresh egg, fold in ground parsley and onion salt. Pan fry, serve over toasted ciabatta with fried potato discs.

THAT SATURDAY

Devon Monk

So when I finally made up my mind to steal a head from across the street, I had to do it fast because Jugg's dad is crazy. Not *crazy ha-ha. Crazy come-meet-my-family-of-stone-heads-and-have-tea-with-us* crazy. If he caught me stealing the heads out of his yard, he'd explode. Worse, he'd tell my mom I did it. My mom's not super-crazy, but she and I aren't really into the same things any more. She likes long walks on the beach, candlelit dinners and grave-robbing. Seriously, I've hated the beach for years.

Jugg's pretty much my best friend now, even though he's a boy and I'm a girl. His house is right across from mine, so I walked over and went into his side yard, figuring I wouldn't get caught taking a head from under the tree.

The head was dark grey, almost black. It had no ears, but a really long nose and its eyes were big as baseballs. It stared straight up at me, mouth half open, like maybe it had just figured out it couldn't breathe.

"You'll get in trouble, Boady." Jugg strolled up next to me.

Jugg was right. I was pretty sure his dad wouldn't like me messing with them. Just like I was pretty sure my mom would go headcase if she ever saw what I kept under my bed in my room. Kids my age weren't supposed to know how to raise the dead.

Still, I had made up my mind. I wanted a head. I needed a head. And I was going to get a head.

I pushed the rock to one side so I could get my fingers under it and I heard a pop—kind of like the sound of a dandelion root breaking. The head finally rolled forward and hit another rock head that was about the size of a bowling ball with a scream on its face. The head-on-head thunk was the same deep sound I remembered hearing inside my ears when my arm broke last summer.

I got a good grip on the loose head and lifted, straightening my knees at the same time. My back hurt, and something in my chest twanged pain down my stomach, but I had that rock off the ground. Oh yeah. The rock was so mine.

All I had to do was hang onto it across the street, then up the stairs to my front door, and inside the house, and down the hallway to my room. A little itch of sweat tickled my lip and I glanced at my house across the street. It suddenly looked a whole lot farther away. Maybe messing with the heads wasn't such a good idea. Maybe putting the rock down would be the smart move. After all, I didn't want to make Jugg's dad mad.

"Wow," Jugg said. "Is it heavy?"

"No," I huffed.

"Yes it is. Your face is getting red."

"Shut up, Jugg."

"You're gonna drop it."

"Shut up, Jugg."

"I never thought you could do it, Boads. You're pretty strong for a girl."

I thought about saying "Shut up, Jugg," again, but needed that breath to start walking. The rock was so heavy my arms hung down to my knees. My thighs bumped into my hands with each step and I kind of wanted to rest the rock on my thighs, because it seemed like it would be easier to carry that way, and maybe I wouldn't drop it and break my foot. I decided to rest the head on my right thigh, and then take one regular step and one nutso-groaning step to push the rock forward.

While I grunted, Jugg sauntered along beside me, chewing a wad of pixie stick paper.

"Man, are you gonna get in trouble."

Shut up Jugg.

"Where are you gonna keep it?"

Shut up Jugg.

"What if your mom finds out?"

Shut. Up. Jugg.

"Doesn't that hurt? Your fingers are all white. Man, you sweat like a hog. Bet you can't make it up those stairs."

Shut up. Shut up. Shut up!

"Want me to open the door?"

"Yes, you idiot," I said, all out of breath. "Hurry!"

Jugg looked mad at me calling him an idiot and purposely took forever opening the door. All I could do was stand there sort of bent in half, the rock resting on my thigh, and both my legs shaking so hard they were pounding in opposite beat to my heart. One little drop of sweat slid down my bangs, slithered into the curve of my eyelid, then down my nose and blipped onto the rock. The rock soaked up the sweat, and—I swear this is what happened—its eyes moved.

"Jugg," I panted, kind of worried now.

The rock rolled its eyes. It didn't have any eyelids, a fact I think both it and I were pretty disturbed to discover.

"Yeah, I know. Shut up." He walked into my house. "Man, I love the smell of your house."

"Uh, Jugg?"

Maybe the rock heard me even without ears. Maybe it noticed it was not attached to a body or, I dunno, maybe it didn't like where my hands were on its bottom. Whatever. It now stared straight at me, and even with no eyelids, I could tell it was angry. Crazy angry.

Another drip of my sweat plopped onto the rock's lips. It moved its mouth, chewed, and smacked, real quietly. Then it smiled a freakishly huge smile.

I wanted to drop it right there, but was pretty sure my mom would notice a head in the hallway. The rock kept smiling, its eyes crazy-angry. It stared at my face, watching the slow dribble of sweat itching down my nose. Maybe it wasn't crazy-angry. Maybe it was crazy-hungry.

So how was I supposed to know rocks liked sweat? I wiped my face on the shoulder of my T-shirt, trying to soak up the sweat. When I looked at the rock again, its mouth was back in scream mode. Oh, yeah, it was angry.

"What is the smell anyway?" Jugg called back. "Cinnamon?"

Jugg the wonder-brain was no help. My hands were starting to sweat and I didn't want to know what would happen when the butt end of the stone soaked that up.

"It's cedar," I said to Jugg. I took a step forward and thumped my way through our living room that was hardwood floor, wood walls and wood ceiling. Then I grunted down the hallway, also made of wood, wood, wood. My fingers were slipping, so I thunked faster, leaning my shoulder and hip along one wall for better leverage. I wanted to look at the rock's eyes, but didn't want to tip my sweaty head down. If a couple drops had made it wake up, I didn't want to find out what more would do.

Jugg strolled along in front of me and did nothing to help.

There were three doors in the hall. The one on the left went to the bathroom. The one on the right was

Mom's workroom and the one on the end, yeah, the farthest one away, was my room.

Jugg just stood there, his hand on the doorknob to my room.

"Please," I said. The rock was sort of squirming now, but I didn't dare look down and drip on it more. Maybe it had teeth. Maybe it even had fangs. What kind of a weirdo did Jugg's dad have to be to carve something with fangs?

Jugg swung the door inward and stepped into my bedroom. I crossed the threshold behind him and groaned. My bed was against the far wall of my room. Even here, I had to walk the farthest to put this stupid rock down.

I hobbled over to the bed and dropped the head in the middle of my unmade covers.

The rock slipped down faster than I thought it would, and I kind of tried to grab it because I didn't want it to bounce off the bed and hit the floor and break, but my grab didn't do much good except put my palm in the perfect place for a rough spot on the rock—like maybe where teeth or fangs would be—to slash it open.

"Ow, ow, ow!" I screamed.

"What, what, what?" Jugg yelled.

The rock hit my mattress and didn't even bounce, it was so heavy. I pulled my hand into my chest so I didn't have to see how bad it was bleeding, because I hated blood, because that would really be a problem and I would really get in trouble and man, I wished I'd asked Mom for more of the really big bandages when she went to the store last and it was a good thing I was wearing a cotton shirt and if I didn't get something to wrap this cut up really quick I was going to pass out.

"Here." Jugg pulled my hand away from my chest and wrapped one of my clean soccer socks around my palm. I hadn't even noticed he had gone to get it. I hissed when he tugged it tight and tied it in a knot on the back of my hand. He put his hand on my shoulder and gave me a friendly pat.

"Wow, Boads. You are so screwed."

"Yeah," I said. See, Jugg knew what my mom's crazy was. Her crazy was all about blood.

I glanced out the window. "Not going to be dark for at least an hour. Maybe I can be somewhere else. Your house, maybe?" I asked.

Jugg shook his head. "She'd find you, and then my dad would get all mad at me having you over when she's crazy. You could go to Nolly's. She's a mile away; that might be far enough."

"Her mom wouldn't let me in, I mean I'm really filthy, and leaking, you know."

Jugg sat down on the edge of my bed. "Yeah. Well, that sucks. But man, I can't believe you stole the rock!"

I sat down next to him. "Jugg, you watched me do it. That counts as permission. Even if your dad gets mad, I'm not the only one who's screwed."

Jugg nodded. "I guess." Then he grinned really big. "So what are you going to do with it?"

I looked at the rock. It was face down in my covers so that only the bald back of the skull was visible. The memory of its eyes moving brought a chill up my arms and legs. Face down like that, maybe it would suffocate. Or maybe it would eat its was through my mattress. I shuddered, feeling really cold now.

"I don't know." I rubbed my good hand down my blue jeans trying to smooth out the goose bumps on my legs. "I just wanted to have one, you know? Maybe I'll put it under my bed until I decide."

"Forget that," Jugg said, suddenly all full of energy. "Let's bury it. Wouldn't that be cool? Dad would never find it!"

"I'm not carrying it out to my yard. I just got it here." I was getting pretty tired. The sock on my hand was warm and really squishy. I just wanted to lie down and rest, but the stupid rock was in my stupid way and there was no way I was getting into bed with it.

"Hey, Boads, you okay?"

I blinked hard and realized I'd had my eyes closed and was falling asleep sitting up. Maybe I was bleeding pretty bad.

"I want to hide the rock before Mom gets up," I said. "Help me push this thing under my bed."

"Sure, yeah, I guess," Jugg said. "I still think it would be cooler to bury it."

"Yeah. Maybe tomorrow." Or maybe I'd get a hammer and break it into gravel. I wondered if that would hurt it. Wondered, for one weird minute, if maybe it really was one of Jugg's relatives or something.

"Jugg," I asked, "when your dad says the heads are family, he's just kidding, right?"

"What do you mean?"

"I mean, he's not really somehow getting real heads and making them somehow into rock heads, is he?" It sounded stupid once I said it, but Jugg didn't laugh at me. He didn't even smile.

"He's, you know, crazy, Boady. Just crazy." And his voice had that flat tired sound to it. Our parents were weird. Super weird. And there wasn't a lot we could do about it.

"Sure," I said. "I know. Help me move this."

With Jugg doing most of the work, and me keeping my bleeding hand completely out of the way, we got the rock off my bed and on my floor without being too loud. Jugg and I crouched down next to it. The head was just a head again, the eyes blank, and not moving. Instead of a scream, it was smiling. I didn't see any teeth, but a red bloodstain smeared the corner of its lips. My blood.

Stupid rock.

I pushed the side of my blankets up on top of my mattress so we could see under the bed.

That was when Jugg saw the secret I kept under my bed. A secret I hadn't told Jugg because I'd figured he'd rat me out. A secret that wasn't a secret any more. My very own raised dead.

"Holy crap!" Jugg yelled. "Dickie's under there!" Jugg shook his head. "Too cool! Didn't you bury him last week?"

I shrugged one shoulder. "I got lonely."

"But Boads—he's dead, dude."

I smiled, and the old excitement came out and some of my tired went away.

"He *used* to be dead."

Jugg's eyes got huge. He stopped chewing the pixie stick paper and swallowed it.

"No."

"Oh yeah," I said. "Watch." I tucked my legs in crisscross style and tapped my good hand on my knee. "Come here, Dickie. Come on. Come on. That's a good boy. Who's a good boy? Dickie's a good boy."

The sound of tail thumping started up. Then a shadow under the bed inched toward us, toward light, and Jugg and I scooted back so Dickie had room to get out. He belly crawled and used his front legs to push up so he was sitting, more or less, on his back legs that didn't work too good anymore. Other than the busted legs and the kind of weird glowing green goo where his eyes should be, he looked almost like he had in life. Even dead, he was the best dog ever.

But Jugg said, "Isn't he kind of flat in the middle?"

"Duh! He was run over by a car." I scratched behind Dickie's ear with my good hand. "He's a good dead dog, yes he is."

"Does your mom know?"

"No, Jugg. And I want to keep it that way. Help

me roll the head under here and then we'll push Dickie back under with it."

Dickie's tail tapped the floor like a slow, hollow heartbeat. He didn't pant like he used to, which made sense, since he didn't need to breathe anymore, but still, there was a look to him tonight that was a little creepy. He kept staring at me and staring at me and wouldn't stop.

"Here, we need to put a T-shirt under the rock before we push it so it doesn't scratch the floor—Mom would notice that," I said.

Jugg got up and pulled a T-shirt off my chair, then we put the shirt under as much of the rock as we could. Jugg gave the rock a push, and so did I, with my good hand. I was so busy thinking about the rock, and Mom waking up, that I wasn't paying much attention to my bloody hand. Until I felt something tug on it. I looked over and Dickie had his jaws sunk into the sock around my hand.

"Hey! Dickie—let go!" I said.

I reached over with my other hand, but Dickie pushed himself to the side, taking my hand along with him so I was kind of stretched out.

"Bad Dickie," I said. "Let go, let go." I slid a little across the floor in my blue jeans.

Dickie shook his head. It made my hand sting so hard I felt tears in the corners of my eyes.

"Crap, Dickie, that hurt! Let go."

Jugg jumped up and stood behind me. "Should I, you know, kill him again or something, Boady?"

"No!" Okay, maybe that was a weird thing to say, but Dickie was the last gift my dad had ever given me. Dickie was my dog and the first undead I'd ever raised. I felt a weird love for him. "Just try to distract him."

"With what?"

That was a good question. Dickie had only been undead for a few days, and since he didn't seem inter-

ested in eating or drinking, or really doing much more
than lying like an undead rug under my bed, I wasn't
sure what he'd be interested in. Dickie shook his head
again and tugged—his sharp teeth tearing all the way
through the sock.

I snatched my hand back, and the sock came off
and I thought Dickie would go for the sock, but he
didn't. Instead, he lunged at me—pretty good for a
dog with only two legs.

Dickie got a hold of my hand and bit down hard.
I screamed.

And then my hand didn't hurt any more. As a matter of fact, I wasn't tired any more, wasn't sore any
more, wasn't worried any more. Yeah, really everything suddenly seemed super, super good. I sort of
slipped back, lay on the floor and liked it.

I think Jugg screamed. I think he said something.
But I just stayed were I was, feeling floaty and fine.

Until I saw my mother's face.

She leaned over me, strands of dark hair like a funeral veil around her pale, pale face. Her eyes looked
worried and maybe angry, but not crazy. I was surprised about that because I figured all the blood I was
leaking would really make her crazier.

"Boady, what have you done?" she asked in her
sad-mother voice.

I worked on thinking about what I could have done
to make her sad. "Uh, Jugg saw me take his dad's
rock. He didn't say I couldn't."

"Not the rock, Boady. The dog."

Oh yeah. Dickie. Man, I should be seriously panick-
ing about my mom finding out about that, but I was
still feeling freakaliously fine.

"Well, I missed him and I wanted him back. So I
used one of your books to, you know, do the undead
thing, like how you get your boyfriends."

Her eyebrow arched and there was a glimmer of
angry mom in her eyes. "They are not my boyfriends.

Not all of them," she said. "Did you read the entire book? Did you read the consequences of raising the dead?"

I blew my breath out between my lips in a big, frustrated sound. "No. I only had about an hour to read the good stuff. I had to put the book back because you woke up." My brain finally hit the danger button. I had just told my mom my secret. I was so screwed.

Instead of grounding me, or telling me what chore I'd be doing for the next six months, Mom tipped her head up so all I saw was her neck and chin. I knew her eyes were closed. I knew she was trying hard not to cry. I'd seen her just like that a lot of times. Every time, actually, after she "broke up" with her boyfriends and sent them back to the grave. But most of all, that first time she really went crazy when Dad died.

"Mom?" I said. I got my elbows under me and pushed up so I was kind of lying and kind of sitting. Jugg was gone, and the room was pretty dark. I had no idea how long I'd been on the floor, but my back was stiff and the room smelled of mint and lemon— things my mom always uses to clean up blood.

The rock head was right where Jugg and I had left it, its face turned upward, the long nose pointing to the ceiling, the eyes, I hoped, unmoving. A puddle of blood ringed the base of the rock. My blood. I had no idea what to do about that.

"Can I keep Dickie?" I asked Mom.

I heard the slow thump of his tail on the hardwood floor and Mom and me both looked over at him. He was sitting on his bad legs, and he looked different. I couldn't quite figure it out, then I knew what it was— Dickie was breathing. Even his green-glow eyes looked more like eyes.

"Look! He's better!" I sat up the rest of the way and put my hands together in front of me. My cut hand didn't hurt so bad, and it was already scabbing. "Please, Mom, please can I keep him?"

Mom nodded slowly. "You *have to* keep him."

My heart soared and I felt like cheering. Then the "have to" part sunk in.

"Why?"

"Because once an undead drinks your blood they are tied to you." Mom put her cool soft fingers on the back of my hurt hand. "That is why we are always careful about blood in the house. Boady, Dickie is your keeper now."

Okay, so I wasn't seeing a down side. I think Mom noticed that.

"Dickie is a part of you. He can make you do things if he wants to, things you might not want to do." She looked over at Dickie, who was still wagging his tail and staring at us.

"That's okay, Mom. He's a good dog. I love him, you know. He's family. Even dead."

Mom nodded. "I understand." And I figured she really did. Then she put her arms around me and gave me a hug. I let her, because even though I wasn't worried about Dickie, I was a little worried she would remember I had snuck into her room and gotten into her stuff. Plus, the rock was making slurping sounds over there in my blood, and I didn't think that was a good thing.

"Come help me make dinner." Mom stood up and walked over to my door. "After that, you can take Giorgio back where he belongs."

"Who?"

"The head."

"Oh." Great. It had a name. Maybe I could trick Jugg into carrying it this time. Or maybe I'd find a wheelbarrow to put it in. I sure didn't want to touch Giorgio barehanded again. He bit.

Still, what mattered was I wasn't really in trouble.

Even though I didn't get to keep the head, I got to keep my dead dog. Things had worked out okay.

I stood up and walked over to Dickie, then bent down and scratched behind his ears.

"Who's a good doggy?" I said.

Suddenly, I knew I should scratch a little more to the left and maybe a little harder, and then a little bit to the right, and then stroke under his chin. So I did, even though I was hungry, and even though my back started hurting, and even though I didn't want to do it any more.

"Bad dog," I said.

Dickie just thumped his tail and licked my cheek with his swollen, purple tongue. Okay. Maybe this was a good thing for him, but so far it wasn't so great for me. Back when he was alive and misbehaving, I would send him to his doghouse and shut the door. I wondered if I could make him go to his house now.

"Go to your house," I said.

Dickie whimpered and I could feel how awful it was to be locked up in that dark little house. I knew how alone and sad it made him feel.

Wow. I always thought I'd been a really good friend to Dickie. But maybe I hadn't understood what it was like for him to be my pet.

"I'm sorry, boy. I'll try to be better this time, okay? No house."

He wagged his tail some more and stood. His bad legs looked a lot better, even though he was still a little flat in the middle.

I patted his head one more time—because I wanted to, not because he wanted me to—and straightened up.

"So, what do you want for dinner? Oh, wait. Do you need to eat anymore?"

Dickie tipped his head to the side and his ears perked up. He yapped. Bones. I knew he didn't need food, but he wanted to chew on a bone.

Awesome.

I found the box of rawhide chews in my closet and took Dickie out into the front yard to a patch of grass still warm from the setting sun. I gave him a rawhide and sat with him for a little while, watching the daylight slowly fade into evening.

"Boady," Mom called through the kitchen window. "Dinner."

Great. I'd forgotten to help her make dinner. That meant I'd have to do the dishes by myself.

"Be right there," I yelled over my shoulder. I patted Dickie's head one last time. "Gotta go, boy. You gonna be okay here?"

Dickie wasn't chewing on the bone any more—wasn't even moving any more. His ears stood straight up and his tail was stiff. He looked like an undead statue, staring across the street at Jugg's yard. Then I saw his nose wiggle a tiny bit, like maybe he smelled something.

"What?" I said. "What's wrong?" I looked at the street, then over at Jugg's yard full of heads. I had the weirdest idea that maybe one of the heads was going to do something, like pull itself out of the ground and roll across the street to take back what's-his-name I'd left on my bedroom floor.

"What, boy? The heads? Is it the heads?" Man, I hoped it wasn't the heads.

Dickie's ears flicked back, then up again. That's when I heard it—the thrum of a car engine veering off the main road and heading our way. Our neighborhood was pretty quiet, so it was easy to know when a car was coming.

And Dickie totally knew it. He shoved up onto his feet and torpedoed across the yard.

"Dickie—no!"

But he didn't listen. He took off like an undead bullet, his bad legs even keeping up with the rest of him.

He reached the end of our yard at the exact time

the car drove in front of our house. My stomach clenched with sick horror. Dickie had always wanted to chase cars when he was alive, but I wouldn't let him. The one time he'd gotten out and chased a car, it had killed him.

"No, Dickie. Stay!" I yelled.

But he did not stop. He went faster, legs pumping hard, body low to the ground, ears back, tail straight out.

If he got crushed to death again I didn't think my mom would let me re-raise him no matter how much I begged. Stupid dog, chasing stupid cars. "Stop!" I ran after him, even though there was no way I'd catch up before he was deader than undead.

He lunged for the front tire. Missed.

Hope fluttered in my chest. Maybe he was too slow. Maybe the car would zoom past and he'd be smart enough to let it go by.

Dickie wasn't that smart.

He ran under the car, jaws snapping at the opposite back tire—which ran right over him. I heard the ka-thump and squeak of the shocks. The car kept right on going like nothing had happened. Like it hadn't just re-killed my best friend.

"Dickie!" I ran into the street.

Dickie was nothing but a flattened lump in the middle of the road. And even though I wanted to cry, I noticed he was not bleeding. And he was still breathing.

"Dickie?" He wagged his tail and slowly peeled himself off the pavement. His legs were working pretty good, and so was the rest of him, I guess. Maybe he was a little flatter in the middle but it didn't seem to bother him. He shook his head and sneezed. Then he wagged his tail harder and barked at the retreating car.

He was fine. More than that, he was happy and excited, like he'd just gotten off a roller coaster ride.

"You're crazy. Do you think you're indestructible?" I rubbed the sides of his face and didn't feel anything more broken than usual. Maybe he was indestructible. Maybe I'd done a really good job when I brought him back to life.

"Promise me no more cars today, okay, boy? I know you like it but it freaks me out."

He barked and licked my hand, still excited about chasing the car. And I knew we had an agreement— no more cars today. But tomorrow was a whole new story.

WALKING FOSSIL

Robert A. Hoyt

I could name any number of strange things to run into while operating a digger in a construction site. But the early morning sunlight glinting off the leathery skin of what looked to me very much like a dinosaur gave me the idea that my list was about to expand. In fact, the only thing that was working against that possibility was the fact that the creature was very much alive for something several million years extinct.

I had been trying to forget about the recent loss of the best hunting dog I'd ever had, a purebred pointer named Rex that I had inherited from my father. After tossing and turning most of the night, I finally just clocked in a couple of hours early. After all, I wasn't sleeping anyway.

Strangely, at the moment, I felt a great urge to be home in bed.

All right, granted, the creature wasn't exactly horrible, but then again, I hadn't really seen any other dinosaurs to compare it to.

It was covered in dark brown soil that obscured most of it, but exaggerated a stiff little frill on the head and a thick tail. Standing on two legs it was still only about six feet tall, with a great big sharp nose and small, comical forearms. Its eyes were slightly yellow, and in some places, it seemed to be missing strategic pieces of flesh, making it seem as though it had been put together from a kit and someone had lost bits from the box.

Brandon, a tenuous friend and my acting supervisor since his father owned the company anyway, came running over from his place near the foreman's trailer, a cheap cigarette in hand and an incredulous expression on his face. In theory, no one was supposed to be in the trailer unless they had a reason to be, but I wasn't about to argue with him.

He hung around there simply because it annoyed the foreman to have the trailer smelling of cigarette smoke.

I jumped out of the digger to talk to him.

"What the hell is that thing, Andrew?" he said, as though I had caused its appearance.

I shrugged and leaned against the digger. "Beats me, Brander . . . looks like a dinosaur, but that ain't possible. At a guess, I'd say it's some kinda lizard from a cave under there."

He looked disgusted and stared at the creature. "Sick lizard, by the look of it. We can't keep the damned thing out in broad daylight. Someone'll get the wrong idea, and the project will be held up for months." Turning to me, he said, "We're gonna have to get rid of it, and quickly. The rest of the crew and the usual heavy traffic will be around any minute now."

Deep down, as he said that, I had some inexplicable grumbling misgivings about the idea of reburying it. There was some ephemeral, distant reason that it wasn't kosher, but I couldn't place it.

On the other hand, I'd have to be insane not to get rid of it. He was right; we were in a city center, and one look at that thing would have a dozen of the investors fighting to get out before some animal rights activist group sued.

But the obvious solution had already made itself

quite apparent in my head. "The best way I can think of that's quick is to push it back in that hole again," I said, slowly. "It can't possibly withstand a few hundred pounds of dirt being dropped on it after that. And, later, if we find a dead lizard while digging, well, no problem, right?"

For a couple seconds, he seemed to be thinking about it, and then he slowly worked it out mentally. The idea clicked. He grinned broadly at me, his smile widening his round, stubble-infested face to a squat oval, and he gestured wildly with the cigarette. "Beautiful. Keep thinking like that, and I'll see you get promoted."

He glanced at the animal, calculating. His grin faded with the effort.

He had the expression of a man with something on the tip of his tongue. An ephiphany struck and he turned to me. "Why push it and *then* bury it?" he said slowly. "I'll hang back, and on the count of three, you charge him with the rig. Two birds with one stone."

I nodded. It was cold, but it made sense.

I climbed on the rig, and Brandon set himself up as a human barrier near the building shell, low to the ground in case he was charged.

One finger up. I moved the ignition into position.

Two fingers up. I juggled the shovel lever towards dump.

Three fingers up. The engine roared to life under my hands. Galvanized by the sudden noise, the creature jumped. Brandon's eyebrows arched.

And my hopes sank.

Unfortunately, the animal didn't have the slightest interest in going back in the hole, and it charged the storage trailers instead of Brandon.

Our beautifully simple plan had just become complex. The storage trailers were right by the road. Any passersby would end up in full rubberneck mode the second they passed. The last thing we wanted was witnesses.

I swore. The rig wasn't agile enough to get between the trailers. We were running out of time. The sun was almost fully crested now.

I jumped off the rig.

"Damn it, Rockhold," Brandon said, turning my last name into a swear word, "Why didn't you move the rig forward?"

Before I could explain that the creature had moved too fast, he cut me off.

"Come on. We haven't got time to wrangle it now. We'll never have him over there in time. Let's just try to shove it in the supplies trailer. We'll deal with it tonight, after the crew leaves."

Glancing at my watch, I decided that this was neither the time nor the place to argue. I ran around and opened the trailer door for him.

Brandon didn't take a moment to catch his breath after the setback. One thing any of his casual acquaintances knew was that he swung a mean right. Three seconds later, that same wicked uppercut caught the animal straight across the jaw, and six feet of dirty lizard toppled into the trailer like a domino.

Brandon massaged his knuckles and turned to me, growling in a low voice. "Don't even say a word. Remember that as far as this project is concerned, Andrew, it's him or us. Get used to treating him rough, 'cause it'll be worse tonight. We're coming back at midnight and finishing this. Until then, you and I don't let anyone else in here. You say anything, even accidentally, I break your jaw." He snapped shut the lock, and tucked his work gloves in his back pocket, wiping his palms on his shirt.

Behind him, the first truck pulled in. We had cut it very fine indeed.

Brandon had already turned away, but his entire back was tense. Something about his tone of voice was entirely too dominant for the part of me that resisted authority. I couldn't explain why, but I felt strangely sympathetic for our recently acquired captive.

The day gradually got progressively worse. I spent a considerable amount of time ducking over to intercept people trying to get supplies from the trailer. The rest of the time I spent thinking about the animal.

Part of the problem was that I felt an odd connection to it. Inexplicably, I felt strangely paternal. I told myself repeatedly that it was simply the fact that it was potentially a very valuable scientific find.

I would have bet the rear axle of my truck that it was a dinosaur, regardless of whatever danger it presented to our future. I didn't know how, but I knew that it was important.

Then, as I was sitting far away from Brandon, who was talking as usual with his crew, something occurred to me. I didn't want the animal hurt. Somehow, it offended the part of me that the only animal I had ever known was closest to . . . the hunter. My dad and my granddad, and even old Rex, knew and taught me the rules; I'd known them since I was a child. If a creature was in pain, if it was sick, it was expected you'd kill it, out of mercy. If it was defenseless and trapped, though, it became something else again.

The truth was that the animal didn't look to be in good shape, but it acted healthy and it seemed aware. I judged that the exact reason for my misgivings was that I couldn't let Brandon harm an innocent animal without at least giving it a sporting chance. Which, seeing as the dino's natural environment was several millennia out of reach, was quite probably impossible.

I was so burdened with this thought that I caught Brandon just after clocking out to try to convince him to reconsider the dino's fate.

But before I could begin, he cut me off. "Andy, go home as usual. Forget about the animal. I'll get some boys together tonight, and we'll take care of it. You—"

He shook his head and spat, then grabbed me by the shoulder and pulled me close so no one could hear, "Damn it, Andy. I can't have you losing your nerve. We've got a lot on the line here, and we've gotta make sure nobody sees that thing. If you're gonna flinch even when I *punch* it, I damn sure don't want you anywhere near here when we kill it and bury it."

I was shocked. "Right here? On the site? Are you crazy? This morning we were desperate, but if you have time, then anywhere else would be better. If someone sees you, you'll be in a bigger mess than before. Finding it while digging is one thing, but not finding it is better."

"Not finding it *is* better," he growled. "I can't risk someone seeing us take it somewhere else. I take no chances. Go home. You and your glass stomach will bankrupt me, otherwise."

My face creased at that insult. "Weigh your words, Brandon. You're talking to the person who has bested you in every hunt. At least my 'glass stomach' is sitting next to a heart." I grabbed his wrist and twisted, suddenly very fed up, "Now listen closely. *Never* mistake good hunting ethics with inability or squeamishness. You know as well as I do that this—" I pointed at the trailer, "—isn't a fair fight."

He stuck his face in mine. "Fair fight nothing. It's threatening the jobs of a lot of hard-working men. That isn't fair either. Life's tough all over."

I couldn't argue that. It was true that it was inconvenient. But it still wasn't right to kill an innocent animal for convenience, and I punctuated the idea with a neat twist of Brandon's arm that sent him away, swearing. I didn't stick around to listen.

Realizing I was crazy even as I thought it, I made up my mind.

No matter what, I had to get to that dinosaur tonight. And I would have to be there before Brandon.

*   *   *

I waited a long while for Brandon to leave. I had
ducked off the road and I was watching from a covered parking lot. They were looking around suspi-
ciously, then one of them headed towards my
apartment. I expected that.

The way I saw it, Brandon would suspect I'd try
something. He'd move back the timetable. I had to
beat him to it. I knew that he wasn't crazy enough to
go earlier then ten thirty, not at this time of year. And
that meant that I would.

It was a long, tense stakeout. As the lights fell, I
had a few candy bars for my dinner and waited.

Finally, after an eternity, the dashboard clock read
ten exactly. I couldn't wait any longer. I had to go
now. If I were going to carry through on this moral
impulse, I had to make sure I did it after heavy traffic,
and I had to time it just right.

Getting to the construction site was simple, because
traffic was minimal in the still-redeveloping part of the
inner city after rush hour. There was relatively little
to do until the abandoned shop fronts were rebuilt, so
the only people out this late were, for the most part,
on their way home.

Unfortunately, a less simple obstacle was the gate on
the construction site, which was barred and locked to
keep people from breaking in and doing some creative
"street art" on expensive pieces of equipment. On the
other hand, I noted that the fence was buried under a
mound of dirt about twelve feet high, just a few dozen
yards to the right of the gate, hidden near a huge maple.

In a sudden crazed moment, I reached down and
downshifted my truck's four-wheel-drive into the low
range setting used for thick snow.

"Ain't nothing like off-roading." I said to myself
as I rolled over the top of the mound and into the
construction site with all the quiet delicacy of a me-
teor strike.

I was out the door before the dust had settled on the fenders, fumbling for the spare key to the supplies trailer Brandon had carelessly left out a couple weeks back. It was fifteen past ten now. I was pushing my time, playing it cautious.

I pulled open the door, and was greeted by the strange sight of the creature belly-up in a pile of cement dust, with its tongue lolling out the side of its mouth ridiculously. I ran to it.

It opened one large eye and said, "rrmuuuurrr?" sounding much like a happy kitten.

"I'm here to protect you . . . come on." I was clearly insane to be talking to a giant lizard.

The creature flipped over and yawned, but didn't seem overly interested in moving. Desperately, I looked around for a rope. Lying underneath the thing's giant neck was a rope coil.

I glanced at my watch. The display read 10:18. I panicked. With strength beyond my own, I pulled the rope out from under the dinosaur and strung it around its neck. It protested, but I braced and started pulling it out the door.

I was halfway out the door when I heard the roar of a pickup truck, accompanied by several other cars approaching at top speed.

Brandon!

I yanked as hard as I could. But my truck was still a good ten yards away, and the creature was stubborn.

There was a tinny metallic crash as the pickup barreled through the gates without slowing down and pulled into a sideways skid. The occupant didn't even bother yelling, instead rolling down the window and pointing a shotgun straight at me.

Where the hell did Brandon find these guys? After a few rounds of beer in a redneck bar?

In the glare of the headlights, I heard a shot ring out just as I dodged aside.

The pickup driver's aim went wide, his shot ricocheting near the lizard's feet. The animal bolted. Going full tilt, I found myself being dragged around my truck. With all my strength, I grabbed the passenger door, braced, and used the animal's own momentum to swing him around. He crashed into the truck full tilt, pushing me into the driver's seat.

The passenger door slammed shut as I hit the accelerator, the vast mass of lizard overflowing the seat next to me and jamming me against my own door. Without thinking, I steered through the framework of the building's front doors, rammed pieces of plywood out of the way with the bumper and drove right between two supports at the back of the building with less than an inch to spare on either side.

My truck rioted onto the road, I stomped the accelerator and raced down the street, hanging a sharp left at the corner. I heard the roar of engines fading into the distance at the crossroads, but I was leaving nothing to chance.

I weaved through the mostly unlit ghettos of the city, not daring to drop my speed below seventy-five for a single moment, lest my pursuers—if there were any—catch up.

At the city limits, I skidded onto a back road that was invisible at night, and ditched the hard gravel for unpaved forest halfway out, cutting five miles off my trip in a wild flurry of tree trunks and dead branches.

My cell phone buzzed as I was driving frantically over a shallow creek bed. I didn't bother to answer it.

A mile or so into the forest, I stopped and sorted out the lizard and the phone.

The phone had a text message on it from Brandon. It read, in full: *You're a crazy bastard. Your problem now. Getting a beer.*

A second text message followed: *P.S. You're fired.*

Given that I had been shot at by some of his goons, I could have been more choked up. The dinosaur was more important in my mind. It was still caked in dirt, so my seats were a mess. It was perched on my seat, with its tiny forearms resting on the dashboard, and a sublimely happy expression painted on its face. After a few minutes, I managed to loosen the rope around his neck a little, and in return he gave an appreciative gurgle.

At last, after much exhaustion, I rolled onto the road near a gated community where my parents had a hunting cabin. I couldn't go back to my apartment, and the cabin up here was furnished well enough for a few days while I sorted out the dinosaur.

My mind suddenly focused as I approached the gate booth. I looked over at my unwieldy passenger, and then at the somewhat sleepy-looking gate guard.

Well, I thought *Let's try the direct approach.*

I pulled the truck right up to the window.

"Hello, sir. Visiting? Or do you have a cabin up here?" he said mechanically, without even looking up.

"Thought I'd surprise my parents," I said through the window. "Just here a bit late. You wouldn't believe the traffic I ran into," I added.

The man looked up as I handed him my driver's license. His face froze. After a long moment, he stuttered, "My, that's an interesting . . . breed. What is it?"

I glanced over at the dinosaur. It was sniffing its reflection in the truck window with great intent. "He's a Great Saurdino Dirtback," I said with a grin. What the hell. I was already having a fun night.

"How fascinating," the man said, returning my ID while keeping his eyes firmly fixed on my passenger, who was now licking my windshield.

His gaze occasionally nervously darted down to his coffee cup, then back up at the creature, as if it might disappear if he looked away too long.

"Have a nice night," he said, and opened the gate.

"You, too," I replied, and drove away.

*   *   *

Getting the animal into the cabin was a Herculean effort. It seemed fascinated by the trees surrounding the site, and I was tugged along on a five-course gastronomic tour of every tuber, weed, tree, shrub, and bush before I got him inside.

In the cabin, I tied him to the coat rack on the wall for a minute, and flicked on the lamp beside me. The modest pine furnishings, a little kitchen, and a half dozen rather nice hunting trophies were illuminated by the warm glow.

I turned around to find that the animal, and my coat rack, had vanished. Behind me, I heard a happy chirp, and then a crunch. Suddenly, the room was pitch dark. I slapped on the overhead light—revealing the ridiculous sight of the creature with its mouth full of my mom's favorite lamp and a very confused expression on its face.

"Aw, for the love of Christ . . . that was a nice lamp," I said, as it spit out the pieces of lamp. It occurred to me that the creature should have gotten hurt by the glass, at least, if not by the live filament.

I took a closer look at the thing's mouth, prising it open while it gurgled in protest. To my surprise its pointed mouth was actually a tough beak, lined with teeth down either side. The creature struggled out of my grip and leapt up onto a worn white couch in a shower of dirt. I heard splintering furniture.

"Squirk!" it chimed from the top of the collapsed couch, eyeing my bookshelf in a way I didn't like.

"Squirk, yourself. I think it's time we figured out just what you are, fella. Do you understand the word 'bath?'"

It tilted its head to the side and chirped musically at me again. It seemed altogether very pleased with itself. But I still couldn't tell what condition it was in while it was covered in all that dirt. Besides which, I hoped that a bath might rescue the remaining pieces of furniture.

With a stolid, resolute hand, I grabbed its leash. This was going to be fun.

To my surprise, the animal did not mind the water. In fact, it took to the bathtub very quickly. In the process, it also took to the sponge and two bars of soap, which were down its gullet before I could utter a protest.

I made a mental note that I would have to feed it after the bath was finished.

But as more and more dirt washed away, I saw that the animal was fatally wounded.

It was definitely a dinosaur, one of the duckbilled ones from the look of it, and I could accept that I didn't know much about it. But I had hunted long enough to know a lethal wound when I saw one, and there was no possible way for it to be alive. Its emaciated torso was more holey than a cathedral, it seemed to have multiple, irregular wounds bad enough that there was no way to patch it up, and it had a gash on its leg that would have had a Marine calling for his mother.

But it was chirping happily as water trickled into it and back out of it like a defective bucket. More curious was the fact that I could find no signs of scabs, even though its eyes were sickly yellowish, and that its pebbly green skin curtained off its raw flesh in some places.

After it had been cleaned up somewhat, I led it downstairs and did some research in a dinosaur encyclopedia I'd borrowed from my neighbor's kid earlier that evening. I pulled some canned corn out of the pantry, dumped it in a bowl and set it out for the beast. For my dinner, I got out a couple bologna sandwiches I hadn't had time to eat for lunch. I dissected one and threw the meat on top of the other while I went back to the pantry for mustard.

Grabbing the dinosaur book on the way, I flipping it open and found a perfect picture before I found the mustard. My guest was definitely a corythosaurus, judging by the little frill and head shape.

What concerned me was that he was a member of a technically extinct species, and he was currently sitting here in my kitchen. More importantly, he didn't appear to be in the best of health, although after that many millions of years, that was to be expected.

Suddenly, my concentration was broken by the bologna sandwich sliding off the edge of the table.

"Oh, no," I said, putting the book down to find the miscreant with a piece of meat in his mouth. "You're a plant eater. You aren't going to like that."

The dinosaur answered by sliding the bologna very neatly into its mouth, and nosing around the bread for the other piece. I cocked an eyebrow quizzically. Then I understood. Like a dog, he was colorblind. As far as he was concerned, round and flat meant that it was edible.

Without quite knowing why, I got up, rooted around in the closet for a moment, and came back with one of Rex's old collars. "You know, you seem to catch on pretty quickly. If I'm gonna take care of you anyway, how'd you like to be a pointer?"

For a moment, he almost seemed to understand what I was saying. His eyes lit up, and he swished his tail in a happy, repetitive arc that beat my guest chair to pieces.

I looked at the collar. Rex had been a big dog.

Carefully, I slid it around the dinosaur's neck. To my surprise, it fit perfectly.

"Well, it's kinda fitting," I chuckled. "Since you're a dinosaur . . . I think that you would make a wonderful Rex."

For just a moment, as I looked at the dinosaur with his new collar, I would have sworn that I saw him puff out his over-worn chest with the solemn weight of his new position.

*   *   *

Over the next couple of weeks, I trained Rex the same as I had trained the hunting dogs, with lots of patience, and strangely enough, with the occasional piece of meat as a reward.

I guessed that the bologna wasn't likely to be very good for him, but in the shape he was in, indigestion could hardly do him in. Besides, he expressed a definite partiality for it, and eventually, I realized that I was never going to train him on canned corn alone.

After a week of training, he simply wouldn't eat the corn.

By the end of the two weeks, Rex was the best dinosaur pointer ever to be seen by the world. In fact, he had a natural instinct for tracking that was nearly unbelievable.

Now that I didn't have the job at the construction site any more, I took some time off before looking for another job. I'd probably have to use Brandon as a reference, but he'd be okay. It's not like I was any threat to him now.

Still. I wasn't keen to have another run-in with him. After all, I may have saved him some trouble, but the least I could expect him to pull if I saw him would be sanctimonious and bureaucratic speeches about how he really shouldn't be seen with the clinically insane, and I didn't have much patience for that.

Rex, meanwhile, started working his way up to bigger pieces of meat. Now and then, I'd toss him a piece of ham, which usually translated in his mind as "extraordinarily large leaf." He even started burying the bones, something I wasn't certain what to make of.

Later, when I went out to tend to the grounds around the cabin one day, one of the little jobs necessary if you keep semi-permanent residence, I saw a small dust storm being flung up nearby; it was of larger proportions then Rex's normal snack hunt.

As I approached, I realized that at the center of the dust was an eight foot hole, from which two absurdly happy eyes were staring triumphantly as Rex pulled the largest bone I had ever seen out of the ground and, after a laborious climb, dropped it at my feet. As it landed, it made a dense thump. It was made entirely out of minerals.

And that was when I realized exactly what my next job would be.

The last time I saw Brandon was from a distance, while I was working on a new dig. There were less fireworks then I expected, but considering that our last engagement had involved firearms, I was more than willing to see things quiet down a bit.

It was sometime after I got my latest job as an excavator on paleontological digs, thanks to a quick discussion with the friend from whom I borrowed the book. I took the courses I needed at the local museum and passed the tests with flying colors. At my interview, I had asked that I be able to bring my "dog" onto the digs, provided it didn't damage anything. It was time to do what had gotten me Rex in the first place, and play a hunch.

Rex soon became popular around the site, because he had an uncanny ability to find fossils where no one else even thought to look. In fact, I even got my picture in the paper as the owner of the semi-famous "rock hound," and no one bothered looking up his species, because after all, he couldn't really be a dinosaur. We couldn't have spilled our secret if we tried. I was his owner and I made sure to file papers to prove it with animal enforcement, complete with a contrived pedigree from a dog breeder in need of a few bucks before he left town. Rex ended up as a rather distant cousin of the Newfoundland.

But one bright spring day when Rex and I took a lunch break in a town near the excavation site, me with a sub sandwich, and Rex with his usual packet of cold cuts from the deli, I happened to look to the side and see a familiar figure in a dark coat. He seemed to look my way, then had an animated conversation with one of the other men on my team, Doug.

After a minute, he stood up straight, glanced at me again, then got back in his car and left.

I got hold of Doug as I was finishing up.

"What was that all about?" I asked, as though I expected the usual press person or similar.

"Oh, it was just someone asking about you again, Ands," he said, business as usual, "From the article, you know. He asked about your dog. I told him it was a—what's the name now?—Sardine Dustback?"

"Saurdino Dirtback," I corrected automatically. "And what did he say?"

Doug leaned against a nearby parking meter. "He didn't really say much of anything. He just laughed and mumbled, 'Damn clever', and then drove off." He glanced up as he started to walk towards the dig. "Know him?"

I smiled and threw Rex the last of my sandwich, a treat he relished if he could get it.

"You could say that," I replied, and headed back to the dig with Rex, the best Saurdino Dirtback I'd ever had.

UNDEAD

Vampires. Blood-suckers. Life-takers. The traditional undead envisioned by Bram Stoker. The Count certainly viewed his undeath as better in some respects. So, in a way, these stories pay homage to Stoker's original view of the undead. But that's only a passing nod; the undead in *these* tales are nothing like Dracula.

Kate Paulk shows us that vampirism doesn't have to be a big deal—even when a would-be slayer shows up. Twelve-step treatment programs get a hilariously unexpected update by Rebecca Lickiss. Charles Edgar Quinn explores vampire hunting as a sport. The things that scare us in the night as children sometimes follow us into adulthood in Amanda S. Green's narrative. Finally, S.M. Stirling takes the undead to a creepy new level with a family squabble that's anything but expected.

NIGHT SHIFTED

Kate Paulk

It was just on half-past eleven when she walked into the store. I gave her a quick look; enough to see who it was, nothing more. At least, that was the plan. The things you see on graveyard shift at a convenience store.

This kid was maybe twenty, and she had "Buffy Fashion Victim" written all over her. She even had a bad bleach job and a Sarah Michelle Gellar haircut. On Gellar—*Buffy the Vampire Slayer*—that style looked good. On this kid, it looked like a straggly home cut. Then there was the big vinyl shoulder bag that was supposed to look like leather but it was cracking and showing white underneath, and the fancy pewter crucifix on a chain around her neck. It was probably supposed to look like silver.

As for the clothes . . . the kid's jeans might have fit someone a bit less on the anorexic side. They hung loose on her. The floaty micromini she wore over them did nothing to help. Then, God help me, there was the tee shirt. White, with pink edging and those silly cap sleeves that make it look like someone burped on the factory floor. And written across the front, in pink puffy letters, "Grrrl Power." I kid you not.

I half expected to see a Powerpuff Girl on the back of the thing.

She smelled of cheap perfume and fear.

Just great. Smelling like that, there was no way she was here to shop, so I kept an eye on her through the security monitors. I can stop your average shoplifter cold, but some dumb kid dared to do it for a fraternity gag? After what happened when I tried to join a frat, I prefer not to mess with the frat stuff.

I had asked myself a thousand times how I was supposed to know the guy who bit me was a vampire, and I still didn't feel any better about it. Then there's what it did to my college schedule. Night classes are kind of hard to get into, especially night classes that run after sundown. I still had to support myself, and while a vampire working graveyard shift had its own irony, the job didn't bring in much above minimum wage.

At least my boss was a decent sort. He always came in early the few days around the daylight savings changeover when sunrise came before my shift was due to close.

The kid wandered around the store, looking at stuff like she didn't really see it. If she was here to shoplift, there was nothing I could do until she actually put something in her bag and headed out the door. Company policy.

She picked up a bag of Doritos and meandered towards the counter.

Now, I'm not your most attractive male, and being changed doesn't magically make you any better looking. You just get paler and a bit skinnier. But that doesn't excuse her for flinching back like I was some kind of monster. I didn't even have my fangs showing.

She dumped the Doritos on the counter.

"Will that be all, ma'am?" I might not be much of a vampire, but God help me, I'll be a polite one.

"You are *so* staked, sucker." She even tried to fake the Buffy accent. With her Texan drawl, it didn't work.

I blinked. This was something the store didn't have a policy on. At least, not an official one.

So there I am, looking at this wannabe slayer, and she's pointing this sharpened dowel at me. I mean, *dowel!* Not even a decent chunk of two by four! She hadn't sharpened it properly, she had it aimed at my gut instead of my heart, and it shook so much in her hand I doubted she could do more than scratch me.

Oh, and the counter was damn near as wide as she could reach. All I had to do was take a step back.

Why did I get all the wannabe slayers? It's not like I'm anyone's idea of ultimate evil. I'm a convenience store cashier, for Chrissake! I don't need more than a pint of the red stuff a week, and I try to get it in daily doses. Preferably with someone who knows what I am and doesn't mind a little nibble, although if I don't have a girlfriend, it's kind of expensive paying for a fifteen minute simulated quickie each night, just so I can get my few ounces in.

Not that I've got much choice. I can't afford to let myself get so low on the red stuff that I can't control what I drink, because it's damned inconvenient trying to hide bodies. If the cops got hold of me over a dead body, well . . . I'd be a dead body. With maybe one or two exceptions, no cop would believe I was a vampire until I went up like a candle, and by then it'd be too late.

I smiled at Miss Grrrl Power Wannabe Slayer, a nice smile that didn't show my fangs. "Pardon, ma'am?"

She shoved the dowel a little closer to my liver while I rang up her Doritos. "Enough with the talking, it's, like, time to die."

I really did not have time for this. I don't get sick pay, and there's no way I was going to go to a hospital. The kid was worse than the potheads who did their best to buy out our stock of blunts each night. At least the potheads were harmless.

I sighed and laid my hand flat on the dowel, pushing it to lie on the counter. "Look, ma'am, you've been overdoing it. Why don't you put this thing away and go home. I'll pay for your food if you like." I didn't usually offer like this, but the wobbly determination the kid showed deserved something from me. I don't even like Doritos.

She snatched the dowel away, glaring at me as she took a few steps back. "Don't try any of your mind, um . . . things!"

Poor kid. I'd like to get my hands on the idiot who sent her out. "I'm not doing anything, ma'am." I spread out my hands so she could see them. "I'm just trying to earn a living, same as anyone else."

She gave me a confused look, and her bottom lip trembled a bit. "But I . . . they said . . ."

I could imagine. "Yeah, I've heard it all before. Spawn of evil, dark angel . . . it's crap." I shook my head. "I never asked to get changed." I moved out from behind the counter, nice and slow. Maybe if she could see I was nothing special she'd calm down.

She backed up against the beer bin, shaking hard enough to rattle the ice. Her free hand fumbled until she got hold of the cross and pointed it at me. "Stay away!"

I sighed. Sometimes it's not a bad thing there are so many dumb myths about vampires, but it gets old. Especially when you're trying to calm down a wannabe slayer who doesn't seem to know the first thing about it.

Like the cross. It might have bothered me if it had been real silver. Or even polished pewter. It's the way the shiny stuff concentrates light, not any built-in holiness. A good set of sequins would do the job just as well—one reason you won't find any vampires hanging around Vegas.

The other reason is, well . . . just about all the ones I know are regular folks, like me. We're too busy making a living to go making out at some glitzy tourist trap.

"Ma'am, I'm not going to hurt you, okay?" I took a careful step back. "I'm not into that kind of thing." Moving slowly, I pulled my rosary out from my jeans pocket. "See? I go to church Sundays—midnight Mass, actually."

She backed up a bit more, sliding around the other side of the beer bin. "But . . . but . . ." Her bottom lip trembled. She had that hollow eyed look the crackheads got after a bad trip. Not good.

I wondered what I was supposed to do now. The kid was terrified, and she sure wasn't thinking. I backed up a bit more. There wasn't really anything else I could tell her about my church. Not while she thought she was a slayer.

The church was a plain old place that had been a country church before Houston's sprawl swallowed it. Now it had a bit of a parish and a small congregation—and about a third of us were vampires. It's kind of nice to be able to go into a church and not be told you're headed straight to hell because you've got this eating disorder.

Me, I went to the midnight service every week unless I was on shift.

I glanced outside. There was a truck gassing up at pump five, and someone pulling into the parking lot. Just what I needed. It was going to look real good trying to serve customers with this kid wanting to slay me. The incident report on this one was going to be a real mongrel. Worse than the incident reports on the drug deals I sometimes saw in the parking lot.

The store manager knew about me—he liked having a reliable graveyard cashier—but it hadn't gone any further than that, at least not officially. No one has equal opportunity employment policies for vampires.

The door chimed, and I automatically turned towards it to see who was coming in and greet them if

I knew them. Habit, really. The store got a fair few graveyard regulars who'd stop in and sometimes hang around and chat until it was time to lock up.

It was a dumb thing to do with Miss Grrrl Power Buffy Wannabe a shade shy of hysterics. Next thing I knew, I was coughing garlic powder, and coated with the stuff. The stupid kid had thrown it at me.

Garlic doesn't hurt vampires any more than onion hurts humans. I coughed and hacked for a while before I could get a good breath.

When I stood up, Miss Wannabe looked liked she'd just lost her favorite puppy, and the customer—Lilah, an ambulance driver who looked like she'd just come off shift, and a regular who often shared a joke when things were quiet—had her cell phone out and was asking me did I want her to call 911?

My eyes watered like crazy as I shook my head. "Just a misunderstanding." If I called the cops on Miss Wannabe, I'd have her whole crazy outfit coming after me. Not my idea of a good time.

"Hell of a misunderstanding." Lilah didn't sound convinced.

I couldn't blame her.

Miss Wannabe shook her head. Now she looked like she was going to cry.

What the hell. I'd had enough of this. It'd be funny when I told Tom, my manager, but right now it was just a pain. "Ma'am, you want to go easy on that stuff. Don't you know too much garlic ruins the flavor?"

Lilah just about wet herself trying not to laugh.

Miss Wannabe cried. The tough slayer act finished crumbling into something soggier than used tissue. "It's not fair!" she gulped. "They said it would be easy! The vampire at the Hollow Tree store's a pushover, they said."

Lilah giggled. "Only if you're trying to get him into bed, kiddo."

I gave her a dirty look, which didn't work too well

because my eyes were still watering. "Just because you never made it there."

"Sweetie, you know I don't hang that way." Lilah blew me a kiss. "Human males only."

"Gee, that only cuts out about three quarters of the guys you date." Okay, maybe it was cruel of me, joking with Lilah while Miss Wannabe sobbed into her oversized handbag. Lilah was a regular, and one way or another I wasn't likely to see Miss Wannabe again. Besides, I was giving her time to pull herself together and slink out into the night. "What'll it be tonight, your usual?"

Lilah nodded. "Yeah, the usual." She shrugged. "I'll quit one of these days."

I retreated behind the counter and snagged her a pack of Newports. "That's what you've said for the last year. I could help you quit . . ."

"Yeah, but your way would leave me with a taste for blood. Not on an ambulance." She mock shuddered as she laid the change on the counter.

I rang up the sale. "I've never changed anyone yet, and I don't plan to." I handed her the smokes, and counted the coins into the register. Lilah was good for the change slots—she'd pay for a ten-dollar sale in quarters and dimes. "Thank you, ma'am."

"And thank you." Lilah winked at me. "Hey, is the kid okay? I could take her home and park her on C.J.'s bed till she gets it together." C.J. was Lilah's son, and about the only thing she'd been able to prise off her ex.

"Oh, God, *would* you?" The kid was still crying into her bag. What a mess. Whoever had taken that on as an apprentice slayer deserved to have his heart ripped out and eaten.

"Sure thing, sweetie." Lilah pocketed her smokes and ambled over to the kid. "Hey there, sweetie." Her voice was softer when she spoke to the kid. I guess it was her "trauma victim" voice.

Whatever it was, it worked. The kid uncurled a bit. She looked more dead than I did, what with the great streaks of mascara running down her face from her tears.

"You won't hurt me?" she asked in a small voice. She looked straight at me.

Aw, crap. Poor kid. I shook my head and went out back for the broom. There was a buttload of garlic powder to get off the floor. While I was out there, I gave myself a good shake to get as much of the garlic powder as I could off me and onto the floor. Lilah could try and talk some sense into the kid and get her home or somewhere safe for the night.

It could get ugly if someone didn't get home safe and you were the last person who saw them. Cops had this problem with, "She left at half eleven and I never saw her after that." They seemed to think that even if that was what the security taped showed you'd somehow met up with her after shift and done the dirty.

Especially if the cop had you figured for a vampire. I mean, they won't officially say we exist, but they know, and if they figure it . . . well . . . not all those police shootings you hear about use normal bullets, you know? Even though I know damn well there's a vampire in the local branch. He's one of the deputy sheriffs, even.

By the time I got back, Lilah had her arm around the kid's shoulder and was guiding her to the door. There was no one else inside—Lilah was about the only customer I'd leave alone in the store while I went in back. She might not want me for a boyfriend, but we were good friends anyhow.

Lilah gave me a thumbs-up at the door, and left me to clean up the kid's mess. And pay for her damn Doritos, since she'd squashed them with the dowel. I paid before I tossed the mangled bag in the trash, then I started sweeping up the garlic powder.

Silly kid must have used a whole bottle of the stuff. My eyes still watered, and the store reeked of garlic. I'd have to mop to get the smell out, and that wasn't happening until after I locked the doors at midnight. I picked up a few other odds and ends the kid had dropped when she tossed the garlic. Mirror, cracked. Empty bottle of garlic powder. Small bottle labeled *Holy Water.*

I took a cautious sniff. The label was spelled wrong. Should have been *holey* water, because there was no way sulfuric acid wasn't going to leave holes in whatever it touched. Did I mention I was studying chem when I got changed?

Two more customers and some cleaning later, I got to lock the doors. After that, it was cleaning the store properly amid the usual parade of potheads looking for blunts and munchies. Five hours of blessed peace, with nothing worse than doped-out morons trying to get themselves together enough to buy the container for their next hit.

Once I reopened the door, I'd need to sweep up all the tobacco they dumped on the porch when they emptied their blunts, but that was normal.

My mind still gnawed at Miss Wannabe Slayer. The little pile of her stuff I'd thrown into a plastic bag had a card for some group calling themselves the "Order of Cleansing." I guessed they were her slayer mentors, although why they'd sent out someone who'd have trouble slaying a dead rat was something I couldn't begin to guess.

Something about the whole setup bothered me, and I couldn't quite pin down why.

The boss got in early and got the real story from me as well as my incident report. He laughed. "You get the best idiots."

"I'll swap you."

He shook his head. "Get on home. Get some sleep.

If she comes back, call the cops on her for assault. Jimmy'll listen.''

Since Jimmy was the county sheriff and his wife was a vampire, he probably would, too. He and Lenny—the vampire deputy—ran the night shift. Unlike most cops, they took a dim view of wannabe slayers staking folks who weren't doing any harm.

So, I changed out my register and finished off my paperwork while Tom took the morning customers.

Dawn was starting to clear the sky while I drove my old pickup to my apartment, but no sign yet of sunrise. All to the better—I was ready to sleep.

There was a message from Lilah on my machine when I got in. "Anna's okay. Can you come over before work tomorrow? Say, eight-ish? Catch you later, sweetie."

Eight . . . that gave me enough time for my evening quickie. I could do it. Heck, I didn't want to disappoint Lilah. There was a lady worth fighting for.

I pulled off my clothes and tossed them in the laundry basket, then stumbled over to the shower. I sluiced off, more a rinse than a wash, and staggered from there to the closet where I kept my mattress.

By then, I was only just conscious enough to kick the closet door closed and collapse onto the mattress.

As always, some inner sense woke me as soon as the sun was below the horizon. I showered again, properly this time, and got myself ready.

I don't like doing the quickies, but Miss Mindy doesn't mind my weird bent and even pretends she enjoys it. It's enough. Better than going out hunting.

It was a few minutes shy of eight when I got to Lilah's place. I knocked on the apartment door.

"Come on in, sweetie. The door's unlocked."

That set off a dozen different alarms in my head. Lilah had come out of a divorce from an abusive ex about a year back. She was paranoid about security.

Nothing in her place was unlocked, and I knew she had a concealed carry license. I knew what she carried, too. That sucker might not kill me, but it'd sure give me a real bad day.

If the kid had . . . I shoved the thought down. The kid probably didn't know better. But I was about to be the star attraction of a nice little slayer demonstration.

Screw them. I wasn't missing a night's work over this crap.

I pushed open the door like I wasn't expecting anything, grabbed the wrist of the guy who tried to stake me right in the doorway, and did a neat little pull and twist I couldn't have done before I'd been changed.

Nice thing about being changed; I could do the coolest physical crap with no training and no idea what I was up to. I was just that much faster when I revved up.

The guy took a header into the cement foyer. There was a nasty cracking sound, and he didn't try to get up.

By then, I was all the way inside and I'd kicked the door shut and got my back against it.

Mister Eager Ex-Slayer hadn't been the only one. I faced about a half-dozen guys with stakes, and behind them I could see a tall skinny fellow with dark hair. He was half-familiar, like I'd seen him somewhere before. He was also on the sofa beside Lilah, and he had a silver knife at her throat.

That pissed me off. Lilah was good people. She didn't deserve to have some jerk poking a knife at her because one of her friends was a vampire.

There was no sign of Miss Wannabe. I didn't know if that was good or bad.

When Mister Eager didn't bash on the door to get back in, the slayers looked at each other. I guess they'd practiced—I didn't want to know on whom— because they all came at me at once.

I grabbed the first stake-holding hand I could, and

swung its owner into the others. A twisty crackling noise almost got drowned out by his scream. I guess I broke his arm. Oops.

They stumbled into each other and then scrambled clear. The one whose arm I'd twisted or broken scurried back, holding the arm.

Four slayers.

"I think that's enough." The fellow with a knife on Lilah sounded angry. "Any more resistance, sucker, and your friend will suffer for it."

I snarled, letting my fangs show. It didn't impress the slayers, but it made me feel better. "Listen, moron. You can come chase me all you want. But if you want to go poking sharp stuff into ambulance drivers, you're no frigging better than the 'spawn of evil' you're trying to kill."

He laughed. "Oh, nobility. Anyone who associates with a bloodsucker is a traitor to the human race."

I thought for something smart-mouthed to say. While he was talking with me, he wasn't concentrating on Lilah, and she was poised to do something. Probably something with that man-killer she had under her jacket. "Oh, har har. Better hope she doesn't remember that when she's called to come get you 'cause you suck so hard your teeth come out your butt."

He hissed and half rose.

Lilah squirmed away from him. She hadn't even gotten up off the sofa before she had her piece out. She aimed for his head.

Guns are loud. Lilah's man-killer in a tiny apartment sounded like the crack of doom on speed. And that was the nice bit.

I was facing the boss slayer, so I got to see what happens when a man gets a high-powered bullet in the face. Let's just say it ain't pretty, and Lilah was going to need new paint and carpet. Not everything that splattered around was blood.

Fortunately for me, the smell of burnt gunpowder

overwhelmed the smell of blood. I can control the cravings some, but that much blood would send me over.

The other four turned, too slowly. Lilah's next shot did really ugly things to one man's chest before they'd turned their backs on me.

I took advantage of that, grabbed a head, and gave a sharp twist. There was a satisfying crunch, and he dropped like a rag doll.

The hammer of doom went off again, making unsavory ketchup out of number three's paunch. Number four got the head treatment from me.

About then, I realized I could hear screaming, and it sure as hell wasn't me. I was panting, and now that I could smell blood *everywhere,* I was trying not to let it take over. I hauled open the door and poked my head out for some fresher air.

A vampire around too much blood gets like sharks in a feeding frenzy. It ain't nice. You don't want to be around me if that happens. My fangs ached.

"Shut up, kid!" Lilah snarled. "You called them here!"

Miss Wannabe's voice rose in a teary wail. "I didn't know! I didn't think they'd hurt anyone, but they . . . they . . . he's not waking up, Lilah, he's not waking up!"

Oh, no. Not Lilah's kid.

I took a deep breath and ran through the blood-soaked living room to the bedroom. Lilah's son C.J. was lying on one of the beds. He had a darkening bruise on the side of his head.

I took a closer look. The boy was alive. He'd better get checked out for concussion and all the usual crap like that, but he'd be okay.

I turned around, and saw Lilah and Miss Wannabe—Anna—crammed in the doorway looking anxious.

"He's not hurt too bad." How did I know? It's a vampire thing. Get close enough to someone and I know how much life they've got in them. C.J had plenty. "You'll want to get him to a hospital to get checked over, though."

The tension drained out of Lilah's body, and she sighed. "Okay. So, what are we gonna do with all the corpses? I can't see the cops taking self defense."

Crap. Someone would have called the cops. The screaming and shooting guaranteed it. If this lost me my job I was going to kill that Anna kid myself.

"Um. Yeah." I tried to think. The smell of blood was getting to me.

"Jason sold drugs," Anna said in a wobbly voice. Her face was all red and blotchy from crying. "He said . . ." She swallowed. "He said it was to finance the war, and to weaken the traitors."

It told me where I'd seen him and his boys. Out in the store parking lot, doing their deals. I'd called Jimmy and given him the car number and a description, but the cops never did get any of them.

Lilah snapped her fingers. "That's where I'd seen the bastard before! Called the cops on him 'cause he and a bunch of others were making a ruckus two doors down. Talked their way out of it, but I know the kid there's a crackhead."

I nodded. "Drug thing gone wrong. You got a crowbar or something in your car? Get it up here and get someone's prints all over it."

Anna's gulped, but her mouth tightened and her chin got firmer. "Get it out of their cars. They'll have keys on them."

In the end, the three of us set up the scene just in time. I got the hell out of there before the cops arrived—driving real carefully—and hoped Lilah and Anna would be okay. Hoped they'd get C.J. to ER, too.

I got to work just in time. Clinton, the evening shift guy, gave me a funny look, and I gave him a "don't you start" one back. He didn't.

* * *

Lilah dropped by a few hours later, about five minutes before I was due to close the doors, with Anna in tow. "C.J.'s in for observation," she said. "They don't think there's any damage."

Anna edged over to the counter. "I'm . . . sorry, sir. I really didn't . . ." She shook her head. Her eyes filled. "I'm sorry."

I glanced over at Lilah and mouthed the word "cult." She nodded.

"Guess it's not your fault, Anna," I shrugged. "You got someplace to go?"

She shook her head. "Mom and Dad . . . they split up six months back. Dad said I was old enough to be on my own, and Mom's boyfriend . . ." She shuddered. "Jason . . . he . . ." Her eyes filled again.

"You're staying with me, sweetie, till we find you someplace." Lilah nodded in my direction. "And you ain't letting toothy here seduce you, either."

I mock-leered at her, but it felt wrong.

"The cops didn't look too close," Lilah added. "Seems they've been wanting to get a hold of this lot for a while. Oh, and Deputy Lenny said to tell you you did a neat job."

Aw, *crap.* All the cops that could have come to the apartment, and Lilah gets the one and only vampire. I'd never hear the end of it. Sure, Lenny was just doing his job, same as I was just doing mine. But . . .

Ah, what the hell. "Tell him I said he can shove it where the sun don't shine." It was probably a good thing, I told myself. Lenny would accept Lilah's self-defense thing, and wouldn't ask any awkward questions. He'd probably also put the word out that Lilah was good folks, and not to be harassed. He was that kind of guy.

"You tell him, sweetie. I got work to do." Lilah grinned at me. It was kind of sickly compared to her usual grin. "See you tomorrow?"

"Sure thing." I gave her my best cheerful wave. "Take care, y'all."

I watched as they left, then locked the doors after them. At least this time, I wouldn't need to do an incident report.

And the way Anna looked back at me as they headed for Lilah's car, well . . . maybe things were looking up.

Maybe life was about to start sucking in a good way.

I started to whistle as I got out the mop and went back to my job.

TWELVE STEPPING IN THE DARK

Rebecca Lickiss

The drab plain door had a small paper sign taped to the inside of the window saying "Free Clinic." Serena looked at the dilapidated building and sighed.

She pulled her floppy, broad-brimmed hat further down on her head. The white gloves made her hands awkward. As she'd expected, wearing a heavy, long-sleeved, cotton shirt with jeans, boots, gloves, and a hat in warm weather drew stares. Serena shrugged her shoulders. She didn't care what they thought. Or rather, she preferred to pretend she didn't care.

Why here? Serena wondered. In the middle of some small town. But then again, why not? Where else would you find a vampire rehabilitation clinic?

Inside the building, the smell of sunscreen was overwhelming. The small lobby looked like a redecorated old store, complete with a dilapidated wooden counter about six feet from the back wall. Shabby blue plastic chairs lined the pastel pink walls. Several paths had been worn into the drab gray flooring. One path led straight from the door to the counter.

The only other person in the room was a quiet young man who sat behind the counter watching her. She noticed first his raven black hair, and pale, pale skin. He smiled cautiously, without parting his lips, so she couldn't be sure. He said, "If you haven't decided on your goal, you'll never achieve it."

A goal. Yes, goals were a good idea. Speaking of which . . . Serena tried smiling at him. "I heard about this clinic." Serena sounded stupid even to her own ears. "It's just that . . . Well, I really don't think anything can help."

"We can help." He stood. "I'm living proof, so to speak." His lips pulled back in a wide smile, revealing pointed canines.

Serena rushed to the counter, and leaned on it to support herself. "I don't even remember being bitten."

"You've come to the right place." He patted her arm with his right hand, while lifting a section of the counter with his left, and kicking a front panel open. "You come on back and sit. I'll get you some juice, and we can talk." He put his arm around her shoulder, steering her through one of the doorways down the hall.

She glanced back the way they'd come. "Don't you need to wait out front?"

"No. You may have noticed we're not real busy right now." He opened a door to what appeared to be a break room or lounge. "We get most of our customers after dark. I can tell you're new. Most won't even go out in daylight."

Sitting in a wobbly folding chair at a cheap round table, Serena watched him open a scratched and dented refrigerator. He pulled out two cans of tomato juice, opened them both, and put one in front of her. She looked at the tomato juice, wondering if it was really a viable substitute.

He sat in another rickety chair. "I'm Boleslaw Woronow. My friends call me Les. It's shorter, easier, and less vampiric." He nodded to her, and sipped from his juice can.

That he'd actually said the word surprised her, nobody else would say it around her since . . . However, since he was one also, and this place was what it was, she supposed that it would be necessary. She braced herself to be brutally honest. "Serena Tropashko. And I don't want to be a vampire any more. I don't even know how it happened. I don't remember being bitten."

"We can help." Les smiled, again without letting his lips part. She wondered if that was to keep others from seeing his fangs, and decided to try copying it herself. It couldn't hurt. "Actually, it's common not to remember being bitten." He patted her hand. "However, with rehabilitation you have to do the work, and it must be something you want with all your heart."

Serena nodded vigorously. "Oh, yes, I want my life back."

"Good, good. First thing," he held up one finger, "No biting. Second," another finger, "You must be completely honest, with us, with yourself, and with others. And third," another finger, "No biting." Les smiled at her, showing his teeth. "Actually, if you're as new as I think, you probably don't have the urge to bite anyone yet, and won't for years to come."

Serena nodded; she didn't want to bite anyone, never had.

"We offer therapy every night. Vampirism isn't an easy thing to overcome, but it can be done. You have to take it in steps, sometimes little baby steps, sometimes giant leaps, but little by little, bit by bit." He took another drink of juice. "First thing, though, we have to take care of your immediate needs. Everyone needs food, shelter, a job, all that stuff. Let's start there. How're you set?"

"I lost my job, when . . ." Her hand touched her neck, and he nodded for her to continue. "I haven't been able to get one since. I live about seventy miles away from here. I didn't want to go where someone might recognize me. I'm so scared my landlord will find out, but if I can't get a job it won't make any difference because I'll be evicted anyway. My whole family is upset. There's never been a vampire in the family before."

Les held up a hand to stop her. "We can get you a job. Employers are more lenient if they're sure you're trying to rehabilitate yourself, and won't bite them. However, you may want to find someplace closer to live. Therapy sessions take a minimum of one and a half hours, and three or four hours isn't unusual. Add a regular work day and several hours of driving on top of that, and you could easily fall asleep at the wheel, maybe even get in an accident."

"But I love my apartment. I love living in the city. Besides, now that I'm a vampire I can't be killed in an auto accident. Right?"

"No, probably not." He shrugged and pushed her tomato juice can closer to her, a broad hint. "It's your decision. Let me get you some addresses where you can go apply for a job."

She picked up her tomato juice after he'd left the room. She'd never cared for it, and one sip confirmed that she still didn't much like it.

Les returned with four business cards, which he handed to her. "You may have some trouble with your name. It sounds like it's from the old country. You're not, are you?"

"No!" Serena sat up straight in surprise. "My family has been in this country for over a hundred years."

"Didn't think so. You don't sound like it. But your name will work against you now. Smith and Brown now, they don't sound so threatening. That's why I'm working here. When Boleslaw Woronow, Vampire, applies for work the employers seem to think I'm from the old country and knew Vlad Tepes personally."

"How long? Ah."

"It was 1743."

"Sorry."

He waved his hand to ward off her apology. "Try these places. Be back here by a half hour after dark for therapy."

Serena nodded, and followed Les numbly to the door. She cringed from the bright sunshine outside, but even that couldn't destroy the tiny seed of hope planted in her heart.

She was back in the shabby, pastel, lobby-that-used-to-be-a-shop long before sunset. Two men and a woman stood with Les behind the counter, gossiping. Of the two men one was as pale as Les, but the other man and the woman were both heavily tanned. They all turned when Serena entered.

"How'd it go?" Les asked. One look at her face and he added, "Not so good?"

Laying three of the business cards on the counter, Serena said, "These three claimed they had no jobs open, even though two of them had Help Wanted signs in their windows. This one," she put the fourth card, for a natural fertilizer place with the motto *Manure Is Our Business,* on the counter. "I didn't get to."

"Don't bother," Les said after looking at the card. "It's probably your name."

"What's wrong with her name?" the woman asked.

"Serena Tropashko." Les turned to face the woman. "She's the newbie I told you about."

"You poor dear." The woman opened the counter, ushering Serena in. "I'm Dr. Felicity Van Helsing, I run the clinic here." Clucking and fussing, Dr. Van Helsing herded Serena back to the breakroom, and forced another can of tomato juice on her.

What followed would usually have been considered a grueling interrogation, except for Dr. Van Helsing's solicitous concern for Serena's welfare. Les finally rescued her by reminding Dr. Van Helsing that Serena needed to eat before therapy that night.

He took Serena to a nearby fast-food restaurant,

and bought them both burgers. They ate in a quiet back booth, where the rays of the setting sun wouldn't reach them.

"Dr. Van Helsing doesn't seem the least bit afraid of us." It was a statement, but Serena hoped he'd take it as a question.

"She's from a long line of vampire hunters." Les grinned, without parting his lips. Serena noticed he managed to eat without showing his fangs. "She has nothing to fear from any of us. Even if we were inclined to bite, the thought of spending the next several hundred years—or several thousand years, or eternity—with her would give anyone pause."

"Do all of you . . . know each other?" Serena asked, a vague suspicion turning her burger into a lump of lead in her stomach.

"No, not all. But since vampires have always been about one hundredth of one percent of the population, most of us get to know at least the ones in our country."

Serena gasped. "Do you know who bit me? Did you?"

"Not me. I haven't bitten anyone for almost a hundred years. I work at the clinic, remember?" He looked wistfully sad. "Don't thirst for revenge. I've seen it happen so many times. I tried it myself. You only end up hurting yourself. And it doesn't change anything." He shook his head, his eyes stared out unfocused, as if lost in some far away thought.

Unready to let go of the desire for revenge, she changed the subject. "Can you tell me, what's true and what's not, about . . ."

Les broke off from whatever memories held him and looked at her, nearly smiling. "Think of it as a disease. It probably is, if anyone would ever do the research to prove it. You're still a human being, but some things are different. We can't turn into bats or fly. That got started because we're so much stronger, so we can jump higher, farther. I guess some people mistook that for flight. We have better reflexes. Sunlight doesn't kill us, but we're very light sensitive. You'll burn much easier than anyone else. A wooden stake through the heart will kill you, as it would everyone else. You do have incredible powers of recuperation. You're nearly impervious to disease and injury. One drink of blood can heal almost anything, completely rejuvenate you. However, I have no idea where the idiocy with the mirrors came from. The laws of physics are still operative. We have all too solid forms, and light still reflects off us."

"If you need blood to rejuvenate you, how have you managed for almost a hundred years?" she asked.

"Therapy." He checked his watch. "We'd better be going, or we'll be late."

That night there were seven in the group, only Serena and Les had old-world-sounding names. Dr. Van Helsing mediated. Each of the others expressed their sympathy to Serena and offered some little insight or thought. The whole idea behind the therapy, and the clinic, seemed to be to support each other in building a new life and to keep up the pressure not to bite anyone. And, of course, drinking tomato juice. Serena wasn't sure she thought much of either purpose. She appreciated the support, particularly the job Dr. Van Helsing offered her, but didn't feel like biting anyone anyway and didn't like tomato juice.

Before she left that night, Les caught her alone by her car and pressed a thick wad of money into her hand. "Pay off your rent and any other bills you have outstanding."

Serena stared at the twenties and fifties in her hand; there had to be a couple thousand dollars. "I can't take this."

He closed her fingers around the wad and patted them. "I've had money in the bank since 1743. The interest adds up. Take it. You can pay me back in a

couple hundred years.'' His grin winked in the dark
night, and the moonlight gleamed menacingly off his
fangs for a brief moment, then he left.

Wrapped inside the money, she found one of the
clinic's business cards, with Les' phone number on the
back. She put the whole thing in her purse, and
headed home, feeling better than she had in months.

Over the next several weeks Serena settled into a
routine, working at the clinic, attending therapy, driving the long trip back to her apartment, sleeping, and
driving back to start all over again. Her family was
thrilled that she'd started therapy, and wanted to
know when she would be cured, but they didn't want
to see her or be seen with her.

Serena considered moving closer to the clinic a
thousand times. She considered it mostly at night, as
she drove back to the city, tired and worn. Still, she
liked the anonymity and diversity of the city. Even
with as different as she was now she could still blend
into the crowd in a big city.

Driving home late one night she saw the lights of
the other vehicle come round the corner up ahead,
realizing that they were in her lane too late.

The pain of her smashed chest, where the steering
wheel trapped her in her car, woke her. The flashing
lights indicated that emergency vehicles had arrived
on the scene. She managed to turn her head, and saw
someone standing by her car door. She tried to think
things through, but the best thought she could come
up with was, *Whatever you do, don't open your mouth.*

She lost consciousness again as they pulled her from
the car, waking when someone shone a light in her
eye. She batted at the hand holding her eye open.

Someone said, "I think she's going to make it."

Looking around, Serena recognized the forbidding
white walls and sterilized smell of a hospital.

"Pulse is weak, but steady," someone else said.

A face hovered into her view. It looked delicious.

She could almost see the blood pumping through his arteries and veins. She suddenly wanted to bite him like she'd wanted nothing else in her life. Without thinking she opened her mouth.

"What's this?" One hand clamped down on her chin, forcing her mouth open; another grabbed her nose, pinching it firmly and pulling one side of her upper lip back. "Code Vee. We've got a vampire here."

Serena watched weakly, as people rushed around her, putting very strange looking clothing on, until they resembled astronauts.

Someone leaned over, peering at her through a bubble helmet. "What religion did you belong to?"

"I'm an agnostic," she murmured.

"Yes, but were you a Christian agnostic, or a pagan agnostic, or a Jewish agnostic, or . . . ?"

What an idiot. She reached toward them, and they moved away. Finally the people in the room settled down and began moving the gurney out of the room.

"This isn't right," someone near her feet complained. "She needs healing."

"She's one of them," the weirdly garbed astronaut near her knee said. "No one, not the administration, not the mayor, not the police chief, *no one* will complain if we throw her out. She'll recover on her own, or she'll wither in the sun. We don't have to risk this kind of stuff."

They wheeled her out of the hospital, off the smooth floors, and through the painful bumpy darkness. It appeared to be an alley, or something, but she couldn't tell for certain from her position. It was hard to focus on anything with every lurch and jolt shooting pain through her body. Someone pulled her off the gurney, and set her gently beside a large, smelly, metal dumpster. He set her purse in her lap, and whispered, "Good luck."

Some time passed before she could move. Finally she managed to stand up, leaning against the building by the dumpster, scraping her hand against the rough bricks. She walked down the alley, heading toward a lighted area, away from the rotten odor of the dumpster. In the opposite direction from where she guessed the hospital was.

She stood, leaning on the building, at the mouth of the alley. Several streetlights on the corner shed a circle of light that reached the alley and spilled a short way in. Closed and barred stores faced her across the wide, dirty, patched street. An empty paper cup rattled down the street, pushed by a stray breeze.

It was just her and the storefronts, on this little side street. Serena walked down to the corner, then pulled her cell phone from her purse and dialed Les' number.

"Hello?" he said.

"It's Serena. I need help." The words spilled out of her, mostly confused, but she managed to tell him what had happened, and read the names off the street signs.

"I'll be there as fast as I can."

She made it back to the alley, trying to find somewhere dark to hide. She ended up sitting a little way back from the mouth of the alley, with her cheek pressed up against the cold brick of the building, watching the little slice of street in front of her, and waiting. Trying to guess how much time had passed, and how long it would take Les to get to her, she listened to the wind, the sound of distant dogs barking, and the rumble of cars passing on other streets. She started up once, when a car pulled onto the street in front of her, but it just rolled past, and she settled back into her wait.

The sound of people failing to be quiet at the other end of the alley caught her attention. Serena looked back to see the oval pools from several flashlights playing over and into the dumpster, the building walls and the alley. They were headed her way.

Frantically she looked around. There was no connecting alley across the street. No dark alcoves where she could hide, only barred storefronts, sidewalk, loose bits of trash and patched pavement. She carefully stood up, keeping tight to the brick building. Watching the flashlights, she quickly slipped around the corner out of the alley and ran to the street corner.

Maybe they were mild-mannered citizens, a neighborhood watch group or something. Serena tried to convince herself that the people in the alley had no connection to her and no intention of bothering her. She tried to ignore the pain in her chest from her wounds.

Distressingly quickly they appeared in the mouth of the alley. One pointed at her. "There she is."

Three men and two women walked menacingly toward her. They all wore dark clothing. Ski masks covered their faces and they reeked of garlic. The impotent cliché would have made her laugh, if they hadn't been so deadly serious.

Seeing no sense in pretending she didn't know what was going on, Serena hissed at them, baring her teeth. As they drew near, she could smell their blood, singing in a rhythmic thump-thump through their bodies. She needed, she wanted, that blood. Vampires were supposed to be stronger, more agile. Serena hoped that even in her weakened state she was still stronger than they.

They dropped their flashlights and spread out in a semicircle around her. Two of the men and the two women held up various items. Serena recognized five different religious symbols, but three of the items mystified her. They all had to be religious symbols, but none held any terror for her. She'd never been a big believer in symbols of any kind, not even Freud's.

"This'll be quick," the man holding a sharpened stick and mallet said. She recognized the voice as the one from the hospital who'd said no one would care what happened to her.

Launching herself at him, Serena grabbed his wrists, pinning them behind him, trying to get her teeth onto his neck. He struggled against her. Pain shot through the wounds on her chest like a burning ember leaping up to a flame, but she decided she'd rather have the pain than death and continued the struggle. The others tried touching her with their symbols. When that didn't work, they tried hitting her with their symbols.

Serena quickly came to the conclusion that she wasn't tall enough to reach his neck, and she'd have to bite him through his thick shirt. At that point someone poured water between them. It seemed a stupid move, and took her by surprise. It didn't hurt, but she breathed in some water, choked, and let go.

Gasping for air and trying to dry her face with her hands, she slipped away from one of the men when he tried to pin her arms behind her. She saw the sharpened stick just as it raked across her bloody chest, thankfully going in the wrong direction to stab through her. She fell to the sidewalk, screaming in pain.

A car screeched to a halt at the corner. Serena saw Les get out of the driver's side of the car and leap onto the roof of the car. He jumped toward the fight, spreading his arms out beside him and a cape out behind him. He landed on two of the men, including the one with the stake, pulling them down to the sidewalk with him.

The others ran back to the alley.

Les stood up, pulling up the two he'd caught by their collars, and threw them at the alley mouth. They too ran.

He turned to her. "Let's get out of here."

Looking up at him, she blinked and asked, "Where'd you get the cape?"

Wrapping it around her, Les said, "It's just a blanket I keep in the car for the winter. The heater's died a couple of times. It does make a rather effective cape in the dark."

Serena rested in the car as he drove, trying to ignore the throbbing mass of pain coursing through her. Somewhere outside of town, he pulled off the highway, negotiated through several two-lane byways, and into a cemetery. He pulled up to a family crypt, white and shining in the moonlight.

Leading her through the doorway, he pointed to a granite coffin. "Sit there. It's the final resting place of an old friend of mine. He won't mind. He might even enjoy the company."

"What now?"

He gently pushed a lock of her hair back from her face. "That depends on whether you can heal up quickly or not."

"I am getting better," she said.

Les patted the granite top. "Stay here. I'm going to get a flashlight from the car." When he returned he examined her wounds in the light of his flashlight, shaking his head. "You'll have to have some blood, or you'll never recover."

"No," she moaned. "I want some so bad, but . . . Didn't you say vampires could recover from almost any wound or disease?"

"Yes, almost any. But at a price." He sat beside her. "Drinking blood enables us to regenerate and rejuvenate. Your wounds are so bad that without a drink of blood you will die, and you'll need a good-sized drink too."

"So I die. Is that so bad?" She already knew the answer. He waited. "I want to live, but not at the expense of another."

"There's something you should know. This," he looked around the crypt as if expected to find the words he wanted written on the walls somewhere, "disease only slows the degeneration of age and time, and keeps you alive through it all. Your body will keep trying to regenerate itself, even though it can't at this point. It will take you hundreds of years of decay before you die. And you'll feel every minute of it, as your body slowly rots until there's finally nothing left of you. Because vampires don't die at their deaths." He looked down at the granite slab they sat on, caressing it with his hand. "That's why we drink blood. It's that, or slow agonizing decay, or asking someone to murder you. To destroy your heart so that the disease can no longer be pumped through your body. There aren't any other alternatives. I've spent over two hundred and fifty years searching. Your choices at this point are a stake through the heart to end it quickly or a drink of blood."

Serena wondered who was under the granite beneath them. And how he had died, or if he was even dead. "I never wanted to be a vampire. I never asked for this. I swore I'd never bite anyone; I'd never make someone else into a vampire."

"No one ever asks for this. Even if you bit someone you probably wouldn't turn them anyway. Most people recover from a vampire bite on their own within a year. Some never notice they were bitten," he whispered. Les looked into her eyes. "There is another way. I'd have to leave you alone for a while. I don't want to leave you helpless." He started to roll up his sleeves then stopped and rebuttoned them saying, "No, that would be noticed." After a moment's hesitation he unbuttoned his shirt, his skin almost as white as the bleached cotton. "Bite me, but don't take too much."

"What? But aren't you already a vampire? I thought your blood wouldn't be good for me."

"More myths." Les smiled, showing his fangs. "Blood is blood. I've had other vampires bite me before, it doesn't seem to matter. Just don't take too much, or I won't be able to do what I have to. Not the neck, I don't want it to be too noticeable. Don't worry, it won't hurt. Much."

Now that she looked at him, really looked at him, she could hear his blood singing to her. She bit. And drank. It tasted so good, and she felt her strength returning to her.

"Not too much," he whispered, tapping her head.

Regretfully, she stopped. He'd aged thirty years in those few seconds. His hair had gone salt and pepper, there were crow's feet around his eyes, and his mouth was deeply lined.

"Stay here," Les said, in an older voice. "I'll be back soon. Don't leave the crypt. The sun might be too much for you."

Again she found herself waiting, alone and scared. She lay down on the granite, and drifted off to sleep. Serena woke to the sound of a car on the gravel road. Through the doorway she could see sunlight and manicured graveyard.

In moments Les stood in the doorway, carrying several bags, filled with blood.

"You stole from a blood bank?" she asked.

"Sort of." He set two bags down on the white granite slab beside her, keeping one for himself. "I stole the ones slated to be today's discards—past-dated from yesterday, not the ones with some dreadful disease. They would have been destroyed anyway. Still, they're good enough for our purposes." He bit off one corner and began drinking.

Serena watched as he became younger before her eyes. The gray in his hair turned black, the wrinkles disappeared, he seemed to stand taller and straighter.

He finished his pint, and licked the blood from his lips. "Go ahead. You'll feel much better."

As she drank, she could feel the strength and health returning to her. He sat beside her, and chatted companionably. "This actually works out better than I'd originally thought. If I didn't get all the surveillance cameras, they'll see an old man rooting through their refrigerator. Won't look a thing like me."

"Fingerprints?" she asked as she reached for the second bag.

"Gloves." He held up his hands.

Draining the second bag made her feel a hundred percent better. "So how will Dr. Van Helsing take our drinking blood?"

"I don't intend on telling her about it." Les glanced at the doorway. "You only bit me, and my intimate life isn't her business. She'll probably find out about the accident, but since you obviously recovered, there's nothing more to it. Is there?"

Serena frowned. "I don't think that's what she intends with her rehab clinic. And you said to be honest."

"Yes, honest. Not stupid. Honesty doesn't mean you have to tell everyone everything. A lot of it isn't their business."

She laid her hand on his arm. "If you don't agree with her, why do you work there?"

Les sighed. For a moment he examined his hands. "She means well, and most people recover on their own no matter what we do. I'm there to meet the newbies. They're the ones she attracts. They haven't yet resigned themselves." He gripped the edge of the granite tightly. "I remember my own first few years. Angry. Vengeful. Foolish. I made," his face twisted up, "many mistakes. I've seen so many vindictive acts, murders, suicides. All out of pain, anger, disappointment." He relaxed, almost smiled. "And I've seen people make incredible sacrifices. Love, to a depth I never imagined could exist. Forgive . . ."

He looked intently at her. "You can't change who you are. You didn't want to be a vampire, but now you are. Without blood you will eventually, slowly, and very painfully, decay and die. Is it really such a bad thing to drink blood every thirty or forty years, or however often?" When she didn't answer, he said, "We're no more evil, and no more good, than anyone else. We're just different from the majority. I hope some day they'll realize that." He started to smile.

"At least Dr. Van Helsing's not coming at us with sharpened stakes any more."

Serena laughed. "And you only drink blood you've stolen from blood banks."

"Sort of. Only when I've had to." Les glanced out the bright doorway. "You ready to go now? I've got a change of clothes in the car you can use. I'll have to get rid of these." He motioned to the empty bags. "You can get changed while I bury them."

They arrived at the clinic to find a police car waiting. Inside, a policeman leaned against the counter, talking to Dr. Van Helsing. He pulled out his badge. "Serena Tropashko?"

"I'm Serena."

"Were you involved in an auto accident last night?" he asked, putting his badge back in his pocket. When she nodded, he continued, "Were you taken to the hospital?"

"And thrown out, without being treated!" she said. "They left me next to a trash dumpster."

Dr. Van Helsing raised her eyebrow, but didn't say anything.

The policeman sighed and pulled out his notebook. "Did you attack anyone at the hospital or later, and try to bite them?"

Serena pulled herself up angrily. "They were trying to kill me. To put a stake through my heart! It was self defense. And I didn't bite them."

"Can you prove that?"

"I saw it," Les said. "She was being pummeled by five people, two women, three men. When I arrived, they ran off. She didn't even try to follow them."

"And you are?"

"Boleslaw Woronow."

The policeman looked Les over carefully, frowning. He glanced back to Dr. Van Helsing, then snapped his notebook shut. "Well, you're both out in broad daylight. Can't be too bad. And no one was hurt. I'll let it go this time."

After he left, Dr. Van Helsing looked at the two of them. "You may have fooled the police, but I'm smarter than that." She looked at Les. "With as bad an accident as he described, she'd need blood to recover. Who'd she bite?"

Les frowned at her. "The police have found no evidence of any crime. I assure you there are no new vampires this morning because of her. That's all you need to know."

"No it's not. Fess up now, or I'm calling that cop back and revoking my endorsement of you two." Dr. Van Helsing put her hands firmly on the counter, staring at Serena. "Who did you bite?"

Serena pointed at Les.

"I don't believe it."

Unbuttoning his shirt, Les muttered, "Believe it."

Shaking her head, Dr. Van Helsing walked away down the hallway muttering loudly, "I ought to keep a stake in my desk drawer. Never know when I'll need it." She called loudly, "Don't forget to order more tomato juice," before slamming her door.

"Tomato juice and sunscreen," Serena said despondently. "I hate tomato juice."

Smiling at her and flashing his fangs, Les said, "I hate sunscreen. Maybe we're going about this the wrong way. Maybe we should bite as many people as we can. We'll be the majority."

After a moment to think over the consequences of that, Serena shook her head. "No. That wouldn't work." But she smiled at him, showing her own fangs. "But I will remember who I am. And who you are. And I thank you."

"Therapy, a half hour after dark tonight."

"I'll be there."

GOOBLE, GOBBLE, ONE OF US

Charles Edgar Quinn

There are no vampires.

I am a vampire hunter.

When the age of reason, unabashed, swept from human minds the cobwebs of beliefs in dark things, in ghosties and ghoulies and long-leggedy beasties and things that go bump in the night, men stopped believing in vampires.

Invisible, unnoticed, vampires swelled their numbers. Unchecked.

My name is Christopher Mauldin. I am the predator who sees them, who moves in their midst unsuspected.

You do not sniff for the scent of the grave, not if you wish to find them. You look for a perfection beyond life, a smoothness that mocks the hot organic. You look for their attraction to their next victim, as desperate and feral and sad as a starving Donner Party pilgrim studying the fresh corpse of her child.

And you do not look in the parties of the fashionable, as if high society would not notice the loss of a debutante or two. Money, if the vampire has it, serves only to attract the lonely and cover their vanishment.

Always the lonely.

Which is how I became the hunted. And the hunter.

It began when I had just left high school. My family's circumstances and a few incidents in school made it impossible to pursue a college education. Not that I didn't work at the same poor jobs as most recent college students and graduates of my generation, but I lacked the caste documentation that seemed to bring some consolation to my coworkers.

I found my first job in a used record store—my mother had been too anxious about my supposed chances at a scholarship to allow me to work for money during high school. The staff and clientele were evenly divided between the hip musicians and partiers on one hand and the lonely collectors on the other, and I found myself very much at home among the latter.

The store was deep downtown, in geography much like that of the Congo, growing more lawless and unknown as one ventured further inward. Carlos, the middle-aged owner, sported a Pancho Villa mustachio and a mane of coal black hair that still went almost to his waist, even though the effect was lessened and made a bit strange by the growing proportion of gray. Poor Carlos did not realize how his keeping the same style of dress and hair for thirty years had left him now looking like a street bum or a lunatic, depending on the social circumstances.

I tried not to let any such judgment show in my face or my words, as Carlos was such a kind soul, and so tireless in teaching me the vast minutia of the used vinyl trade. The color of the label, or the seemingly forbidding appellation "mono," could raise an old record from twenty-five-cent Goodwill castoff to collector's item worth ten thousand dollars. In my first two months of work I had spotted two such prizes in batches from estate sales, testimony only to my photographic memory of the clues I was given and not to any love of the collecting game.

But to Carlos my mastery of the details was a sign

of natural fellowship that put me far more in his graces than the other-workers, who had been there longer but never went beyond their own personal obsessions in music. So he wanted to make me more social, happier in life.

Which undoubtedly involved getting me laid—which had not happened yet, in a general environment where this was rather like not getting wet when it rained.

He wasn't gross about it, of course, which might have worked. Instead, he pointed the young girls at me, the interesting ones who had somehow developed a taste for forty-year-old items from Moby Grape or the Flying Burrito Brothers or Tom Rapp. More accurately, he aimed them at me like guided missiles.

That night, it was music I was truly interested in. Carlos was roaming about the store, long black hair and raggedy black whiskers in full glory, only the lack of cannon fuses sputtering in his beard keeping him from looking like an illustration from a book about Blackbeard the pirate. Two girls had already glanced at him and then found something interesting well out of his path, but then the girl I had been watching since she came in the store realized that he was the real expert among us.

She had long, thick, straight dark hair, and she was quite tall, but not skinny. Sharp features, pale creamy skin, rimless wire glasses of the kind that barely seem to be there. The eyes behind them were blue, I guessed, but they seemed just bright and indeterminate. She spoke to Carlos very softly and politely, and I could tell that he thought she was an unusually good prospect for me only by the friendly glitter in his eye as he pointed her across the store to me.

I went on filing, completing that small corner of the store that Carlos had decided should be set aside as a shrine to obscure psychedelia. I felt my blood rise as she approached me; I did not look up but rather watched her out of the corner of my eye. I had learned that something in my manner offended some women if they caught me looking at them.

She moved like a cat. I don't mean that she was slinking or anything like that, rather she moved shyly, but her shyness, like that of the cat, was entirely physical. She was shying away even as she neared me, tacking aside and then returning to her course like a small sailboat.

When she was right before me, I sensed none of the command that you get from so many right-thinking folk, the retrograde urge to treat the employees of a store as if they were slaves. Rather, it was as if she had seen me in the street, carrying some book or record that she just had to ask about, and was trying to think up an excuse to speak to me without seeming too forward.

"Excuse me," she said softly, so softly. "Do you have anything by Pentangle? I heard something on *The Thistle & Shamrock*—'Willy O' Winsbury' I think it was. Great musicians, acoustic guitarists and a woman who sang like an angel—"

"Jacqui McShee," I said. "That track is on *Solomon's Seal.* One of their two Warner albums. Their one shot at the big time, though they still record, a different lineup with the same singer. I have it at my place, but I know the store doesn't. About fifty dollars if we ever get a copy. Warner lost the tapes, if you can believe that, so it's only on vinyl. And one German CD, probably just copied it from the album . . ."

I suddenly became convinced that I was babbling, so I trailed off.

"I just have to have that song," she said. "I need to be able to hear it when I feel like it." She grinned; she didn't smile, but drew her mouth back hesitantly, as if she were embarrassed by her teeth.

"I could tape it for you," I stuttered, as I flipped pointlessly through the records of so many forgotten pioneers who had blown their one moment of opportunity and inspiration.

"I have a few tapes," she said, and seemed to fumble for a handbag that she did not have. Then she felt at the huge pocket of her long black coat, and grinned again. "When do you get off?"

I glared around in panic, and Carlos read the moment perfectly, from a third of the way across the store. It was fifteen minutes to closing, but the hours of this business were erratic at best.

"You can go on ahead if you want, Chris," he said, looking in the register and then looking at the other employees as if he just happened to be working out who he needed for closing. "Gerry and I can handle the close."

True enough. I was there to buy and file records, and the older fellows always took care of the till, with an out-of-place care they probably learned in the drug trade they abandoned long ago. The girl smiled and walked toward the door, looking back every once in a while to see if I followed. I did, not even remembering to take the backpack in which I stored all the lists I had made for the job and anything that I thought I could not do without.

I suppose it's still there.

For a moment, outside the door, I followed her like a lost puppy, until I caught myself and stepped up beside her. She told me her name was Karen. We made the smallest of small talk, nothing about the music that had thrown us together, but only about the current topics that were common property. We were at my place before I knew it, walking around the old van that Dad had signed over to me when I left home.

She waited so patiently while I unbolted the door.

In a moment we were in. I went straight to the record rack, as if to deny any other reason she might have had to enter my place. Most of my Pentangle albums were on CD, but *Solomon's Seal* I had on vinyl—I had sought it out and bought it even before I went to work at the store, had found it at a Goodwill and hadn't even known it was a collector's item. I placed it on the the turntable, and took the cassette tape she offered me.

"It's blank," she said. "Could I get the whole album?"

I nodded and started both the record and the tape. It was a forty-five minute tape, long enough for both sides. The futon where I slept was the only place we could both sit, and I was glad that I had folded it up into a couch for some reason that morning. She took off her long black coat before she sat down, and she was wearing a knee-length skirt, that rode up as she sat down, and a delicate white cotton shirt.

It just seemed natural to sit there together quietly, and listen to the great music without talking. I had wondered why she hadn't explored the apartment in any way and just stayed there near the door. Then I saw the mirror on the door on the far side of the room. I thought that she must be as uncomfortable at seeing herself as I was.

She looked at me far more than I looked at her. She stayed on the futon while I got up at the end of side one, ran the tape to the end before turning it over, and turned the album to the other side. When I sat down, she moved closer to me and smiled, touched my hand. I had a hard time keeping from pulling it away. Her hand was so cool, it made me feel that my own was hot and sweaty.

"Willy O' Winsbury" was the first track on side two. It was the story of a king who had been held captive for many years in Spain, and was overcome by doubt of his daughter's chastity when he finally returns. *He asks why she is so pale.*

Karen moved toward me, so slowly.

Have you been sick, he asks. Or have you slept with a man?

She touched my shoulder.

The king orders his daughter to take off her gown, so that he might know whether or not she was still a virgin . . .

To see if she was pregnant? Or did he think loss of virginity changed a woman's very form?

Karen's arm was around my shoulder, tentatively, as if not to frighten me, and her other hand touched my chest.

Her hips so round . . .

She kissed me, slowly and thoroughly. I don't know even now how long it lasted. I grasped her to me—I had none of the skill she showed; I just held her as if she were something afloat in a fatal sea.

I feared acting too soon, being too eager. The kiss alone was too much for me, too much to be believed.

But she was the one who was too eager. Her mouth left mine and worked its way down my chin, down to my neck. She nuzzled there like an abandoned kitten, and I felt the teeth of her lower jaw to the side of my Adam's apple. Her charming, slightly protruding front teeth.

I opened my eyes and saw the mirror across the room. Her face in the mirror flickered, and would not resolve. My God, I thought, of course I would have a migraine at this time. But then her teeth brushed my neck.

And her fangs.

It didn't hurt much, the piercing. But suddenly I knew what was happening. I pushed her away and stumbled to my feet. My hand went to my throat, where there were the tiniest cuts. No more than I got when I shaved my too-soft skin.

I ran to the door, then remembered it was my own apartment. I longed to escape, but I thought madly that I was already in the only place I could run to.

Karen was standing now, brushing herself off and trying not to look at me.

I fell to the floor as the song ended, down to my knees. No, that's the wrong song, I thought madly. The Kinks.

She walked toward me, hesitantly. Still shyly.

She had her coat over her arms. She looked away from me and slid it on. She was breathing so deeply that she could not keep her mouth shut, and I could see her gleaming white fangs, so much whiter than her other teeth, slowly retract into her upper jaw and slowly become regular incisors. Like a viper's fangs folding up.

"I'm sorry," she said. "I thought everyone wants . . ."

She was acting as if she had been merely a bit too forward. You were after my life's blood, I thought madly, you were after my soul . . . everyone wants to lose his soul?.

She stepped carefully around me, not looking at me, as she opened the door and left. She did not close the door, and she ran down the steps to the street.

I might have thought that she would just try to forget me, forget the embarrassing thing that had happened to her, get on with her life—

Her life?

Those two words stuck in my head, and they changed everything. All that went after. All that I could think of was that a vampire knew where I lived.

It took far less time than I would have thought to throw all the indispensable things that I owned into the van. Clothes, the futon, a few books. I even threw the records and all the stereo equipment in there.

It took less time than I would have thought to find another job, another place to live.

It took less time than I would have thought to find her again.

I worked the second shift at an all-night copy shop. The job was easy to learn, easy to perform competently. And I got out every night at midnight, when the undead were just getting to their most serious stalking.

I stopped at the grocery store the day after. At a hardware store. At an odd martial arts place. I had what I needed.

Just in case.

It was about eleven-thirty one night and I was running off a church bulletin when I saw them pass. It was so close to closing, just like the last time, that I could take off a bit early. And follow them.

I had another backpack this time.

Karen had found someone. Good for her.

A charming couple, I thought bitterly. She in her long dark coat, he in his new leather jacket. He was very pale and wore a scarf around his neck. Short dark hair. Only the scarf to get in the way, I thought. I tracked them deep into the city, to the heart of the jungle. There was Goth music booming from a club, their obvious destination.

Karen had been glancing behind her uneasily for quite a while, but she only took a few unexpected turns. The boy's instincts were not as well formed, and he tramped on innocently until I blatantly kicked a bottle at the mouth of an alley.

He turned and confronted me. He smirked at the image I must have presented, but for the first time in my life I was glad that I was not trying to impress someone in the slightest way.

I let the backpack slide off my shoulder carelessly, as if by accident.

"You following us, creep?" he snarled. He smiled, and I saw the newest, cutest baby fangs start to unfold themselves.

I felt the handle of the kukri I had bought at the martial arts store. Made in Nepal. The other trade of the Gurkhas, besides fighting for the British as mercenaries. I whipped it out, giving him only a second to admire the blade that started out from the handle as if it were a normal large knife, maybe a Bowie, and then bent inward about forty-five degrees, the blade of the second half rounded luxuriously to the tip. I had seen someone behead a cow with one in *Apocalypse Now*—not a faked scene—and the odd clerk at the martial arts store had assured me that it was the best beheading tool ever invented.

The boy drew his breath in, and did not look so confident. The scarf slipped down from his neck, revealing two small scars. That was all I needed to remove my doubts.

The blade seemed alive in my hands.

There was a thud on the pavement, but the body still stood. No life's blood spurted, but rather, there was a sucking sound, as if the body expressed its longing for blood in its last moment and drew in only air.

The body fell. Karen was standing right behind him. She did not scream, but only began to weep. I heard an odd crinkling sound, and smelled something foul. The body at my feet was hurrying to catch up to the time that had passed since it should rightfully have died.

Karen did not run, but only wept pitifully; she stared into my eyes with blue eyes full of guilt at what she had created and I had destroyed.

There was a commotion in the club, dark forms ran out, and I used them as an excuse to run. A coward I was, not to do the same to poor weeping Karen.

But I made up for it in the following months. She never sought me out and I never saw her again in my haunts. I suppose she fled under cover of night, the darkness hiding her in the few hours it would take a late night bus to carry her to another town.

But there was other, easier prey. Those who had been where I had been that night, and had hesitated as I had not. Had given in to this latest fad. To the 'esire to walk the night, every night, forever.

I could tell how long each had been a vampire by the state of the body immediately after death. Some looked as if they had died a few days before, others almost turned into dust. The papers carried the story of the mad serial killer who hid his victims for months, and then displayed their wrinkled mummified bodies in staged scenes, making it look as if the victims had just fallen where they had been beheaded. The police did not reveal by what weapon, but I kept my kukri out of sight.

I only began to long for the end of my crusade when Elizabeth joined the late shift at the copy shop.

The shop was so desperate for help that they often allowed me to work on past midnight and into the third shift, all night if I wanted. I could earn a lot in overtime. And dodge my responsibilities as the city's only Van Helsing. And it was on such a night that I met her.

She was so pale and delicate. So small. Sickly, but in a way that inspired me to the most morbid romanticism. I wanted to protect her, though I could rarely work up the nerve to talk to her. Even her soft blonde hair seemed strawlike sometimes, starved and dry. She explained to the boss that she had lupus, and needed an all-night job to avoid the sun that would eventually kill her. She had worked for the Red Cross and other such charities while she had insurance coverage, but now she needed to work for pay. Part-time, she came on at midnight and left well before dawn.

One evening I walked across the street on my nine o'clock break, and saw her in the health food store across the street. I went in to get a snack and lingered nearby as she talked with the person at the counter, discussing how the eating of meat empowered the sexual aspect of the body—not that she felt female meat-eaters were to blame if they were raped, as some vegetarian extremists held.

Yes, I had my doubts, but she wore a gold cross around her neck, and I had by experiment confirmed the power of holy symbols.

I had just begun to be comfortable with her, was considering asking her out, when the man with the magazine came into the store.

He was the most blatant and indiscreet vampire I had seen yet. Black leather jacket, pale smooth skin. Slick black hair. Too perfect by far.

And as soon as he came in, he latched onto Elizabeth. He explained the job in excruciating detail, how this was the new free weekly in town, and would cover all cultural activities. A bit short on funds, so far, so they needed to print it here. He did not seem to notice or care that she shied away from him, that she was obviously counting the minutes until she could be freed from his presence.

"You know what I want, and what you want," I heard him say at one point, from across the room.

And then the job was explained and done. The magazine sheets he left with the experts in the back room to print and collate and staple. And Elizabeth and I were both free to wait the few hours till dawn.

"I'll walk you home," I heard him say.

I knew she lived nearby; she left work far later than the last bus, and I knew she did not own a car. I had often worried about such a frail defenseless soul making her way home, and had only hoped that the worst of street life was exhausted and spent by four in the morning.

Her shoulders went limp under the coat she had already put on. She nodded to him, and gathered the handbag that seemed too big a burden for her to carry, and allowed him to follow her out the door.

I left seconds later, grabbing my backpack and not even making sure that the other late-night men had heard my shouted explanation.

I followed, more careful than I had ever been before. Never had I slipped from one doorway to another with greater stealth. I slowly peeked around the corner of the common path that led into a cul-de-sac of quaint old townhouses. Spied the doorway that the two of them had gone into.

She was standing there, more frail than ever. He was whispering to her, and she shook her head. He reached out and grabbed her shoulders, and she glared into her eyes with hopeless defiance.

I emerged from hiding. I don't even remember grabbing the kukri from my pack. I was on him in an instant, and I did not even notice the sudden impossible strength with which she tore out of his grasp, backed up against her humble door and shouted out an inarticulate warning.

He never turned his head, while he still had it. He only looked at her, in puzzlement, I suppose.

His head came off more easily than any of the others. Practice, I thought, as it fell.

And then his hot life's blood painted the walls around us. Splattered me.

His body fell to the pavement, alive, for a moment. Alive.

Not undead.

Elizabeth, unstained yet, flinched against the doorway. She tried to keep her eyes pressed closed, but she opened them to the bloody scene before her.

And she looked at the rivers of hot blood with a longing I was already far too familiar with.

Then she closed her eyes and grasped the cross at her throat.

"Plenty to spare at the blood bank I help at," she whispered. To me, I suppose. Or to an imaginary confessor. "Like a restaurant, so much gets old before it's needed, and has to be thrown away. Cold blood," she said, and dared a glimpse at all the hot blood before her. "Good enough for the likes of me. Keeps me going, more or less.

"For the blood is the life," she whispered, and I first heard shouting, someone in the townhouses across the way yelling about 911.

She opened her eyes and looked at me.

"I did have lupus, before—that wasn't a lie—and it was killing me, slowly, painfully. I went everywhere, all the health cults, until someone introduced me to the new cure. The fad the month before had been cocaine, then meth, for a week, then everyone wanted the new drug. Blood. I'm surprised that there are any mortals left, what with all the young dudes and dudettes coming to this side of town to get bitten. I suppose most of the vampires disposed of the victims they didn't want to share the street with.

"But I couldn't kill. I couldn't *make* another like me. This method of avoiding a painful, drawn-out death was my salvation, in a way, but the price . . ." She looked down and sighed. "It's too much to ask of another. I wasn't sure I could pay it myself. Believe me, there were opportunities to kill, to feed, but I couldn't do it. Ironically, after a few months, I'd nearly wasted away to nothing, unable to feed, unable to die, when an old man found me crouched against the cathedral and helped me live again, on blood from suppliers at the hospitals and the meat markets supplied him. And so I stepped . . . out of fashion.

"I could hunt these streets for a thousand years," she said, in a conspiratorial whisper. Then she grasped her cross again. *"But I will not. It is my choice. I can choose not to harm anyone. I will wither away before I will become what he wanted to be."*

She stared at me in disgust. "Or what you are."

I stepped toward her, hardly noticed that I stepped over the smooth corpse. Hardly noticed the sirens that approached. I looked around me and noticed our reflections in a window. There was a mirror in the room behind the window that faced us, across the way, and I looked at it. I saw myself, and a mere flicker where

Elizabeth's face should have been. I had seen that with all the vampires, they could hypnotize the person in front of them into seeing living vibrant flesh, but the illusion was too difficult to extend to a mirror.

Then, as if by force of will, the flicker went away. And I saw Elizabeth as she was. Like a china doll. Unspeakably beautiful. No flaw of living flesh. Perfect. It was the perfection they hid, I suddenly understood, so as not to inspire lethal envy in the living.

I dropped the kukri to the pavement, just as the sirens came to a stop just out of sight. I looked into Elizabeth's eyes and let my longing show.

"You want the same thing he did, the same thing everyone on these streets seems to want now," she whispered in horror. "And that I cannot give."

I fumbled for words to deny what she had said. Become one of the undead, search the darkness every night for prey?

She turned and fumbled at the lock. She entered the doorway and turned to me.

"You would be the worst monster of us all," she whispered, and closed the door, leaving me to the shouts and the recriminations.

BUMP IN THE NIGHT

Amanda S. Green

*I wake as I have so many times before. Fear quickens
my pulse and I fight the almost overwhelming urge to
move. My heart pounds so hard anyone nearby will hear
it. Blood pulses an almost deafening beat in my ears.
Every nerve seems alive, on fire, as I lie there struggling
not to scream. I have to remain motionless, silent, or
whoever, whatever had awakened me will pounce.*

*Even so, it takes every ounce of self-control I possess
not to snake my arm out from under the covers. I desperately yearn to turn on the lamp beside my bed, to
flood the room with light. Light is good, so very good.
It chases away the shadows and the monsters hiding in
them. I hesitate, not yet ready to face the unknown.*

*One small part of my brain tries to tell me to quit
being foolish. There's no one waiting to pounce the
moment they realize I'm awake. I'd locked up the
house and set the alarm before coming to bed. There's
no way anyone could have gotten inside. I'd been
awakened by a nightmare I couldn't remember. That's
all. A nightmare brought on by too much bad pizza
and a horror movie marathon I knew better than to
watch so late at night.*

*Still my pulse pounds and the cold fingers of fear
tighten inexorably around my heart. No matter how*

hard I try to will myself to simply roll over and go back to sleep, I can't. So I lie here as I have so many times in the past, ears straining for any sound that might identify who or what had awakened me. Every instinct screams on a primal level I know so well, warning me to run away as fast as I can. If I don't, I'll regret it for the rest of my life, a life that might end at any moment.

How can I ignore that feeling? Surely this must be more than simple imagination. Everything seems so real, so close. Just as it had when I was a child, when I knew things went bump in the night and monsters lived under the bed.

Dear God, help me.

Drea glanced up from the page she was reading and I breathed an almost silent sigh of relief. I'd done it and had somehow survived. The earth hadn't opened up to swallow me nor had the heavens sent down thunder and lightning to wipe me from existence. That had to be good, right? After all, a large part of me had anticipated at least one of those improbable acts happening. Honestly, I still expected something to reach out and strike me down without mercy because of what I'd dared to write.

Truth be told, part of me wanted it to.

What in the world had possessed me to put those particular words to paper? I knew better. By doing so I'd broken a code of silence as ancient as it was necessary. Those words hinted at things best left unsaid— for me and for those like me, as well as for the rest of the world. How could I have been so foolish?

More to the point, why had I ever said anything about them? Drea certainly hadn't held a gun to my head when she'd unexpectedly shown up at my front door and asked what I was working on. I could have mentioned several other projects. So why in the world had I mentioned this particular one?

Something perverse must have taken hold of me. The words were out of my mouth before I could stop them. Without conscious thought, I'd told her about this story, and there was no way I could turn back the clock and swallow the words before they'd been spoken. All I could do was hope some flash of inspiration would come to me that would help explain why she couldn't offer this project to my editor—now or ever.

Unfortunately, that hope hadn't come to fruition yet and, with my luck, it never would.

Still, I couldn't give up. Perhaps Drea wouldn't like it. That would be the easiest, most painless solution to the problem. Then I could simply put the pages back in a drawer so they would never again see the light of day.

That was the only possible solution that would keep both of us out of trouble, out of danger.

So how could I convince her?

Drea read on.

How different it had been when I was a child.

My parents expected, even accepted, that I would see monsters under my bed, in my closet and outside my window. They knew that a child's imagination is a wonderfully wild and untamed resource, good for hours of entertainment. Imagination takes the ordinary and turns it into the extraordinary, the mundane into the magical. It allows a child to fly to distant planets or be a fairy princess. What could be more exciting?

They'd even encouraged me to use my imagination. But they hadn't warned me about what would happen when night came and those wonderful flights of fancy turned dark and terrifying. Every sound and shadow foretold some disaster to come. They held me in a grip so firm and unyielding that I became trapped in the nightmarish hell of my imagination without hope of escape.

Then I'd wake, knowing the bogeyman was waiting,

ready to pounce the moment I let my guard down or turned my back. Fear held me and I knew I'd never be safe again. Then, miracle of miracles, Mommy and Daddy were there to comfort and protect. Oh so calmly they'd assure me there's no such thing as the bogeyman. To prove it, Daddy would look under the bed and in the closet. Mommy would hold me close and promise to keep me safe forever.

Remember, there are no such things as monsters. That's what they told me over and over. It was all my imagination. If I'd think happy thoughts, I wouldn't be afraid.

Funny thing, they actually believed it. They'd forgotten the nightmares from their own childhoods. They didn't remember just how real those nightmares could be. I knew how real they were; but how could I convince my parents?

I couldn't. So I let them reassure me and I believed their explanations. After all, Mommy and Daddy wouldn't lie. If they say the nightmare's nothing more than my imagination running wild, they must be right. So I'd listen and believe. In short, I grew up.

Then the nightmares returned, coming with a force and fury far eclipsing those of my childhood. Perhaps it's because there is more I hold dear. Therefore, I have more to lose. All I know is that the fears of my childhood are somehow magnified to such an extent that a normally confident adult once more becomes that terrified child desperately wanting her mommy and daddy to protect her.

That's even more frightening than the nightmare itself. So I look for some logical explanation. I listen to the so-called experts who all too easily discount the fear and sense of doom the nightmare instills in me.

So smug and sure of themselves, these experts say the nightmares are simply extensions of whatever is bothering me. They are my subconscious trying to draw my attention to a problem so I can find a solution.

There's nothing to be afraid of because monsters aren't real. I simply have to figure out what's wrong with my life and fix it. That's all.

So simple. So easy.

And so much bull!

Because the truth is that the monsters are there, under my bed and outside my window. They're lurking in my closet, just waiting for the right moment to pounce. I know. I've seen them.

Haven't you?

Please let her hate it.

I repeated it over and over like a mantra. My only hope was Drea would tell me I'd missed the mark this time. After all, I couldn't always write something that would sell. No one can. Let her think this lacked that special spark editors look for. Please let this fall into that category. It has to fall into that category.

Unfortunately, all it took was one look at the woman who had been my agent for almost two years and my hopes were instantly crushed. She didn't hate the story. Quite the contrary, in fact. Excitement danced in Drea's light blue eyes and a smile touched the corners of her mouth. I could almost see her adding up the dollar signs as she all but rubbed her hands together in glee. This was my newest nightmare, one I would not awaken from—unfortunately. My only hope was to find some way to convince her she was wrong, that it would be a big mistake to try to sell this story. But how?

"Jess, this is simply amazing."

Drea leaned back and reached for the glass of wine I'd poured her a lifetime ago. When she lifted it in a toast, I knew I needed to say something. But what? She'd think I'd lost my mind if I told her she couldn't have the story. Still, she hadn't heard all of it. There was still a chance she'd change her mind. Until that happened, I had to keep her from guessing how I felt.

But how? I'm not that good an actress, one of the main reasons I never play poker.

"Do you really think so?"

"Oh, yes." She gave that cat and canary smile of hers that always made me just a little uncomfortable. "It's similar to what you've written before, yet different. Darker, more intense. It also feels more personal, somehow. I like it."

I swallowed hard and closed my eyes. What was I going to do? I desperately needed that flash of inspiration. Unfortunately, it didn't come. Instead, emotions warred deep inside me. I wanted to shout in triumph even as I cursed my foolishness. I had created something my agent obviously liked, so it was a pretty sure bet my editor would as well. Wasn't that the dream of every writer?

Then reality returned with the speed and devastation of a tornado cutting a path of destruction across the plains. How could I have been so foolish? I never should have told her about the story, much less let her read it. That seemingly innocent narrative was far more dangerous than I wanted to think about. It threatened everything I held dear. But what could I do?

Nothing. There was absolutely nothing I could do. The damage was done and there was no turning back. Now I simply had to figure out how best to contain the fallout.

"Jess, I can't wait to get this to Greg. He's going to love it."

She gave another of those cat and canary smiles and I fought the urge to squirm. Dismay surged for a moment only to be dimmed by the faintest glimmer of hope. Maybe Greg wouldn't like it. Maybe he'd hate it. If he did, I could forget I'd ever been foolish enough to write the story, much less let Drea know about it.

"Now, how about the rest of it?" Drea placed her

wine glass once more on the table at her elbow. "Please tell me there's more."

Oh, there was more all right. Much, much more.

"All right." As I reached for more pages— compulsively doling them out to Drea like candy, like a reward—I glanced out the window and my heart skipped a beat to see the moon begin its slow trek across the night sky. "Drea, don't forget you need to leave soon if you're going to make it back to the city before midnight."

And so you won't be here when things get really interesting.

Maybe I should start at the beginning. I've known I'm different from everyone else for almost as long as I can remember. So many mornings I'd wake, excited and energized because I'd spent the night soaring high in the sky or creeping silently through the deepest, darkest shadows in search of—something. Those dreams had seemed so real, so much a part of me. Nothing anyone said could change that.

The beat of the drum fired my blood. Playing tag brought out the thrill of the hunt. I felt so alive then, so ready to meet the challenges of a new day. How could anyone not revel in such a feeling?

Unfortunately, I hadn't understood. Those wonderful dreams were simply a prelude to the nightmares to come. The nightmares were a dark warning of what life could become if I let it.

I was fifteen when things changed. That's when I had the "accident." That's what my parents called it. I really don't remember much. We'd been in the country, near the woods, on a picnic. It was getting late. The sun had already dropped below the horizon and the first evening stars twinkled overhead. Mom and Dad had been gathering everything for the trip home and I'd wandered off, bored and sulking because they'd dragged me away from my friends on one of the last days before school began. I remember following someone, something, into the woods and then nothing else before I woke in the hospital, Mom sitting beside my bed, crying.

For several days, they wouldn't tell me anything about what happened. Whenever I asked, they simply said the doctors wanted me to try to remember on my own. The police came to ask questions I couldn't answer. Finally, when I demanded an explanation, Mom told me they had searched for me for hours, calling in the local police to help. Finally they'd found me lying in the creek bed, my head just inches from the water. It looked like I had fallen and hit my head on a large rock nearby. Later I learned that I hadn't been breathing when Dad found me and that the doctors had thought me gone by the time I got to the hospital.

That's the day everything changed and the nightmares returned. Nightmares so terrible I'd wake, screaming in terror, convinced the flesh had been ripped from my bones, my blood drained away, leaving nothing more than a dry husk. Nothing my parents said reassured me. It was all so real. Just as those wonderful dreams had been.

That's when things started going bump in the night and I knew the monsters were real.

All the experts, all the shrinks and counselors my parents sent me to, told me there was nothing wrong with me. It was all in my head. I simply needed to believe in them and take my medication. I just needed to be a happy kid and everything would be all right.

How little they knew—then or now.

Sure the doctors had saved me that day so long ago—or so they thought. All they'd really done was postpone the inevitable. Twice more I'd disappeared. The first of those happened the night I graduated from high school. At first no one, not even my parents, had been too worried. After all, so many seniors spend graduation night celebrating that transition into adult-

hood. Surely I'd come home the next morning, a little worse for wear but still fine.

Only I didn't return home the next morning. Or the morning after that. Three days after graduation, a police officer found me in a field near the high school. Once more, the doctors worked like Trojans to save me from massive blood loss from tearing wounds to my neck and left forearm. And, like before, I couldn't remember what happened.

The next time, the last time, happened the night of my thirtieth birthday. Only this time, there was no last minute reprieve, no heroic lifesaving efforts by the doctors. That night I died. I know that just as surely as I know my own name. Since then, I've lived my dreams—and my nightmares. There's no escape, not for me.

Even now, as I write this, I can feel it. My blood pulses with a growing heat as my hunger builds. The anticipation of the hunt fills me. The moon is slowly trekking across the night sky, welcoming me just as the sun of a new morning once did. A part of me looks forward to the night and the hunt to follow because no hunt is the same as the one before it. What will happen this time?

Outside my window, the last hint of day loses the battle against the dark of night. As it does, I close my eyes, remembering the evening of my thirtieth birthday. The beauty of the setting sun washed over and through me then. The blues, reds, yellows and purples are like an artist's palette, so lovely and awe-inspiring. Such beauty should never be the harbinger of anything but good. It's at times like this, as the memory of the splendor of a sunset fills me, that I almost regret what's happened.

But, as with most regrets, it quickly fades. The dark mystery of night is as invigorating as the beauty of a sunny day. Too many overlook or never see the true

*majesty of the night. Now the night is my milieu and I
revel in its mysteries, its challenges and its dark beauty.*

*The song of countless crickets fills the air and the
hunger once more asserts itself. At least I don't have
to be picky about what I want. The city just beyond my
window offers a whole smorgasbord of possibilities . . .*

I leaned back with the remaining pages on my
knees, my hands resting lightly on top of them, guard-
ing them. As I did, a sense of something new filled
me. It wasn't peace, not exactly. It was more like a
sense of calm, of acceptance. Come what may, I'd
written the story and Drea's reading it somehow made
it real. Depending on Drea's response, I had some
decisions to make.

Drea reached for the pages. My first instinct was to
slap her hands away. Then the irony of it hit. Why
stop her? She'd already read most of the story. It
wouldn't cause any more damage to let her see the
rest of the pages. While it wasn't exactly a "no harm,
no foul" situation, that philosophy certainly seemed
to apply.

"Jess, tell me something."

Drea spoke softly, almost hesitantly, and hope once
more flared. Maybe she hadn't liked the second part
of the story and was finding it difficult to tell me.

Please, God, let that be it.

"It's obvious you've drawn on your own childhood
for parts of this story. Why? Why choose something
so personal?"

I didn't answer immediately. I couldn't. If I said too
much, she'd realize more about the story than was
safe for either of us. If I didn't say enough, she would
keep probing, prodding. But I needed to say something before she started putting it all together.

To give myself a moment to gather my thoughts, I
reached for my wine glass. I should have realized she'd

recognize part of the story. She knew how my parents had institutionalized me twice during my teens. They'd been at their wits' end because I kept disappearing at night. The next morning they'd find me, sometimes battered and bloody. All too often, the blood had been my own. No matter how hard they tried to convince me to tell them what was going on, I wouldn't. How could I? They'd no more understand what was happening than I did. So, worried I was trying to harm myself, they'd turned me over to the "professionals" to cure.

Not that any cure for what ailed me was available. The only cure was to die—again—and I wasn't ready for that. Not yet, at any rate.

Any way, I'd told Drea about it, without going into too many details, a year ago. She'd needed to know before some reviewer dug it up. She'd jumped to the conclusion I'd expected. She thought I'd had a drug problem my parents couldn't deal with and I was satisfied letting her think that. It was so much safer than the truth—for both of us.

"You're always telling me to write what I know."

And I had made a fairly successful career out of it. Over the last five years I'd had five books published, each of them steeped in the paranormal. Oh, they weren't horror stories like those of King or paranormal romances that made tragic heroes of hunky vampires or tormented werewolves. Still my paranormal mysteries had made me enough money to allow me to move to the country, away from the prying eyes of nosy neighbors and the cameras of those fans who simply didn't know how to respect personal boundaries.

Out here I was safe. Whenever the urge to hunt came over me, I could indulge it with a short trip to the city. There was no one to ask uncomfortable questions, no one to see something they shouldn't.

In short, I was living the life I'd always wanted and enjoying it.

However, if I didn't think of something to say pretty soon, that might all over.

Once more I glanced out the window. My pulse beat a quick staccato at the sight of the harvest moon moving inexorably across the night sky. It was later than I thought and Drea had to go—now. But how was I going to without bodily throwing her out the door?

"Well, you certainly captured the pain and fear of your narrator." She looked up and smiled, approval lighting her eyes. "You outdid yourself. Especially when you described how she slowly changed. It's almost as though you've been through it yourself."

Oh, she had no idea.

"Really, Drea. You know that's impossible."

"I do. Even so, I'd love to know how you managed to tap into not only how it feels to die but also how it feels to be someone who's no longer quite human."

"To paraphrase the old adage, 'If I told you, I'd have to kill you.' "

Damn it, why wouldn't she leave?

Pain flashed and muscles tensed as a shaft of moonlight streamed through the window. If Drea didn't get out of there soon, it would be too late. She'd get the answers to her questions, but the cost would be too high—for her, at least.

I flowed out of my chair, unable to sit still any longer. As I did, I felt my control slipping even as my senses sprang to life. Fighting the sudden hunger that demanded satisfaction, I fisted my hands at my side so tightly my nails bit into my palms. My breath hissed from between my clenched teeth as my lips peeled back, revealing those telltale fangs I'd been so careful to hide.

Damn it! It was too late. She'd waited too long.

Drea looked up, her eyes widened and her mouth

formed a perfect O of shock. The wine glass slipped from her fingers and shattered against the hard wood floor. With a small cry of fear, she shrank against the back of her chair, almost as if she were trying to become part of it. No longer did she look like the cat that had swallowed the canary. Now she reminded me of the canary—a very tasty canary.

Why had she so foolishly shown up without warning, without giving me the chance to feed before her arrival?

Well, she'd wanted to know how I'd been able to describe the changes my narrator went through. Now she was about to find out, up close and personal. But it was a shame. I really didn't want to kill her. Besides, in those high heels and tight skirt, she wouldn't even lead me on a good chase. That would be no fun at all.

Then inspiration struck, bringing with it the answer to all my problems. It was perfect. If I controlled myself, I could turn her, make her one of us. There'd be no uncomfortable questions to answer when she didn't turn up for work for a day or two, since she worked out of her house. Even better, I wouldn't be faced with having to look for someone to replace her.

After all, it's so very hard to find a good agent, and Drea had been a very good agent indeed.

SEPARATION ANXIETY

S.M. Stirling

Jacob Carrol Graff stood at the head of his casket, watching mourners file past his body with a deep sense of satisfaction.

Distinguished, if I say so myself, he thought, looking down at the form that had been his.

Tall, impressively fit for a man in his eighties, face ruggedly handsome and still with a full head of iron-gray hair, all set off by the immaculate pearl-gray Armani suit, the tasteful dark velvet of the rubbed-teak casket, and the soft rainbow light that filtered through the chapel's stained-glass windows. The one right behind the coffin showed the Lamb of God. He had commissioned that himself, years ago.

If you looked *very carefully* you could see that the Lamb had disconcertingly sharp teeth, and a rather un-Jesus-like expression of mocking irony in those curiously slanted, slit-pupiled eyes. The glass also filtered out the elements in sunlight that would be fatal to his discorporate form.

The wonders of modern science, he thought happily. *Monkey curiosity has its uses.*

He wasn't really standing; that was a perception he imposed on himself, as he imposed the sensation of feet resting on the carpeted floor, or the touch of the silk ascot against his throat, and the scent of the floral arrangements that glowed along the walls. He'd worn that body for eighty-odd years, and the floating web of energy held together by sheer will which now constituted his being remembered it at a level far below thought. It had been that lump of gray matter and tangled net of nerves that gave rise to the quantum net that held his being.

But I am free of it now, he thought.

Free of all the nagging little aches, the soreness in his right hip, the pain and weakness in the hands. The body he . . . hypothesized . . . on the evening of his funeral was young and taut and trim. It had become more and more distasteful to return to his birth-form for decades now, as it failed him bit by bit. He'd have gone over much earlier, if he'd been *certain* that he could survive. And at last . . .

I am become Literalized Metaphor, he thought with a chuckle. *How that English professor at Harvard would hate me.*

One of the mourners looked up in uneasy suspicion, one who shared the Blood, a member of a lesser Family. Jacob diminished his presence with practiced ease, fading even to his own perceptions.

He had survived death; most of his breed could walk free of the flesh while it lived and slept, walk free to hunt and feed and amuse themselves, but those who could go on after their mortal shell died the final death were much fewer. In a few weeks he would be able to manifest an artificial body from available matter. In the meantime he could begin practicing his ability to influence minds . . . and then material objects. Inspiring psychological torment by haunting dreams and the edges of perception was all very well—delightful, in fact—but there were times when the sheer atavistic joy of fang and claw were best.

Ah, he thought, as one man in the line paused gravely to look at the body; he could see the fantasy running through the mind (behind the solemn expression) of spitting into the corpse's face and dancing about the coffin snapping his fingers.

Sergio is discourteously gleeful to see me gone. Sergio, Sergio, I'm not gone . . . I'm just changed. Death is not necessarily the end . . . as you will find out to your eternal regret.

The emotions of the mourners filing by were marvelously clear to him without the muffling effect of a link to living meat; the deep satisfying crimson heat of hate, the delicious musk of fear . . . even the occasional waft of grief, like the taste of salt and acid. The lavender-and-cut-grass scent of *relief* was predominant. But he made a careful note of those who were enjoying themselves *too* much.

He would visit them first.

He glanced at his daughter, Carol, who had taken her name from his to honor him, and approved the cool, controlled demeanor she projected. It was very much in keeping with her detached personality. His son Jason was there too; the name was as close to his own as possible without becoming an impossibly vulgar *junior*. Next to his half-sister's detached calm the boy was milk-pale and visibly shaking, a line of sweat along the edge of his fine blond hair.

Well, Jason's seventeen to Carol's twenty-four. It's to be expected that he'll be more emotional. I suppose it's even flattering.

His son had been a surprise in many ways, starting with the pregnancy—it was all very well to play with your food, but you didn't expect *that*. Vastly more talented than he had any right to be, given his mixed blood. As Graff had told the boy more than once, it was obviously quality of genes, not quantity, that counted.

Then he caught a look from Carol, directed at her brother. One that should have boiled the blood in his veins . . . though that would take considerable power, and killed too quickly to be very amusing, despite the lovely sound of the words.

Tsk, he thought. *My little girl is about to show her true colors. Better watch yourself, son.*

In truth, he was pleased; the girl's swift flicker of deadly intent might have escaped him when he wore the body, perhaps even when he night-walked from it. There were definite advantages to being dead, rather like a butterfly bursting free of its cocoon. Of course, Carol would never have allowed herself to show her animosity if he were still alive . . . or if she thought he was dead-but-present. The breeding program hadn't anticipated that before *her* generation.

This is going to be interesting. Jason will either survive and prove his right to the Blood . . . or keep the next few weeks from being too *boring.*

Dad would never forgive me if I lost it, Jason thought, looking down on the time-scored aquiline features.

"Good-bye," he murmured very softly. *I'll never be able to make you proud of me now,* he thought, and blinked fiercely against a prickle under his eyelids.

Then something *struck* him. Something like an enema of ice; he had to exert all his will to keep from screaming and leaping before he realized that it was not material. He looked up to meet Carol's huge violet eyes as she brushed back a fall of hair red as an autumn maple leaf.

It's OK, he thought. *I know you've got your own grief to work through. It's natural to lash out.*

Particularly natural for one of them; and Carol was nearly purebred. It was a pity she hadn't conceived from their father—among the Brethren of Night it was a matter of simple survival to cross back that way. The future of their species hung in the balance. If they wished to hold the powers they had, and breed back to the godlike powers their ancestors had once possessed, only fools or humans would balk at a little incest.

If only I had more of the Blood! he thought. *And you know, Carol and me . . . the children would be over three-quarters. As pure as Father. . . . Why not now, when we're both lost and in pain?*

Of course, she had Jeff, her fiancé, to turn to. Looking around he hunched his shoulders at the sight of the tall dark-haired man, so calmly assured and indefinably amused.

I, on the other hand, feel like a bait fish in shark-filled waters.

His training was far from complete and he needed a mentor. Which meant, should he even be able to find one, that he would effectively be a servant for the next ten or fifteen years.

That's if I'm lucky and get a generous master who wants me to leave eventually.

Most of them were looking for a lifetime commitment or no deal. His sister would be able to help him, but she was acting so cold. For the life of him he couldn't figure out what he'd done to upset her.

"That was quite a look you just shot at your brother," Jeff murmured in Carol's ear. "What did the infant do to offend you?"

The crowd was milling around the reception room. Tall French windows stood open on the stairs that led down to the gardens and the pool, and the warm California air bore the scents of pepper trees and flowers. Servants circulated with trays of refreshments; Carol took a tall flute of pale Roederer Cristal Rose 1999 in one hand and a little sausage on a toothpick in the other. She savored the aromatic bouquet, then sipped the honey and white chocolate flavors. Then she nibbled at the sausage; that was delicious—either pork delicately spiced with ginger and garlic, or that secretary Father had said was asking too many questions. In which case it was not only tasty, but a wonderful joke on the human majority attending the funeral of the distinguished San Francisco philanthropist and financier Jacob Carrol Graff.

"That *monkey's* existence offends me," she hissed. "I had to play nice while my father was around to dote on it, but that's over now."

Her fiancé chuckled. "What do you intend to do about it?"

She looked up at him and smiled faintly. "Let's just say I have no intention of sharing my inheritance with a meat-animal."

"*Do* save some for me."

"My boy."

Jason dropped the toothpick and turned to meet the cold, assessing eyes of Michael Bundt, a contemporary of his father's. He took the hand the older man offered and shook it. Bundt held onto Jason's and placed his other hand on top of it.

"My condolences. When you're settled we really must talk. I can be of help to you. And a young boy on his own in this world will need all the help he can get."

Ouch, Jason thought. *Do I look* that *vulnerable?*

Bundt was exactly the type of man he'd hoped to avoid. Rumored to have an appetite for boys and cruelty, not necessarily in that order. Still, it was the only offer he'd received, he couldn't afford to be overtly hostile.

"Thank you, sir." He tugged on his hand and after a moment Bundt released it with a little smile.

"Here's my card," he said, producing one as if by magic. As Jason took it he slapped the boy's shoulder. "Call me."

Graff senior narrowed his gaze on the older man. Certainly, they'd been rivals for most of their lives, that didn't mean it was good form to take advantage of his underage son. *Oh, you're in for a surprise, old friend.* And not a pleasant one if he had anything to say about it.

He felt a spear of will come from Carol and decided to follow its course, passing through the wall of the mansion out into the parking lot. Moonlight prickled on his skin like the bubbles in champagne, and tempted him to turn wolf and run across the Marin County hills. He resisted it, and traced the scent of power to a little silver roadster. His pseudo-senses were already acute, smell particularly . . . and fluid began to pool beneath the Italian import.

Oh, Carol, he thought.

He traced the silvery cords of might-have-been that marked her Wreaking. Yes, a push at the probabilities of corrosion here in the gasket . . .

How crude! Not that he begrudged her success in killing her brother if it was done with sufficient savage artistry, but this was so clumsy. And so easily countered.

I thought the girl had more style. Perhaps she needs a lesson.

"Jason."

He hastily finished his glass of champagne—he'd lost count how many, and his attempt to neutralize the molecules in his blood had only succeeded in giving him a headache—and turned to find Mildred Manz confronting him; leading, as she always was, two attractive young men.

You followed me out into the parking lot? he thought. *I'm flattered. Harassed and threatened, but flattered.*

"Now that your father's gone you'll need a mentor," she said, oozing sincerity. "I would be happy to take you on, dear. Here's my card. No rush, think it over, then call me." She patted his hand and turned to go.

"What's that under his car?" one of her followers said.

What? Jason thought blurrily. *That sounded like* Father's *voice.*

"What's that under your car, Jason?" the young man said again.

Jason looked, then squatted down, hitching the knees of his dress slacks. "I don't know," he said. "But it doesn't look good."

It was dark—only a three-quarter moon and the low glow of the lamps from behind the garden wall—but they were all of the Blood; night was their natural element. The young man turned to follow Mildred; Jason was mildly surprised he'd let himself be separated from her for even the space of three steps. As clearly as speech he picked up the words formed in the other man's vocal centers:

Looks like brake fluid, you back-bred bastard.

Bastard yourself! Jason thought, and saw the other man's back stiffen; he'd made no attempt to damp his response. *It's not as if any of us are* completely *pure.*

But it *did* look like brake fluid; Jason reached out and touched thumb and forefinger to it and brought it to his nose. Even in the flesh he could scent more keenly than a human, and the oily-bitter smell was unmistakable.

"Damn," he said, reaching for his phone. "Oh, well, I'll be safer in a taxi anyway."

Carol noticed her brother staring under his car and hissed with annoyance. Jeff followed her gaze and laughed.

"You didn't," he said. "I'm impressed at the raw power, but I'm also shocked. I expect more finesse from you, my darling."

She pouted. "Well, I didn't think he'd notice. He's pretty distracted."

It had seemed like a good idea. The Graff country

mansion was on a clifftop, a Spanish Gothic pile built over a century ago, with a very winding and, unless driven slowly, dangerous road leading to it. She'd imagined the sympathy she'd get for losing two such close relatives in such short order, and the way she'd take advantage of it. But that was the way of things among the Brethren; they were lucky, it was the root of their power. Luck didn't have to be an accident, if you had the Blood.

"I guess I'll just have to think of something more subtle," she said sullenly.

And more definite.

"Do," Jeff said, amused.

Carol ground sharp white teeth; suddenly the universe seemed to mock her, even the crow going *gruck . . . gruck . . .* in the tall eucalyptus overhead. With a flick of her mind she reached out and *pushed.*

The bird probably wouldn't have had a stroke just then. But then again, it might have. It *did,* and toppled to fall dead at her feet with a fading flash of pain in its ravaged brain. She absently drew in the power of the passing; it was blandly unsatisfying, as animal pain and death always were.

Tastes like chicken, she thought.

"Oh, petty," Jeff said, shaking his head. "Call me when you're in a better mood."

Carol turned her shoulder on him and walked over to her brother, her heels crunching in the crushed shell surface.

"What's the matter?" she demanded.

"I've lost my brake fluid. At least I think that's what it is. With what this car cost, you'd think it would last from checkup to checkup!"

"Buy a Beamer, if you want quality, for heaven's sake, Jason. I don't know why you didn't ride in the limo with me anyway; then this wouldn't have been a problem. I can't wait. I've got to get back to the townhouse to greet our guests."

"I know. But I didn't think you wanted me with you," he said sheepishly.

"Oh, Jason." She looked at him in sorrow, letting her eyes go large. "Of course I wanted you with me. How could you think otherwise?"

Maybe it was the way you were glaring at him.

Carol blinked and forced herself not to look around. Was someone eavesdropping? No, she could block far better than anyone likely to be within range . . .

"I'm sorry," Jason mumbled. "I guess I'm being too sensitive."

Carol sighed and patted his shoulder reluctantly. "I suppose that's to be expected. Well, I'll see you when I see you." She turned and walked back to the limo and Jeff.

Jason watched her go and sighed. With her face turned away—and her mind carefully shielded—Carol let herself smile. She could feel his desire; it was like holding a palm over a candle-flame.

I think my darling daughter has a plan, Jacob thought, walking through a wall into what had been his favorite room.

And it still is, he thought.

The townhouse looked out over Nob Hill. San Francisco made a fairyland below, a glitter many-colored to eyes that could see as much of the spectrum as he pleased. The Bay stretched darker, yet alive with the sea's more subtle energies, until the lights of the cities on the eastern shore rose in firefly brightness against a windy sky where the wings of his kin rode. The great two-footed step of the Bay Bridge stretched there, and north you could see the lovely double curve men had thrown across the Golden Gate.

Jason was sitting in a lounger, moodily watching a movie on the thin screen television that covered most of one of the solid walls. Jacob cocked an immaterial eye at it—the boy had an adolescent crush on Catherine Deneuve's image, which at least showed good taste—and waited for his daughter to appear.

She did, the long ruddy hair falling around slim shoulders, and the aureoles of her nipples showing through the sheer fabric of her gown. Jacob watched with detached appreciation at the performance; it would take a while for *those* desires to return. The effect on a seventeen-year-old male would be somewhere between suffocation and a sharp blow on the temple with a ball-peen hammer, of course. She turned off the set with an effort of will and her father smiled.

He'd been getting a bit bored. He'd been pleased at the flood of flowers and condolence messages that were pouring in; they were testimony to the power he'd wielded, in the worlds of men and Brethren alike. But he'd been waiting on his daughter and her nefarious plans.

. . . and I've never liked to be kept waiting. I find that doesn't change.

"Jason," she said, sitting on his footstool and touching his ankle, "I've been thinking about Daddy."

Her brother licked his lips. "Oh?" he said, looking down at her hand and swallowing visibly. "Uh . . . I've been thinking about him a lot too."

"If any of us would be able to survive death, I'm convinced that he would."

Jacob Graff shouted laughter from behind her shoulder.

"But he might be having trouble getting through."

Carol looked into her brother's eyes with liquid sincerity.

If the old buzzard had made it, he'd have made contact before now, she thought, unaware that her parent teased the patterned energy out of her brain.

This is far too amusing, he thought. *I can see why haunting was such a popular sport!*

She held up the book. "But we can help him."

"You've found a ritual?" Jason said eagerly.

Oh, do my work for me, she thought.

"I think so. But," she hesitated, "it requires . . . that we become . . . intimate."

Jason took a deep breath. "Anything for Father," he said.

Control! Graff thought. *If you laugh too loudly they* may *hear you, and that would spoil things entirely!*

"I can count on you then?"

Jason nodded.

"Tomorrow night. I just need to get a few ingredients."

"The stars will be favorable so soon?" Jason asked. "Uhh . . . I know that planetary alignment is important."

"No," she said, blue eyes serious, "but with this ritual, the sooner it's done, the better. Remember, Father is only a net of energy, he could dissipate at any time."

That should convince him, she thought. *Now, a little bit of a tease . . .*

She kissed her brother on the lips, a lingering soft touch. "I've got to go, I've a lot to do to prepare."

"What about me?"

"Well, to be honest you'll be my altar."

He wrinkled his nose. "Doesn't that mean I need to be a virgin?"

"In this case," she grinned, "an about-to-be-deflowered virgin." Carol turned away and then turned back. "You *are* a virgin, aren't you?"

He nodded.

"Well, that's a relief."

You poor little sod, she thought. *What a thing for a man of the Brethren to say! Maybe I should just boff you out of pity. Nah! Unlike Daddy, bestiality isn't my thing.*

Jacob chuckled as he sensed the thoughts flow and writhe, part words, part the darting flicker of desire and intuition. His son's blazed hotter than lava.

It doesn't get any better than this! the boy thought, and his father drank the glee that poured off him. *It does, tomorrow night!*

Jason punched his fist in the air repeatedly and slid down on the couch, giggling delightedly.

The elder Graff shook what he thought of as his head. *Was I ever that easy to lead about by my reproductive urge?* he thought. *Be honest with yourself, Jacob. Of course you were! And in a little time . . .*

In the Silverado hills, a woman with a delicately sensitive mind whimpered and tossed in a sleep full of evil dreams. The pull of her pain was like the intoxicating scent of a raw wound. Jacob Carrol Graff turned and ran at the window, leaping headfirst. The glass passed through him with a shock like the embrace of a glacial river, and then great wings beat the night as he rose and turned northward, on pinions that stretched reptile skin over traceries of bone.

Nightmare rode the wind.

After careful consideration, Carol had decided to wear a concealing robe for her "ritual." She didn't see any reason to catch cold and she didn't want to see her brother in an aroused state. He was going to be naked. It would make her feel more in control. And control was what it was all about.

Jeff shouldn't have laughed at me!

It wasn't her fault. Who would have expected him to notice the brake fluid?

Half the time he doesn't notice his own perpetual teenager's hard-on, or what or whom he's eating.

He just had more of the luck than he was entitled to, that was all. Or Daddy might have managed to concentrate enough to ensure the genes matched in an optimum pattern, even then. He'd never really lost control.

Jason entered their father's workroom, barefoot and wearing a bathrobe. He ignored the murals—oddly, he usually did even when he *wasn't* preoccupied. Carol had always loved them, the more so as most of them were done from the life.

"Excellent," Carol said. "I'm almost ready. Why don't you just strip off."

She ignored him while she stirred the crushed sleeping pills in the brandy. She'd been told that thirty-five should do the trick, and the liquor should disguise the taste.

Not that he'll suspect anything, and if he did I'll just say it was herbs. By the time he's sure, he won't have enough mental control to do anything.

She placed the goblet on the stone altar, then turned her attention to marking out a circle on the stone floor, murmuring as she went.

Got to make it look good, she thought. Jason had a lot to learn, but he knew *some* things.

When she had finished she went to the altar and Called.

"Tezcatlipoca, Jaguar in the Night, Smoking Mirror, Obsidian Heart of the Secret World—"

Ooh, little girl, Graff thought, *that's not a name I'd use lightly. That One is far less likely to be indulgent with you than I, if He were to notice. Even now He has the strength of eaten lives beyond counting.*

Carol picked up the goblet and took a sip, grimacing at the taste.

"I used Daddy's best brandy, but I'm afraid it's still awfully bitter. And," she bit her lip prettily, "I'm afraid you have to drink the rest." She handed him the goblet. "Then just lie down and try to relax."

Jason took the goblet. Then brandy slopped over the edge. Graff concentrated; sound was only vibrations in the air, after all. The mind could move it, just as it commanded lungs and vocal cords to the same end. He *was* strong enough, even so soon. Molecules just outside his son's eardrum *might* move thus . . .

and so . . . and thus . . . and so . . . stroke the threads of might-be . . .

"Just how stupid are you, boy?"

Jason *hesitated,* then took a sip, grimacing at the taste.

"She's trying to poison you, you dolt!"

The boy blinked. *Is that . . . Father?* rang through his mind.

"If you drink that, you deserve to die and you're no son of mine!"

"Dad? The ritual's not done!"

Jason's face had lost most of its puppy fat, beginning to take on the long saturnine lines that went with the Blood. For a moment it went slack with bewilderment.

"Yes, we're doing this for Daddy. So he can come back to us." Carol pushed the goblet toward her brother's lips. "So let's get started."

Jason opened his mouth to drink.

"*Drop it!*" Graff told him, with the snap of command.

Startled, the boy bobbled the cup. The slick surface of the multicolored Sabbiata glass trembled and crashed to the black basalt of the floor. Liquid splattered Carol's robe.

"I'm sorry," Jason said. "I thought I heard . . ."

Carol took a deep breath and closed her eyes. "All right," she said. "So that didn't work. I have a plan B." She pulled a gun out of her pocket. "You tried to rape me. You threatened me with a gun, but we struggled and it went off. Too bad, so sad, I'm down a brother."

Graff sighed. His little girl was really determined. Time to interfere. The chill iron made him wince as his fingers combed through it. But weakness *here* and *here* . . .

Carol stared at the pieces on the floor and dropped the few parts that remained in her hand.

"Daddy?" she whispered, and then her eyes went wide.

Graff *felt* the stone beneath his feet. It was no illusion; the stone was pushing on the soles of his feet. Just for a moment . . . but he could feed, now. The strength would grow.

"Father!" Jason said. "You lived!"

"Lucky for you, boy. Never, never, never let yourself be led around by your pecker."

He turned to Carol. "And I'm just as disappointed in you, girl. First for trying to murder your brother, and far more for being so *clumsy* about it. And a *gun*? Have you no sense of style at all, girl? It didn't occur to you that in any 'struggle for the gun' he'd win because young as he is he's stronger than you are? And if he won he could then beat you to death. Or rape you. Or beat you to death and *then* rape you. Or simply swallow your *persona* and . . . entertain . . . you in perpetuity?"

Carol licked her lips. "Daddy," she said. "I can't help it, he's just a half-breed, he's *nothing*!"

Jason was finally looking angry, a soundless snarl parting his lips and his face pale, long-fingered hands clenching and unclenching.

Good, Graff thought, feeling the murderous rage. *I was beginning to think you were soft, boy.* Aloud—the manifestation's voice was soft as yet—he went on:

"Of course I would never let him beat you to death any more than I'd let you shoot him." He held up a finger to forestall her desperate explanations. "However, being beaten *almost* to death could be a valuable and much needed life lesson."

He turned to Jason. "I'll watch to make sure you don't go too far. Enjoy."

"You lied to me," Jason growled, closing in on his sister. "You tried to use me, you humiliated me and I trusted you!"

Graff smiled contentedly as his son's fist sank into

Carol's solar plexus. She fell to the ground, gagging, and then lunged. Jason tore his ankle loose from her teeth and kicked her in the ribs . . .

Ah, family, Jacob Carrol Graff thought to the sound of blows and cries of pain and pleas for mercy, *there's nothing like it.*

ABOUT THE AUTHORS

Alan Dean Foster's sometimes humorous, occasionally poignant, but always entertaining short fiction has appeared in all the major SF magazines as well as in original anthologies and several "Best of the Year" compendiums. His published works includes more than one hundred books. The Fosters reside in Prescott, AZ, in a house built of brick salvaged from a turn-of-the-century miners' brothel, along with assorted dogs, cats, fish, several hundred houseplants, visiting javelina, porcupines, eagles, red-tailed hawks, skunks, coyotes, bobcats, and the ensorceled chair of the nefarious Dr. John Dee. He is presently at work on several new novels and media projects.

"Hello, my name is **Dave Freer** and I'm a poet."

"Don't be ashamed, Dave. Here at Poets Anonymous you're among friends. And with the sonnet program and accepting that you were in the grip of a muse greater than yourself, you can free yourself."

"Um. Okay. I used to write meaningful epic poetry during class at school and inflict it onto my unfortunate girlfriends. Yes, friends, there really are such sick people at large out there. But I'm reformed now and have ten SF/fantasy novels in print which I have either written or co-authored with Eric Flint or Mercedes Lackey. I also accept moral responsibility for an increasing number of short stories. All of the above I blame on my cats. Or even in extremis the Old English sheepdog. I would blame my sons, but they're taller than I am now. What about rock climbing as an excuse? Or having been a fisheries biologist? Perhaps I can claim it was the influence of the African sun that I live under?"

"Part of freeing yourself of the grip of poetry is accepting responsibility for your own actions."

"Really? Well. I . . . I like writing, I love amusing and entertaining readers. And writing about the living dead was just perfect for me. They say you should write about what you know, and until the third cup of coffee I am a zombie."

Esther M. Friesner is the author of over thirty novels and over one hundred fifty short stories, two of which won the Nebula Award. Most recent publications include *Temping Fate* with the sequel *Nobody's Prize* to appear in spring 2008. Her most popular claim to fame is for creating and editing the *Chicks in Chainmail* anthology series. She is married, a mom, and lives in Connecticut.

Amanda S. Green grew up in Texas, land of tall tales and big hair. While she never liked the big hair, she loved the tall tales. She's been a teacher, a lawyer, and worked a myriad of jobs in her search for what she wants to be when she grows up. Her ultimate goal is to become the crazy cat lady who writes stories people enjoy. She currently lives near Dallas in a multi-generational home that includes her mother, her teenaged son, one dog, and a crazy kitten. Everything else is subject to change.

Over the past twenty-five years, **Nina Kiriki Hoffman** has sold many novels and more than two hundred

About the Authors

short stories. Her works have been finalists for the Nebula, World Fantasy, Mythopoeic, Sturgeon, and Endeavour awards. Her first novel, *The Thread That Binds The Bones,* won a Stoker Award. *Spirits That Walk in Shadow,* a young adult novel (nominated for the Mythopoeic Award), and *Catalyst,* a science fiction novella (shortlisted for the Philip K. Dick award), came out in 2006. Nina does production for *F&SF,* teaches short story writing, and works with teen writers. She lives in Oregon.

Daniel M. Hoyt aspires to be *that* Dan Hoyt—you know, the one who writes those cool short stories and novels everybody loves. Realizing a few years ago that rocket science was fun, but unlikely to pay all the bills, Dan embarked on a new career choice—writing fiction for fun and profit. Since his first publication in *Analog,* his short stories have appeared in several magazines and anthologies, most recently *Something Magic This Way Comes* (DAW), *Transhuman: On the Edge of the Singularity* and *Witch Way to the Mall.* While marketing his first novel, he is working on his next one. Curiously, after a few years of this writing thing, Dan's mortgage is still outstanding, but he remains hopeful that will change. Catch up with him at www.danielmhoyt.com.

Robert Anson Hoyt has always wanted to live in Jurassic Park, but has currently settled for Colorado Springs, where he lives with a multitude of cats who help keep things interesting. He is currently working on a new novel, but keeping up with short stories under the watchful eye of his felines. He believes that the pets you love the most never truly die.

Sarah A. Hoyt is the author of an acclaimed Shakespearean fantasy trilogy (*Ill Met By Moonlight*, *All Night Awake*, *Any Man So Daring*) and is in the midst of a shape-shifter novel series (*Draw One In The*

Dark, Gentleman Takes A Chance) as well as of an historical fantasy series (*Heart Of Light, Soul of Fire, Heart and Soul*) which takes place at the closing of the Victorian era in a magical British Empire. Soon she will debut in science fiction with her novel *DarkShip Thieves*. She has also edited the DAW anthology *Something Magic This Way Comes*. She has published over four dozen short stories in various magazines and anthologies, including *Asimov's, Analog* and *Fantastic, Modern Magic* and *The Book Of Final Flesh*. She is also in the midst of a foray into mystery under the name Sarah D'Almeida, with her Musketeer's Mysteries series: *Death of a Musketeer, The Musketeer's Seamstress, The Musketeer's Apprentice, The Musketeer's Inheritance*. She lives in Colorado with her husband, two teen sons and an illassorted clowder of cats. Catch up with her at www.sarahahoyt.com.

Jay Lake lives in Portland, Oregon, with his books and two inept cats, where he works on numerous writing and editing projects. His current novels are *Trial of Flowers* and *Mainspring,* with sequels to both books in 2008. Jay is the winner of the 2004 John W. Campbell Award for Best New Writer and a multiple nominee for the Hugo and World Fantasy Awards. Jay can be reached through his blog at jaylake.livejournal.com.

Fran LaPlaca lives and writes in Connecticut, and has finally managed to keep one guppy alive for over two months. She's had better luck with her children, who are all thriving and well, though she suspects them of hiding the other fish in a bid to get their allowance raised. She's been married to the perfect man for many years now, and promises not to resort to any extreme measures to make him more perfect. A promise she will keep if he promises to load the dishwasher the proper way, which would, in fact, be her way.

A passionate reader, **Rebecca Lickiss** began telling stories at an early age. She finally decided to write them down for publication, since it was better than cleaning house again. Her husband and children humor her; otherwise, they're making their own dinner. Her husband also writes, 'cause he doesn't want to clean house either. Worried that taking care of her house, five children, going to work, and writing stories wouldn't be enough to keep her busy, Rebecca has returned to school to get her master's degree.

Devon Monk lives in Oregon with her husband, two sons, and a dog named Mojo. The first book in her urban fantasy series, *Magic To The Bone*, will be released November 2008. Her short stories can be found in a variety of genre magazines and anthologies including *Realms of Fantasy* and *Year's Best Fantasy #2*. When not writing, she is drinks coffee, knits toys, and wonders why the dog is looking at her so strangely. For more on Devon, go to www.devonmonk.com.

Kate Paulk is a working zombie by day and a crazy writer by night. Her friends invoke the Mad Aussie clause to explain the trail of destruction and weirdness she leaves. Her most memorable exploit to date is driving fifteen hundred miles with an untreated broken right ankle. People would worry for her sanity, but she claims not to have any. She's been published in several anthologies, and lives in semi-urban Pennsylvania with her husband and two bossy lady cats.

Charles Edgar Quinn's last published short story appeared in last year's DAW anthology *Something Magic This Way Comes*. He collects recordings of Celtic and British folk music, especially the creepy songs. While he's worked with several pale blondes in the past, he's *pretty* sure none of them were vampires.

A member of an endangered species, a native Oregonian who lives in Oregon, **Irene Radford** and her husband make their home in Welches, Oregon, where deer, bear, coyote, hawks, owls, and woodpeckers feed regularly on their back deck. As a service brat, she lived in a number of cities throughout the country before returning to Oregon in time to graduate from high school. She earned a B.A. in History from Lewis and Clark College, where she met her husband. In her spare time, Irene enjoys lacemaking and is a long-time member of an international guild.

Laura Resnick is the author of such fantasy novels as *Disappearing Nightly*, *In Legend Born*, *The Destroyer Goddess*, and *The White Dragon*, which made the Year's Best lists of *Publishers Weekly* and *Voya*. She has also published more than sixty short stories. You can find her on the Web at www.LauraResnick.com.

S.M. Stirling was born in France in 1953, to Canadian parents—although his mother was born in England and grew up in Peru. He graduated from law school in Canada but had his dorsal fin surgically removed, and published his first novel (*Snowbrother*) in 1984, going full-time as a writer in 1988. In 1995 he suddenly realized that he could live anywhere, so he decamped from Toronto, and moved to Santa Fe, New Mexico. His latest books are *In the Courts of the Crimson Kings*, and *The Sunrise Lands*. His hobbies mostly involve reading—history, anthropology, archaeology, and travel, besides fiction—but he also cooks and bakes for fun and food. For twenty years he also pursued the martial arts, until hyperextension injuries convinced him he was in danger of becoming the most deadly cripple in human history. Currently he lives with his wife Janet, also an author, and the compulsory authorial cats.

Carrie Vaughn is the author of a series of novels about a werewolf named Kitty who hosts a talk radio show. The next adventure, *Kitty and the Silver Bullet,* was released in 2008. She's also published over thirty short stories in anthologies and magazines such as *Weird Tales* and *Realms of Fantasy.* She has a master's in English literature and lives in Boulder, Colorado, where she seems to be collecting hobbies. For more information, see www.carrievaughn.com.

A professional writer for forty years, **Chelsea Quinn Yarbro** has sold eighty-five books and more than ninety works of short fiction, essays, and reviews. She also composes serious music. She lives in her hometown—Berkeley, California—with three autocratic cats. In 2003, the World Horror Association presented her with a Grand Master award; the International Horror Guild honored her as a Living Legend in 2006.